A TAPESTRY

OF

VICE AND VIRTUE

A TAPESTRY
OF
VICE AND VIRTUE

A Novel by

Clara Challoner Walker

© Clara Challoner Walker, 2014

Published by Ings Press

A CIP catalogue record for this book is available from the British Library.

ISBN 978-0-9931418-0-5

Book layout and cover design by Clare Brayshaw

Prepared and printed by:

York Publishing Services Ltd
64 Hallfield Road
Layerthorpe
York
YO31 7ZQ

Tel: 01904 431213

Website: www.yps-publishing.co.uk

… 'Hypocrisy is the homage vice pays to virtue'…

Francois de La Rochefoucauld –
seventeenth century writer

CHAPTER 1

Gabriel's Cottage and 'Bennets', Market Hamilton, Yorkshire, United Kingdom

July 2013

Gabriel forced herself to concentrate on breathing. The simple rhythm and gentle sensation of sweeping air, helped to distract her from the threats to her life and the horror of what had happened, just a stones-throw from the holy city of Mecca.

Last Friday, in advance of her return, Gabriel had telephoned Shylah at the delicatessen.

'Shylah, I'm sorry to interrupt you at work. I'm coming home. I wanted to let you know, so I don't disturb you at the cottage.' Her voice grated across the thousands of miles between them.

'Gabriel, is everything OK? We didn't expect you back for months, what's wrong?'

'I need to get away from here ... this place is ... evil ... they're murderers. Despite all their praying and their big acts of religion, not one of them has any sense of mercy or compassion, not even the women ... I can't speak about it at the moment, someone might be listening. I'm sorry,' Gabriel's voice had become tearful, shrunken to a whisper.

'Don't worry; everything will be ready for you, when you arrive. Do you have any idea when you'll be here? I can leave stuff in the fridge to save you going out and give you some peace to rest.'

'No, don't worry, I don't know exactly when I'll be back … as soon as I can get a flight. I have to be somewhere where I can put a stop to this evil and I can't do that from here. It's too dangerous.'

Upon her return, Gabriel entered the cottage garden through the iron gate, walked along the short, straight path and through the green front door. She crossed the chessboard-tiled floor of the hallway to the sitting room and her chair, where she sat stone-still and silent throughout that first evening in Yorkshire. Thin layers of motionless air held still between the folds of her multi-layered clothing, insulating her frozen body. Her exposed hands lay joined, in silent prayer, on her lap.

She stayed shattered and immobile, until darkness engulfed the room. Throughout the night, she suffered bouts of tortured sleep, punctuated by horrific, sweltering dreams.

As the early, summer dawn broke, Gabriel awoke weeping, unable to extinguish the nightmare wherein a tiny, distraught child, grazing his knees and knuckles on the filthy concrete, was trying to reach his young mother's mutilated corpse. The infant's progress was impeded by a crowd of men in blood-soaked, white garments cheering and dancing, trampling his fragile fingers, as he crawled.

Years before, Gabriel had rearranged the sitting room to position her chair for maximum enjoyment of the neat cottage garden. Now at daybreak, within touching distance of the sun, the chair's window-facing surfaces glowed ruby and crimson, smudging to purple-black in its many folds and undulations. The overall impression of the chair was a huge, thunderous cloud on the horizon of a verdant sunset. It was the focal point in the Bedouin richness of the room; walls tessellated with souvenirs from her own and her late parents' travels.

She willed the early morning hours to pass until she could go to Shylah. Eventually she rose and made her way unsteadily to the kitchen. Her uniform rows of glass jars and bottles sparkled, as shards of sunshine pierced the window. She drew a glass of cold, clear water from the tap, raised it to her lips and swallowed, revelling in the freshness of British water, untainted by desalination, processing or chemical pollution.

Gabriel climbed the narrow, twisted staircase, tipping her head out of habit, to avoid the beam at the top and turned towards her bedroom, to get ready. On her way, she paused and smiled to appreciate the exquisite, golden gentleness of the framed early 14c Byzantine icon, one of many depicting a female Archangel Gabriel, at the Annunciation. Among her most treasured possessions, it had been a gift from her parents on her thirteenth birthday.

She gathered her bag, drew an extra crimson layer of warmth around her trembling shoulders, descended the staircase and stepped outside into the gentle sunshine. She hesitated, to experience the unfamiliar sensation of cool, European air in her nostrils, the slight tightening of a chill breeze on her skin. As she walked along the straight path and out through the gate, a robin stoked his chest chock-full to sing three, shrill arpeggios from his perch on a branch in the apple tree.

Despite the effects of a tortured night, Gabriel's muscular strides devoured the half mile distance to the centre of the medium-sized Yorkshire market town. Shylah smiled with visible relief as Gabriel appeared in the doorway of Bennets, the deli'. She felt a tingling renewal of strength as the familiar scent of her friend wafted through the clattering door, into the warmth of the shop. Gabriel had always been handsome but today, still with her characteristically striking clothing, her face suntanned and her hair a little lighter than before, she brought with her a fresh, atomic energy and the presage of progress.

'Gabriel it's just great to have you back,' Shylah exclaimed, sweet smile phosphorescing under the skin of her lineless face. She stepped out from behind the simplicity of the counter to embrace the much taller, broader woman, 'how long are you staying?'

'I'm staying: I've come home for good now. I've things I need to do which can only be done from here,' answered Gabriel, stretching her long arms forward. They held together, silent and still while Shylah breathed in the scent of ginger which clung to the fibrous folds of Gabriel's clothes.

'Ella, look who's here, she's come back to us,' called Shylah to a sturdy black Labrador, who bounded from the stock room into the usually out-of bounds concession of the real shop, with its infinite promise of edibles.

'I missed you, Ella, and you, Shylah, my beautiful friend. I loved your Haiku, those little bursts of verse really kept me going at times, amidst the madness out there.'

Within the first few weeks of Gabriel's easterly absence, it had become clear that the familiar dialogue which accompanied Gabriel and Shylah's deep, tactile friendship

4

did not lend itself to the crackle of electromagnetic media. Rather than compromise, they had settled into a humorous Haiku-based exchange, evoking thought, often laughter but with no space for in-depth discussion or transmission of high volumes of information. Gabriel ached with joy at the prospect of resuming where they had left-off, eight months before.

'I'm glad you liked them, I've kept them all, yours and mine … Was it really that bad? Whatever happened, Gabriel? What did you mean about it being dangerous?' Shylah, noticed the bruise-black smudges beneath Gabriel's eyes, the bloodshot pinkness of their whites and the unsteadiness of her hands as she reached down to pet the, now ecstatic, Ella.

'It was fine … at first,' Gabriel's voice faltered as she forced herself to confront the memory. Shylah waited, exuding love and strength to enable her friend to continue.

'It was all new and interesting in the early days, an opportunity to learn, a platform upon which to try to make great things happen, and I think we did. It's not the Muslim religion that's the problem, it's just … the... the thuggishness of some of the people, some of the men.' Gabriel hammered the word 'thuggishness', her face held still as granite, her steely, grey eyes lifted to meet Shylah's warm, moss green pools. Silence seized the air between the two women.

Shylah's gentle intonation bade Gabriel, 'Come to the back of the shop, my dear friend. We'll have coffee and a little something to eat and we can talk properly. Rosemary's out so Colm will be moping upstairs in the flat somewhere. I'll get him to come down and mind things here.'

Shylah placed Gabriel's coffee before her, in the Poole pottery mug she had kept carefully and exclusively over the preceding eight months.

'This is something I absolutely longed for over there. Decent coffee was impossible to buy, along with a whole lot of other things, including medicinal Lebkuchen like these.' Gabriel sensed the tension in the back of her head dissipate gently for the first time in several weeks.

'Do you want to talk now about the Haiku you sent me last week?' asked Shylah, placing her tablet on the table between them, scrolling to 'Haiku 62 – July 2013'. They both looked down at the small screen, sitting together, knee touching knee.

Haiku 62 – from Jeddah to Market Hamilton via email
Greatest tragedy
Radiant beauty gone. Purpose
Becoming clearer.

'That's something to do with why you came back early, isn't it, Gabriel?' Shylah said eventually.

'She was so beautiful. Very clever too and only eighteen years old,' Gabriel replied softly, joining her hands in the manner of the previous evening and closing her smarting eyes. 'I was there that night. I know she couldn't have done it. It was because she was female, and considered by the local population, to be a low class foreigner.'

Shylah preserved the silence in the cool, grey room.

'She didn't stand a chance. And the worst of it was, no one cared. Not one single person. She was completely worthless to them all.'

'I still don't really understand what happened Gabriel, but what about Mubaarak and the other people you were working with out there? Couldn't they have helped you with whatever it was?' asked Shylah.

'No one was interested. They were only worried about their own reputations and avoiding danger themselves. There was a growing resistance to what we were doing for women in the country and … for various reasons, people didn't want … other things exposed. We're all in danger and it will only get worse.'

Ella lay down just outside the office door during the pause in the conversation.

'Will you be alright at the cottage on your own, Gabriel? I've never seen you like this before,' Shylah asked eventually.

Gabriel hesitated, remembering her parents, Bill and Catherine who used to fill the, now silent, cottage with music and laughter. Once their adoptive daughter, Gabriel was an adult, Bill and Catherine's work had been complete. They died, with their Yorkshire terrier, Brisk while walking on the Yorkshire Downs, shortly after Gabriel's graduation. As their sole beneficiary, Gabriel was housed and provided for; everything had been meticulously planned.

'I'd rather not be alone any longer, to be honest. I'm really missing Mum and Dad and I seem to be haunted by these awful dreams. I just can't get the images out of my head. You said that Colm has Rosemary here now. Would there be any chance they could spare you to come and stay with me for a bit?'

'Of course I'll come. I feel a bit like a gooseberry here anyway now. I'll pack my things and come over later.'

Gabriel sighed, settling deeper into her chair.

'Shylah, I'm clear now, for the first time in my life, about what I'm here to do. What happened in Saudi is just the start. It's my role to stop this evil getting worse.' She looked intently at Shylah, trying to establish the extent of her understanding; wondering what Shylah had already guessed over the years.

Shylah looked back and smiled tenderly as Gabriel's exhausted eyes closed, her head fell gently forward onto her chest and her breathing deepened.

After a few moments, Shylah left a snoring Gabriel and returned to the shop. She touched her son, Colm lightly on the upper arm without need of words or explanation between them, as she relieved him at the counter. He galloped at the stairs, two or three at once, ungainly, trippingly, to resume his recipe-testing in the flat.

When Gabriel woke up, she reflected that a cricked-neck was a small price to pay for waking free from the haunting visions of the last few weeks. Shylah was talking to customers in the shop, so she waved as she left, mouthing, 'see you later.'

She emerged into the busy High Street of the town where she had lived for the majority of her thirty-eight years. With her dominating stature and imperious bearing, she was a recognisable figure, clashing like a beautiful, exotic bird with the sludgy green waxiness and bewellingtoned rubberiness; preferred countryside attire among the majority of the locals.

She passed the school where she and Shylah had met. They had both started late, one year after everyone else. Gabriel had been gently extracted from the Comprehensive following her adoptive parents' despair at the lip-service

8

Church of England philosophy, wallpaper paste politics and flabby academic lassitude. Shylah had been ignominiously plucked from her private school when money, in the Cook household, became tight.

Gabriel entered her cottage and took her bag with her into the sitting room. She opened her laptop and waited for the screen. An email had arrived while she had been at the shop. With quivering hands, she opened the text.

Gabriel,

I am aware that you have been corresponding with Sister Anthony on the subject of our return from Ghana. As she is so efficient, I didn't wish to interfere with the arrangements, hence my silence until now! I did, however, want to take a minute to connect with you directly before we leave, to let you know how much I am looking forward to meeting you.

Sister Anthony has told me all about you, she remembers your late parents very well and has spoken many times about what a brilliant pupil you were at school. She has also explained the great work you have been doing in Saudi Arabia. I am already in awe, Gabriel, and very much looking forward to meeting you soon.

My very best wishes

Michael

Gabriel gasped, her heart quickened and her hand flew to her mouth. For the first time in many weeks, she allowed a smile to soothe the tension which clung to her face.

CHAPTER 2

Market Hamilton, Yorkshire, United Kingdom

September 1990

Lilith and her gang had started on Shylah from the first day back at school. Shylah and Gabriel had been told that they were no longer in the same lessons. It was all Sister Anthony's fault, she was head of year as well as Gabriel's chemistry teacher; not Shylah's any longer though, now she was in the dunces' group. Just because Gabriel was so brainy at everything. If everything hadn't been ruined, the two of them could have gone to lessons together like they had for the last two years and Gabriel could help her with the answers. Gabriel always finished everything miles before anyone else anyway. This year though, everyone kept saying that things were more serious, there were exams to work for. So everything got turned upside down and she was alone in class with those bitches while Gabriel was with the clever ones.

Until now, Shylah had Gabriel, the tallest, strongest girl in their year to protect her but from today, she was just lonely, weakling Shylah. Her poshness, her drunken Mum, brothers at the private school, her 'lezzie' friend Gabriel, whose parents played in the Sally Army band just compounded her long list of inadequacies. Gabriel wasn't even there at break or lunchtime when things just got worse. All because of Sister Anthony moving Shylah and changing their lunch and break rotas when she must have known what would happen.

Lilith had told Shylah on Thursday lunchtime that there was a party at her house tomorrow. Lilith's parents would be away so there would be alcoholic drink, boys, cigarettes and everything that Shylah, the thick lezzie, wouldn't be interested in.

'Strange, when everyone knows your Mum is a drunken slag. She must be interested in alcohol and shagging even if her lezzie daughter isn't,' hissed Lilith, cornering Shylah in the playground and crushing her against the dining hall wall.

Shylah clutched at what could be the only chance she would ever get to escape the bullying. She turned down Gabriel's invitation to spend the evening watching the new comedy with her, and her Mum and Dad. She told her Mum she would be at Gabriel's and then walked to the bus stop. On the bus, alone, cold, she dreaded the walk in the drizzly dusk, through the rough bit of Hull with no street lights. She thought about Gabriel's sitting room with the fire lit and her Dad popping to the kitchen to fetch a tray of hot chocolate and some of those lovely gingery biscuits. Last time she had been at the cottage, a week ago, before term started and her life was ruined, Gabriel's Mum had bought some new German biscuits for them all to try. They had been very crumbly but Gabriel's little dog Brisk had bumbled around their legs, hoovering.

Shylah felt the tears well in her eyes as she sat on the draughty bus with rain slapping the windows. There was an awful smell, like someone had weed themselves all over the floor. She wished she were there in the cottage now watching 'Never the Twain' with them all. Would Gabriel speak to her again? She had stayed silent when Lilith called out that Shylah wasn't going to Gabriel's crappy cottage... If it didn't work out tonight, she would have no friends at all at this rate. And was it true what Lilith kept saying about her Mum and the guy from the garage? She felt sorry for her Dad but why didn't he just stand up for himself? It wasn't normal for Dads to sleep on a sofa in the attic while their wives lolled alone in the marital bed, why didn't he do something about it instead of being such a wimp?

She reached the address Lilith had written down for her on a page torn from her exercise book, tried the bell, then after a few minutes silence knocked on the door. There were no signs of a party, she couldn't hear any music. Shylah hoped she had been the butt of a joke, sent to the house of a stranger, that she could get back on the bus and go home before it got too late. She saw Lilith's silhouette through the frosted glass door, which had an odd tree trunk texture. Not like a real tree trunk, because the pattern repeated in precise, uniform squares about twenty centimetres by twenty centimetres each.

Lilith opened the door, cast a dismissive eye over her shivering guest and turned her back. Disappointed at the welcome after such a crappy journey, Shylah followed her through the grubby, smoky-smelling hallway. There were dents and paint marks along the walls and it looked as though someone had ridden their bike into the skirting board time and time again. There was a hole too, half way down, about the size of a football and head height. A cold draught whipped through the hole disturbing her rain-soaked hair as she passed. Shylah wondered why no one had bothered to ring a workman to come and fix it.

When they reached the kitchen, she was relieved to recognise the rest of the gang, waiting for her with a group of boys who looked older than they were; sixth form at least. Everyone fell silent as she walked in and the boys nudged one another, whispering and laughing. Lilith positioned herself slightly to Shylah's left and slightly behind her, where she couldn't see Lilith's face. A cold sense of unease crept deeper into her chest as the others all started to make eye contact above her head, excluding her from some sort of silent joke. Someone shoved a glass of wine towards her.

'We've only got wine,' said Lilith, despite the tins of beer and bottles of lurid blood red, fiery orange and poison blue liquid the other guests were holding.

'It's OK, I always drink wine. I like wine, thanks,' replied Shylah.

Everyone laughed and she scolded herself silently for forgetting to use her other voice, to drop her t's and d's like they all did. She took a tentative sip and flinched at the bitter taste. She'd had wine before and knew she could drink at least one glass before she started feeling slurry. When Mum was in an OK mood, sometimes the family opened a bottle of wine on a Sunday lunchtime. Once Dad had been allowed to join them, they all had a glass together and for a few hours it had felt like things were getting back to how they were before he changed jobs and started at the Council.

Shylah swallowed the sip. It tasted awful, like chemicals, probably because it was cheap. Lilith's family couldn't have much money if they lived in Hull in a house like this, tiny with damaged walls, only a sink, an ancient gas cooker and a Formica table in the kitchen. She couldn't even see a fridge. There were no cupboards, no fitted units like they had at home. Lilith and the others continued their silent dialogue above her head.

'How's your Mum? I heard she likes a good servicing at the garage,' said one of the boys.

Everyone laughed as Shylah shrugged, confused at the idiotic question. She looked around at Lilith for support. Lilith looked back and showed her small, sharp, yellow teeth, her mouth stretching, grinning while the rest of her face remained motionless like steel. Shylah continued to drink the cheap wine, not wanting to be rude to her hostess.

* * *

When Shylah woke up shivering, the place beneath her ribs was burning and heaving, her head was banging as if someone was inside with a hammer. Her throat was scratchy like the wire wool they used to clean the sinks in the chemistry lab at school. With mounting horror and disgust she realised she was naked, lying on a pile of what felt like coats, in a freezing cold, shabby, empty room. There was no furniture, just a stripy purple and grey nylon carpet. Shylah tried to sit up slowly, dizzily. Her right shoulder hurt, so did the three middle fingers on her left hand which were swollen and bruised. She felt sore grazes on the back of her shoulders and hips. Once she had managed to raise herself, she felt the hot, searing pain between her thighs and the tear of something like glue on her legs and stomach which pulled apart and stretched every time she tried to move. She felt around for her clothes in the semi-dark, curtainless cell; where was her watch? Her purse? The house was silent. It was still night time outside.

Despite the pain, Shylah knew she needed to hurry. She must cover herself and get out of this freezing place, away from the smell of toadstools and smoke. Among the grubby pile, she found a pair of tights, they were probably Lilith's; she wouldn't mind Shylah borrowing them. She could give them back to her at school next week. As she pulled the tights up over her filthy thighs, waves of sickness and sweat boiled over her, she retched, she smelt vomit. She pulled an anorak from the pile, doing up the zip to cover what remained of her shame. The hammer hammered harder in her head as she opened the door.

Shylah looked neither left nor right, too afraid of what may be waiting. She walked, single small step by single small step, wobbling down the steep, narrow staircase. There was no banister to hold onto and the same wiry nylon carpet crackled, synthetic beneath her feet. She saw the glass from the tree-trunk door now lying in razor sharp, cubic particles on the hallway carpet. It was impossible to avoid them and the pain as they pierced her feet felt real and delicious through Lilith's tights. She opened the door, stepped outside and saw the police car in the road. The police officer in the driving seat and the lady police officer beside him were asleep. Maybe they had been there all night and were tired. Shylah crept silently past the car and started to walk, following the route the bus had taken when she had come yesterday.

* * *

Brisk knew something smelt wrong when his beloved Gabriel opened the door. His other beloved, Shylah, who stood on the doorstep that morning, only smelt half like herself today and half like something unfamiliar, very big and very frightening. Brisk shuffled backwards away from the half person and uttered a small bark as she entered. He must take care of his beloved Gabriel while Catherine and Bill were out.

The half person had no shoes diluting the smell of her footsteps. Beloved Shylah normally wore shoes but these feet were leaving smelly, bloody marks on the carpet. Brisk licked up some of the marks. Beloved Gabriel and the half person were going upstairs and they shut themselves in Gabriel's room. Brisk curled up outside the door. He would be able to protect them both from here, just in case things were wrong today, as he suspected. Bill and Catherine were out so they could not do the protecting themselves, it was all down to him again.

Brisk's eyes were heavy and the floor was warm, he fell asleep for a while. When he woke up he could hear one and a half beloveds talking quietly behind the door. He could hear a person crying. Had he accidentally let something bad pass him by and go into the room while he was asleep? Had that something bad made beloved Shylah cry? Brisk paced up and down on the small landing, looked up at the picture on the wall in front of which Catherine, Bill and beloved Gabriel sometimes stood, still and quiet. It was still there and looked the same as usual to Brisk. That was good, a very good sign. He barked once, just in case.

Gabriel opened the door and came out. She walked into the bathroom and started to run steamy water into the tub adding some smelly, smelly like the garden, liquid to the water. This was a strange day. Baths were for evening time when it was dark, after he had eaten his dinner, not morning time before lunch, when he often benefitted from a few little left-overs.

Shylah lowered her body with relief into the comforting, warm bath. Her grazed skin smarted as each patch made contact with the clean, flowery water. Her upper thighs and the area between her legs stung like acid. The honesty of pain was a relief from the hurricane in her brain. She laid her head back against the hard edge of the bath, flinched as she realised that the back of her head was bruised too. She closed her eyes, breathed in the steam and waited until the stinging subsided. When the water had started to cool and the bubbles had burst she scrubbed, scrubbed and scrubbed herself until her skin burned raw. Whatever it was that had happened at Lilith's house last night was filth and she was infected with filth. The pain would take away the filth which injected and infected her.

She remembered nothing at all after the silent, signed conversation and the chemical-tasting wine in the kitchen. She knew that she had done something terrible in the bedroom. She was sure that by Monday, everyone at school would know about whatever it was and about what a filthy slag she was too.

Gabriel sat with Brisk on the floor outside the bathroom, her back flat against the wall. She looked upwards at the exquisite, golden gentleness of the framed early 14c Byzantine icon, one of many depicting the Archangel Gabriel in female form, at the Annunciation. She concentrated hard, listened and waited. Something very bad had happened to Shylah – a part of her world, a part of Gabriel herself – but no sign nor message had come yet, it was still too early.

Later that day, shortly before Gabriel's Mum and Dad were due to return from band practice, Gabriel walked home with Shylah.

'I'm dreading this weekend, trapped in there with them all,' said Shylah as the Cooks' house loomed before them.

'It's only thirty six hours until Monday. I'll come and call for you on Monday morning, if you like, and we can face everyone at school together,' offered Gabriel.

'Thanks. That'll help. I suppose I can just count the hours at home one by one and get through them. Hopefully they'll all either be out or, in Mum's case, too drunk to notice me.'

Gabriel reluctantly turned for home, leaving Shylah to endure the hours of anxious agony. Despite Shylah's tears, ramblings and incomprehensible self-recrimination, Gabriel still had no idea what had happened at the party. Shylah had said she had no recollection of events following a glass of wine in Lilith's kitchen. Whatever had gone on had been terrible, had something to do with Lilith and had made Shylah injured, ashamed, filthy and very sad indeed. Gabriel suspected her friend had been raped but with Shylah so confused and upset, could not find the right words to say it.

She approached the cottage, where her adoptive parents had lived since their marriage in 1965. Bill and Catherine were stoic Salvation Army officers, their marriage a devoted, Christian partnership, secure and safe in the shared certainty that their life here on earth was to perform a duty for God. Before Gabriel was brought to them, already christened with her traditionally male name, they worked as Salvation Army missionaries in Africa and the Far East. Once Gabriel had come however, their sole priority was to raise their beloved, adopted daughter, their special charge, entrusted to them. Bill and Catherine provided not only the support needed to nurture her talents ready for her future, but with an appreciation of art, music, nature, good comedy and laughter.

Shylah entered the house and listened, trying to gauge the mood before walking through the hallway into one of the proper rooms, where real life would be taking place. She gently touched and read the Braille which would identify the species of today's silence. Was it the tense, gravelly silence when her Dad unusually summoned the courage to leave the attic and inhabit the same room as her Mum or brothers? Was it the silence wherein a dishevelled, slumbering Mum languished on the sofa exhaling sour-sweet fumes and farting? She approached the drawing room and heard a small snore from behind the door.

Shylah climbed the stairs to her bedroom, closed the door and took off the clothes she had borrowed from Gabriel. She hauled on her familiar, soft, warm pyjamas with the childish Eeyore motif on the front. She grabbed her ancient teddy which had been her father's when he was a boy, lay down in her bed and curled into a ball to make herself as small as possible. She was so disgusting and so filthy that she didn't deserve to waste space in the world any more.

When Gabriel came to call for her on Monday morning, Shylah saw her friend halt uncertainly outside the back door upon hearing the strains of an exhausting Cook family row. Mum had seized upon Shylah's lost coat and the impossibility of affording a replacement, as an opportunity to highlight her Dad's multiple failings as provider, father and husband.

'So Peter, what am I supposed to do? Shylah's lost her coat and because you wanted to work for the Council instead of keeping a proper job in private practice, we can't afford another,' carped Mary.

'Mum, I'll ask around at school. I probably left it there. Stop making such a big thing out of it. It's only a coat.'

'Big thing, big thing. It wouldn't need to be a big thing if HE,' Mary jabbed her lacquered finger in Peter's general direction as he fumbled with the toaster. 'If HE wasn't such a bloody failure and brought a living wage into this household.'

'Mum, I'm going to school now, just leave it, please.'

Shylah joined Gabriel on the back step deciding not to reveal the loss of her watch, clothes or purse to her parents for as long as possible. They would be easier to hide anyway. Also, her mother was unlikely to notice grazes and bruises particularly under the androgynous layers of clothing she had worn since Saturday. They walked together in tense silence to school and when the bell rang, went their separate ways.

'Good luck,' said Gabriel.

'Thanks.'

'What time do you finish? I'll meet you after if you like.'

'Quarter to four. Thanks.'

At registration, Shylah realised that Lilith was not at school. Relief flooded through her crushed body like arnica on a bruise. The gang was avoiding her for the most part too and by lunchtime it was clear that the day was passing without incident apart from a single, whispered threat in the corridor

'You tell anyone about Friday and you're dead.' The messenger ran off before Shylah was able to say that she couldn't tell anyone anything because she didn't remember anything except standing in Lilith's parents' kitchen.

After an uneventful lunch break, Sister Anthony was called out of the classroom. When she came back, her face was stern. She stood behind her desk and rapped with her knuckles for silence.

'Harriet, Liz, please come with me. The rest of you, please make your way to your afternoon lessons and wait quietly outside until your teacher is ready for you.'

Shylah didn't see any of them again that week. Lilith and the gang became famous overnight. Even the sixth formers were whispering in the corridors. Parents quizzed their daughters after school. No one knew the truth; school gossip was in mega drive.

'…there was a party last weekend at an empty house…'

'…they all come from that council estate in Hull with all the druggies and squatters...'

'…they're in serious trouble with the law, something to do with drugs…'

'…they're bound to be expelled from the school. Quite right too, it's a Catholic school…'

Shylah was the last person anyone would have expected to be invited to such a risqué occasion. Only Lilith, her gang and the nameless boys knew she had been there. She kept her silence, piecing together the complex splinters of the shattered Saturday night. The address she had gone to hadn't been Lilith's house at all. There may be an explanation for the disgusting taste of the wine. But what had happened in the room with the pile of coats and which of the sneering boys in the kitchen had been there with her? Where were they now? In some sort of institution with Lilith?

The weeks passed and life at school improved. As each day dawned, Shylah found a new, more creative technique for dissolving the images of the party, which clung like parasites inside her brain. It helped that Lilith never came back to school. Only one of the gang reappeared, a couple of weeks later. She avoided Shylah as though she were a poisonous snake and Shylah reciprocated, unwilling to awaken the unbearable memories she stirred.

It was November before Shylah realised she was sick. Every morning as she was getting dressed for school, she had to rush to the loo and throw up. She went to breakfast in the kitchen, pale and shaking. On one of the rare mornings when Mum had appeared from her room before everyone left the house for school or work, Dad spoke to his pale, trembling daughter.

"Shylah, are you OK? You don't look well at all this morning, love.'

'Leave her alone, Peter, there's nothing wrong with her, she's just on her period or something,' snapped Mum.

The realisation was like a slap on Shylah's head. She couldn't remember when she had her last period and the horrific conclusion started to crystallise, in a way that even her most effective evasion techniques could not crush.

The following Sunday, at mass with both parents, she played one third of the model Roman Catholic family while the boys went to rugby practice. Shylah prayed on her knees until they were stiff and she could pray no more, to every saint, deity and holy hanger-on. She prayed that it was all a terrible mistake and her period would come during mass. After the final hymn, she set-off with Dad towards the car.

Mum intervened. 'Shylah, come and stand with me here and give out the lady's stickers.'

Shylah had blocked out the sound of the lady's voice when she stood up at the pulpit and spoke after the homily. She made herself look at the lady's leaflet which had been forced into her hand, instead.

'LIFE' was written in light green letters at the top of each of the round stickers. In the middle was a line drawing of a foetus with sweet, closed eyes as if sleeping contentedly and the slogan 'every child is a wanted child' curved around the bottom.

Shylah looked at her Mum to see what mood she was in. It was always helpful when planning Sunday, a high risk battleground every week, to know what frame of mind and state of sobriety she was dealing with. It struck her then, outside the church, like a gunshot. However many stickers she and Mum stuck on the lapels of the white, posh parishioners, there was no way Mum would support Shylah, fifteen and unmarried, throughout a pregnancy.

Shylah swiftly weighed up the certainty of the eternal damnation an abortion would bring, against the shame and struggle of a pregnancy alone on the streets. Dire warnings of Hades had been issued during RE a couple of weeks ago and reiterated by the LIFE lady during mass today. She considered her Mum's likely reaction. Her daughter's eternal damnation would undoubtedly be preferable to the disapproval of the neighbours. Shylah concluded that the only course of action was to do nothing and hope it would all prove to be a mistake after all.

Another fortnight went by; the sickness came, went and came again. Shylah became more practised at hiding it and her prayers on the way to her frequent trips to the loo became longer and harder. She made bargains with God, her favourite one being that if he made the pregnancy a mistake, she would become a nun. She would be even more dedicated to the school than Sister Anthony, who was the only one of the nuns who actually did any teaching or proper work anyway. None of it made any difference, her breasts ached, she started to put on weight and, as a consequence, took to wearing more layers, cardigans and jumpers to hide herself.

The Christmas holidays arrived and passed with marginally fewer than the normal quotient of violent incidents and slanging matches in the Cook household. Still no one guessed her terrible, filthy secret about the little foetus with sweet, closed eyes, sleeping contentedly inside her... 'every child is a wanted child'.

CHAPTER 3

Market Hamilton, Yorkshire, United Kingdom

January 1991

'Can you tell me about what happened at the party at the start of last term, Shylah?' asked the lady in the soft, green cardigan from somewhere which sounded a very, very long, echoey way away.

Shylah closed her eyes more tightly, wrapped her arms around her knees and shrunk lower into the chair. She pressed the heels of her woolly-socked feet back into her buttocks, trying to make herself as small and colourless as possible. If she closed her eyes and screwed up the eyelids until tears stung and her head hurt and if she pulled on her knees hard enough to squash her disgusting, veiny, hard, fat stomach, Sister Anthony, the soft, green lady and she, might just slip out of the floor. All three of them would disappear from Sister Anthony's office, through a gap in time, fall and fall and fall spinning and spinning into another place where everything could be back to how it was before…

Shylah didn't answer. The three of them continued to sit in silence, ignoring the shrill of the bell for last lesson. Shylah wondered what would happen at a quarter to four when the home time bell rang. For now, she would sit it out and see.

After a little while, the soft, green lady spoke again.

'Shylah, last September Lilith Tilston and some other girls from your form were at a party in Hull, just after you all started the fourth year. Were you at the party, Shylah?'

Shylah realised she was about to be sick; the hiccoughy feeling in her chest, the lemon-juice mixed with cough syrup welling upwards into her throat. She heard Sister Anthony and the soft, green lady scuttling around the office trying to find something to catch it all as it soaked through her layers and layers and layers of clothes and its stinky smell wafted back up into their faces. She kept her eyes shut as they dabbed and mopped with tissues and then a cool, damp cloth. It felt nice to be fussed over and the cool, damp cloth was lovely on her sweaty face. She lay down across the two comfy chairs and felt the headache start to drift away taking the awful sicky feeling with it.

It had been easier than being sick at home in the Christmas holidays. For three whole weeks, she had to disguise herself under baggy jumpers. Thankfully, despite being the nosiest people in the world, neither her Mum nor her brothers had noticed her repulsive, fat tummy. They were all too busy bullying each other or criticising Dad.

The soft, green lady came, sat near her head and started to talk again.

'Shylah, is there anything you need to tell Sister Anthony and me in complete confidence?'

The home bell rang. Shylah knew she couldn't get away with staying silent for very much longer.

'I'm pregnant Miss, Sister. My Mum doesn't know and she'll throw me out.'

Sister and the soft, green lady kept on talking and asking her things but Shylah locked herself back inside a little space under the fridge and turned herself grey again. Sister and the soft, green lady were bustling around Sister's office, looking through cabinets, opening and shutting squeaky drawers, using the phone. Shylah just needed to lie still and small now. Later she heard Mum's late-in-the-day slurry voice shouting, shouting and shouting at Sister and the soft, green lady; shouting at Shylah, calling her names, telling her she was stupid to leave it so long so they couldn't sort it out now.

Not 'every child is a wanted child', after all then, Shylah reflected, and Shylah's banishment to Hell was a small price to pay for the neighbours' continued approval. She had been right all along.

After more shouting from Mum, opening and closing doors and phone calls, Sister Anthony and the soft, green lady spoke to her again. It was evening now and she was starting to feel hungry

'Shylah, we've spoken to your parents and they have agreed to let you stay at the convent for a while until things calm down a little. Would you like to come and lie down in your room?'

'And I am from the Social Services, Shylah. I will come to the convent tomorrow morning and talk to you about the options, medical care and so forth. Get some rest now though if you can.'

Shylah opened her eyes, looked into Sister Anthony's smooth, kind face and smiled her sweet smile at the nun. Sister Anthony was moved with tenderness as Shylah's face phosphoresced with gratitude.

Later that evening, Dad called and dropped off a case at the convent. Shylah assumed that neither Sister Anthony nor Dad knew that she could hear them talking.

'Thank you for coming, Mr Cook. Shylah is very distressed and tired, I am sure she would like to see you though, just to have some reassurance that you and her mother love her as I know you do.'

'Ahh umm, no, Sister. With respect, Sister, I umm, I don't think so. I'm sorry, Sister. I don't think it would be a good idea at all. I will just leave the case with you if I may, Sister.'

The door slammed.

Sister Anthony brought the case into the small, pale room of which Shylah would be reminded some years later when visiting Gabriel at the top of the spiral stone staircase in college. Dad didn't love Shylah enough to face up to Mum, even though Shylah had stood up for him so many times at home. She did not see anyone from her model Roman Catholic family for many months.

The predictable routine of the convent was a welcome contrast with the war zone of the Cook household. Every morning Shylah had tea, toast and jam with the Sisters, then at 8.45 she passed through the large wooden connecting door into the school for lessons. Gabriel was allowed to come to her room for an hour after school and one of the Sisters would usually pop in with glasses of milk and biscuits. On Saturdays, she was free to go over to Gabriel's cottage for the afternoon, do homework and then watch television with Gabriel and her family in the evening. It was a welcome distraction, since the convent had no television, radio or music playing equipment other than the squeaky organ in the chapel. At nine o'clock, Gabriel's Dad would drive her back to the convent where Sister Anthony would wait up for her. At Gabriel's house, her pregnancy was never mentioned, other than in the most practical terms:

'Bill, I think Shylah may be a little more comfortable in that chair with a cushion behind her back. Please could you pass her the one beside you, unless that is you need all the cushions we own for yourself?'

'Ah Catherine, you found me out. I was thinking of starting a cushion stall at the market, we've got so many.' Bill threw the cushion over towards Shylah as they all laughed together.

Shylah attended mass in the convent chapel each Sunday, joined in the Sisters' reedy, discordant hymn-singing and had not felt so secure since before Dad lost his job, moved into the attic and everything at home had gone crazy.

The soft, green lady came to see her every week and talked to her kindly about 'options' and 'choices'. Shylah listened politely and never said anything about the party. Nor did Shylah tell the soft, green lady that she had already made all her choices. If she could, she would live at the convent with Sister Anthony, the other nuns and the little baby with sweet, closed eyes, sleeping contentedly until she was old enough to live on her own and care for him or her.

CHAPTER 4

Magdalen College, Oxford, United Kingdom

February 1996

Shylah visited Gabriel only once during her three years studying anthropology at Magdalen College, Oxford. The practicality of transporting her son, Colm, from Market Hamilton to York railway station and thereafter all the way to Oxford was unthinkable. Furthermore, Gabriel's return to Market Hamilton every weekend in the trusty, if aged Austin mini, Patrick, rendered the unthinkable unnecessary.

In February, while Gabriel was in the final year of her degree, during one of her weekend visits, Bill and Catherine offered to take care of Colm for the weekend.

'It would give young Shylah a little break from her routine and you girls could spend some time together, you could show her around Oxford, have some fun,' Bill had been nominated as spokesperson for the couple. Catherine nodded with encouragement. Gabriel's heart warmed at their unassuming kindness. It was very clear that there had been numerous preparatory conversations between her parents during the week.

'Dad, are you sure you and Mum can cope for a whole weekend?' asked Gabriel, struck by the selflessness of the gesture. Four year old Colm was the height of an average six year old and had developed the clumsy inelegance which stalked him throughout his life. 'That wee boy has a whole arsenal of weapons-grade wrecking skills, well-honed and ready to be launched on the cottage and garden. A whole weekend is a long time and it's a while since you've both had a small child to care for.'

Bill and Catherine went on, anxious to close off all avenues which risked even an iota of offence. 'It would be a pleasure for us. We can move anything breakable up high. We won't be at all upset though if Shylah's parents aren't happy about Colm spending the whole weekend with us instead of them.'

'It's a really kind offer. I'm seeing Shylah later. I'll suggest it to her then. I doubt if it will be a problem with Mary and Peter but I'll check and let you both know.'

In actual fact, Gabriel was aware from Shylah's relayed conversations with Mary that Colm's maternal grandmother, had already announced zero intention of becoming involved with Colm or his care.

'I can't be expected to put up with small children and their snot,' she had said to Shylah after being informed of her grandson's birth. Gabriel had suspected that this applied in particular to small children born to a daughter out of wedlock.

Mary had more recently validated her absolution of responsibility by telling Shylah and Gabriel about a recent procurement:

'I bought a beautiful new downstairs carpet from Brintons, the ones with the royal crest, you know, so it simply is not possible to have a small child in the house, in case of spillages. Colm's very clumsy too, Shylah, you ought to get him checked out at the doctors, there's probably something wrong with him.'

Gabriel suspected that Peter, on the other hand, would have enjoyed the company of young Colm, clumsy or not. The lively laughter of a small child in the chilly hallways would surely provide a welcome distraction from the desiccated Mary. On the few occasions Gabriel had accompanied Shylah on visits to the Cooks recently, Mary had unleashed a tirade of unrelenting complaints, delighted at having an audience. The majority of complaints centred on Peter's various inadequacies, backed up by exhortations of how he was unworthy of any respect or authority. He would never be forgiven for leaving his well-paid job to go to the Council and reducing them to their current, penurious state.

Gabriel and Shylah sat in Gabriel's college room throughout the Saturday afternoon and into the evening. They drank the strong, rich Yorkshire tea provided by the scout, Stan, who was delighted at the opportunity to care for his favourite charge over the weekend.

'It's great that you have found a nice, pretty girl to spend time with here in Oxford, Gabriel. It always takes some students longer than others to make friends. Now you girls just sit here in the warm and enjoy your tea,' Stan was beaming, genuinely pleased that Gabriel had finally found some company.

At four o'clock Stan returned, bearing a plate of dripping crumpets and a pot of home-made strawberry jam, lovingly boiled and bottled at the hand of Beryl, his wife.

'This'll set you girls up for an evening of dancing. Beryl's won prizes for her jam, you know.'

Instead of dancing but certainly fortified by Beryl's splendid jam, Gabriel and Shylah spent the evening developing the concept and the ideas behind a delicatessen. They chose its name, 'Bennets'.

'We should name it something English, something Jane Austinish. How about naming it after Mrs Bennet from Pride and Prejudice? Do you remember we had to read it in English? Her marketing skills were amazing,' suggested Shylah.

'That's a great name, we'll bring fresh, exotic tastes to the inhabitants of Market Hamilton in the manner of Mrs Bennet bringing her fresh, exotic, spinsterly daughters to the marriage market,' replied Gabriel.

Amidst excited laughter and yet more gallons of Stan's tea, they shared ideas, built on each other's suggestions and crafted their plan. They worked late into the night, made product lists, designed signage and drew up floor plans on the sheets of A4 lined paper Gabriel used for her lecture notes. That evening they germinated the seed of an ambition which sustained Shylah's sanity over the coming years, until the dream could be realised.

At ten o'clock, they huddled in their pyjamas around mugs of hot chocolate and Gabriel's pint-sized portable television to watch the news.

'How can a computer play chess?' asked Shylah as the geeky reporter enthused over the capabilities of Big Blue, the chess-playing computer.

'I'm not sure, it seems a bit like we're in danger of computers taking over the world,' replied Gabriel.

'I'd much rather hear about a human story. I saw a fantastic Horizon programme the other day about the spread of AIDS. It was mostly about the USA but a bit about charity workers in Africa too.'

'Well, it sounds more interesting than this cyber intelligence nonsense.' replied Gabriel.

'Do you ever fancy doing charity work, Gabriel? There was this guy called Michael on the programme I saw. He's only about our age but he's already doing so much good out there.'

'Well I'd better finish my degree first but I'd like to do something worthwhile when I'm working. Shall we turn this off and go to sleep? We can talk some more about saving the world tomorrow.'

On Sunday morning in Oxford, Gabriel and Shylah rose early and enjoyed yet more of Stan's tea, absorbed in part by toast. They conducted themselves companionably to the bus stop to board the Oxford tourist tour. Sitting upstairs on the open air deck, they huddled together in their coats, gloves and scarves as it gently started to snow; diamond light over Oxford's somnolent, morning spires.

'This is Alice's sweet shop, let's get some sweets for Colm?' suggested Gabriel when they reached the erstwhile haunt of the Reverend Dobson's indelicate, unripe obsession. Over coffee they reminisced about their shared time at St Anne's and the joint peculiarities of the clergy and exclusively female religious environments. Despite Gabriel's wide-eyed disbelief, Shylah insisted that the majority of their classmates had shared a schoolgirl obsession with the fresh-faced, tidy-figured chemistry teacher, Sister Anthony.

'Everyone was so in love with her, how can you not have noticed, Gabriel?' she exclaimed laughing. 'It's not about lesbianism, it's just about the sort of obsessions that young girls in all girl environments have for the people in authority. They are all probably in relationships with men now, time moves on and people grow up.'

Shylah smiled and shook her head. Despite her intellect and confidence, Gabriel remained an endearing stranger to matters of the heart.

They journeyed onto the next stop on the tour and Shylah posed for a photograph with the English copy of the Bridge of Sighs in the background.

'What a daft name, 'Bridge of Sighs.' Quite romantic though,' she smiled then sighed and sighed in exaggeratedly dramatic fashion and they collapsed together with mirth at the non-joke. Why had it seemed so funny at the time, they would wonder in the future? The senseless nonsense which only those on top of the world and in the company of those they love find intoxicatingly funny.

They continued around the colleges arm in arm, head leaning on head. Shylah breathed in the delicious ginger scent of Gabriel's hair, sighed dramatically and they collapsed once more with mirth. They barely noticed nor did they care about Mubaarak, one of Gabriel's fellow students, whom they spied lurking and frowning in one of the college quadrangles. He issued a snide snort of disapproval as they passed.

'He comes from abroad and has a thing about women touching each other. Especially Western women. Apparently that sort of thing isn't allowed wherever it is he comes from. I wouldn't be surprised if he didn't come knocking on my door after you've gone to make a point of mentioning it to me.'

'Oh heck, he sounds awful. I should just send him packing if I were you.'

Gabriel hesitated. 'Well... he doesn't really have any friends. I feel a bit sorry for him. He's a bit of a misfit here in Oxford. No one knows much about him except that he's always sending enormous parcels of books back to wherever it is he comes from.'

'Sounds like a right weirdo and it'll be his own fault if he hasn't got any friends. Anyway let's not waste time talking about grumpy men who lurk about in the colleges. Let's grab another cup of tea in your room before I get the train.'

After walking Shylah to the railway station, Gabriel returned to her room alone, delighted that she now had the weekend among the treasured entries in her memory bank. She sat at her desk, carefully chose a sheet of handcrafted paper and wrote a short letter to her parents, describing in detail the sights she and Shylah had seen, the joy of being together and thanking Bill and Catherine for 'coping with' Colm. She knew already that their reply would be fulsome about the young Colm's many capabilities, skills and wonderments and scant on detail of the wreckage sustained at the cottage.

Gabriel's heart dropped as she heard Mubaarak's knock, later that evening. She opened the door to his friendless form and allowed his usual Sunday evening monologue to float unheard in the air above her head. After all, she expected that he had been alone all weekend and unusually this Sunday, she was not tired after a long drive. Moreover, she reflected that she and Shylah had created a vision, a purpose and a crystallising future in Bennets. In her head she listed their first stock order of sausages, pâté, Scotch eggs and Yorkshire ham. Mubaarak droned ever onwards and listed (again) the poisoning propensities of all pork products and the harlotry of close friendships between females. In his opinion, he espoused, indivisible from lesbianism, appropriately punishable by execution in civilised countries and rife, apparently, in Oxford. Mubaarak had clearly studied lesbianism very, very carefully.

CHAPTER 5

Magdalen College, Oxford, United Kingdom

July 1996

Gabriel suffered successive, choking waves of protectiveness throughout the tense, disappointing day. Bill and Catherine huddled together in the unfamiliar, uncomfortable surroundings of her Oxford College for her graduation celebration. After such a build-up, despite their excited anticipation and the fervent efforts at jolliness from all three, genuine enjoyment of the actual occasion proved to be a Sisyphean task. The day's memory was doomed perpetually to create sadness for all three of them. Bill and Catherine's gentle physical and vocal presence was diminished and fragile alongside the braying Amazonian parents of Gabriel's student contemporaries. The two small Salvationists stood straight, still and tidy in their new clothes, bought in honour of the occasion.

Gabriel had helped her Mum to procure a boxy, navy, lightweight woollen suit (Catherine's preference), classic court shoes (recommended by the shop assistant), a smart navy coat (practicality) and a swirling fiery silk scarf (Gabriel's choice) in Marks and Spencer.

'Mum, you look great; smart, sophisticated and then the scarf makes you look a bit modern too. You know I like you in something a bit brighter, it's time to experiment a bit,' encouraged Gabriel.

She had sat with her mother on the sofa in the cottage sitting room to admire her father as he laughingly 'modelled' his choice of suit and tie on his return from his own shopping trip to the local tailor.

'Wow, Dad, you look twenty years younger, they'll mistake you for one of the students.' They had all hugged laughing, eagerly looking forward to the occasion.

Gabriel left early on the morning of the graduation in her trusty conveyance, Patrick, the elderly British racing green Austin mini, to collect her parents from the station. Eschewing the profligacy of Gabriel's suggestion that they spend the night in a hotel, as a bit of a treat, they had stayed with some fellow Salvationists in Bicester.

When Gabriel saw them peering nervously through the glass door of the train, it was clear that neither of her pale, tired-looking parents had slept through their state of nervous excitement the night before. Throughout the entirety of the sweltering, stormy day they stuck closely, shakily together. They were permanently conjoined from shoulder to knee, walking slowly in step with one another, emulating a pair of small, dull fish huddling for protection in the face of a hungry predator.

Gabriel found herself over-providing the protection she sensed they needed, drawing upon her own imposing physical stature in the face of their unease.

'Don't worry, Mum,' she said, struggling to dissipate the tension with levity, 'I'll hold your arm and Dad will be just the other side. You don't need to worry, we won't let you trip on the cobbles in your new shoes.'

She positioned herself between her parents and the herd of other guests like a mare protecting her foals. After the interminable roll-call of the graduation ceremony, Bill and Catherine declined champagne and the successive lakes of alcoholic offerings before and during lunch. Silently and without fuss they said grace and then dutifully cleaned their plates of the unfamiliar fare so as not to cause offence to the college kitchen staff.

Gabriel and her parents, a physically mismatched threesome, had been positioned at the far end of the refectory table with the other college misfits. Some of the others in their state-school contingent stepped up their decibel output and espoused throughout lunch.

'Don't you find that timeshares in the Algarve are very reasonably priced these days? With all the money we will save on holidays, Simon will be able to buy a new BMW,' preached the most proximal dining companion, trying desperately to 'fit in' with the public school majority. Harold, the only person in Gabriel's year in a wheelchair (or indeed with any visible deviation from the Aryan standard) had table manners which could not be relied upon and hence had been secreted away, too, in the land of misfits. He was eagerly accompanied by his tall, grey, able-bodied parents, university lecturers from one of the aspiring red-bricks, keen to make the right impression among the academics and simultaneously make the most of the free food and drink on offer.

Mubaarak, the Muslim, was nearby; a solitary figure, he was unfettered by relations or friends. True to form, he was rudely hectoring, questioning college staff about food preparation practices, as each course was laid before him.

'Has this been prepared in a kitchen where pork has been present? I have told you all about this before, my meals must not be contaminated with everyone else's food.' He emphasised the final word, making it clear from his facial contortions, that 'mess' would have been a more apt description, but that he was too polite to say so.

The staff seized upon their well-rehearsed answers. Mubaarak had been hectoring in the same ill-mannered way for every course of every meal in the three previous academic years.

Grateful to escape the refectory after lunch, Gabriel offered to show her parents around her alma mater. She sheltered them through the complex cobbleways, gently guided them away from the forbidden practice of 'walking on the grass', chivvied them up her steep, stone, spiral staircase. She led them into her compact room with its pale grey light, unbleached cotton fabrics and Spartan minimalism. The ordered rows of books around three of the four walls, the pale, unglazed pottery mugs filled with pens and the piles of stationary and papers in wickerwork baskets dominated the place where Gabriel had spent solitary hours studying for her first class honours degree in anthropology.

'This is a cosy space Gabriel; you have made it lovely and homely,' said Catherine, relaxing and placing her trembling hand on top of Gabriel's which was larger, squarer, and stronger.

Bill paused by the exquisite, golden gentleness of the framed early 14c Byzantine icon, one of many depicting the Archangel Gabriel in female form, at the Annunciation. It had been a gift from Bill and Catherine to their beloved daughter, on her thirteenth birthday. He looked to his wife, then to his daughter and they smiled in synchrony in the harbour of the room which had been Gabriel's home from her real home.

'Your mother and I are very proud of you, Gabriel. We really did appreciate you coming home every weekend too. I know it must have been tiring for you, I hope you didn't feel we were putting you under any pressure,' said Bill. A diamond tear at the left hand side of his eye crept loose and gently dampened his suntanned, garden-lovers cheek.

'Dad, don't be silly. I wanted to be back in Yorkshire at the weekends. It's my home and I missed you and Shylah and of course I didn't want to miss out on seeing little Colm. I love you both dearly, you have been the best parents I could ever have wished for. You have made me ready to take on what I need to do.'

In silence the three of them embraced, the warm umbrella of Gabriel's long arms forming an impenetrable canopy around the family in the centre of the diminutive space.

Stan, the scout, knocked quietly on the door, entered and silently left a tray of tea and shortbread biscuits. Shortly afterwards, Bill's indigestion launched its attack in retaliation against the luncheon and having brought her new handbag in place of her usual trusty portmanteau for the occasion, Catherine had left his tablets at home.

'I'll tell you what, Mum, why not wrap the shortbread up in a tissue then you and Dad can enjoy it when dad feels better, back at home.' They stowed it in the new, smart, navy leather bag, it would be a treat for later when they were back amidst more comfortable surroundings.

Shortly after Stan's unimposing entrance and swift exit, Mubaarak also knocked at the door, substantially more loudly. He entered uninvited, sat on Gabriel's bed and started to lecture the small family on the dangers of alcoholic drink and the inappropriate quantities consumed by their contemporaries and their parents. Harold's parents came in for particular criticism in the face of an illogical expectation that the academically inclined parents of a disabled offspring should know better.

'You'd think that God has already shown them that they need to be more careful.'

Bill and Catherine were a confused, captive audience, too kind and embarrassed to interrupt Mubaarak, who quivering with rage, was warming to his virtuous purpose. He complained bitterly about the general lack of respect for his Muslim heritage which had sullied not only the last three years but also this, the hallowed day of his graduation. However, despite the many evils which reportedly stalked Mubaarak in the corridors of Oxford, he explained to the family, impervious to their rapidly waning interest, how he intended to remain for a further three years and secure the title of 'Doctor'.

'When I return to Saudi Arabia, I will be treated with proper respect in my country. Did you know that my parents emigrated from Morocco when I was small? My family have done very well in Saudi Arabia and as the only son, I intend to do even better when I have my PhD.'

After approximately five minutes, Gabriel decided enough was enough and fearful that a fresh and all too familiar cavernous well of subject matter was in danger of opening up, she stood to announce that her parents had to leave soon and catch their train. The move precipitated Mubaarak's reluctant retreat.

Extricated from Mubaarak's reverie, Gabriel and her parents enjoyed a fresh pot of tea. Together they contrived to conceal, in Catherine's now bulging handbag, the three slices of Beryl's special sponge cake, proudly borne into the room by Stan.

As Gabriel waved them goodbye, she reassured them. 'You were both great, thanks for coming all this way. I hope I made you proud today.'

'So proud love, so proud,' whispered a still tearful Bill.

'I'll be home in a few days and we can all be together again. I'll make you an apple pie when I'm back, Dad. You probably won't need it though with all that shortbread and cake.'

Bill and Catherine smiled weakly as they looked back through the rear window of the taxi at their treasured daughter who stood and waved. More diamond tears creeping from the left hand corners of each of their right eyes and gently dampening their respective regimental faces. As she walked back through the quadrangle to her room, Gabriel heard a robin sing from one of the trees, three shrill arpeggios ending unusually on the minor chord. She looked upwards and saw the coal black of the robin's eye before he flew upwards and away.

As she had promised her parents, Gabriel returned permanently to Yorkshire later that week after clearing her room and saying her very few goodbyes. As she parked outside the cottage, a kind lady police officer helped her from the car, held her forearm and informed her, in a professionally sympathetic tone that her return had coincided with the day of a tragic accident.

Bill, Catherine and little Brisk had all been killed in a cliff-top fall while walking on the Yorkshire moors, a few hours before her arrival.

CHAPTER 6

Kingston upon Hull, Yorkshire, United Kingdom

Spring and Summer School Terms 1996

Colm's Mummy looked forward to the weekends, so Colm looked forward to the weekends too. On Friday evenings, just before Colm had to go to bed, Mummy talked on the phone to her friend, Gabriel. They usually started talking just before bed time. Sometimes when Gabriel's traffic at Oxford had been bad or when they talked for an extra-long time about something special, Colm was allowed to stay up late. That meant Colm was allowed to watch telly until late on a Friday which was a good thing to look forward to.

The telly in the flat was about the same size as the cardboard box which Colm had to put his toys away in at night time, or to tidy up, if someone was coming round. The telly was smaller than the one at Gabriel's Mummy and Daddy's house and smaller, too, than the big black one at his Nana's house (but he had never been allowed to watch that one). Mummy's was made of white plastic and was going yellow like a dirty egg around the sides and also on the sticking-out curvy bit at the back.

There was an unwound coat hanger stuck into a little metal buttonhole at the back of the telly. When the picture went all grey and snowy, Mummy stood up and fiddled with the coat hanger. When she was holding onto the coat hanger, the picture went clear again and the sound came louder but then usually when she let go, the picture went back to how it had been before. Sometimes she would let go and then creep in a very funny way back to the sofa where they cuddled together, so the telly didn't notice and forgot to go snowy again. That made them both laugh. Sometimes she stuck the coat hanger in the right place with a bit of Sellotape. Sometimes she got sad and said she was sorry that they couldn't afford a proper telly and they cuddled under the green blanket made of special fluffy, holey knitting and looked at a book or did something else instead.

If the telly went snowy on a Friday, Colm had to do something else on his own because he mustn't interrupt when Mummy was talking to Gabriel. He had to be very careful not to knock things over or break them while Mummy was talking. Things broke and fell over very easily in the flat.

Colm had his own bedroom. Gabriel's Daddy had come round one day without Gabriel or Gabriel's Mummy and helped Mummy paint the walls so they looked nice with the Rosie and Jim cover and pillow case which Mummy had bought him for his birthday. In the space next to the bed, all his teddies sat in a straight line like nice, tidy soldiers. Gabriel's Daddy was a soldier but Colm thought he must be too old to be a proper one because he was always at home instead of with the other soldiers. Mummy explained that he was a Salvation Army soldier, a different type of soldier than the ones on the telly when Mummy sometimes watched the news. Colm thought she must have made a mistake about all that. He was definitely too old.

The tidy, soldier teddies sat next to the books which were in a tidy row on the floor of Colm's bedroom too. The books and the teddies were presents from the nuns who were ladies who lived in a special, big house together and wore black or blue dresses and little matching towels on their heads. Colm and his Mummy were very lucky because they were allowed to go and see the nuns in the special, big house where they all lived together. It was very nice when they went to visit the nuns. They sat in the nuns' big, woody kitchen with the paddling pool sized sink and Colm had a glass of milk or some orange juice, which was nicer than the orange squash they had at home. Colm had to be very careful not to drop or spill his drink. His Mummy told him he needed to concentrate.

The old nuns with bent hands gave him biscuits and sometimes little cakes in paper which he had to peel off before he could eat them. Most of the nuns wanted to cuddle him which he let them do because it was polite but their bent hands and papery faces felt very strange. Not at all like his smooth, soft Mummy or strong, cool Aunty Gabriel who smelt like lovely biscuits. Gabriel's Mummy cuddled him sometimes and that felt a bit nice but Gabriel's Daddy shook his hand like a grown up. When the nuns gave him presents, he always said 'thank you' because it was polite.

Going to church at the nuns' special church on Sunday was very boring. The nuns made coughing, burping and other impolite noises and all of them except Sister Anthony (who had no little towel on her head and wasn't very old) sang in squeaky, windy voices. It all went on for a very long time. Sometimes when one of the nuns made a very rude noise, Colm started giggling. Father Jim often winked at him when he saw him giggling or fidgeting in his seat but

Mummy always looked very cross so he tried hard to stop even though Father Jim liked it. Mummy looked cross too when he fell off his seat sometimes and it made a very loud noise and the old nuns jumped.

Mummy always went to bed after Colm because she had to pull up the top of the sofa and then heave out its very heavy insides, to turn it into a bed. She had to get the sheets and pillows out of the wooden box and sometimes it all hurt her back too much. When Colm was big and strong, he would be able to help her more. Mummy couldn't go to sleep before him because if he was still up, there wasn't enough room for him to walk around the bed made of the sofa's insides in the sitting room. In the mornings he sometimes went and got into the bed with her though and they cuddled. He didn't need to walk around then so it didn't matter.

Before Mummy went into the kitchen to make breakfast she had to take down the broom. Every night before she went to sleep, Mummy put a broom under the handle of the door to the hall and kitchen. The hall and kitchen had windows which faced out onto the grey outside corridor which went along everybody's front doors. Sometimes people walking along the corridor banged on the front door and the windows so the broom made it safer for Mummy and Colm in case the banging people jumped through into the flat.

Colm went on the bus with Mummy two mornings every week to playgroup. The bus ride was nice but it sometimes took a long time if the traffic was bad or it was raining and the windows went foggy. His Mummy always stayed and helped the other ladies at the playgroup while Colm played with the toys, painted, sang, danced and did all the other good fun things. His Mummy kept an eye on him and if he was getting too clumsy or things were breaking, she helped him put it right again. He had some special friends at the playgroup called James and Jonny. Sometimes they played soldiers together, just the three of them but it normally got too rough very quickly and they had to stop and sit down again with the others.

Colm remembered one very bad day when he had gone with his Mummy to see Nana after playgroup. They had to sit in the kitchen which had a hard, cold floor because Nana said he couldn't take his drink into the other rooms because of the carpets. Nana and Mummy were talking about schools. Mummy was saying that the school James and Jonny were going to was good and some others were bad. They were talking about very complicated things and Nana started shouting at Mummy. Mummy started crying and Nana shouted louder, saying horrible words to Mummy. Then Nana didn't come to the door when they went to the bus stop. After that Mummy talked very, very happily like she was singing a song when she talked to Colm about the school near the flat. She said they could not rely on any help from Nana either and had to cope on their own. Colm thought that they had been on their own for a long time anyway, so that should be OK.

Colm was looking forward to school but he felt scared too. He was going to the school Mummy had taken him to visit, just down the road from the flat, so Mummy would be able to walk with him in the mornings and come and get him afterwards. James and Jonny were going to school in Market Hamilton and he wanted to go to school with them so they could play soldiers but his Mummy said he couldn't go to the same school because they lived in Hull and Nana wouldn't let them say they lived with her.

On his first day at the school, Colm was very frightened when his Mummy went and he cried. The teacher was called Mrs Wilkinson and she was cross all the time. She said she didn't have time to deal with Colm and he needed to stop skriking. Colm asked her what skriking meant and she shouted very, very crossly at him about 'playing Mrs Wilkinson up'. All the other children laughed and he felt sadder so he still couldn't stop crying. Colm had seen some of the other children before, playing on the piece of grass with dog muck on it outside the flat. They always played without their Mummies there with them and Colm's Mummy wouldn't let him play with them because she said it wasn't safe. All the other children knew each other's names but no one knew his name. They whispered and laughed at him when he asked if they wanted to play animals with him, so he asked them whether they liked Rosie and Jim and told them about his bed cover; they laughed even more at him.

When it was playtime, a lady helping Mrs Wilkinson took them to the toilets. In the toilets, something terrible, very terrible, happened and Colm got poo on his hands. He pulled more and more and more of the pink, scratchy paper and tried to clean up the mess but the more he pulled, the more the paper spread the poo out, onto the wall, his hands and his trousers. The helping lady knocked on the door and shouted so Colm had to open it. There were other children outside the door when he opened it and the helping lady shouted, very, very loudly and very crossly. All the children were laughing and pointing at him and saying 'yuk'. At playtime and lunchtime and afternoon playtime, the other children didn't play with him. They called him 'Shitty' and even though the helping lady had washed his hands, they still smelt of poo and so did his trousers. He smelt it in the classroom creeping up to his nose from his trousers and the other children said 'poo' and held their noses shut with their fingers.

When his Mummy came to pick him up, Mrs Wilkinson made her go into the classroom to talk about something.

'You can just sit there quietly, young man, while I speak to your mother about your disgraceful behaviour today,' said Mrs Wilkinson in her shouty voice, pointing her waggy finger at Colm.

He sat on the bench under the coat pegs just outside the classroom door. There were no coats now, everyone had gone home and a man was sweeping the floor. He put his fingers to his nose when the man was looking away, they still smelled of poo. He sat very still so the smell of poo from his trousers didn't creep up to his nose or to the nose of the sweeping man.

His Mummy had been crying when she came out of the classroom, her eyes and nose were red. Colm was not surprised she had been crying, Mrs Wilkinson was a nasty, cross lady. He walked back to the flat with his Mummy but his Mummy didn't say anything all the way. They walked past the grass with dog muck on it, some of the children he had seen at school were playing on the grass. He waved at them and they shouted back, 'shitty Colm, stinky little bastard,' as he and his Mummy walked past.

When they got to the flat, Mummy ran him a bath, took his clothes away and brought his pyjamas. She sat on the lid of the toilet where she always sat while he was in the bath and looked very sad.

'Mummy, I'm sorry I made the mess,' said Colm.

'You've nothing to be sorry for, Colm. It's Mummy who's sorry today, love. It just isn't working out and it's Mummy who needs to make it better.'

After a little while Mummy spoke again.

'Chin up, love. I've got an idea who might be able to help us. You be a good boy and sit and eat your tea while I make some 'phone calls.'

He had toast and jam and was allowed to watch telly after the bath. His Mummy spoke to someone on the telephone in the kitchen for a very long time. Colm didn't think his Mummy was speaking to Gabriel because it wasn't a Friday and she was not laughing at all while she spoke even though it was a very long time. Two times Mummy stopped talking and then a bit later the phone rang and she started talking again. He lay down and cuddled up to his Eeyore on the couch while his Mummy kept talking on the telephone. In the morning, he woke up in the lounge on the couch and Mummy had slept in his bed.

Instead of walking to the school the next day, he and Mummy went to the bus stop.

'Mummy, aren't we going to Mrs Wilkinson's school today?' he asked, hoping not.

'I hope not, Colm. If everything works out for us today, I hope not ever again,' said Mummy. She was wrapping her tissue round and round and round her thumb in her lap as she spoke so Colm decided to be quiet in case she had a headache.

The bus was extra bumpy, the sun was shining and Colm looked into the gardens as they drove down the long, straight road to Market Hamilton. Mummy was very quiet for the rest of the journey and at the other end, Sister Anthony was waiting for them on the pavement. Sister Anthony kissed Mummy when they got off the bus and held her arms around Mummy for a long time while Colm waited and tapped his feet in a little puddle on the pavement, just little splashes, not so it went on his shoes properly. They went with Sister Anthony to the other school near the bus stop. He saw Jonny and James in the playground and waved as they walked past the windows with little grey wiggly squares in the glass stretching from top to bottom.

He had to sit in the corridor while his Mummy and Sister Anthony went into a room inside the other school. It was nicer than the corridor yesterday with the sweeping man. Lots of children were following their teachers to their doors in lines. The teachers put their fingers to their lips and said 'shhh' when the children were noisy, or pushed them back into their lines very gently if they were in the wrong place. No one was cross and loud like his teacher, Mrs Wilkinson.

After a very long time, Sister Anthony and Mummy came out of the room. Sister Anthony looked at Colm with her special face that made him feel like he was very strong and that he wouldn't knock anything over or break anything that day.

'Make me proud, my little man. This is a very special school and you are here because you are a very special young man,' Sister Anthony said, 'and don't forget to say a proper, grown up thank you to God.'

She kissed Mummy on the cheek. Her blue dress blew up like a round balloon with the wind when she walked away down the corridor and Colm could see the colour blue still there in the corridor even after Sister Anthony had turned the corner.

His Mummy smiled and said, 'Colm, please go to your classroom at your new school with Mr Downs. I will be here to pick you up and take you on the bus at home time.'

Colm felt very important walking through the blue corridor beside tall Mr Downs with his deep voice. He was saying 'Good morning' to everybody he passed and everyone was saying 'Good morning, Mr Downs' back. They went into one of the classrooms and Colm was very happy to see Father Jim at the front of the class with a lady who must be the new teacher, both of them were talking to the children.

Mr Downs talked quickly to the teacher while Father Jim continued with his story and the teacher told him to go and sit down in the spare seat next to Jonny and James. Father Jim winked at him as he sat down and Colm felt very proud for the second time that morning. The new teacher was called Miss Stevens. She had two helpers called Mrs Cooper and Mrs Taggert. The three ladies were very good at making all the children listen and go the places they were meant to go to. Everything happened properly in the classroom at the new school without any shouting or getting cross.

Colm and his Mummy went home on the bus together from the new school every evening. Sometimes they went to see the nuns first and had their biscuits and cakes with paper on. One day when they went to see the nuns, there was a little girl at the convent too and Colm was allowed to show the little girl where the biscuits and cakes were in the nuns' kitchen. Mummy told Colm he had to be kind to the little girl because she didn't have a Mummy or a Daddy and was living with a fostering Mummy instead.

'What's your name?' Colm asked the little girl.

'Rosemary,' she answered 'what's your name?'

'Colm. I'm five and I go to school.'

'I'm going to school soon too.'

Colm felt very grown up and proud looking after Rosemary and the nuns smiled funny eyes-closed smiles and made 'oooo' noises whenever he showed her how to do anything or told her where anything was.

Whenever it wasn't raining, the children from the old school were playing on the grass with dog muck on outside the flat. They shouted 'Shitty little bastard' when Colm and his Mummy walked past. One day when Colm and his Mummy got back to the flat there was a very nasty smell when they opened the front door. There was a piece of cardboard with a pile of dog muck falling off it onto the carpet on the floor. There was dog muck on the letterbox and on the inside of the door too. Mummy shouted a bit crossly at Colm.

'Oh God, I can't stand it anymore. This is disgusting. Just leave me to deal with it, Colm, and go and sit in your room.'

Through the door of his bedroom, Colm saw Mummy walk in and out of the lounge, through to the kitchen and back again with buckets and cloths and bottles of orange, yellow and green liquid. They had tea very late that night because Mummy had so much cleaning up to do in the hall. The smell of the dogs muck didn't go even though Mummy had worked so hard cleaning up.

Another day when they got back to the flat, someone had written something in big, brown, smelly, muddy letters all across the door and the front wall of the flat. The person had painted the smelly mud all over the kitchen window too. Colm was sad. His Mummy and Sister Anthony had made everything better at his new school where he played with Jonny and James and said 'Good morning' and didn't have Mrs Wilkinson shouting. But the people from the old school were still making him and his Mummy very sad at the flat. He had to go and sit in his bedroom again that evening, too, and have his tea on his own in front of the telly. Mummy spoke to Gabriel for a long time on the telephone from behind the closed kitchen door that night. She was crying a lot, Colm could hear.

There had been a lot of crying anyway in the last few weeks, ever since the weather had got sunny, because Gabriel had been very sad too. Her Mummy and Daddy and her little dog Brisk had died and gone to heaven and Gabriel was all on her own like Mummy. It made Colm's throat ache very painfully whenever he thought about not seeing Gabriel's Mummy and Daddy again and it made him cry properly when he thought about Brisk. Gabriel's Mummy and Daddy had let Colm throw Brisk's ball for him in Gabriel's Daddy's garden whenever they went to see them on Saturdays and on other days too. Brisk always brought the ball back and dropped it at Colm's feet. He never minded when Colm didn't throw straight or threw the ball too high. Brisk just ran and got the ball and brought it back. Throwing the ball for Brisk had been Colm's favourite game except for when he played soldiers with Jonny and James.

Mummy brought him a slice of toast and a glass of milk while he was still in bed the next morning. She was smiling and when she smiled, Colm saw a special shiny thing happen under her skin. He touched her cheek and it felt warm and soft.

'Hurry and eat up, Colm, while I pack up your things for you,' said Mummy. 'We're going to stay with Gabriel for a while. It will be nice for us to look after her, now she's all alone. It will be nearer your school too and, best of all, we can get away from the horrible people here and the horrible things they say and do to us.'

Colm finished his toast, put on his clothes all by himself and then helped Gabriel and Mummy take the carrier bags and boxes along the grey, windy walkway with flying papers, past the other people's front doors and kitchen windows. He carried them down the concrete steps which smelt of wee and cut you if you fell on them. The three of them put everything in Gabriel's little green car called Patrick. Patrick winked as Colm came towards him with the heavy carrier bags, just like Father Jim had winked when he first got to the new school. Mummy was smiling her special shiny smile again like she had been all morning. Gabriel was being big and strong, helping Mummy with the bags and boxes in her special swingy red clothes with a big black scarf and jangling metal things on both her wrists.

Colm looked into the concretey eyes of the children on the grass with the dog muck from his safe place in a small gap between the bags piled onto Patrick's back seat. No one would hurt them now and Mummy could stop crying. Colm felt his own smile shine warmly under his skin, just like Mummy's did. Maybe Gabriel would get a new puppy for him to play with in the garden at her house; but he knew he mustn't be greedy.

His bottom bounced and danced on Patrick's back seat and they drove along the very straight road from the flat in Hull back to Gabriel's cottage. Colm loved Patrick's gurgly engine and his wobbly windows. Patrick was all uneven and up and down, like talking, not the brooooooom, broom-broom of a bus or the hummy, whirry sound of other cars. Gabriel stopped in a squeaky, jumpy way outside the cottage and Colm was allowed to run round the back on his own to see the garden.

Bill stood by the vegetable patch, looking into the distance over the fields. He turned round just as Colm reached the apple tree, looked at Colm's eyes, smiled and made the special 'thumbs-up' sign which he only made to Colm, never, ever to the ladies. Colm stood completely still and watched as Bill melted slowly into the air until he was invisible again. A pretty bird with an orange chest sat in the tree and sang a pretty whistly song with three, long, wobbly verses. Colm ran back round to Patrick to help Mummy and Gabriel with the carrying.

CHAPTER 7

Market Hamilton, Yorkshire, United Kingdom

July 1996 to 1999

Shortly after graduating, from the many offers she received, Gabriel chose a job as a graduate management trainee in the Yorkshire-based office of a major global Superbrand. At first, during the vanilla familiarisation tour, the job was indistinguishable from any of the other 'graduate management trainee' offers from the brands and Superbrands who courted first class honours graduates from Oxford. The location, however, was ideal and with Bill and Catherine's recent demise, she would be able to build her life at the cottage and support Shylah as they realised their dream – Bennets.

She commuted daily to the office in trusty Patrick, still functional if a little tired following his weekly pilgrimages from Oxford. On her return each evening, she tried hard to listen through the silence for a signal as to where her priorities should be, what direction she should follow.

No guidance, no message and no clarity came to Gabriel throughout those long, lonely evenings. She concluded that it was too soon and instead clung morning 'til night to the repetitive news briefings on Radio Four to fill the silent spaces previously occupied by the beloved Bill and Catherine.

On one such evening, she was entranced by a programme which explained how many African leaders had simply failed to acknowledge the existence of AIDS, its relationship to HIV or to admit that there was a problem. As a result, AIDS was spreading in their countries, where prostitution and extra marital relations were rife, like a plague. Africans were resorting to unthinkable 'traditional cures', the result of which was to spread the scourge even further. She wondered whether this was where her priorities should be and continued to seek the guidance she craved.

She became depressed by the vortex of scrutiny afforded to the Dunblane Massacre squeezing out more humanitarian concerns like the affordability of antiretroviral drugs in African countries.

After the intellectual thrill of lectures and peaceful studiousness of her room in Oxford, the work in Superbrand's corporate vortex in those early days was a depressing blend of the monotonous and the pointless. The Superbrand was a greedy, slave-driving taskmaster, penny-pinching and quality-quashing across his entire valueless supply chain. Her graduate management trainee contemporaries were a shallow pool obsessed with the price of everything and oblivious to the value of anything at all.

'So Gabriel, do you actually own the cottage you're in? No mortgage or anything.'

'I'd rather have my parents alive and them owning it instead. Wouldn't anyone?'

'Well, a house without a mortgage would be nice. I don't get on with my parents anyway.'

Gabriel was horrified at their materialism, their prying interest in her personal and financial situation and their cliquishness; reminiscent of some of the worst school days at the convent.

Gabriel started to carve a reputation for herself as an excellent Human Resources project manager. She transformed the Superbrand's recruitment, training and retention practices and relentlessly drove an agenda to maximise the contributions of minority groups in the workforce. The senior management at the Superbrand were quick to see the potential to secure personal gain as a result of Gabriel's talent and hard work.

Spring transitioned to summer, and Bill's garden transitioned from order to disorder. His rambling roses rambled a thorn or two too far and his vegetable patch vegetated weedily. Shylah and the young Colm were already visiting the cottage so frequently that when they moved out of their terrible flat in Hull to live with her at the cottage, Gabriel reflected that she had hardly noticed the transition. Her Radio Four addiction was rendered superfluous and she was released from the more gruesome details of the Dunblane catastrophe by the comforting chaos of their company.

'Are you sure we're not too noisy for you here, Gabriel? Colm is a bit boisterous.'

'Boys are meant to be boisterous, Shylah, and I was climbing the walls here on my own without Mum and Dad. I don't think I can cope with the garden either without some help.'

'Don't worry, we'll have the garden back to how it used to be in no time, leave it to me and Colm,' smiled Shylah.

'Yes, leave it to me and Mummy. I'll ask Bill how to do the jobs in the garden next time I see him,' added Colm.

Shylah shrugged at Gabriel and they silently both decided not to remind Colm of Bill's recent death.

While Gabriel was at work that autumn and winter, Shylah tackled the cottage garden. She returned it to its previous order, readied it for another spring and managed months of productivity of which Bill would have been proud.

In the evenings, Gabriel and Shylah worked together on their business plan for the deli'. Colm was at school in the town and one Friday afternoon while he was engaged in painting a portrait of Gabriel, the physical Gabriel and his mother shared a bottle of champagne and a box of gingery Lebkuchen as they signed the lease. Bennets was soon to be a reality in recently emptied premises which matched the dimensions of the floor plans drawn up in Oxford on a Sunday afternoon three years before.

'There, that's all the legal stuff done. Now we just need to work towards the opening,' said Gabriel

'What do you mean 'just', there's so much to do,' Shylah's voice was infused with a hint of panic.

'Don't worry, we'll do it together, I'm thinking of leaving my job soon anyway.'

'Why? I thought you liked it. It's a handy commute, much better than London.'

'Well the job's OK and I really enjoy creating opportunities for women, the disabled and that part of it, but the people are not really very inspiring.'

'What will you do, Gabriel, will you be able to stay and work in the shop with me?' Shylah was hopeful.

'You won't need me for good, but I want to be around at the start. I'm thinking of going freelance, being choosier about what I take on so I can focus more on equal opportunity projects. I'd like to work more internationally too, if I can.'

'Are you sure you're not being too hasty?'

'No, I've thought it through and it's the right thing, I'm sure. I want to take a bit of time off to concentrate on Bennets, just while we get it set up. I don't want to miss out on all the fun now it's actually happening.'

'Well, if you're sure.'

'I am, Shylah. When I see things on the telly like the work people like that guy Michael are doing in Africa to help AIDS victims, it makes me realise how much I am wasting my time and my talents where I am now.'

When Gabriel announced her intention to shake off Superbrand's shackles and escape to the fresh fields of freelance freedom, her Superbrand bosses were horrified. Their crutch had been axed from beneath them, and they hadn't seen it coming.

She had been diligent, making the most of Superbrand's training and had avoided the nightly drunken revelries and inter-office liaisons enjoyed by her graduate contemporaries. Working for herself, she would chose her projects carefully and turn away those which did not fit with her values. Away from the imprisonment of the Superbrand, she could work hard, receive a fair return and utilise her talents to deliver outcomes of which she could be proud.

The majority of those who had ignored her as she studied alongside them at Oxford, were subsequently in awe of her achievements. To the many people who worked for her over the years she became a trusted mentor, coach and friend.

The perpetually friendless Mubaarak was periodically in touch when he needed Gabriel's skills to further his own ambitions. As predicted, he had completed his PhD, earned himself the title of Doctor and returned to Saudi Arabia where he had joined the ranks in the oil business. Gabriel thought he may have married and had a family like most men of his age but was unsure. In truth, Mubaarak's private life remained a mystery and he was always unwilling to enter into private discussions. Mubaarak's preferred subjects of conversation were now his own professional excellence, the professional inadequacies of others and the extent of his personal success. Compelling conversation indeed.

CHAPTER 8

Market Hamilton, Yorkshire, United Kingdom

November 2012

The phone was already ringing inside the cottage when Gabriel returned from Bennets.

'It's Doctor Mubaarak here, I have been trying to get you for over a week now, Gabriel.' The receiver rattled with his irritation. 'I have some Saudi Arabians coming to the UK to see some recruitment centres next week and I need you to do a presentation. Please book your ticket to London as soon as possible. Your presentation will be ninety minutes, about the work you did setting up the women's recruitment centre in Bahrain. The one where we won the prize. It's an excellent case study for what they are trying to do and I really need to be selected as leader for this.'

'Hello Doctor, it's so nice to hear from you, it must be about three years since we spoke,' Gabriel smiled to herself. Despite the passage of time, Mubaarak's exclusive focus on his own priorities and insensitivity to those of others could always be relied upon. 'Why didn't you leave a message on the machine and I would have called you back, Doctor?' Would she be able to get the word Doctor into this conversation ten times, she ventured silently to herself? She fancied the challenge!

'I needed you to confirm immediately, Gabriel, these are very important people from Saraco, you need to realise that.'

Gabriel could picture Mubaarak ruffling his feathers in London as he immediately launched into details of time and location and finished with the emphatic requirement that Gabriel send her presentation materials for his review 'by tomorrow, six o'clock UK time.'

'You're staying in London, how nice, how long have you been there? Are you at a hotel?' Gabriel's capricious attempt at small talk was bound to rile.

'Gabriel, I need you to concentrate on preparing for the meeting. Yes, I am in London. You don't need to concern yourself with where I am staying. Now please focus on the meeting.' Mubaarak had adopted the petulant tone he reserved for occasions when others endeavoured to steer the conversation towards their own agenda. Many years of experience in Mubaarak-management had taught Gabriel that more small talk was inadvisable.

Gabriel reflected some time later that she could have refused there and then to Mubaarak's unreasonable and (as usual) entirely self-motivated request, interrupting her Sunday afternoon. After years, however, of playing the role of the only person with any patience at all for the friendless Mubaarak and his unique approach to human relations, she acceded. She enjoyed the sport of teasing him and hoped to prove to herself eventually that his 'heart was in the right place'. She would need to find the elusive organ first, of course.

Gabriel's accession to Mubaarak was not entirely selfless either. She had never worked with Saudis before and was fascinated by the country. In the wake of 9/11, over ten years previously, amidst the troubling emergence of Christian – Islamic tension, Saudi was growing in world importance. Mubaarak had mentioned that the Saudis were travelling from Jeddah, a city very close to Mecca, the Holy City of Islam and birthplace of the prophet Muhammad.

'Could this be a sign?' Gabriel reflected.

Her presentation was duly 'quality checked' by the pernickety Doctor Mubaarak on Tuesday morning. Predictably, she hadn't needed to rearrange her plans to help Shylah and Colm in Bennets and rush to finish it by six o'clock on Monday at all. She smiled wryly, sitting at her laptop in the cottage, when it reappeared in her inbox bearing several inconsequential changes which served the sole purpose of making Doctor Mubaarak feel important. This wasn't the first time and wouldn't be the last. Wearily patient, she agreed to run through on the 'phone what she planned to say and having passed Mubaarak's personal censorship panel, all was deemed ready for Thursday, London and the visiting Saudis.

Gabriel stood under the soaring Victorian roofs, among clanging tracks, inaudible announcements and other commuters on York station. She caught sight of Shylah's Dad on the opposite platform and waved. He was looking so old and tired these days. Unsurprising, having lived with Mary's unrelenting criticism for so long. Peter Cook didn't see her nor did he wave back, too absorbed in whatever he was doing there on a Thursday morning.

Despite Mubaarak's exhortations to travel on Wednesday evening, stay overnight and run through the presentation one final time face to face with him, Gabriel had erred on the side of caution where saving her sanity was concerned and avoided an interminable evening being told how to do what she already did very well by the Doctor. Mubaarak's stress, conveyed to Gabriel via phone, text and email that week, was becoming more viral by the day, would probably be infectious in close physical proximity and was hence best given a wide berth.

Gabriel towered at least six inches above the diminutive frame of Mubaarak in the foyer of the Park Lane Hilton. With a full two hours to spare before the meeting, Mubaarak was panicking about lack of preparation time. When they reached the allocated room, Mubaarak's flapping intensity escalated exponentially. Gabriel did everything possible to ignore him as she ran through her usual preparations; connecting her laptop, testing the projection equipment, focussing her presentation, ordering her notes.

'Doctor Mubaarak, are you able to tell me something about the people who will be in the room today?' Gabriel's pen was poised above her black, leather-bound notebook.

Mubaarak, already sweating profusely in his vest, jacket and tie, reddened, furtled through his laptop bag and drew out an ungainly heap of papers. Irrespective of Gabriel's question, the perspiring Mubaarak pursued an oblique agenda.

'These clients are not used to working with women, Gabriel. You need to understand that Saudi is a very strict Islamic culture and women are not allowed to be with men in the workplace. They have only agreed to meet you because I have told them about your professional achievements and how you are too tall and large for them to worry about your being a woman.'

Gabriel knew that to allow the volcanic spume of laughter to escape from her throat could be the final straw for the now hyperventilating Mubaarak. 'Thank you for that,' she replied. The irony was lost.

'I am also glad to see that you are modestly dressed, Gabriel,' he added, 'I meant to mention that on the 'phone.' Again the volcano promised to erupt as Gabriel reflected that she could not remember a time when she had dressed immodestly in her professional life, not one bikini or basque at the board table, Islam, Saudis or neither.

'In Saudi Arabia, of course, women wear abaya,' Mubaarak smiled contentedly, clearly approving of such garments to fetter the globes and crevices of the female form. 'You will need to sort all that out if we are successful today.' Mubaarak's presumptuousness knew no bounds; they hadn't even discussed how her expenses for the train journey to London were to be covered.

The Saudis arrived, smart-suited, handsome, olive-skinned and gentlemanly; no visible signs of discomfort in the presence of the non-woman, Gabriel. As instructed (by Mubaarak) Gabriel offered her hand to each Saudi first to prove that she did not feel defiled by the unwelcome invasion of a handshake. Mubaarak obsequiously meandered through an interminable introduction to the hotel, London, the UK, the world, and the Saudis started meddling with their phones. At the bleep of an alarm, Mubaarak announced a break for Asr, the afternoon prayer. The Saudis looked at one another in surprise, there was some muttering and discussion in Arabic following which they casually confirmed that they intended to take advantage of the leeway allowed during times of travel, and bunk-off prayers for the next two days. They continued to meddle with their 'phones instead.

Having raised the subject of prayer, with no viable excuse for bunking-off himself and terrified that leaving Gabriel in the meeting room alone with the Saudis would result in professional catastrophe, Mubaarak announced a coffee break. The Saudis would use the meeting room, he would go and pray in solitude and Gabriel would implicitly make herself scarce for fifteen minutes. Gabriel smiled as she wandered alone through the opulent spongy-carpeted corridors of the hotel, reflecting on events so far. You could say one thing about working with Mubaarak; despite his complete absence of any sense of humour, it was always good comedy for everyone else involved.

Gabriel wandered into a side room where a gargantuan TV screen flickered on the wall. An on-screen orator stood head and shoulders above everyone around him. As Gabriel listened, she felt his black, velvet voice vibrate through every neurone. The highlights on his rich chocolaty skin reflected golden in the African, evening sunshine. The camera panned outwards to scan the crowd, thousands of people gathered outside in the African heat, rapt, barefoot on the dusty earth. The camera panned back to the stage and Gabriel noticed that the man was flanked by African men in suits, women swathed in vibrant cloths, with architectural millinery shading their dark, privileged faces. As the man spoke, his muscular arms, luminescent through his shirt, gestured with strong, graceful movements, drawing the silent crowd and dignitaries into his message, into his heart, into his mind.

He was speaking not only to those people but to the people of Africa, his message extolled respect, dignity, clean-living and self-restraint. The subject was the spread of AIDS in the continent. Gabriel was physically unable to move from the room, transfixed for every one of the twenty minutes she was there. She realised that the orator was Michael and he held thousands in the palm of his expansive hand. Every single one of those people would leave that dusty place committed to following his word. She had heard mention of a charity leader, Michael, many times already, but only now did she realise the extent of his charisma. She was consumed with tingling elation at the realisation they were sharing the same time on the same earth.

Unmoved by her rapture, the TV switched to a story about the solar eclipse and a shocked Gabriel realised the time. Fearing the wrath of Mubaarak, she ran back to the meeting room, entering as Mubaarak concluded his opening dialogue and the Saudis remained fixated on their phones; stark contrast with Michael's command of the thousands of Africans a few minutes before.

As Gabriel delivered her presentation, the Saudis, possibly more respectful in the presence of a woman, however unwomanly her physique, took notes and asked questions. Phones lay sleeping on the tables throughout and Gabriel enjoyed herself as she told her story. The Saudis explained they had been given a target to recruit and train one hundred women by 2015, the government having recently introduced a Saudiisation points system: one for a Saudi man, two for a Saudi woman, three for a Saudi handicapped person and deductions for employing foreigners. Gabriel wryly considered how such a patriotic approach to employing the British workforce might be received in the United Kingdom. The Saudis had work to do, the London visitors knew it and Gabriel's experience in setting up minority recruitment and opportunity schemes was music to their ears. Mubaarak's vested chest was swelling, his smile threatened to split his ears; the session had been a success and Doctor Mubaarak was poised to slurp up every dram of credit.

A trip to the bar was proposed (by the Saudis), Mubaarak launched himself decisively into the role of coordinator for ALL follow-up, lest any credit for today's good meeting should dare to dribble in the direction of another, and the group temporarily dispersed. Mubaarak took the opportunity to remind a smiling Gabriel how she should be grateful that his ingenuity and genius, having coordinated this afternoon, had enabled her success and broadened her professional network.

'Gabriel, you are very fortunate that I have engaged you in this opportunity. Now may I remind you that these very important people are strict Muslims. On no account whatsoever, must you order an alcoholic beverage.'

'Thank you, Mubaarak, for your advice. I'm so glad you thought this afternoon went well.'

'It has only gone well so far, Gabriel. If you slip up and cause offence in the bar now, the whole project could be off.'

'I'll do my best to control myself, Doctor.'

Mubaarak shot Gabriel a withering glance which he swiftly sequestered, rearranging his features into a sycophantic smirk as they entered the bar.

As they took their seats in the dimly-lit booth, the Saudis had just finished pouring the first bottle of Chateauneuf du Pape. Another was ordered, two more glasses appeared and Mubaarak declined, alone with his mineral water. Clearly the excusements of travel were broader than the good Doctor had expected. They stayed an hour or so, the Saudis procured bottle number three and Mubaarak announced that it was time for him and Gabriel to leave. He stood and his expression bade a surprised Gabriel to do likewise. Goodbyes said, hands shaken and promises to be in touch made, she followed the Doctor out onto the street.

'Would you like to share a cab? Or maybe we could have dinner?' Gabriel asked. Mubaarak twitched uncomfortably, fidgeted with his bag and started tutting.

'No, I will go home alone, thank you, Gabriel, I have some things I need to do this evening.' He hailed a cab and jumped inside leaving Gabriel alone on the street.

Home? Mubaarak's home was in Saudi, she thought. The Doctor was being very mysterious about his domestic arrangements in London.

On her walk to the tube station through crowded, rainy streets, Gabriel reflected on the afternoon. Mubaarak hadn't changed but she still felt loyalty to one of the few people who had bothered to talk to her at Oxford; she wanted to help the little vest- wearing Doctor if she could. The Saudis were clearly interested in her subject and impressed with her experience, and the project and the Saudi approach to eliminating imported labour sounded fascinating. Her glimpse today of the complexities and conflicts of Muslims in today's world, the haphazard observance of Islam's numerous rules and regulations were similarly captivating. She was interested in a professional sense. She also allowed her mind momentarily to reflect that Saudi Arabia was closer to Michael in Africa than she would be in the UK.

She bought a paper at the station, boarded the train and settled into her prickly seat for the two hour journey. She was hoping to read more about Michael and his message in Africa and was delighted to find that coverage of the African AIDS epidemic was at once extensive, fascinating and horrific. Gabriel gorged on her newspaper, hungry to understand everything about Michael and his message, chastising herself for her foolishness at not having realised before the brilliance and significance of the charity leader. Gabriel did not see the English countryside flash past the train window that night, mesmerised by her newspaper, her Michael.

The paper explained how Michael's message was the only thing making any difference to the behaviour of the African people. Numerous commentators from around the world were in awe of how an articulate but ordinary man was able to create such a following and through delivering a simple message, make such a positive change. Michael had found his platform, he had been guided towards the AIDS epidemic; Gabriel was still waiting.

Gabriel telephoned Shylah shortly before the train reached York.

'Did they have tea towels on their heads?' Shylah was laughing as she answered the 'phone. 'Did Mubaarak make you cover your face with one of those black things with only a slit for the eyes? Was the good Doctor on odd-bod form?'

'They were all very westernised, as far as I could tell, unless it was all an act to try to get me out there to help them. And you'll be pleased to hear that the Doctor was on absolute top form, odd-bodishness well under wraps today,' Gabriel replied. 'By the way, have you heard the latest news about Michael, the guy in Africa who's getting so many people to listen to him, when he talks about AIDS?'

'Of course I have. He's been on the TV this week, people are travelling miles and standing for hours in the hot sun, just to listen to him,' Shylah replied. 'Everyone says that despite all the money being spent on AIDS by the churches and charities, over the years he has been in Africa, he's made more of an impact than all of it added together, just by talking to people and asking them to change attitudes.'

'Yes, he is brilliant. I'm so glad he's here.' Gabriel lapsed into reflective silence before stirring herself again. 'By the way, Shylah, I saw your Dad on the station, I waved but I don't think he saw me.'

'I wonder where he was going. Mum never mentioned anything, although she probably wouldn't have done anyway. I'll see you in the morning, Gabriel, I need to just go and finish off in the shop with Colm.'

Later that evening, Shylah 'phoned Gabriel at the cottage. She had just received a call from the police advising her that Peter had died on a train from York to Edinburgh that morning.

'Gabriel, I know it's late but please would you be able to come and help me tell Mum what's happened. The police say they haven't been able to get hold of her.'

Gabriel and Shylah reached the Cooks' house where, despite the darkness, three magpies were still fighting over something dead on the front lawn, pecking at one another, jumping, landing, pecking at their prey. They didn't notice Gabriel and Shylah as they engaged in their nocturnal greed.

Gabriel and Shylah heard doors slamming and lights being switched on in the hallway. Mary must have been in the sitting room when they rang the doorbell, she took several minutes to open the front door and release the deafening reverberation of canned laughter from the TV. There was a half empty bottle of wine in her hand and a less than welcoming expression trapped her pinched features as she opened the door.

'Mum, I'm really sorry but we've come with some bad news. Can we go inside?'

Reluctantly Mary stood aside and let them pass.

'I have a guest arriving soon,' she said 'You can't stay long'.

'Mum, this is important. I'm afraid that Dad died this morning. The police called me, it happened on a train,' said Shylah, her voice trembling.

Mary didn't pause and her facial expression remained unaltered. 'The Council 'phoned me this morning to say he hadn't turned up at work. I wondered where he was,' she tossed at them in a matter of fact tone, ushering the horrified pair out of her hallway before the arrival of the anonymous guest.

In public, Mary played the role of bereaved widow with Victorian, post Albertine aplomb. She sat beside Shylah, Colm and his three uncles at the front of the church for the funeral and forced a delicate tear for her audience. In private, she cleared the attic of Peter's effects, filling black plastic sacks and leaving them outside for the bin men, within twenty four hours of his death. The extra attic space would be handy. Peter had been very well insured and the Council took their responsibilities for death in service and employees' dependents very seriously. She cleared the mortgage within the week and booked herself on a luxurious cruise with her windfall; just reward, she observed, for putting up with the worthless Peter for as long as she did. Despite the gluttonous hints from her sons which swiftly metamorphosed, after the funeral, into outraged demands for a cut of the winnings, she had no intention of allowing anyone else in the family to share in what she described as her 'bit of good fortune'.

Gabriel went to the Cooks' house with Colm as Shylah's stand-in after the funeral for the obligatory sherry and nibbles. Mary intended to play her bereaved part to the full and Shylah, unable to cope with another helping of hypocrisy with her sherry, returned home alone.

'Thanks for going in my place, Gabriel. I can't take any more. I'm sorry. Please just say I don't feel too well.'

She let herself in to the back door of Bennets and crept silently upstairs; the girl minding the shop could cope for another thirty minutes, she told herself. As she sat and drank her tea, wrapping her fingers round the heavy mug for comfort, her mind churned.

What had Dad been doing on a train to Edinburgh? He didn't know anyone in Edinburgh as far as Shylah knew, and he hadn't let anyone at the office know where he was going, which was odd. The police said he had nothing with him, no bag, only his 'phone and wallet with a picture of Shylah, a nun and Colm as a baby. Shylah didn't know he had a picture of them and couldn't remember it being taken. Mary certainly hadn't allowed any pictures of Shylah and Colm in the house in case the neighbours asked difficult questions.

'Shylah is such an unusual name,' the kind police lady had said, 'that's how we found you on his 'phone.'

If he had been going to the hospital or something, he could have done all that in York or Leeds. As she struggled in confusion, Shylah was struck with the sudden realisation that Dad's funeral had been the only time the Cook family had all been in the same room together since she moved into the convent, over twenty years previously. She barely recognised her three overweight, middle-aged, affluent-looking siblings in their suits and black ties and was confused which of the horsey-looking women who accompanied them belonged to which brother.

Any one of the parishioners of St Francis Xavier's RC Church, Market Hamilton would describe the Cooks as a 'nice, close Catholic family,' Shylah reflected. How little any of us really know about what happens behind the closed front doors of other executive, four bedroomed, detached homes. Dads live in the attic, Mums have long term liaisons with the local garage owner and care so little that they ignore 'phone calls from work heralding potential disaster. Moreover, unmarried teenage mothers are ostracised for years on end and estranged uncles first meet their nephew at his grandfather's funeral.

Shylah was shocked at the rising bile in her trachea and the excoriating bitterness towards her Mum. Mary had always had it her own way, had treated her Dad, Colm and Shylah appallingly. Rather than get what she deserved in the end, she had got it all her own way again with Peter's early death, leaving her free to do whatever it was she did, while still comparatively young, and with a financially secure future.

The bile rose again.

CHAPTER 9

Market Hamilton, Yorkshire, United Kingdom

December 2012

'Of course we'll all miss you but it's only twelve months,' said Shylah as she and Gabriel shared lunchtime risotto and a bottle of Chablis at Gabriel's dining table.

'Mubaarak did say they had never had a woman manage anything in Saudi, so it is breaking new ground and that interests me, but it still makes me nervous.'

'Go for it Gabriel, we can take care of the cottage and everything here for you. We are so proud of you, you'll be great and the time will fly.'

The robin sat on the bare branches of the apple tree outside the sitting room window; waiting. As soon as the women came from dining room to sitting room with their coffee, he would sing, three shrill arpeggios and Gabriel would call Mubaarak to confirm that for the next twelve months, she would be working close to the birthplace of the prophet Muhammad.

The following morning, Gabriel braced herself before the teetering pile of paperwork on her table. Mubaarak had explained that the process to secure her Saudi work visa required the intervention of several middle-men, 'normal practice,' he said, in the Saudi culture. So far, Gabriel had encountered three of the middle-men, all named Muhammad (albeit the spellings varied between each), all clear on the scale of their charges and all vague about what they would do to get the visa. While equality in the workplace was commonplace in the rest of the world, securing work visas for women had passed the Muhammads by! Things were moving too slowly for the ever-anxious Mubaarak who intervened and pointed out to the Muhammads that had Gabriel been single and attractive (rather than single, well over thirty, very tall and unattractive), the process would have been far more complex. The Muhammads agreed to redouble their efforts, sent Gabriel more forms and requested a new set of 'unattractive' photographs. The Saudi authorities were clearly fearful of the crowds of young, attractive, single women all clamouring at the airports to travel to the Kingdom in search of a Saudi husband.

This was going to be an interesting year. Gabriel moved on to the second item on her list of tasks. Despite fervent online searching, she found information about the appropriate attire for professional women in Saudi to be scant. Mubaarak had counselled vaguely on the need for an abaya and she sourced descriptions and diagrams of the garment without too much trouble. She read that she would require a floor-length, long-sleeved, black article which must not cling to or stretch over the female form and was to be worn at all times outside the home or in the presence of men. She further learned that failure to wear an abaya in public would guarantee arrest; Mubaarak had not been quite as open as he might have been about that.

Gabriel duly travelled to Bradford that morning (the internet's recommended Northern British seat of Muslim attire) to seek an appropriate purveyor. She travelled by train from York, arrived at 10 a.m., found every shop in the recommended Muslim shopping area closed and the streets deserted. It wasn't Friday, the Muslim day of prayer, so what was going on? She consulted a shop doorway to find that opening times aligned with another time zone and were from noon until late in the evening. She settled down to a long, long coffee break in one of the Lebanese cafes. Eventually at 12.30 there were gentle signs of life behind one of the shop windows. Gabriel approached and entered a dingy establishment piled high with dusty boxes, books, bottles and shisha.

'I am looking for an abaya please,' she said to the assistant who avoided eye contact at all costs, and shrunk behind his boxes.

'Fatima!' he called through a curtain at the back of the shop and Gabriel waited in the dusty silence.

Eventually Fatima, a challenging glint in her deep, brown eyes and somewhere in her twenties appeared and inquired why she wanted to buy an abaya; maybe the shop had been beset by Christmas fancy dress partygoers preparing to emulate notorious Arabs and vigilance was required... Gabriel explained to an aghast Fatima and the gentleman assistant, standing at a discrete but carefully calculated earwigging distance, that she was going to work in Saudi. Fatima's face exploded, she was clearly horrified.

'Have you been to Saudi before?' she asked incredulous. 'Do you know that women can't even drive there? I got out as soon as I could get my Dad to allow me to come and live with my Aunt and Uncle in the UK.'

Shaking her head in disbelief, Fatima hauled a murder of abayas from a rail, looked up and down at her lofty customer and summarily deemed them all too short.

'It has to be floor length,' she said, 'they are very strict in Saudi and you need to cover your hair too, let me see if we have any longer ones.' Fatima disappeared and Gabriel rummaged through the hectares of heavy darkness piled on top of the rail. So long as Fatima could find something long enough, there was nothing to distinguish one abaya from another and she should be able to get back to the train station early.

'This is the longest we have,' said Fatima heaving a sweltering, shroud-like garment around Gabriel's shoulders.

'What do I wear underneath?' she inquired.

'Oh anything.' Fatima made a casual arc with her hand. 'You can wear really sexy things underneath, sexy underwear, miniskirts, hot pants, stockings and suspenders, anything you like.'

Gabriel stood aghast in the shop, the gentleman assistant skulked smirking behind his boxes and Fatima's face stayed steady; she had not been joking.

'Thanks for letting me know,' Gabriel replied wondering quite what she was letting herself in for. 'I didn't think I had to cover my head as a Westerner, is that right?'

'Well, you don't really but if you get caught by the Muttawa, they will shout at you and might beat you if you don't,' Fatima was warming to her role as cultural advisor. Gabriel added a headscarf to the funereal mountain of cloth before her.

'And you'll need perfume too,' counselled Fatima. 'You can't wear perfume from here because it has alcohol in it.' She started spraying samples of a cinnamon-smelling oily substance on Gabriel's arm and Gabriel recalled one of the visa forms she had signed that morning wherein she had promised faithfully to observe that alcohol is illegal in Saudi. She hadn't expected it to extend to inhalation.

'Come back if you need anything else,' said Fatima, withdrawing through the dusty curtain. The financial elements of the transaction precipitated her uncle's re-emergence from his dusty hiding place.

Her purchases safe in a rough, brown paper bag and no VAT receipt having been made available for reasons unclear (Mubaarak would not be pleased when she tried to claim her expenses), Gabriel set off back to the train station. Once out of the Muslim area of the city, she passed shops bedecked with the green, red and gold of Christmas, heard the strains of familiar carols and smelt the tingle of snow in the air.

She would create a list of questions and go back to see Fatima again, she decided.

On reaching the cottage, she opened her inbox to find that her visa was en route via courier and her flight was confirmed. Clearly the unattractive second set of visa photographs had done the trick nicely and the adventure was underway.

Later that week, Fatima and Gabriel sat in the small Lebanese café opposite her uncle's shop, drinking mint tea (Gabriel) and Diet Coke (Fatima). She was explaining how it would have been impossible for her to get a job or any sort of independence, had she stayed in Saudi.

'I wasn't clever enough to be a doctor or a teacher which are thought to be the only jobs suitable for women, Gabriel. And if I am honest, they are only considered suitable because men and women can be separated easily in hospitals and schools. So there's no danger that women would have to work alongside men,' she went on.

'Other jobs which I would be clever enough to do like working in a shop, as I do here, or a restaurant are simply not possible. Over there, they're all-male workplaces.'

To leave the country, Fatima had needed permission from her male sponsor, in her case her father, and he was not keen, not keen at all.

'He told me that he would never allow me to leave and that I must stay and help my mother look after the relatives. I just couldn't stand it, Gabriel, I was going mad.'

As each year went by, however, she explained how she became less and less marriageable and hence less and less financially viable for her father. When she reached twenty five, her parents concluded that the only offers she was likely to get were as bargain basement wife number three or even four and they relented, happy to get Fatima off their hands.

It had taken her many years of wheedling and negotiating to be allowed to go and stay with her Aunt and Uncle in Bradford, to work in the dark, dusty shop and start to build for herself some self-respect and independence as she reached her late twenties. No wonder she was so horrified that Gabriel, a British woman, was voluntarily going to Saudi to work.

'There are really only five things you need to know before you go,' she said. 'The five big rules applying to Muslims will help you to understand Saudi and why it is so different to here.'

She pulled a small card from her handbag. The card depicted pastel-coloured flowers in modern sweeping curves. Fatima explained that it was a postcard from the Sheikh Zayed mosque in Abu Dhabi.

'The most beautiful building in the world,' she said, unusually wistful. 'My parents took me there when I was sixteen, to meet a guy who was looking for a wife but he didn't want me.' Fatima looked briefly sad then jolted herself, looked up and smiled at Gabriel. 'Just as well really, or I wouldn't be here in the UK helping you now.'

She turned over the card where she had written in careful, childlike, Western script:

1. There is 1 God and Muhammad is his messenger

2. Must perform ritual prayers 5 times each day

3. Must do payment of alms

4. Fast with no food or water for the month of Ramadan

5. Pilgrimage to Mecca once in the lifetime

'Thank you,' said Gabriel. 'I have come across the Hadith of Gabriel once or twice before, but this is a very useful reminder. I will keep this with me throughout the whole of next year.'

Fatima looked momentarily confused at the mention of the Hadith of Gabriel but, not being one for deep reflection, quickly let it pass and returned to the moment.

As they left the cafe, Fatima kissed her on both cheeks and wished her luck. She hugged Gabriel warmly and was gone, swinging her silken, straight dark hair over her shoulder and flinging her shoulder bag in an energetic parabola.

Gabriel had warmed to the wild young woman with her honesty and balanced views on her culture. Fatima was not bitter after the disappointment in Abu Dhabi but triumphant that, by avoiding conflict, biding her time and playing the long game, she had beaten the restrictions she faced and secured for herself the future that she wanted in the West.

In the cottage that weekend, Gabriel, Shylah and Colm shared their last meal together for what they anticipated would be a full year. Shylah had brought crackers so they could 'wear hats and be Christmassy together early.' Colm had cooked the meal, banishing his dining companions from Gabriel's kitchen for the entire afternoon as he banged and scraped behind the door. They toasted Gabriel's adventure and the ongoing success of Bennets in 2013, listened to carols and resolutely remained positive about how quickly the year would pass.

CHAPTER 10

Heathrow airport, London, United Kingdom and Jeddah, Saudi Arabia

December 2012

Gabriel waited in the check-in queue, standing out from the crowd like the sculptural ironwork of the Eiffel tower on the stony Paris skyline and attracting a similar measure of attention.

She was delighted at the opportunities for people-watching afforded by the trip. As expected, professional women travelling alone were conspicuous by their absence; Gabriel was the only one on the whole plane. Smart-suited business men, mostly travelling alone, were more numerous, hailing from the West or the Far East. There were a multitude of Saudi family groups; returning home from a shopping trip in the West End, if the carrier bags were anything to go by. The groups were large, spanning the generations and with a hoard of unruly children, largely ignored by the adults. The patriarchs wore long white thaubs and white gutrah headdresses and their womenfolk were, as expected, in abayas. Saudi women's headwear ranged from a veil covering only the hair, via the face covered with a split for the eyes, to a fully covered veiled face with black gloves on their hands, so not a morsel of potentially tempting flesh was visible.

The vast majority of the passengers to Jeddah, however, were pilgrims bound for the nearby city of Mecca. These were easily identifiable by their regulation pilgrim attire; for women a white version of the abaya and veil but for men a tantalisingly revealing garment comprising a bath towel wrapped around the lower body and no other clothing at all.

Gabriel reached the desk and without raising his head, the clerk inquired, 'are you on a pilgrimage, madam?'

Box ticked, the desk clerk confirmed that her visa was in order; she did not need to pay the extra fees for pilgrimage visas and Gabriel proceeded to sit with her fellow travellers in the alcohol-free, family section (no single men or all-male groups allowed) of the waiting area.

She wondered how much the additional cost of a pilgrim visa would have been. With a visit to Mecca accounting for twenty percent of the Five Big Rules, the commercial possibilities were endless. She ventured further what the motivations behind all the sexual segregation were about, was it fear that the women would ravish and defile the single men (scantily clad for pilgrimage in many cases) or fear that the single men when confronted by the sight of the feminine form would be unable to control their primal urges? Fatima and she had discussed the Prophet Muhammad's teachings on holiness and modesty, Fatima had actually used this teaching to explain the requirement for the abaya and veil. However, the bare chests, hirsute shoulders and flabby tummies of the unclothed male pilgrims around her were challenging even for Gabriel's relaxed Western standards. Surely the prophet would not approve of such immodest flashing of the male person? This sort of attire wouldn't be allowed in a hotel or restaurant in Europe. It was just as well that the rules for women were so stringent, some sort of barrier against all that male nudity was not only mandatory but desirable.

Gabriel was relieved that her most proximal travelling companion was a fully clad, pleasant-looking gentleman.

'May I help you with your bag? My name is Amr, I am an Egyptian working in Saudi,' he explained, shaking her proffered hand.

'Thank you, Amr, this is my first time.'

Amr was polite, quietly spoken and kind. 'I can help you with your case again before we land. I have worked in Saudi for many years and I would recommend you put on your abaya before we disembark. There are often Muttawa in the airport in Jeddah and some people are very … ignorant.'

Gabriel noticed that Saudi Airlines had dispensed with the need for film entertainment on the aircraft, preferring instead shared screens descending from somewhere near the oxygen masks, playing scenes of Mecca, with its myriad pilgrims, circulating like a swarm of white bees, on a continuous loop. Amr and Gabriel settled down to read.

The airline had similarly dispensed with the requirement for alcoholic beverage, to the very vocal disappointment of several of the British pilgrims, shortly after take-off.

'They'll have something to say in a few hours when they have to sign a declaration that they understand the penalty for alcohol is execution, before they can get off the plane,' laughed Amr.

Some hours later, Gabriel heard a humming sound build within the confines of the plane; the male pilgrims had started singing.

'It's the pilgrims chanting the Talbiya,' Amr explained; the chanting continued for over an hour, becoming louder and more fervent as the plane approached its destination.

In the latter phases of the flight, the crew made several announcements associated with the approach to Miqat. The first was a warning to complete ablutions and the second was about Talbiya (already well underway and in full voice). Her companion explained that Miqat was the holy place in Mecca and that the airspace above was included in the definition and hence was also holy. For that reason, all pilgrims on the flight, or indeed on a spacecraft should one venture that way, needed to complete their ablutions and sport the risqué ihram, however far above the ground they were.

Gabriel marvelled at the extent of ritual surrounding the pilgrimages and the universal compliance with its various rules and regulations. Young and old alike were drawn into their shared experience and she was reminded of Michael drawing the thousands into his message.

A silent, brooding driver reluctantly met Gabriel at the airport, sneering as she recognised her name on his card and waved. He walked at speed ahead of her from the gate to his car, offering no assistance with her case nor her nerves. After a supersonic, perilous drive, Gabriel was alarmed at the level of security within which she would exist in the compound; a fourteen foot wall, topped with coiled barbed wire, armed guards, stringent security questions and passport checks at the gate. The driver accelerated away immediately, as if escaping a crime scene, once he had dropped her off at the compound office.

As Gabriel watched the driver leave, an intense, clip-board wielding Pakistani gentleman approached and handed her a set of keys accompanied by a fresh mountain of paperwork.

'You don't need to wear abaya in the compound, ma'am. Alcohol, drugs and adultery are prohibited and there is a shop, library, gym and restaurant in the clubhouse complex,' he recited, reading from his clipboard, never once looking at Gabriel's face. 'Ladies sessions in the gym are on a Thursday morning and a Sunday evening. You are allowed to use any of the outside gardens and the outside terraces and pools.'

He started off across the car park ahead of her, entered the building and held the door as she struggled into the lift with her cases. Once they reached the first floor, he opened the apartment door and turned on the light to reveal brown décor and furnishings reminiscent of a 1970s interior stage set and equally flimsy. He ushered her forward at arm's length, reluctant to enter the apartment with her and as soon as she was inside, backed away from the doorway. He confirmed hurriedly over his shoulder that she had no other questions and ran away to sanctuary.

Gabriel removed her sweltering abaya as soon as he had gone. She scanned the small apartment which would be home for the next twelve months, imprisoned within the weapons-grade fortifications.

There were three rooms, a lounge with kitchenette at one end with milk chocolate coloured, fitted units of the type to be unsteadied by the weight of more than one tinned product at a time. These were topped in mocha hue by a puny, scratched Formica top. The couch comprised Spartan planks, with carpet tacked in place for user comfort, to the rear. Its sides bore a Styrofoam seat covered in chocolate sandwich spread curtain fabric. The air conditioning, dripping condensation from a cavernous square duct in the ceiling, maintained a threatening roar and the temperature inside the apartment was glacial; presumably to stop the whole chocolate creation from melting, smiled Gabriel to herself.

She tackled the air-conditioning first, adjusting it to a temperature more ambient for Western attire and set about making her dismal surroundings feel more homely. Gabriel opened her two Stonehenge-proportioned suitcases in the bedroom, the walls and floor of which were cocoa brown and bare. A double bed floated like an island in the middle of the room. A set of collapsing fitted wardrobe doors clung precariously to one wall.

She stuck the list of five rules from Fatima in pride of place on the utilitarian tiled wall in the kitchenette and stood her photographs on the counter top. The first was of her parents, smiling, straight and proud in their band regalia, in front of York Minster. Their band had won the Northern England Salvation Army Band prize and they had all been treated to tea at Betty's by the bandmaster. The second was a picture taken last Summer of Colm and Shylah standing in front of Bennets, just after the vegetable delivery. Colourful globes, cones and cylinders, green, brown, orange and purple tumbled out of baskets onto the pavement in the sunshine and Colm and Shylah bore matching smiles. The next was of Brisk, sitting in the garden at the cottage, guarding Bill's apple tree while his master was out. The final picture was of Ella sitting proudly in the doorway of the deli', no doubt enjoying the smells from inside. Gabriel tentatively arranged some of her books in a stack on one of the feeble shelves, tenuously attached to the wall in the lounge area.

Gabriel had brought many of her characteristic scarves and wraps with her; brightly coloured silks, wools, pashminas in reds, mossy greens, golds. Gabriel's plan was to brighten up the abaya with colourful neck scarves but she needed to test the water in her first few days. In the meantime, she swathed the scarves across the chair and couch, the bed and on a couple of plain tables in the sitting room. The apartment was starting to recover from its chocolaty sickness by the time she sat down to prepare for the morning.

Before retiring, Gabriel descended the depressing staircase (also brown) and stepped outside. After nightfall in Jeddah, the air was cooler and more gentle, the temperature nurturing. She sat down on a bench in a small walled garden, listened to the soothing music of flowing water and the gentle breeze among tall grasses.

The sneering, silent speed merchant had been sent again to collect her at 9 a.m. and take her to the office. He was late and unapologetic, but knowing that the penalty for women driving in Saudi was several lashes, he was well aware that she needed him more than he her and had clearly resolved to take full advantage. The wordless drive drew upon Gabriel's steeliest of nerves as the virile road-using population raced and barged through the potholed byways of Jeddah. The only rule which applied was survival of the largest and roughest. Traffic signals were merely decorative pennants around the battle ground. Leaving her to struggle with her bags, the driver sped off again without a word.

It took a full twenty minutes, several phone calls and the descent of Mubaarak to reception before the security guard would allow a woman into the building. Once beaten down by the insistent Mubaarak, the defeated security guard required that Gabriel travel alone in the lift and that Mubaarak follow separately. The Saudis must be quick workers, Gabriel mused, to descend to debaucherous acts within the time taken to ascend to floor three.

Gabriel's exclusively male fellow workers had dressed with care for the office, she noticed. All but the ex-pats (conspicuously Caucasian, Indian or Pakistani) sported flowing, floor-length thaubs, their peripheral vision impeded by their wedding veil-like gutrah and heavy black ogals to keep everything in place and ship-shape. In addition to traditional white, several of the younger employees sported navy, yellow, cream, brown or even black thaubs. The sportier, more colourful examples were worn generally by men with heads bare (and enhanced peripheral vision which could be useful when tackling the roads) but white gutrah or red and white checked shumagg were undoubtedly the norm.

At the start of each meeting, attendees rejected manly hand-shaking and backslapping but hugged and kissed, often lingeringly on the lips. Men walked around the office in pairs, holding hands and occasionally with their arms around one another; one young man had his head on the shoulder of his colleague as they circulated the office. Gabriel was amazed. The extent of physical interaction which went on between men would not have gone down well in the UK, particularly in the virile county of Yorkshire. Fatima had also explained at length how Saudi is a country where penalties for homosexuality are steep.

Everyone she met in the first week had clearly been briefed by Mubaarak and shook her hand (frequently hesitantly) when proffered. Most of those to whom she was not introduced eyed her with contempt as she passed by their desks and offices. The majority of men chain-smoked in the workplace and by the afternoon, a bluish haze hung around the building. One of the lifts was swiftly repurposed as a 'Ladies lift' and having been told not to use the stairs as the exercise would be unhealthy for her, Gabriel was delighted to sail up and down the building unfettered, as queues at all the other lifts lengthened. Despite the nicotine imbued atmosphere which pervaded everywhere except the canteen, lunch was reluctantly brought to her daily in her office on a tray by one of the many Indian tea boys; the canteen being out of bounds to women.

Despite the steady flow of tea and coffee provided to her colleagues, Gabriel went thirsty until Mubaarak or one of the others intervened on her behalf. The tea boys, she was told by a frustrated Mubaarak, considered it beneath them to have to wait on her. Mubaarak had explained the strict pecking order, where Indians, Pakistanis and Philippinos were at the bottom with Arabs, followed by white Arabs (from North Africa) and then Europeans or Americans at the top. Working women must be a very lowly bunch indeed, she thought, a very clear sign of the extent of work before her.

Gabriel's biggest logistical challenge that first week was the toilets. There were no women's facilities in the building and the issue was not discussed. On days one and two she had to ask Mubaarak to call the driver (who wouldn't take her calls directly) to take her back to the apartment after lunch.

'Mubaarak, I cannot continue like this. You need to speak to someone and get them to sort the toilets out. Calling the driver whenever I need to go is nowhere near a permanent solution.' In reality, Gabriel had noticed that the driver delighted in keeping her waiting when called in the middle of the day. Also, the greater time spent on the roads, the greater was the risk of death!

'Gabriel, I have more important things to think about. These matters are not discussed here in Saudi. Please behave with decorum and concentrate on the project.'

'Mubaarak, how can I concentrate when I need to go to the loo? Please will you ask someone to get it sorted this weekend, or sooner if possible. They will just need to change one of the men's toilets into a ladies one … Or would you like me to ask them?'

'Alright, Gabriel. Please, I do not wish to discuss this anymore.' An embarrassed, exasperated Mubaarak stalked from the office to arrange the second 'repurposing' of the week.

Later that day, Gabriel received a message via the Doctor that under no circumstances was she to avail herself of the new facility (which would be repurposed overnight) until the doorway had been 'adequately screened from the eyes of passing men.' Gabriel snorted with laughter but was delighted the next morning to see a new sign on floor three.

'LADIES WC'.

Several carpenters were still working on the doorway, constructing a sanitary antechamber to which only Gabriel had the key and which would protect against the prying eyes of men into the inner recesses of the facility. By the afternoon, the job was done.

Gabriel's workload at the behest of Mubaarak's demands, coupled with the three hour time difference and Shylah's commitments at the shop meant that Gabriel could not share her experiences (nor laugh about them) with Shylah. During the week, she swiftly emailed a couple of Haiku to convey the high-spots and was delighted to receive responses in kind, the start of a pattern for the year.

Haiku 1 – December 2012 – Jeddah to Market Hamilton via email

Driver is awful,

Office guys kiss and cuddle,

Multi-coloured thaubs.

Haiku 2 – December 2012 – Market Hamilton to Jeddah via email

Put up with driver

Don't risk lashes! Or ask the

Good Doctor for lift!

Haiku 3 – December 2012 – Jeddah to Market Hamilton via email

No ladies toilet

New one, exclusively mine,

Fortified at door!!

Haiku 4 – December 2012 – Market Hamilton to Jeddah via email

Just as well no drink.

Insist new one has bidet

Have been reading up!!

The reference to a bidet was lost on Gabriel who resolved to ask Shylah what she meant at some point!

After a productive, if logistically demanding first week, Gabriel asked Mubaarak if he would care to join her for dinner or a coffee to review progress and make some plans for the coming months. They agreed to meet in the restaurant at her compound. Any other restaurant in Jeddah was out of bounds due to the restrictions on unmarried, unrelated mixed sex couples being together.

'Why don't you bring your wife, Mubaarak? I would love to meet her,' said Gabriel and Mubaarak swiftly declined.

'She doesn't like to go out,' he said.

'Maybe she would like you to take her out,' answered Gabriel to be dismissed with a wave of Mubaarak's hand accompanied by an impatient snort. The subject was closed.

Gabriel looked out of the office window at the sandy, smoggy city.

'What's that garden over there in the distance?' she asked, hungry for some green amongst the concrete.

'It's not a garden, it's a square,' Mubaarak replied. 'The expat's all call it chop-chop square. It's where they carry out the executions and other punishments.'

Gabriel was horrified. 'But I can see it from my window,' she said.

'Don't worry,' said Mubaarak, 'they normally only use it on a Friday. People are not at work, so they can go and watch. It gets very crowded around there on a Friday.'

Gabriel descended into stunned silence. The combination of barbarous roads, misogynist practical arrangements, excessive male on male affection and uncompromising punishments brought to mind the book she had been forced to study in English Literature.

'Lord of the Flies' by William Golding had disgusted her and she had asked the unyielding Sister Bernard if she could read something else instead. That same feeling threatened to engulf her again unless she jolted herself back to the reason why she was there, to bring opportunity to the women of Saudi Arabia. It occurred to her then that she hadn't ever actually seen any of the women of Saudi Arabia since she left the airport. Were they all like Mubaarak's wife, not wanting to go out?

Dinner at the compound restaurant started well with a review of the week's progress and plans for next week. The food was adequate, the ambience an eccentric mixture of Middle Eastern and Mediterranean with pantiled partitions, checked tablecloths, shishas and an invasive, living vine. Mubaarak was enthusiastic, he was glorying in several dollops of reflected praise and Gabriel was dutifully delighted for him. As they chatted companionably over their meal and shared a jug of lollypop fresh mango juice, Gabriel admitted how she had found the overt physicality between men in the office surprising in a culture which considered homosexuality to be such a serious crime. She added, without looking up from her plate to calibrate Mubaarak's reaction that men in the UK would be horrified at such behaviour which would only ever be conducted in private between gay men. She started as Mubaarak's bearing became immediately tense, he drew his mouth into a tight, thin line and his eyes narrowed.

'It is nothing to do with homosexuality. It is fraternity and is part of the Arab culture,' he hissed, throwing down his knife and fork.

'So why were you so upset at university when Shylah and I were linking arms?' asked Gabriel. She had already decided not to let Mubaarak get away with everything tonight.

Mubaarak erupted to a standing position, clattering back his chair on the tiles; all to the delighted curiosity of the other diners (hoping for some entertaining marital discord in the compound). He leant towards Gabriel and spat into her face,

'That is different. Women should keep their bodies only for their husbands. I will see you at the office at 9 o'clock on Sunday.'

He turned on his stormy heel and thundered out of the restaurant leaving Gabriel dripping with embarrassment, his unfinished dinner and the bill. Reeling from the unpredictable strike, Gabriel sat motionless, pinned to her chair. She had never seen Mubaarak so angry in all the many years they had known one another; she had inadvertently lit a touch paper.

December 2012 – Haiku 5 – Jeddah to Market Hamilton via email
Doctor had tantrum
Homophobia raw nerve
Wife is a recluse!

December 2012 – Haiku 6 – Market Hamilton to Jeddah via email
Typical; ignore!
Suspected issues for years.
Not surprised re wife.

CHAPTER 11

Jeddah, Saudi Arabia

December 2012 (Gregorian calendar)

Mubaarak was smiling a plastic smile and being resolutely brisk in the office at the beginning of the following week. He had evidently decided to expunge, from their collective memories, the episode in the compound restaurant. Gabriel doubted that it would ever be mentioned again. He briefly inquired about Gabriel's weekend, then, before she could answer, with eyes cast heavenwards, explained how he and his wife had visited Mecca. His wife's voluntary confinement to the marital home did not extend to trips to the holy city, therefore. Mubaarak explained in infinite detail how they had stayed in one of the best hotels, performed the Hajj and returned late on Saturday night.

'Gabriel, after performing Hajj, we emerged from our sins like a new-born babies, in the words of the prophet, peace be upon him,' he smiled an 'uplifted' smile. Gabriel did not press Mubaarak on the specific nature of the sins he, or indeed the mysterious, housebound wife, had in mind, nor their relation (if any) to the conversations of Thursday night. The trip had definitely improved his mood and that was something for which to be grateful.

'I would like to visit Mecca while I am here. May I come with you and your wife next time you go?' she asked.

Mubaarak looked suspicious, as though Gabriel might be setting some sort of cultural trap.

'Only Muslims are allowed to visit Mecca, you know that,' he snapped.

Gabriel had not, in fact, 'known that' at all. Having spent most of the weekend alone in the flat or sitting in the compound's walled garden on the bench, reading about the Muslim faith, the Qur'an and Islam, she was shocked. The prophet Muhammad had espoused the importance of interaction with other faiths, respect for others' beliefs and in his lifetime, had supported a Jewish family and their ailing son, living close to him. How would the Muslims in London react if they were prevented from enjoying the cathedrals and other monuments of the Christian church? She wondered whether Mubaarak had availed himself of the guided tours of Westminster Abbey and St Pauls when on one of his extended stays in London. After Thursday's fiasco however, she decided to leave well alone conversations which might risk upsetting the hypersensitive Doctor.

'Did your children go with you to Mecca, Mubaarak?' she asked, still unclear of the precise make-up of Mubaarak's family. It was progress that he had at last started mentioning the existence of a wife.

'We don't have children, Gabriel,' Mubaarak's bearing was becoming tense, his face reddening, she was moving back into dangerous territory. 'Will you please refocus on the project, Gabriel.'

The deteriorating conversation was aborted as one of their colleagues, Samir, a graduate from Harvard, recently returned to his home country, banged into the office, flustered and apologetic. He explained that there had been some 'trouble' that morning at the Starbucks he frequented on his way to work.

'All the cups had to be changed. The queue was out the door. Sorry I'm late, Doctor Mubaarak,' Samir gestured to a plain, white cardboard cup, in place of the usual Starbucks red, white and green jollity.

'I went to the mall at the weekend and the Muttawa were everywhere because of Christmas. We had Christmas when I was in the States. I can't see what the problem is.'

Samir explained how the Muttawa had decided to crack down on all establishments celebrating the 'pagan festival' of Christmas. Starbucks and several other international brands whose winter livery bore red, green and gold among their palette had come in for particularly harsh sanction. This morning, any people emerging from Starbucks bearing suspiciously Christmassy coffee cups were being beaten with sticks by the Muttawa, hence the switch to white cups. He sat shakily and consumed his colourless coffee while Mubaarak outlined plans for the week. Gabriel made a mental note to hide the Advent calendar which Shylah and Colm had given her before she left.

That evening, once the sneering, silent speed merchant had finally deigned to arrive and collect her, Gabriel asked him to call in at the shopping mall on the way back to the compound. Silent and with additional measures of both sneering and speed he acceded, visibly horrified and slapping the steering wheel at her audacity as she asked him to wait outside. She could not face another night working her way through the carbohydrate-laden fare of the compound restaurant nor battling to create something edible from the restrictive ingredients available from the compound shop. Also, since the incident with Mubaarak on Thursday evening, she had become a compound curiosity, the subject of stares and whispered comments among the other compounded dwellers.

Over the weekend, Gabriel had become clear that her fellow compoundees were bound in close knit groups, defined and segregated by employer. Following whole days and weeks working together, so strong was the herding instinct that the noisy groups dined and socialised with their wives and families at the compound facilities throughout the evenings and weekends. Gabriel swiftly realised, studying the demographics, that not only was she the only working woman on the compound but also that she was the only person working alone among the local people, without a non-Saudi team around her.

The shopping centre was vast, its sweeping roofs reminiscent of the largest of London's railway stations. There was a gargantuan fountain in the centre surrounded with gaudy, plastic cartoon fish. No music was playing, in accordance with Saudi laws (Gabriel had read at the weekend) but the echoing cacophony of voices and air-conditioning was deafening. The centre's clientele were almost exclusively local Saudis, traditionally clad, in large, cross-generational family groups. Women and children outnumbered men who strode purposefully ahead of their entourages. Multiple wives, offspring and in laws, straggled behind them. At the rear of each group was one or more tiny Indian, Pakistani or Far Eastern ladies, laden like donkeys with an assortment of shopping bags and small children while the rest of the family strode on, unhampered by their burdens.

She reached the door of the supermarket just as the shutters descended and the call to prayer echoed over the speaker system. Fellow shoppers dissipated, filing towards the separate men's and women's prayer rooms. The shopping centre sank swiftly into silence and the corridors were deserted. She sat down on the floor outside the supermarket alongside an evidently Western couple.

'Did you get the time wrong, too?' asked the woman in a Scandinavian accent, pulling a Mills and Boonish paperback from her handbag.

'I didn't realise the shops actually shut for prayers,' replied Gabriel.

'Oh, you've not been here long then,' added the husband. 'They will be shut now for over half an hour then open for thirty minutes or so, so you can run round and get what you need and then they shut again for the last prayer. It's even worse if you are in a restaurant. You just have to sit and wait. They lock the door so you can't even go in or out.'

'Is everyone praying all that time?' asked Gabriel.

'No, most of them are outside or down in the car park having a smoke,' laughed the man.

The three of them sat together, on the floor, in oddly companionable silence. The Scandinavians read their books and Gabriel fretted that the driver would abandon her and she would be stranded at the mall overnight. Some forty minutes later, the shutters rose and the Scandinavians bade their encouragement, 'Go round quickly before they shut again.'

Gabriel seized a rusty, crippled shopping trolley and bolted for the aisles. As she sped round the shop she noticed that the majority of what was on offer was international, mostly American. Notably absent from the store were the alcohol section and women's sanitary provisions. She grabbed some basic ingredients, marvelled at the diversity and quality of fresh juices, dates, fruit and vegetables and hastened to the checkout.

The enormity of the centre was such that it took Gabriel several minutes to identify the correct exit. The call to last prayer was just getting underway as she left. This served to put her driver into an even worse frame of mind than usual. He pretended not to hear her requests that he open the boot. She tried the word 'trunk', in case of basic misunderstanding, then gave up and piled her bags in beside her on the back seat.

While she had been shopping, Jeddah's roads had filled with traffic. The eight lane highway from the centre to her compound was gridlocked and the driver was furious. Almost every car on the road was a large four wheel drive vehicle, most were full with multigenerational families or groups of young, boisterous men. Drivers were blasting their horns, playing out vuvuzela rhythms together. Many vehicles played music at ear-exploding volume, their windows wide open. The atmosphere was like a carnival! No one appeared to mind the traffic jam; being on the road, in their cars with the rest of the city's population was the event for which they had left the house. With no theatres, bars, cinemas or clubs in Jeddah, in deference to the religious laws, the people of the city were making their own entertainment.

They made very slow progress through the traffic, her driver periodically lurching forward into any gap he could find, much to the annoyance of the partygoers. As the evening wore on, the mood of the crowd became ever more electric. People climbed out of their sunroofs and sat on top of their cars, waving and shouting to one another. To Gabriel's horror, small children were hanging from the waist upwards out of car windows and being lifted by their parents onto car roofs, where they sat and waved. Babies and toddlers sat on their father's laps as they drove. Seat belts and child safety seats had definitely passed Jeddah by. Gabriel, who had grown up in the world of the Green Cross Code and 'Clunk Click Every Trip', found it almost impossible to watch. It took the car two hours to travel the three miles between the shopping centre and the compound. Two hours earlier, their normal departure time, the same journey took ten minutes.

Haiku 7 – December 2012 – Jeddah to Market Hamilton via email

Jeddah traffic hell,

Child safety non-existent.

Christmas illegal!

Haiku 8 – December 2012 – Market Hamilton to Jeddah via email

Roads sound horrific,

Better if women could drive.

Christmas – bah humbug

Gabriel asked Samir the next morning whether the street carnival was a nightly event.

'There are people out every night but it's better on a Thursday and Friday, absolutely everyone is out on the roads on a Friday. We sometimes stay out all night,' he replied, a delighted smile smothering his face.

'And when it is National Day,' he continued, 'we decorate the cars with flags and green, white and orange paint. Sometimes a crowd of us line up our cars across the Corniche and block all the traffic. The police came for us one year,' Samir's face lit up at the memory.

'What about the children, Samir, isn't it a bit late for them to be up at ten o'clock in the evening?' Gabriel continued.

Samir looked confused. The concept of children's bedtimes was not something he had encountered while growing up.

'We have picnics too.' Samir was becoming excited, 'at the side of the road and on the grass, normally on a Friday.'

'That sounds great, Samir. Maybe I could come and join you one Friday.' Gabriel was infected by Samir's enthusiasm and desperate for the opportunity to do something, (anything, in fact) which was not confined to the compound.

Samir started to look worried, shuffling embarrassed in his seat. 'It's only for men and families. I'm sorry, Gabriel.' He skulked outside for a cigarette.

The initial wave of female Saraco candidates were due to arrive at the office in January. Gabriel would host them for the first of a planned series of assessment events and had developed a programme under the critical gaze of Mubaarak. The initial cadre of twelve women were all exceptionally well educated, having been part of the first group of women to benefit from the Saudi Royal initiative to fund overseas university education for girls. Mubaarak considered this of itself to be sufficient evidence that there was no gender equality issue in Saudi and was quick to point this out to Gabriel.

'Mubaarak, I do agree it is a start but there is still a long way to go while women remain unable to travel without their male guardian's permission.'

Mubaarak sniffed and retreated to his usual position during such debates. 'Gabriel, you need to try harder to understand the culture if we are to be successful.'

Gabriel reflected that she had never expected this project to be easy!

The logistical complications surrounding the first assessment event were monumental. Despite her recommendations, the board insisted that women be referred to as 'Ladies' and the word 'women' expunged from the lexicon. Gabriel spent many hours with them explaining how the day would run and taking feedback from them all. During face to face encounters, the board would nod, smile, toss their long white gutrah head-dresses over their shoulders and agree with all her suggestions. In subsequent emails or messages passed via 'third parties' however, their true feelings and concerns at the unfamiliar (and unwelcome) invasion of women into their world would emerge. Several colleagues had taken the time to bring translated, printed copies of relevant workplace legislation to her office specifying the stringent segregation requirements stipulated in the country and enforced by the HAIA. The HAIA, it was explained, was the Saudi authority for the prevention of Vice. Gabriel reflected on her time as a graduate management trainee; the HAIA would have had their hands full at the Superbrand!

She compiled a list of 'rules' for the day from the mountain of emotional traffic which had descended into her inbox or been imparted with exaggerated intensity (by the brave) across her desk:

RULES FOR LADIES' ASSESSMENT DAY

1. The foyer must be cleared of all men except for one single security guard when the Ladies arrive

2. One lift in the building must be designated as a Ladies lift and kept exclusively for the use of the Ladies

3. Ladies will not use the stairs at any time. If there is a fire alarm, Ladies will gather in Office 321 and await the arrival of a security guard to escort them from the building.

4. Ladies will use the canteen between 12.30 and 13.00 only.

5. Ladies will use rooms 321, 322 and 323 and will remain in these rooms for the duration of the day. All internal windows for rooms 321, 322 and 323 will be curtained throughout the day

6. All Ladies will share the key to the Ladies WC on floor three and will ensure that the door remains locked at all times

7. Ladies must not smoke in the building during the assessment day and are not permitted to stand outside in the designated smoking area.

8. A separate Ladies prayer room will be created in room 324 and Ladies will use this facility as required.

Gabriel circulated the list of rules and the board were delighted. Observance of rules was something they could handle, having been brought up within the framework of the five pillars of Islam and precisely stipulated rules for prayer.

In light of the sanctions on non-Islamic religious festivals (or pagan ones as Christmas was referred to in Saudi), the anniversary of Christ's birth in 2012 passed without mention or acknowledgement. Behind the safety of the compound walls and security measures, several festive souls bravely erected Christmas trees and lights, and a traditional, turkey dinner was arranged in the restaurant. Gabriel decided to try to create a little jollity alone in her flat, rather than sit lonely amongst the cliquishness of the expat community in their office groupings. She cooked the closest approximation to a roast dinner that she could muster from the ingredients available. With her gravy and stuffing bereft roast chicken breast, roasted (rather than boiled) new potatoes and multiple cling wrapped salad before her, she toasted the season and number of air food miles the feast had travelled, with mango juice.

She played a selection of Christmas carols on her laptop. The Saudi authorities had not thought to block the relevant material. Perhaps she should offer them some technical help to render their censorship fully effective.

Haiku 9 – December 2012 – Jeddah to Market Hamilton via email

Alone for Christmas,

Couldn't face compound cronies.

Carols on You-tube!

Haiku 10 – December 2012 – Market Hamilton to Jeddah via email

Sad for you alone
We'll make up for it next year.
Wet and windy here!

After her festive dinner, Gabriel stepped out into the warm evening. One thing you could say for Jeddah in the wintertime was that the temperature outside was sheer perfection, neither too warm nor too cool, no rain and few clouds. She looked upwards at the sky but sadly not one single star was visible through the light pollution of the city. She sought out her usual bench in the walled garden, sat and closed her eyes.

'Happy Christmas, ma'am.' A kind, quiet, Far Eastern voice tendered the only Christmas felicitation Gabriel had received all day.

She looked up and met sympathetic, chocolate-brown eyes looking down at her. The young woman's round, pretty face was the colour of milky coffee; she was dressed in a lilac overall with her head covered in a matching scarf.

'Thank you, what's your name?' replied Gabriel.

'Thanuja, ma'am. I see you sit here alone many times. You have no husband ma'am?'

Gabriel leant forwards so she could hear the gentle, soft voice more clearly as Thanuja sat down on the bench and placed a feather-light hand on her forearm.

'I am alone here, Thanuja, I am not married. I work at Saraco and I don't know anyone else on the compound. They all work for other companies.' Gabriel shrugged as she spoke and felt a pang of sadness as she thought of Shylah and Colm who would be enjoying Christmas day together either in the flat above Bennets or, she hoped, at her cottage.

No doubt Colm would have cooked the Christmas dinner with his usual mesh of military precision and flourish. The previous year, the three of them had shared goose. Colm had laboured, forbidding entry to the kitchen until three in the afternoon when he flung open the door with such force that it reticulated on its hinges and dented the wall,

'The feast is ready,' he had announced at town crier volume.

The goose was outstanding and sufficient to serve twelve or thirteen. They were eating it for days in soups, curries and risotto. Colm was delighted and vowed to start a campaign to bring the traditional British goose back to the Yuletide plates of Yorkshire. Gabriel wondered how the two of them had managed this year and whether Colm had downsized his poultry ambitions. If not, Shylah would be dining on goose until New Year at least. The merry widow Mary wouldn't be taking any of it off their hands, reflected Gabriel. She had left for an eight week cruise shortly after Peter's funeral.

'Do you have a family in the States, ma'am?' asked Thanuja, assuming as most people did, that Gabriel was American.

'I come from England, Thanuja, not the States. From a place in the North of England, called Yorkshire. It is very nice there, I think you would like it if you enjoy coming to the garden; there are many gardens in Yorkshire.' Gabriel spoke softly, maintaining the gentle ambiance Thanuja had imbued into the warm garden.

'Are your family in England, ma'am?' Thanuja was not going to let the subject drop.

'No, I have no family, Thanuja, but I do have some very, very special friends who are like a family to me.'

Thanuja's face was suffused with concern; she placed her hand again on Gabriel's forearm. 'I am sorry, ma'am,' she said.

'What about you, Thanuja? Do you have a family?' asked Gabriel.

'Yes, ma'am. I have son, he is very small. He is in Sri Lanka with my family,' Thanuja replied head downwards. She removed her hand from Gabriel's arm and joined her hands together in her lap, where her eyes were focussed.

The two women sat silently together in the garden, grasses whispering and the distant car horns calling from the city, both remembering previous Christmases in their respective homelands, thinking about the people they loved and missed.

'Goodnight, Thanuja, I have to go now. It has been lovely meeting you, I hope to see you in the garden another evening,' said Gabriel.

Thanuja stayed behind and watched her go, the touch of her eyes warm, gentle and kind on Gabriel's back.

Back inside the apartment, Gabriel opened her laptop to find an email from Fatima. Despite her earnest promises, Fatima had turned out to be an infrequent correspondent but Gabriel was fascinated to read.

Gabriel

I hope you are well. I have been doing English lessons. Aunty and Uncle let me have a Christmas tree in my room so I am celebrating myself.

I met someone at my class!!!!!

HAPPY CHRISTMAS habib'ti

Remember the five rules!!

Fatima x

Gabriel smiled to herself. Now that she had experienced the misogyny of Saudi Arabia for herself, she could empathise with the enigmatic Fatima more closely and was delighted to imagine her working in a country she loved and sitting beside her little tree. The news about a possible relationship was similarly heart-warming after Fatima's rejection in Abu Dhabi.

Gabriel decided to leave her response to Fatima for another day but to send just one final Haiku to Shylah before bed.

Haiku 11 – December 2012 – Jeddah to Market Hamilton via email

Did you both have goose?

Remembered last year's monster!

Mary still away?

Gabriel was delighted to receive an immediate reply.

Haiku 12 – December 2013 – Market Hamilton to Jeddah via email

Colm's goose campaign!

Mum, food poisoning on cruise

Confinement to ship!!

Schadenfreude at Christmastide, Gabriel smiled to herself.

Boxing Day was another normal working day in Saudi. She and Samir arrived at the office before Mubaarak. Samir quaffed from his albino Starbucks coffee cup and yawned.

'Tired already, Samir? Were you out picnicking last night?' she asked.

'My wife just had a baby. My mother didn't like the girl we hired to look after him at nights so we're on our own until she finds someone else,' he replied, yawning again.

'Oh dear, I'm sorry. What was the problem?' Gabriel enquired.

'My mother said she had the evil eye,' Samir replied, eyes circling skywards. 'She asked her sister round to look and she agreed with her, so we had to send the girl back to India.'

'What's the evil eye, Samir?' asked Gabriel entranced. For a culture which called Christmas a pagan festival, this flirtation with the occult was fascinating. She hoped to get some answers before Mubaarak arrived, expecting him to put an immediate stop to such flippant conversation.

'Well, it's when you have a baby and all the other women are jealous. They give it the evil eye and then it gets ill or dies. That's why everyone keeps their babies hidden and if anyone looks at them, they ask God to look after them. It's mostly the old women that talk about all this stuff,' he added with a wave of his hand, trying to distance himself.

'My baby sister had the evil eye from one of my mother's grown up sisters, who would have been her aunt, and she died while she was still a baby. But this will not happen to your baby Samir, mash'Allah.' Mubaarak's unexpected voice came from the doorway.

Gabriel certainly hadn't predicted that Mubaarak would hold any truck with such superstition. She shook her head silently in disbelief and carried on with her work.

That evening, after a Boxing Day which had closely resembled the preceding Christmas Day, she descended in the lift. She wondered how long she would have to wait for the hateful driver tonight and was amazed to see him, out of the car among a small crowd of other men encircling a single spot by the wall. The driver was scuffing the toe of his shoe. As she approached, she saw with horror that he was kicking something small and orange/brown, which was huddled beside the wall.

The other men were encouraging him, some smoking, some occasionally giving a small kick in support. She strode over. They didn't hear her approach and continued to kick at the small, ginger kitten, squealing with pain and terror. Gabriel felt the fire of rage seize her blood, she grabbed the driver's upper right arm, heaving him backwards. He was lighter than she had expected, lost his balance and fell heavily onto his buttocks with a yelp. She towered over him in the car park, deserted except for the drivers. She brought her face close to his so she could smell stale smoke and, to her shock, something which resembled whisky on his breath. She pointed to her left eye.

'Do you see that, you hateful little man? It's an evil eye, and do you know what? There's another one just here! They are both looking right at you.'

She moved her finger hypnotically from eye to eye.

The deflated bully followed her finger with terrified eyes.

'I have had it with you, you appalling little arse. You drive like a maniac and nearly kill me every single day, you treat me like dirt and now I find that you are just a pathetic little bully, as I suspected,' Gabriel continued.

The driver shuffled on his buttocks towards the car. Gabriel followed him, towering above him, her abaya creating a threatening cloud, blocking the sun. She stared hot, hard into his eyes. He reached the car and with a girlish squeak climbed into the driving seat and drove away, clipping the gate as he left. She turned, her voluminous abaya assuming a circular arc around her, and faced the small crowd of accomplices cowering by the wall. Open mouthed and with terrified faces they ran to their respective vehicles and tyres squealing, they sped away too.

Gabriel went back to where the kitten lay, its skull crushed and bloody and its tiny limp body twitching slightly as it died. She turned away, tears stinging her eyes. She would cope with this. The country may be run on the moral principles of a boys' boarding school, its citizens may behave like the characters from Lord of the Flies, but she was there to change things. Why did the Saudi women do nothing about it? Where were they while their husbands and sons were driving like maniacs, killing people on the roads or their drivers were murdering small animals?

She stormed back up in the lift to where Mubaarak was meticulously packing his bag.

'Mubaarak, I need another driver. The one you found for me has drink on his breath,' she insisted. Mubaarak fumbled and his bag fell from the desk with a crash. He gathered himself and endeavoured to assume an air of authoritative order.

'This is absolutely shocking, Gabriel, leave it with me.' The suspicion of alcohol consumption was sufficient evil to precipitate Mubaarak to action. The murdered kitten, dangerous driving and lamentable lack of courtesy would not have been, Gabriel was certain.

Mubaarak spoke in rapid, angry Arabic on his phone and told her to wait downstairs until the new driver arrived.

The tall, smartly dressed gentleman drew up and braked smoothly in front of the office. He climbed from his vehicle and bade her, 'Good evening, ma'am, my name is Priyantha,' opened the door, relieved her of her bag and conveyed her along quiet back streets, well away from the battleground of Jeddah's perilous highways, to the compound.

CHAPTER 12

Market Hamilton, Yorkshire, United Kingdom

March to April 1999

Shylah and Gabriel gathered the plans and lists they created together in Oxford into a blue and white striped box file. In her flamboyant handwriting, Gabriel emblazoned 'Bennets' across its lid. On one of their weekend trips home, shortly after Shylah's visit to Oxford, Patrick and Gabriel conveyed the file to the cottage. Rather than being stowed tidily away with Bill and Catherine's other papers and their bills, the file stayed out and open on top of the bureau, a growing, moving, living entity and frequently the central character in their conversations. Over the years, the file rose like dough, doubling, quadrupling in volume. Shylah, Gabriel, Bill and Catherine all participated, adding scribbled ideas, snipped cuttings, pictures, advertisements, dreams. Soon, rather than one blue and white striped file, there were three, together with a collection of magazines, books and brochures, piled precariously on the bureau.

Before their accident, Bill and Catherine had been eager participants in the project. Afterwards, Shylah, Colm and Gabriel were its guardians into perpetuity. With cameras, notebooks, Ordinance Survey maps and Colm's new dog, Bonny (he had his way in the end against minimal resistance!) they piled into Patrick at the weekends to visit and sample from similar businesses in nearby Yorkshire towns. They took notes, photographs and souvenirs, they worked out what made the businesses popular and what didn't work well. They listened to what customers asked for and watched what they bought.

When Mr Dalton, owner of Market Hamilton's second most popular off licence, felt the time had come to retire, his son, already a borderline alcoholic, decided that accountancy was a profession more suited to his proclivities. The premises became available and Gabriel and Shylah knew it was time to face the thrilling, daunting reality.

'It's perfect, Shylah, even the floor layout is similar to the ones we drew up in Oxford and the position on the High Street is just where the footfall is highest.'

'Yes, I know, but it's an awful lot of money.'

'I can afford it. It makes much more sense to buy the freehold, shop and flat above, then we save on rent and insurance too with someone living on-site.'

'I know it makes sense, Gabriel, and it's all we dreamed of. I just feel so nervous talking about sums of money like that.'

'Don't think about it then. Leave all that to me and Mr Betteridge. He helped me with Mum and Dad's estate. He's really honest and astute. Let's just think about the shop and leave all the money and legal stuff to him.'

Shylah knew Gabriel was right. It was time to turn the box files on the bureau into boxes, bottles and packets on the shelves of the shop. Having been stripped of all fittings, furniture and light bulbs by Mr Dalton, a careful Yorkshire man, and his financially astute son, 45 The High Street,

Market Hamilton was a very blank canvas on which they could start work; the sooner the better.

They purchased matching navy blue boiler suits, an industrial strength hoover, buckets, cloths, tools and cleaning products and set to work. Having recently left the Superbrand, Gabriel prioritised Bennets over her initial flurry of lucrative offers of work. They started in the main shop, an expansive, bright space with an office and bathroom at the rear and a huge, dusty cellar down a set of precarious concrete steps.

Bonny made sure she was ahead of Colm every time they walked down the steep, concrete stairs. Bill had made particular mention of the fact that it was Bonny's responsibility to ensure Colm didn't fall down, especially as Colm was a bit of a clumsy boy who (despite having only two) had trouble getting his legs in the right order. Bonny took her duties very seriously, particularly those conveyed by Bill on one of his visits to the vegetable plot at the cottage before he disappeared again, melting into the air.

Once they were at the bottom of the stairs in the lovely, big boxy space with a special high up window, through which you could see people's shoes, Colm threw Bonny's ball. The ball bounced very high, very excitingly on the flat, hard floor. Bonny could run the whole length of the boxy space, right to the window with the shoes, catch the ball on it's up-bounce and run back to Colm for another go, and another, and another, and another …

Behind the concrete stairs, Bonny had found some delightful smells reminiscent of the small, brown, scuttly, furry creatures with long tails, who sometimes came to the cottage. When Bonny was absolutely certain that Colm was otherwise engaged, rolling his toy vehicles along the smooth floor, for example, Bonny made it her business to sit, watch and enjoy the delightful scuttly, furry animal smell. If she waited long enough, one of the actual scuttly, furry animals might emerge. Bonny was uncertain what the next step would be, should this eagerly anticipated event occur but was confident that the smell of the actual scuttly furry animal, rather than the already delectable smell of the place where they had been, would be more than worth the wait.

Gabriel and Shylah worked with the strength of Amazonians, painting the walls and ceiling white, hanging wooden shelves, building pine display units. Several of Market Hamilton's interested inhabitants peered through windows or took the time to come into the shop, introduce themselves and promise future custom.

One morning, Peter came. His silhouette approached and hesitated, knocking timidly on the glass before entering. He and Shylah had spoken only a few times since her abrupt ejection from the family home to the convent, over seven years before. He had put on weight, his face was flushed and he looked very tired.

'Hi Dad, how are you?' said Shylah smiling gently and touching his shoulder.

Gabriel marvelled silently at Shylah's pervasive goodness; no recrimination, no hint of surprise at his unheralded appearance after so long. Peter was stuck near the door, an invisible force preventing him from making a complete entrance.

Gabriel descended the concrete steps and offered her services as fielder to Colm and Bonny who were just reaching the exciting climax of a game of 'fetch the tennis ball' in the cellar.

'Can I join in please, you two?' she asked.

'Oh good, you can stand over there and catch the ball when I throw it. You are called a 'fielder', Gabriel. Jonny, James and I play cricket at school.'

Above the clattering of paws on the concrete and the mounting volume of Colm's excited whoops and cheers, Gabriel caught the strains of a quiet conversation in progress upstairs. She hoped that the conflict-free accessibility afforded by the shop could be the catalyst which would enable Shylah to rebuild her relationship with Peter. Trips into the centre of Market Hamilton to fetch something to eat would surely be permissible, even under Mary's crushing regime.

She heard chairs moving upstairs and concluded that Peter must be preparing to leave.

'Come on, Colm, come and say goodbye to your Granddad,' Gabriel held a confused Colm's hand as he embarked unsteadily upon on the bottom step and then she almost toppled to the ground herself as Bonny hurled herself at the staircase.

The lovely, big ginger smelling person is very lucky I came to help her and Colm on that dangerous staircase, reflected Bonny as the threesome climbed slowly, entangled together into the embryonic emporium, Bennets.

Shylah and her Father were embracing. Colm ran over to join the cuddle, anxious not to miss out despite daily overdoses of affection from Gabriel, Bonny and Shylah. Peter blew his nose, looking downwards but Gabriel and Colm saw the curved course of tears on his purple, blue and red veined cheeks.

Bonny realised immediately that the old, fat man needed special gentleness and pressed her head against his spongy thigh as he blew his nose again. The old, fat man shook Colm's hand then blew his nose, yet again.

Colm knew exactly what to do, Bill had showed him how gentlemen shake hands a very long time ago, right from when he and his Mummy used to visit the cottage on Saturdays to watch TV.

Shylah walked with her father to the door, her hand gentle, on his back encouraging his meandering step.

'Please come again, Dad. It will be easier for you to visit now I am here at the shop every day and it will be lovely to see more of you.'

As he left and Shylah shut the door behind him, she turned to Gabriel.

'I cannot help but feel he wanted to tell me something today but didn't quite have the courage to say it,' she said.

After that first visit, Peter called regularly, his confidence and the ease with which he and Shylah re-learned their facility with conversation, rebuilding. Neither Mary nor Shylah's brothers were ever discussed. The shop and a mutual interest in its development and success was the basis of their rejuvenated relationship. Peter developed a cautious affection for Colm and integrated clumsily into his small-boy consciousness. Very much better late than never, in Gabriel's opinion.

Over the next few weeks, in the evenings and at the weekends, Peter helped Gabriel and Shylah with the painting, became adept at arranging the shelves and made a start on the upstairs flat. When Peter was painting Colm's bedroom walls, Colm told Peter about the walls at the old flat.

'Bill helped Mummy paint my bedroom wall at the old flat, Grandpa. I used to have a special Rosie and Jim quilt cover when I was little and he painted them the right colour to match. The flat wasn't very nice though. We were happier when we came to live at the cottage with Gabriel and I could get Bonny.'

Peter immediately engaged in a flurry of nose blowing and going red, so serious that Colm had to fetch Shylah.

After Bennets had opened, over subsequent years until his death, Peter was a regular customer. Usually he called on his way home from the office and occasionally at the weekend. Early on a Saturday morning, he would frequently gather a collection of favourite fare in a hessian RSPB bag and leave with a wave and a smile.

'You must eat like a king on a Saturday lunchtime, Dad,' joked Shylah. She and Gabriel wondered at Mary's reaction to Peter's solitary gourmet lunches and evident emerging interest in ornithology.

Bennets was due to open on Friday morning in the week before Easter. Colm was delighted, primarily because he was not at school and could join in the full scope of the excitement. He had secured promises from both Jonny and James that they would come with their parents on the opening day and buy Easter eggs.

Peter was reticent about the opening, saying he wouldn't come because he didn't want to 'draw attention to himself.' He had recommended the shop to everyone in his office though, he reassured Shylah and Gabriel, and would be amply represented.

By Wednesday evening, the shelves were stacked with multi-coloured packaging, bottles, jars and boxes, the fridges gleamed white-edged and stainless-steeled, awaiting deliveries of fresh produce on Thursday. Gabriel and Colm had worked together on a small yellow and gold Easter display to tempt the last minute purchasers (including, they hoped, Jonny and James' parents). A local producer was scheduled to deliver Simnel cakes and other fresh seasonal fare on Friday morning. On the pavement outside, shelving and baskets had been erected, ready to bear fresh vegetables and fruit.

They did not know whether Peter had spoken to Mary about the opening or whether she intended coming.

Shylah called at the house on Thursday morning, while her Father was at work and told a disinterested Mary about their new business,

'We're opening tomorrow, Mum. It was an idea which Gabriel and I had when she was at university in Oxford. We found an ideal premises in the High Street, number forty five. We thought you might like to call in on Friday for the opening.'

Mary's sole preoccupation (apart from her sherry) that particular day, was the new house that one of Shylah's brothers and his wife had just bought.

'I'll see, Shylah. I am hoping to go and see their new house. They've got five bedrooms, all en suite and an au pair's apartment.'

'Gabriel and I have worked really hard for this, Mum, I really do hope you can make the opening. Surely it won't take you all day to go round their house, even though it is enormous.' Shylah concluded that a small shop on the High Street was unlikely to divert her mother's attention from her brother's materialistic bragging fodder. In any case, she reflected, Mary was of the belief that wise women avoided work at all costs having entrapped a man (or a couple of men if one proved insufficiently lucrative) to provide whatever they fancied. Shylah decided to cut her losses.

'OK Mum, well if you can make it, we'll be pleased to see you. I had better get back now and help Gabriel.' She left in a hurry.

With unexpected time on her hands, Shylah diverted to the convent instead to visit Sister Anthony and the nuns. She always tried to call every couple of weeks and give the nuns the latest news about Colm. With the pressure of work as Bennets' opening loomed, she had not been since Shrove Tuesday when she and Colm had helped Sister Anthony make pancakes and hand them round to the other nuns. As the years passed, with the paucity of noviciates choosing a life of prayer, Sister Anthony was rapidly becoming the only capable or indeed compos mentis member of the Yorkshire based branch of the order. The elderly nuns' bland, sheltered existence at the convent, unviolated by TV or radio, elevated even Shylah's most quotidian accounts to the level of breaking world news. Their reactions to news about Bennets assumed a level of excitement which would normally be reserved for a second coming or at the very least, the election of a new Pope. Shylah had her bag with her, she would show the nuns some pictures of the metamorphosis of Bennets' interior, the burgeoning shelves, Colm and Bonny in the shop.

Sister Anthony opened the door as usual and with no question or recrimination about Shylah's lack of visits during the now, almost concluded, period of Lent, welcomed her into the draughty grey corridor.

'Shylah, it is great to see you and so good of you to come. The Sisters will be over the moon. You must be so busy, it's great of you to make time like this.'

Shylah noticed a slalom of buckets weaving its way along the corridor's rattling parquet floor. It was not only the nuns who were showing their age, the convent building was looking tired and wrinkled too. Sister Anthony followed Shylah's eyes.

'It's a mess, isn't it?' she was uncharacteristically negative. 'I don't know how we are going to carry on here.'

Shylah, who had for weeks, been poring over cash flow forecasts and stock turnover plans with the business-like and thorough Gabriel, realised that she had never considered the economics of the convent. She had simply assumed its continuity, funded from some invisible, spiritual force into eternity. She had stayed there during her pregnancy until Colm was two years old, and she seventeen. As far as she knew, her period of residence had been entirely free of charge. Certainly there was minimal probability that any contribution had been made by her over-borrowed parents. Sister Anthony had insisted that she keep any government funding which she and Colm secured, thanks to the intervention of the lady in the soft, green cardigan, 'for their future'.

She knew there had been other girls, too, who had been at St Anne's, had 'got into trouble' and who had enjoyed peace and refuge in the windowless, plain rooms, silent corridors and the utilitarian catering. While Shylah had been resident, a few other women had passed through. She didn't remember any of their names, nor did she know their stories, most had stayed either in their rooms or in the chapel throughout their stay, appearing only at mealtimes. But like Shylah and Colm, they had been made welcome and been provided for until they were ready to leave.

'Sister, I'm sorry, I just never realised that convents had to balance their books too.'

Sister Anthony smiled. 'No one ever does, everyone assumes that nuns are just nuns, above worldly considerations like book-balancing, love, temptation, sexuality. Few people think about the diversity of reasons why we choose or are driven to this life or how it is sustained.'

They reached the kitchen. Shylah noticed how the paint was stained nicotine yellow on the looming, plain walls where they met the mitred ceiling. She saw the cracked light fitting spewing frayed cable and the bare light bulb.

'Let's have some tea, Shylah, and you can tell me all about how you and Gabriel are getting on with the shop.' Sister Anthony placed the kettle on the stove, opened the door, threw in some coal and prodded the beast to spattering life.

Shylah was thoughtful.

'Sister, is the convent going to have to close and the school just become a normal school?'

'I would expect the school to continue as a Roman Catholic school, Shylah, I don't think that is in question. The role of the nuns here is, maybe; the debate has been underway for some time. With the level of poverty and need in the rest of the world, the order is questioning whether it is right to continue to allow its Sisters to spend their time educating the 'daughters of the rich'.'

'But this isn't a private school. The parents of the girls here aren't rich,' Shylah was shocked.

'Shylah, compared to the children with no parents, no shoes, no running water and no food in some of the war-ravaged African countries, where our Sisters are working, our girls' parents are rich beyond their dreams,' Sister Anthony bit her bottom lip and circled her eyes to the right, a gesture Shylah had not seen before. She stood and poured the tea, her familiar, square, straight back was balanced, reliable, permanent … but just at that moment, Sister Anthony's back wavered slightly.

'What will happen to the older Sisters?' Shylah asked.

'That's what I am most concerned about, Shylah,' Sister Anthony replied. 'Some of them have been here for sixty years or more, I don't think they'll cope well with moving to another convent to sit all day with the rest of the dying. Also, to be frank, some of them do say some very odd, some would think shocking, things, they are sinking into dementia as many of us will in time.'

'And what about you, Sister?'

'I will be expected to go abroad and help those whom the order feels are genuinely needy rather than do my duty here, Shylah,' Sister Anthony made the nervous gesture again. 'I always wanted to be a science teacher, Shylah. I had planned to do that via a more conventional route when I left college in Ireland but then I was very badly let down by someone,' Sister Anthony sat at ninety degrees to Shylah at the rough wooden table, riddled with knife marks and teacup rings. 'I couldn't deal with what happened. I couldn't face anyone, my parents, my family, my friends, I was too humiliated. So I joined the order, but my real vocation was always the teaching.' Sister Anthony looked down at her hands, she seized a tissue from somewhere within the multi-layered folds of her habit and started to twist it round and round into tight spirals in her fingers. 'That's not the case with all the nuns here. Many of them came for different reasons although, to be honest, very few as a result of a pure calling from God. Most of us have a dark story somewhere in our past.'

Shylah was horrified. For so long, she had taken for granted the hospitality and kindness of the nuns at the convent, believing it was their vocation to care for unfortunates such as unmarried mothers, expulsed wives, battered girlfriends. It had never occurred to her that these nuns were 'real women', had pasts, regrets, dashed hopes and aspirations. She had believed that the odd visit, some pictures of Colm and a bar of chocolate at Christmas were sufficient to keep them happy.

'Sister, I am so sorry. I had no idea,' she said finally. 'I thought it was your vocations to be nuns and the life you lead here which fulfilled you all.'

'Don't get me wrong now, Shylah, I will do what the order wants me to do. I made my choice and came here, I've had years and years teaching in the school, I've met some great people like yourself,' she put the compressed tissue back into her pocket, stood up and bade Shylah to follow.

'Come on, Shylah, let's go and tell some of the older nuns about your new shop and about Colm. Let's go and make their days.'

The stable, square bearing returned, Sister Anthony smiled and flicked quickly away what may have been a tear with her sleeve. They spent the next hour together, as a team, making teas, showing pictures and telling the story of Bennets to the delight of the other nuns.

Sometime either very late on Thursday evening or very early Friday morning, Peter had posted a card through the letterbox of 45 The High Street saying how proud he was of Shylah and Colm, wishing them luck and thanking Gabriel for being their wonderful friend. The card, with a picture of a robin in an apple tree, stayed permanently attached to the wall of the shop, just behind the counter.

By six o'clock the following morning, Shylah arrived at the shop to meet the first of a procession of delivery men. They were, to a man, delighted to encounter such a charming businesswoman and more than willing to do a little more of the carrying and heaving than they did for their usual customers. The vegetables and fresh produce were in place and Shylah warmed, her skin phosphorescing, lineless, bright, feeling for the first time confident that Bennets would be the success of which she and Gabriel had dreamed in the room at the top of the spiral stone steps, three years earlier.

Just after eight o'clock, Gabriel and Colm were nearly ready to leave the cottage. Shylah had taken Patrick earlier, so they would walk. Before they left, Colm asked Gabriel to wait by the iron gate.

'I just need to check something in the back garden. Will you wait here for me and face the other way?'

Bill was by his vegetable patch. He made the special sign. Thumbs up, just for the men. That was the last time Colm saw Bill in the garden. Many times after that special Friday, he tried to remember how it had felt seeing him, what he looked like, how he melted into the air. As the years passed and his memory of the day faded, Colm began to wonder whether Bill was really there at all or whether, as a little boy, he had imagined augmented longevity for the only father figure he had known.

The robin in the apple tree sang its pretty tune with three long wobbly notes. Colm ran back to Gabriel, they waved goodbye to Bonny who was watching them go, her paws up and head proud on the cottage windowsill.

'Come on, Colm, Bonny will be fine here for the morning. I need you to be a real grown up today and help Mummy and me.'

They set off to work. Gabriel was wearing her big, orange, swingy clothes. She had no coat, just extra swingy red colours on top which billowed and rustled as they walked along together. Colm felt proud to be walking with Gabriel, holding her warm, dry, strong hand as she waved and nodded to the people they saw, her jangly bracelets clanging and ringing. Through adulthood, when Colm closed his eyes and concentrated, he could remember the feel of the walk that morning. The cool, clean air on his face, the music, warmth and scent of Gabriel beside him, the delicious feeling of anticipation and hope that his Mother would be even happier once the shop was open.

At nine o'clock, Gabriel lifted Colm up so he could reach the Yale lock more easily, turn the stiff key and open the shop door.

'OK Colm, let's countdown to lift-off together. Ten, nine, eight, seven, six, five, four, three, two, one and …. Door open!'

The sun was shining, the deliveries had all arrived and Shylah was ready to welcome her first customers. Gabriel stood back, this would be Shylah's venture, her life and, when with Peter's help, they had finished the flat upstairs, her new home of her own for herself and Colm. Gabriel had to get back to work. The opening was Shylah's day, Shylah's turn for the limelight.

Between ten and twelve o'clock, Colm received the two eagerly anticipated bursts of Easter custom from the families of both Jonny and James. Both sets of parents, already familiar to Shylah and Gabriel, were affable, complimentary and generous with their wallets, adding an assortment of products to the main focus of their visits, the Easter eggs. They joked at how the boys' social lives: play dates, sleepovers and parties outsmarted those of the adults. They compared notes about the school and complimented the headmaster, Mr Downs. They expressed complete surprise when they heard that Shylah and Colm intended to move out of Gabriel's cottage and into the flat above the shop.

'Oh, that will be handy for you but we thought… we thought you were all quite settled together at the cottage. It'll be great to have some more space.'

They had thought Colm would stay with his two Mummies. Gabriel and Shylah reflected some years later on the (mistaken) assumptions made and the kind, open-mindedness they had enjoyed from both families over the preceding and subsequent years.

Later in the morning, little Rosemary and her foster parents entered the shop. Colm immediately adopted an air of authority, recognising Rosemary from their meeting at the convent several months before.

'Hello, Rosemary. I helped you find things in Sister Anthony's kitchen, didn't I? I can help you find things here too if you like, this is where I work.'

Rosemary was clearly impressed with Colm's accomplishments and followed him around faithfully while he pointed out the features and benefits of the majority of the products on the lower shelves.

'She's a lovely little girl, isn't she?' Shylah remarked to the pale, fat lady with Rosemary.

'Yes, she's a poppet but she's had a hard time. We're her third foster home already. The first couple moved abroad, her last foster Mummy is ill with cancer and sadly we will not be able to keep her long term for various reasons.'

'Well, you're obviously doing a great job, she seems very happy and confident.' The woman smiled with relief acceding to Colm's recommendation that Rosemary be allowed an Easter egg in a mug bearing a yellow rabbit in a purple waistcoat.

At one o'clock, Gabriel and Colm took a break, returning briefly to the cottage, laden with fare from Bennets.

'Hmmm, are we going to have big lunches every day now? Because of all the hard work we are doing,' asked Colm.

Gabriel laughed. 'Well you can, Colm, because you get plenty of exercise playing with Bonny and helping Mummy. I'll need to cut down though when I go back to work and leave everything here to you and Mummy. If not, I'll end up the same size as an elephant.'

After their lunch, they spent time with Bonny in the back garden, throwing her ball.

'Gabriel, when you go back to work, can Mummy and I still play in the garden with Bonny?'

'Of course you can, Colm. I'm relying on you and Mummy to keep an eye on the cottage and garden for me while I am working and to keep Patrick running, please, when I'm not using him.'

'Are you going to work with the funny man called Montezuma who Mummy says is an odd-bod?'

A flicker of confusion swept across Gabriel's face before she realised what Colm meant. She smiled to herself at Shylah's insightful description of her erstwhile college contemporary, Mubaarak.

'No, I don't think I will be working with Montezuma at first, Colm, but he does do work in some very interesting countries, so maybe I will work with him another time. I'll keep you posted.'

Colm nodded seriously, satisfied that he was sufficiently abreast of Gabriel's professional endeavours and they were ready to set-off.

A gentle shower left pearly droplets on their clothes and Bonny's fur. The plants in the garden glowed green, refreshed. Colm insisted on settling Bonny for the afternoon with a cuddly toy to keep her company before they left.

While Gabriel and Colm were at the cottage, Shylah enjoyed the relative tranquillity of an ebb in footfall. The shop was momentarily empty when Shylah sat down behind the counter to enjoy her locally sourced, organic pork pie, enhanced with apple chutney and washed down with rhubarb cordial of similar provenance. Just when her mouth was full of the salty savoury snack, the shop door opened. Shylah hurriedly chewed, swigged the cordial, swallowed exaggeratedly and endeavoured, unsuccessfully, to issue a greeting without showering the shop with detritus.

'Carry on with your lunch, dear. I'm fine browsing for now,' said the woman, in an accent which sounded like springy, purple heather. The woman had an aura of the nineteen fifties about her. Nothing she wore was conventionally fashionable but together the understated, coordinated ensemble sang with style. She had swingy chestnut hair which moved in synchrony with her graceful gait as she circled the shop looking intently at each shelf, picking up items and placing them in her gaping raffia shopping bag. She moved to the counter, looked up and smiled at the card with the robin in an apple tree, pinned to the wall. The card had been joined by several others but the woman picked it out for special attention.

'That's a lovely card for a lovely new shop. You have done wonders in here, I am told,' she said.

'My friend and my son have helped me, and my Dad has been wonderful,' Shylah replied. The woman smiled more broadly, piling purchases onto the counter.

'My Dad likes these biscuits too. He has been eating them with his coffee and taking them home with him ever since we received our first order. This is the second batch already and we're only on day one!' Shylah commented.

'There's no Scotswoman on earth either who doesn't like her Tunnocks caramel,' joked the woman, paying and gathering everything back into the bag.

'You've done such a great job here, you should be very proud, Shylah,' she said as she left.

It wasn't until later that afternoon that Shylah wondered how the woman had known her name. Over subsequent years, the woman became a regular albeit infrequent customer. Her home was in Edinburgh but her work often brought her to Hull. She preferred to stay well out of the city in a small hotel in Market Hamilton. She never used Shylah's name again and Shylah grew to wonder whether she had misheard, until the memory of that first unusual encounter dissolved completely from her mind.

At three o'clock in the afternoon, a jerky, carbuncled youth shot through the doorway into the shop. Black plastic photography paraphernalia clanged from cords and straps around his neck, a brick-like mobile phone was welded between his ear and his hand.

'Hi, I'm from The Market Hamilton Post. Been sent to cover the opening of your shop,' he shouted, forgetting he was no longer on the phone. He removed his Dictaphone from its holster, slammed the brick on the counter and swung his tripod in a potentially catastrophic arc.

'What's your angle? What's different about Bennets? Why shouldn't we just drive to Tesco's in York or Hull?' he barked without making eye contact, pressing the Dictaphone towards Shylah's mouth.

'Well, we are sourcing locally wherever possible, we're prioritising organic and additive-free produce and we are offering products which are just that little bit different from the norm.'

Shylah got into her stride and the interview continued constructively for a few minutes.

'Great, can I get some photos of you and your partner and the little boy?

Standing together in the shop and then some outside,' he knelt down, stood up, spun round, sprung onto a chair, jumped off it again before a bemused Gabriel and Shylah and an uncontrollably giggly Colm.

Outside the shop, things became worse. The young David Bailey decided he needed a wider angle to capture the shop front and three proprietors. He walked backwards, eye glued to the eyepiece of the camera and stood in the middle of the road. Oblivious to the danger around him, he obstructed the traffic on the High Street, deaf to the horns and profanities. Mary's car turned at the traffic lights and embarked upon the High Street in a meandering swerve.

'Oh God. It's Mum and she looks like she's been on the sherry,' hissed Shylah to Gabriel. 'She's a liability, she'll run him over out there.'

Gabriel stepped out into the road, grabbed the journalist by his sleeve and propelled him, his equipment assuming a following trajectory, back to the pavement. Mary, amazed to see Gabriel and Shylah, the abortive conversation about the shop having slipped her mind, and not even noticing Colm, forgot that she was in charge of a vehicle. She took her eyes off the road, craning with curiosity at what her daughter and her friend were up to and crashed into the door of a parked car directly opposite.

The journalist was over the moon, his acne pulsating as he ran treacherously across the road again to secure first coverage of the accident and ensuing slanging match between the slurry-voiced woman and the owner of the parked car.

Shylah walked sadly back inside the shop. 'Things were going so well, she's ruined everything. She'll get her licence taken off her now, I'll bet.'

'Don't worry, the chap from the paper got some good pictures and business is going well. We've had over one hundred paying customers already today. You and Colm carry on here and I'll go and see what needs doing with your Mum.'

Six days later, the Market Hamilton Post bore a beautiful photograph of Gabriel, Shylah and Colm, arms around one another outside Bennets, under a headline which read:

'Market Hamilton ready for the twenty first century'.

The article started:

'Shylah Cook, her partner and their child Colm are taking Market Hamilton High Street into the twenty first century. Their new store Bennets, was conceived by the pair in their bedroom at Oxford University.'

Gabriel, immediately recognising the innuendo, considered sending a copy of the interestingly worded article to her old friend Mubaarak who was badgering her to help him with a project he was running in Bahrain.

Shylah was delighted with the article which extolled the quality and virtue of the shop with its organic, local concept; she missed the innuendo entirely.

Six weeks later, Mary appeared in court, was charged with drunk driving and had her licence confiscated.

At six o'clock on the evening of the opening, as Shylah was about to close the door, Sister Anthony slipped quietly inside.

'I am sorry I am so late, I wanted to come and see how you are getting on. I have to go and report back to the Sisters. It's all they've been talking about today.'

'It was great. Thank you, Sister. Colm and Gabriel have gone back to the cottage already and I'm just packing up now. We had absolutely loads of customers, Gabriel will know all the figures and everything but it feels like a great first day. A guy from the paper came so we'll be in next week. I can bring a copy to the convent one evening.'

'That's great, Shylah, I am so pleased for you and you will have made their day again back at the convent. I hope we see you again soon, Shylah. I will be off to Africa in two weeks. The best news though is that there are a couple of noviciates from Sri Lanka who will be coming over to look after the older nuns and live at the convent here, so everything will go on as normal.'

Shylah hugged Sister Anthony.

'That's great news, Sister, but please think about yourself for once instead of the other Sisters or the school? I know you wanted to stay here but it could work out really well in Africa. People need to learn there too, you may get the chance to teach while you're there.'

'I hope so, Shylah but it may be time for a different type of calling now. Please come and say goodbye before I go. I'll let you get on. And thank you for your support the other day,' Sister Anthony looked downwards, bashful, unsteady.

'Sister, let me just get you something to take back with you.' Shylah stowed several packets of biscuits into a carrier and handed it to Sister Anthony who had sat down on the small stool by the counter. She looked up and smiled as she took the bag.

'Thank you so much, Shylah. The Sisters will be so happy.' Still smiling, she turned and left the shop.

Within two paces, Shylah saw from the window that she had gathered herself and assumed her usual steady stride back towards the convent.

Two weeks later, Shylah drank tea, shared a box of chocolate biscuits (snaffled from the shelves at Bennets) and said goodbye to Sister Anthony in the convent kitchen. Sister had already placed her small bag of possessions by the large front door, ready to move onto the next calling, without fuss or complaint.

Then, the week after Sister Anthony left for Africa, two young, kind girls arrived from Colombo. They cared for the elderly nuns as if they were queens, spoke in sweet, slightly accented voices, sang like angels in the chapel and retrieved a pair of ladders from the convent garden shed to set about mending the holes in the roof.

CHAPTER 13

Colombo, Sri Lanka

2012

Thanuja, the eldest of ten children, had been proud of her school exercise books. She always stayed in the classroom to do studying and homework after all the other girls went home. It was the only way she could do things properly, there was no room and no quiet at home with her parents and the nine younger ones all in one room.

She got good grades, better than most of the other girls in the class, especially in maths. Thanuja's favourite subject was maths. She set her work out neatly on the pages of her exercise book. For every equation and calculation, she set the 'equals signs' in a soldierly, vertical line, constants and variables springing to left and right like fronds on a crooked palm tree.

One afternoon, Sister Mary, the maths teacher from Ireland, a Sister of the Holy Family, came and sat with Thanuja after all the others had left.

'Thanuja, you are a very gifted girl and a delight to teach. If you continue to work as hard as you do now, I could see you going to university,' she said, placing her palm gently on Thanuja's bare arm.

'But Sister, the universities here are very hard to get into, there are far more applicants than places and my family has no money.'

Thanuja realised, embarrassed, as she spoke too soon, that Sister Mary probably had more understanding of the Sri Lankan university system than she did, having worked in the country for over twenty years.

'There are universities all over the world, Thanuja, not just in Sri Lanka. With a good degree and your talent for maths, you could be an accountant, or work in IT.'

Thanuja's chocolate-brown eyes opened wide and she looked into Sister Mary's face. The nun's eyes were greeny brown with fiery flecks.

'You would be able to earn very good money abroad, in the US or Europe and you could send some home to your family, maybe help your sisters to get an education too.'

Thanuja remembered every word of the conversation and replayed it over and over in her mind throughout the evening and for days afterwards. Sister Mary could see the future. A future Thanuja craved, yearned for.

When Thanuja was sixteen, she took her exams. Her grades were better than all the other girls in her class. Sister Mary asked to see her again.

'Thanuja, I have some ideas for you for the next two years. We are recommending the International Baccalaureate as the most rounded grounding for further education. I would suggest that you follow a sciences route and perfect your English as a priority. That will enable you to become a really viable candidate for universities across the world.'

Sister Mary's confidence in Thanuja's capability was viral. Thanuja could smell the scent of opportunity. She could feel on her fingertips, the patina of the book covers she would use at university.

'There are government and church sponsorship schemes for gifted girls like you, Thanuja. With a talent for maths like yours, accountancy, IT, management ... all of those are within your reach.'

Sister Mary's view of the future was not just a dream, it was backed up by a plan, and she would help Thanuja to execute the plan. Thanuja felt her insides swell, warm, like yeast in bread.

'Thanuja, you can be a great example for the girls in Colombo.'

Thanuja thought about several of her cousins. They were gifted Sri Lankan girls, working abroad; the Middle East mostly, as manicurists, beauticians and housemaids. They were in dead end, badly paid jobs, and were bullied and disrespected, they told her on their infrequent trips back home. The girls were near starvation in the Middle East, sending money back to Sri Lanka; their potential, their futures, crushed. Sister Mary wanted more for Thanuja and Thanuja was desperate to grasp the tiny, golden thread of opportunity, roll it into a ball and throw it high into the air where it would shine like a planet of promise for all the poor, gifted girls in the city.

Thanuja casually slipped notice of her plans into a conversation with her mother at home. Her mother must have swiftly relayed the conversation to her father because he came immediately, furiously into the school, interrupting lessons, to the amusement of Thanuja's classmates. It was a very good thing that Sister Mary was a Westerner and a nun, reflected Thanuja subsequently. If she hadn't been, Thanuja's father would have been a lot angrier and probably violent too.

He explained in Sinhala (which he insisted Thanuja translate), that he would decide when his daughter would be allowed to leave school and come home, where she belonged, to help her mother with her sisters and brothers. He added that he did not appreciate Sister Mary putting other ideas into Thanuja's head and forbade Thanuja to stay on at school after the end of her compulsory education.

Sister Mary remained calm and dignified throughout the tirade. She had encountered exactly this situation more times than she cared to remember. The opportunity for girls to make a lasting difference to the poor in Colombo depended on people like Sister Mary. In turn, Sister Mary depended wholly on the support of the fathers. Her success rate was poor. For every ten girls with the potential to continue their education past sixteen, Sister Mary had calculated that only two were allowed by their fathers to do so. It was always pointless to argue. When the Sri Lankan patriarchs felt threatened by their educated daughters, logic and reason had never, in Sister Mary's experience, enabled progress. On occasion, such encounters resulted in black eyes or a bruised jaw for Sister Mary. Black eyes and bruised jaws were nothing compared to the suffering the girls endured once their fathers had got them home.

Thanuja's father left on his bike. A sneer smeared across his gaunt, pock marked face. He was pleased with himself, very pleased indeed, he had shown the Western nun who was more powerful around her stupid school. He had told Thanuja, far too big for herself these days, in front of all her upstart classmates what he was going to make her do. He pushed down on his pedals with an extra surge of power. He tossed his greasy, black hair over his shoulder. He was the big man. He would make sure everyone else realised that, just in case they had any doubt. He would show Thanuja who was boss with a very good beating when she finally came home.

As her father rode away, congratulating himself on his performance, Thanuja wept in the school toilet until the tears were gone and the blood in her veins threatened to emerge from her tear ducts. Sister Mary found her crumpled on the toilet floor among used tissues, hair and grime.

'Sister, please help me.'

But Thanuja knew there was nothing Sister could do.

She felt the slice of stainless-steely hatred in her chest; not for her father, but for her mother who must have taken her usual appeasing pathway when relaying Thanuja's plans to her father, protecting herself at Thanuja's expense.

A few days later, Thanuja's father told Thanuja that he had identified a suitable husband for her. He was sure the boy was from a family who owned a phalanx of pharmacies in the city.

'Thanuja, you have let me and your bitch of a mother down with your talk about schools. You try to make me, a big man, look small in front of your teacher. I told her though, and I tell you too, that I make the rules. You will meet this boy and marry him quickly. I am a big man and a big man will get money from these people when his daughter marries.'

Thanuja's father had seen the boy with his parents, driving around the city in a big, silver car, from pharmacy to pharmacy

'They drive around in their big car while I, the big man here in Colombo, am left riding a bike with so many children to feed.'

The boy had a moped too,

'If I don't see you on the back of that moped, Thanuja, by the time the rain comes, I will make you sorry, properly sorry, not just little suffering like you had so far with all your talk of your school and teachers. I am a big man. I deserve a moped and you will make sure I get one by marrying this boy.'

The desired coupling with the pharmaceutical son was doomed to failure. Thanuja had never met the boy and didn't know how or where to find him among the dense population of Colombo. Her father had only ever seen his parents in their car from his bicycle, didn't know their name and had never spoken to them. As in everything else, her father had failed to embrace logical thought or common sense when he had planned his daughter's marriage.

With no school to take her away from the oppression of the apartment and her Father's megalomaniacal rants and schemes becoming ever more preposterous, Thanuja took to languishing, with some of the other girls from her old school, around the bars near the port of Kolomtoto. Her father wanted her to find a husband, she had no alternative; the bars were the best place to go. So she went. None of the other girls in the bars had grades comparable with Thanuja's, none of them had glimpsed the golden thread of Thanuja's side-lined future. They were happy to be on the marriage market, hanging around the bars.

Thanuja met Chanuka in one of the bars. Chanuka's grades had been poor, his family did not own pharmacies, they had no big, silver car, they had no car at all and Chanuka did not own a moped. Thanuja didn't particularly like Chanuka but the beatings at home had escalated exponentially after the incident with Sister Mary and subsequent lack of progress with the pharmacy/moped boy. Chanuka enthusiastically pawed and slobbered over Thanuja in the crowded, muddy alleyway outside one of the bars. His crooked teeth bruised her lips as he pressed his dribbling mouth over hers. His hands kneaded at her flesh underneath her tee shirt like an apprentice baker trying to coax his sticky dough into good behaviour.

Thanuja's father swiftly adjusted his eligibility criteria for Thanuja's husband.

'You let me down again, Thanuja. You are a disgrace to me and to your useless mother. I will be kind and let you marry this boy so long as he brings money to me and this family. If there is no money, you will suffer, Thanuja.'

Thanuja, her dreams dissolved and spirit crushed, trod the path of least resistance. She was unable to fathom how to escape from the vortex, slowly drowning as it pulled her further and further away from the golden threads of hope. Within three months of the Sister Mary incident, Chanuka and Thanuja were married in the expansive local Roman Catholic Church, filled with the numerous multigenerational families of both bride and groom.

The couple spent their wedding night in one of the two bedrooms in Chanuka's parents' home. On the plus side, her father's beatings had stopped, conversely, it took less than a fortnight for Thanuja's irritation with Chanuka to mature into excoriating contempt. She gritted her teeth and muttered curses under her breath as she endured his incompetent, unpleasant lovemaking. Unwilling to contemplate the life into which she had been sucked, she lazed silent, sullen, about his parents' house, returned occasionally to see her mother and found her siblings insufferable.

Chanuka's mother complained at the laziness of her new daughter in law. 'Look at this useless girl, Chanuka, she just sleeps and lays about all day. Why could my only son not find a decent wife?'

Thanuja ignored her, contempt spreading on top of contempt. As the weeks passed, the love and admiration Thanuja had fostered for Sister Mary turned to bitterness. If Sister Mary had never spoken about universities, careers, accountancy and IT, Thanuja fancied that she might even have been happy with Chanuka, sharing his parents' fairly pleasant house, staying in the city. It was Sister Mary's fault for showing her the possibility of an alternative which had thrown the dim, grey future which now presented into such unfavourable contrast.

After three months enduring Chanuka's heaving and grunting, Thanuja fell pregnant and delightedly forbade Chanuka further relations lest the baby be damaged. During the long, sticky months of her pregnancy, she did nothing but lie on one of the mattresses either in Chanuka's parents' house or at home, being climbed over by her numerous, unbearable siblings. Night and day were inseparable, both interspersed with episodes of unrefreshing sleep, haunted by terrifying dreams. Thanuja now at least had a viable excuse for her depressive behaviour and Chanuka's mother eased off her complaints in light of Thanuja's new fecundity.

Six months into her pregnancy, Chanuka secured work as a cleaner at one of the hotels in the centre of the city and was thereafter, to Thanuja's delight, absent from his parents' home. The hotel preferred staff to stay on-site so they could maximise their working hours without them wasting time on travelling through the city's congested streets or on personal matters such as wives or families. As her father had hoped, Chanuka's money was dutifully handed over to Thanuja who under threat of further beatings, pregnancy irrelevant, handed the money on to her father.

Thanuja's waters broke at Chanuka's mother's house.

'For goodness sake, girl, look at the mess you have made. Get outside,' cried the imminent paternal grandmother. Thanuja was bundled alone, her clothes dripping, with a small carrier bag of essentials, into a taxi and sent to the hospital.

The baby, a boy, was born while Chanuka was at work. The labour and delivery progressed with little drama in the sole presence of Thanuja and an Australian charity worker. The Australian girl's knowledge of midwifery was equivalent to Thanuja's facility with racing car maintenance but Thanuja enjoyed her company and laughed to herself at the girl's 'school hockey captain' approach to motivating her charge during childbirth.

'Come on, Thanuja love, one more push for the team!'

It was the first enjoyable verbal interaction Thanuja had experienced since leaving school.

In the twenty four hours after her son was born, infused with beautiful, multi-coloured love and fizzing with hormonal energy, Thanuja planned their lives. As soon as she could walk the distance to the school, she would go and see Sister Mary to ask whether there was charitable assistance available and somewhere she and the baby could stay while she continued her education. The golden thread of hope had temporarily unravelled, it was time to wind it up again into a ball, throw it high in the air and jump, with her son on her hip, to catch it as it fell.

As Thanuja concluded planning and evening darkness was falling over the city, the message finally reached the hotel that Chanuka's wife had given birth to a baby boy. He finished his shift and borrowed a bicycle to make the five mile journey to the hospital, his wife and day old son. Chanuka hoped, as he cycled, that the baby would help Thanuja shake off the laziness and silence of the last twelve months and return to him the sensible, meek girl he had married.

A truck was driving without headlights through Colombo's congested, unlit streets. It swerved onto the opposite side of the road to overtake a bullock cart, directly into the path of an oncoming car. Swarms of pedestrians, cyclists, mopeds and rickshaws at the side of the street scattered centrifugally. The car veered to the left to avoid a collision as Chanuka's cycle assumed a trajectory perpendicular to its side. Chanuka was thrown from the bike, over the roof of the car on impact, his body propelled five metres into the middle of the road where his cranium connected at speed with the narrow strip of tarmac between the two muddy outer lanes.

News of Chanuka's death took two days to reach Thanuja via Colombo's overburdened transport and communications infrastructure.

'Thanuja, I am sorry but we have just had a message from the hotel where your husband works. There has been an accident. I am so sorry, Thanuja'.

The Australian charity worker, who was helping Thanuja pack her carrier bag with donated baby clothes, wept as Thanuja calmly absorbed the news, which had been delivered in the matron's sonorous, Scottish voice. Thanuja continued, throughout the matron's message, to make her preparations to leave hospital in a taxi with the baby. She would need to tell the taxi driver to take her to her own mother's home rather than Chanuka's, in light of the news. Her other plans need not change, she would go and see Sister Mary in the morning.

Thanuja's father's reaction to his daughter's newly widowed status was predictable. To his abject disappointment, the proxy wages from the recently deceased Chanuka had sustained for fewer than four months, he had nowhere near enough money for a moped and he was now left with not only his daughter back in the single roomed apartment, but her baby too.

'Thanuja, you are again a disappointment to me and not the daughter that I, a big man in the city, deserve.' He raised his hand but let it drop again as Thanuja, sitting on the floor before him feeding her child, met his eye.

'No husband will take you now, Thanuja, with a baby. I will speak to my cousins tomorrow to see what can be done with you.'

As planned, Thanuja visited Sister Mary. She timed it carefully so she would catch her as soon as she finished teaching.

'Thanuja, it is great to see you and who is the wee man?' Sister Mary reached out and took the baby, holding him expertly in the angle of her arm, his face turned slightly into her body, comforted against her cushioned chest.

'He doesn't have a name yet, Sister. I want him to have a European name so that when I am working in the West, it will be easier for him. Can you help me choose one?'

Sister Mary pressed the baby closer into her body and smiled like a cup of sweet, warm tea. Thanuja saw the golden thread in front of her face, reached out, pulled it towards herself and held on tight.

'My brother's name was Sean, Thanuja. How about Sean? I have to go now to meet one of the parents but will you come back soon and we can talk some more?'

Two weeks after Thanuja's seventeenth birthday, one week after Sean's birth and two days after the conversation with Sister Mary, Thanuja's father had a new plan. He pressed his face into Thanuja's, clamped her upper arm in a bruising grip.

'You are a very lucky girl, Thanuja. I am such a big man in Colombo that one of the cousins has found you a job in Saudi Arabia, through an agency. You will be working for an Arab couple, looking after their baby.'

Thanuja could smell his rotten breath and felt droplets of his spit on her lips as he spoke, telling her, 'It is your duty to me and your family to go and work abroad, to send money home so we can care for your bastard son.'

Thanuja did not speak. She had learned thoroughly by now that resistance was hopeless. With no husband to provide, she had no choice but to go and do what lots and lots of other Sri Lankan girls did.

'Good, you are silent for a change, daughter. I am the big man, I say what you will do. You will walk with me to the agency in the morning. We will meet the cousin who is getting your papers.'

Not one scintilla of time passed over the next three weeks when Thanuja's father was not watching her. The prospect of regular money being transferred from a family member working in the Middle East was something he had dreamed about. He would not let anything derail his plan; in particular, he didn't want Thanuja going anywhere near the school or the interfering Sister Mary. As soon as Thanuja was in Saudi Arabia and his wife was caring for the baby, they would get him christened and give him a proper Sri Lankan name; Sean indeed!

Barbed wire wound itself around Thanuja's heart. She would travel to Saudi to look after the Arab couple's baby while Sean would be under the careless, casual charge of her incompetent, weak mother and immature sisters. The barbed wire screwed tighter, extending from her heart to her other organs. It tore as it wound through her veins, slashing, slitting. The beatings had started again, motivated by the slightest look or move which caused her father to suspect, or to choose to suspect, that she was planning to escape. Her mother knew exactly what was happening. She did nothing to help, avoided being alone with Thanuja and made no eye contact. The golden thread of hope was frayed, the ball unravelled and started to tarnish.

In the evening, the cousin arrived with the papers while Thanuja and her family were eating. Thanuja had been positioned that day, by her mother, with her back to the door, feeding the thriving Sean, her tee-shirt rolled up, her cardigan sheltering his velvety, vanilla-scented head against which she rested her cheek. Her father gripped her upper arm, smarting the bruises sustained in beatings over the preceding days, and pulled her to her feet. Her mother snatched Sean out of her arms, tearing his mouth from Thanuja's breast. Sean's eyes opened, their whites marbled with shock, his arms and legs involuntarily, immediately poker straight, emitting terrified, piercing shrieks. The smaller siblings complained, putting their hands over their ears.

Thanuja was manhandled by her father and the cousin into the car. Her mother sent her sister out with a lilac-coloured, cylindrical sports bag, already packed. Thanuja couldn't scream or fight any more. The pain of the barbed wire had vacuumed the air from her lungs, the blood from her arteries. She wrapped her arms around herself in the back of the car, lay down in the foetal position on the back seat, her head crashing, echoing rhythmically against the hard, metal door over the ruts and ridges in the road; the pain comforting.

The cousin, bribing officials to let him pass, accompanied her all the way to the gate and watched her board the 'plane. He handed her a long, black garment, instructing her to put it on over her clothes before she landed.

Nothing had been left to chance, her mother and father would have their moped.

She sat numb, silent for the duration of the flight and stood resigned, frozen, following the heaving, stinking crowd of pilgrims, into the cavernous immigration hall in Jeddah. She sat on the floor with the pilgrims throughout the ordeal of immigration. Bullying officials in bottle green uniforms poking, pushing, shouting, relishing every crumb of power. After four hours, she emerged confused into a wall of humanity, shouting, waving papers bearing names, in the arrivals hall. She stood static amidst the flow and press of the pilgrims, unsure where to go.

'Hello, I am your cousin Priyantha. Immigration is always like this, I think you were about four hours. I will drive you to your sponsor,' said the tall, quietly spoken man, taking her bag. 'Is this all you have with you?'

She nodded and followed him to the car. He watched the road carefully as he navigated the mortal combat of Jeddah's congested traffic.

'Thanuja, you need to be very careful here, the roads are dangerous. You should only travel with the driver you know. The couple you will be working for have a house on a Western compound and they have their own driver. They don't really mix with the Western people as they are very strict Muslim, they stay with the other Egyptians and Moroccans. The baby is only a few weeks old and the mother needs your help, Thanuja. I know you can do a good job for them.'

'The same age as Sean,' she answered, too softly for Priyantha to hear from the front.

CHAPTER 14

Jeddah, Saudi Arabia

February 2013 (Gregorian calendar)

For Gabriel, trips to and from the office in the competent care of Priyantha provided a fascinating study of the nature of stress. She had not recognised the extent of tension and fear which built before each trip with the kitten murderer (as she and Shylah had named him in their Haiku) until she no longer had to endure them. She found herself surprised to be relaxed as departures approached and similarly discovered that her nails no longer cut deep into her palms en route. One morning in mid-February, during one of their small-talking trips, Priyantha broached the light-hearted subject of St Valentine.

'Ma'am, do you know Valentine's?' he enquired.

Gabriel wondered whether she was about to be asked for counsel on which gift or card might generate the greatest favour from someone whom Priyantha had in his sights.

'Yes, I know about St Valentine's Day, Priyantha. In England and in fact in lots of Western countries, people exchange cards and flowers.'

'Yes ma'am, I know this. Please be very careful while you are here, ma'am. The authorities here in Saudi Arabia do not allow St. Valentine's.'

Gabriel was not particularly surprised that extramarital boy/girl interaction was discouraged but remembering the staggering overreaction to all things green, red or gold at Christmas, she pressed Priyantha further.

'What specifically is not allowed, Priyantha?'

'Well ma'am, last year the HAIA ordered that all florists shut over the fourteenth of February, from a few days before to a few days after. And anyone wearing anything red could be arrested if they are out in public.'

Gabriel realised that having been in Saudi Arabia for nearly three months, she was no longer surprised by the bizarre strictures imposed by the ruling bodies in the country.

'Thank you for keeping me in the picture, Priyantha. I will make sure I avoid wearing anything that might offend,' she answered, suppressing a smile at the thought of her red slippers in the flat and resolving to wear them more frequently.

Mubaarak had enjoyed a very easy ride over the last few weeks, reflected Gabriel, as they approached the office. The first Ladies Assessment Day had gone extremely well, thanks to her leadership. She resolved to check all this Valentines business out with him more thoroughly later.

They arrived at the office and Priyantha left with a cheerful wave. Mubaarak was in chipper form that morning, having received another flurry of emails congratulating him on the success of the first Ladies Assessment Day. Ten of the twelve ladies who attended would be offered jobs in Saraco and the board was delighted. For company leaders seen to be embracing the Royal and governmental decrees associated with inclusion in Saudi Arabia, there would be trips to the palace, pictures in the paper and opportunities to speak at conferences. So far the board, soaked in the soothing balm of kudos, had been unreceptive to discussions about the practicality of accommodating the ladies, should they accept their offers. Gabriel would leave the subjects of one Ladies toilet between a potentially substantial number of lady users, the lack of access to the canteen and other 'small' practical matters for another day.

She decided to tackle Samir in the first instance on the question of Valentine's Day, now that their relationship had developed into one of gentle older sister, younger brother teasing. She waited until Mubaarak was out of the room before embarking.

'Samir, I have been doing some reading about the prophet Muhammad,' she started. Samir smiled delightedly and tossed the peripheral, snowy vestiges of his gutrah over his shoulders.

'This is excellent news, Gabriel. If you would like to convert to Islam, you would be welcomed like a queen in Mecca.' His young face looked upwards in wonder and delight at the prospect. 'Westerners who have changed their ways and embraced Islam are treated with much respect in the Holy City and in the mosques. And I would be applauded for leading you through the conversion, habib'ti,' he winked.

'Thank you Samir, I will think about what you say but I was reading about how devoted Muhammad was to Khadija, his first wife, and how in the Qur'an it talks about the value of love and compassion between married couples.'

Samir warmed afresh to his subject. Being comparatively newly married himself, he considered this to be his area of authority over the lamentably single Gabriel.

'Yes, the prophet cherished marriage, Gabriel, and the Qur'an has many passages celebrating marriage and married love.'

'So why then Samir, do people not celebrate that love by giving gifts, cards and flowers on Valentine's Day?' asked Gabriel trying to sound relaxed and casual. She was determined to avoid the 'clamming up in the face of difficult challenge' issue she sometimes faced when discussing the subject of religion.

Samir was silent, thoughtful. It was the first time he had considered the question. The education system within which Samir had spent the majority of his scholarly life did not encourage inquiry where matters associated (however tenuously) with religion were concerned.

'At Harvard some people celebrated St Valentine's Day. It's not allowed here though because it is a pagan festival,' he answered falteringly just as Mubaarak bounced, still triumphant and revelling in his positive feedback, into the room.

'Mubaarak, why are we not allowed to celebrate St Valentine's Day?' asked Samir, delighted at the opportunity to offload the difficult question.

Mubaarak stopped mid step, spun around and shot a withering glance at Gabriel whom he suspected of having started the insurrection.

'It is not a Muslim custom. St Valentine is a pagan concept, Samir, you know that. We need to get back to the project, please.' He redirected his rebuke towards Gabriel, the suspected root cause of the distraction.

That evening, as had become her daily habit, Gabriel sat in the garden after the scorching Jeddah heat had subsided, reflecting on the day's events and revelations. She was frequently joined by Thanuja, who was allowed a short break each day once she had settled the baby to sleep. She heard Thanuja's soft, balletic footstep and turned. Thanuja was excited about something.

'Hello ma'am. I am very happy to see you. I have been speaking to my cousin Priyantha today and he told me he drives for a lady in our compound who works at Saraco. This is you, ma'am?'

'Yes, Thanuja, it is me. If it is the same Priyantha, your cousin is a very good driver'

'He is a very good man. He has spoken to the cousins in Sri Lanka and helped me get the job here in Saudi Arabia. He took me to my sponsor when I arrived and he helps with my money and papers. He does not take anything from me. He is not like the other cousins in Sri Lanka.'

'That is a nice coincidence, Thanuja. It is good of him to find you a job and it must be enjoyable looking after the baby.'

Thanuja's eyes dropped and her hands joined in her lap. 'Ma'am, it is hard looking after the baby when my own very young baby is in Sri Lanka. I am very sad. When I first came here and I held baby Mohamed, my milk would come and I would have pain here.' Thanuja placed her palm flat on her lower abdomen. 'It was like when I held my Sean before.'

Thanuja went on to explain to a silent, rapt Gabriel about her family in Colombo, her bullying father and careless mother, in whose care Sean had been left, to Thanuja's perpetual terror. She explained how all the family lived in the tiny one roomed apartment, about her truncated marriage to the tragic Chanuka and how her parents wanted a moped. Thanuja's faltering voice tossed words into the air between them which weaved together into a web of abuse, exploitation, powerlessness and the ultimate grief of being parted from her child. Despite this, Gabriel marvelled, Thanuja was still balanced, calm, happy and articulate.

'Ma'am, I worked very hard at school for a better life but my father would not let me stay.'

Thanuja then explained about her talent for maths, Sister Mary, the glimpse of hope she had been given and then how, at the hands of her father and complicit mother, the hope had been strangled.

'Thanuja, have you tried to contact Sister Mary from here?' asked Gabriel. 'It is still worth trying. With Priyantha here liaising with your sponsor, there must be something which can be done.'

'But ma'am, how can I do anything from here? I have no 'phone and I am not allowed to use the computer.'

'Leave it with me, Thanuja, I will see what I can do if you would like me to,' answered Gabriel. 'It may take me a few days but tomorrow is Friday so I can spend a little time on it for you.'

Thanuja put her small, smooth arms around the taller woman's neck and her tears dampened Gabriel's upper arm. She had to return to her employers' house. During the latter part of their conversation that evening, her face had warmed as though a golden flame had been illuminated behind her eyes. As she released Gabriel and stood to leave, the moon caught the shoulder of her utilitarian working outfit. Gabriel saw the glimmer of two golden threads woven fast among the lilac fabric. Thanuja saw them too and placed her hand protectively over her shoulder. She would never let the golden threads slip through her hands again.

Back in the apartment, now a more homely place of sanctuary after several weeks and the expansion of Gabriel's Saudi based possessions, Gabriel decided to enlist Shylah's help.

Haiku 33 – Jeddah to Market Hamilton via email
Sister Anthony
Are you still in touch with her?
Thanuja needs help

Haiku 34 – Market Hamilton to Jeddah via email
In Africa still
Working on an AIDS project
We email weekly!

Under the Haiku, Shylah had typed Sister Anthony's email address.

Gabriel lit the jasmine-scented candle on her table, inhaled its sweetness and installed herself among the deep purple, velvet cushions with which she had now covered the carpeted sofa. Weekends alone on the compound were difficult. Socialising for single women in Saudi was non-existent, unless she braved the cliquey clubhouse complex, and since the disastrous dinner at the end of her first week, Mubaarak avoided any contact outside work. She sat with her laptop on her knees, a glass of strawberry juice beside her, delighted to have found useful endeavour to occupy herself over the two days which stretched before her and overjoyed that she might be able to help Thanuja. She composed her email, realising with shame that she had not had direct contact with Sister Anthony since the opening of Bennets, many years previously, when Sister was leaving for Africa.

Sister

I am very sorry that I have not been in touch for so long. I am aware that you are in regular contact with Shylah with whom I remain very close friends, so I have been getting your news, albeit second hand. I resolve to do better in future.

I do not know whether Shylah has mentioned it at all but I am working in Saudi Arabia at present and have met a young girl here named Thanuja. I will not go into detail about her background but having encountered many difficult circumstances, she now finds herself working as a nanny, away from her own baby and on very low pay.

She was educated in a school in Colombo where a Sister Mary of the order of the Holy Family took a special interest in her because of her extraordinary talent for maths. Sadly Thanuja was forced to leave school at sixteen.

Sister, do you have any idea whether there are any charitable organisations which would provide help to gifted girls like Thanuja to help them break out of the cycle of poverty and exploitation and get back into education?

It occurs to me, Sister, that Thanuja has striking similarities to both myself and to Shylah at her age but that by a simple stroke of good fortune, we were children in a market town in Yorkshire while she was dealt a poor suburb of Colombo...

I would very much like to help her, if I can. Sorry for several years of silence. ☺

Yours, Gabriel

In her inbox, she was delighted to find another communication from the elusive Fatima.

Gabriel

I hope everything is OK there in Saudi. The guy I met at my English class sent me a Valentine's card and gave me twelve red roses! I have never had anything on Valentine's Day before.

By the way, my Mum says if you want to go round and see her and her (mad) sister at our house, you can. I haven't given you their address here because I will quite understand if you don't fancy it.

Your choice Gabriel, let me know if you want the address of the mad ladies!

Love Fatima x

She responded quickly to Fatima

Fatima

I am delighted that things with the guy are going well. Sadly no Valentines here for me (or for anyone else in Saudi Arabia I am told)!

Thank you for the offer to make an introduction to your family. I am pretty busy at work, so I think I'll pass for now! Is that a valid excuse?

By the way, I still have your five big rules stuck on my kitchen wall (just in case I forget the Hadith of Gabriel!).

Take care and keep in touch

Gabriel

Sister Anthony, as diligent in her cyber communications as she had been formerly in the stewardship of St Anne's responded by the next morning. She was familiar with the Sisters of the Holy Family and would be back to Gabriel soon with contact details for Sister Mary in Colombo. She had also made some parallel enquiries about charitable schemes relevant to Thanuja's needs. In her final paragraph, Sister Anthony described to Gabriel the AIDS project in Africa with which she had been working. The approach being used by Sister Anthony and her cohort sounded very similar to that espoused by Michael, the glorious orator from the TV in London several months before. Gabriel had hungrily devoured all written and electronic media covering Michael's work ever since.

As she thought about Michael, Gabriel sensed an unfamiliar, rising warmth, starting deep between her thighs, penetrating slowly through her abdomen and spreading upwards towards her heart, catching her lungs en route, rendering her breathless.

In her late thirties, Gabriel remained a stranger to the physical experience of love. She had observed with (sometimes) amused interest how many of her contemporaries at St. Anne's, Oxford and in her professional environments lived their lives in a perpetual state of heightened sexual tension. She observed how the tension, unchecked, created, in equal measure, paroxysms of delight, schisms, tears and betrayals. Gabriel had frequently been engaged as the sage source of advice in matters of the heart (and loins), probably she concluded, because others sensed her impartiality.

Drenched in confusion while at Oxford, she had consulted the University GP seeking a physical explanation for her lack of sexual interest. Dr Marguerite Harris, petite, high heeled, black stockinged and the owner of an enviable festoon of spiral, curly hair, explained in a competent, unpatronising tone.

'Gabriel, asexuality is a very well understood concept. In fact, studies suggest that between one and ten percent of the population are asexual, depending on which study you choose, of course.'

'It doesn't feel like there is anyone else like me, Doctor. I feel like there's a big secret going on out there that I've just been somehow been left out of. I'm worried people will think I'm weird.'

'Try not to worry, Gabriel. I think that all the media obsession with sex means that asexual people feel more embarrassed about their condition than homosexuals or lesbians. Also, the condition is not always permanent. Things may change one day.'

Ever since the pivotal conversation, Gabriel decided to accept asexuality as her norm. Shylah and she never spoke seriously about sex, Shylah's own shattering experience aged fourteen at the party in Hull had never been discussed in detail between them. Gabriel respected Shylah's decision to excise the memory. Many had assumed over the years that Shylah and Gabriel were themselves an item; a misunderstanding which neither of them felt was sufficiently important to challenge.

On a Friday morning in Jeddah in 2013 however, Gabriel, on considering the proximity of Michael, sensed the power of an unfamiliar urge. She was uncertain. Was this a sexual urge or something else, something more spiritual? She imagined the feel of his firm, muscular physique beneath her hands, she smelt the moisture on his black skin as it shone golden in the African sun. She heard his deep, chocolate, intelligent voice.

By the end of the day, after multiple email exchanges, Gabriel and Sister Anthony had identified several potential sources of charitable funding. It looked like it would be possible for Thanuja to continue her studies and be reunited with Sean, living in charity-funded accommodation outside Sri Lanka. Sister Mary in Colombo had been engaged in the dialogue and had explained that with Thanuja in Saudi, away from the physical control of her father, once they were able to secure her Saudi sponsor's authority and she reached age eighteen, she could travel without difficulty. Plans would still need to be made to help Thanuja retrieve her son from her parents and reunite them but the irrepressible forces of Sisters Mary and Anthony backed up by the intelligent and business-like Gabriel were up to the task, they all concluded.

Gabriel hurried to the walled garden that evening, sat and read some papers for work as she waited for Thanuja. The graceful footsteps were later than usual and an almost imperceptible shuffle punctuated each step. Thanuja's head and back as she sat, lacked the usual balanced, dancer's poise.

'Are you alright, Thanuja?' asked Gabriel as she was joined on the bench.

'I am fine, ma'am, but Mrs Taha is unwell today and will not feed the baby. I am very sad for him.' Thanuja was evidently agitated, glancing back at the Tahas' substantial, modern villa. 'I cannot stay long this evening, ma'am. I am sorry but he is crying and I cannot make him stop unless she will feed him.'

'That's terrible, Thanuja, is Mrs Taha OK? Does she need a doctor?'

'In Sri Lanka, ma'am, many women become sad after a baby and the hospital has medicine to help them. I was not sad. I was happy and strong after the baby.' Thanuja hesitated at the memory before hauling herself back into the present. 'Mr Taha will not let Mrs Taha see a doctor even though she asks. He says that curing Mrs Taha's mind is not a medical matter. One of his lady relatives will come and talk to her about submitting more fully to God.' Thanuja's usually round, smooth face was hardened into unaccustomed, angular tension.

Gabriel swiftly decided that this was not the night to share her news with the distracted Thanuja, already standing and anxious to return to the Tahas' villa.

'Shall I walk with you back to the villa, Thanuja,' offered Gabriel.

'No ma'am, it is best if I am alone. Mrs Taha is crying, the baby is crying too, I can hear him. Mr Taha was shouting, he is very angry.'

Gabriel strained her ears to hear the baby. The Taha' villa was only three buildings away from the garden. She couldn't hear a sound. She remembered similar phenomena at the convent shortly after Colm had been born. Shylah would hear him crying in her room from the kitchen while Gabriel and the other childless nuns would strain their ears but hear nothing. Gabriel wondered what it would be like to hold her own child in her arms, to give birth, to breast feed a helpless human, fully dependent upon her for its survival. Her purpose on this earth did not include procreation, as far as she was aware, a probable explanation for her asexuality.

As Thanuja left, Gabriel's thoughts meandered, she remained confused as to what her purpose on earth was.

She was still waiting for a sign. She harboured an illogical suspicion that Michael would be able to help her find the answer. Perhaps that explained the strength of her feelings for him.

After a restless night, interrupted by unfamiliar sensations and unwelcome dreams featuring the Tahas, Thanuja, her two babies and inevitably, Michael, Gabriel woke early on Saturday morning.

Sister Anthony

Thank you so very much for your ongoing help with Thanuja. I will try to speak to her later today, she was very busy last night with the baby for whom she cares.

You mentioned that you are working for an AIDS project in Kenya. I was wondering whether the project is anything to do with someone called Michael whose progress in Africa I have been following closely over the last few months on TV, in the papers and the internet.

I am just curious, Sister.

Yours Gabriel

She hesitated before sending the email. Did it sound inappropriate? Would Sister Anthony think it odd that she was showing such an interest in Michael? Would she, to Gabriel's abject embarrassment, tell Michael about Gabriel's interest and Michael think it inappropriate or worse still, amusing?

Sister Anthony's response later that morning was both revealing and a shock. Gabriel had thought that she was alone with her secrets following the death of her parents.

Gabriel

Before you contacted me a few days ago, I had already spoken to Michael about you. When you joined St Anne's, I spent a long time talking with your dear late parents. You will remember that I also spent seven years close to you while you were at school, watching you, trying to understand you and asking God how he wished me to help you. I do know, Gabriel, who you are and why you are here on earth. Since you left for university, Shylah and I have corresponded regularly and through her, I have been keeping very close to what you have been doing and where you are, as is my duty.

As you have probably deduced by now, Michael is here on earth for a similar reason to yourself. He and I have already agreed that you and he should meet soon. He is committed to helping you fulfil your purpose just as others helped him in the past.

I will always be here to support you, Gabriel. I am yours and God's servant.

Sister Anthony

Gabriel sat down heavily on the cushions, all strength having departed her legs. The revelation that both Sister Anthony and Michael were aware of her background, her purpose on earth, was simultaneously a shock and a comfort, each of equally megalithic proportions. Perhaps she should have contacted Michael as soon as she had suspected who he was rather than waiting and facing the near humiliation of having to rely on Sister Anthony to bring them together. Why hadn't Michael contacted her before now if he knew who she was? Gabriel was glad it was the weekend and she had time to reflect on the complexities of the situation.

She sensed that time was running out; Michael had already made a substantial impact on the people of Africa. Gabriel became aware that expectations upon her would grow, her time was near. She resolved to meet Michael as soon as she was confident that Thanuja would be reunited with Sean and that the project at Saraco, starting the process of giving equal opportunities to Islamic women, could continue under Mubaarak and Samir's stewardship.

Mrs Taha did not improve either that weekend or throughout the subsequent weeks. The tone of Gabriel's meetings with Thanuja in the garden shifted from relaxed companionship and conversation to tense, snatched opportunities for Thanuja to share her worries and Gabriel to offer suggestions which she knew would go unheeded. On every occasion when Gabriel tried to broach the subject of Sister Mary, Thanuja became tense, unable, in the face of her exhaustion and stress, to cope with challenging conversations or life-changing decisions.

Mr Taha's female relative came to stay and a few days later, after a tirade of shouting which could be heard from the garden, left again for good. Black blinds were drawn at the windows and no one from the Taha family was ever seen outside the villa except for Mr Taha leaving for work in his car and returning late in the evening.

According to Thanuja's brief, nervous updates on the situation, the post natal depression continued unameliorated. Mrs Taha stayed in bed all day, crying, refusing to eat, shower or get dressed. Young Mohamed switched from breast to bottle and Mrs Taha's interest in him (as in everything else) dissipated to obscurity leaving a flagging Thanuja in sole, lonely charge of both household and child.

The second and third Ladies' Assessment Days identified a further forty four highly educated, talented candidates to swell the female workforce at Saraco. Female toilet and refreshment facilities were built, a ladies prayer room created and a sumptuous ladies lounge with coffee machine, snacks, billowing cushions and couches, all photographed and featured in the newspaper (with none of its young lady inhabitants). Saraco was serious about equality came the message, loud and clear, even if Saudi labour law required that the new recruits be segregated from their male colleagues, unable to interact fully in professional life from behind wickerwork, zigzag screens, procured especially for their concealment.

Mubaarak continued to wallow in the glory of success, popping in and out of the office to circulate and receive compliments, leaving the camel's share of the work to Samir and Gabriel. While Mubaarak was on one of his forays, Samir and Gabriel were sitting together in the office, finalising the plans for the induction training for the first cadre of Saraco ladies.

'Twenty nine minutes past two, Gabriel, his 'phone will ring in a minute,' said Samir glancing from the clock on the wall to the 'phone which Mubaarak had inadvertently left on the desk.

'How do you know that, Samir, some kind of divine insight?' Gabriel raised her eyebrows at the risqué suggestion, challenging as it did the principle of a singular deity. Her relationship with the young Samir could take

175

that level of Christian teasing by now!

'You wait, Gabriel, it has rung at two thirty every day since we started the project. I am amazed you haven't noticed, my friend. He is normally here when it rings and he takes it outside to have the conversation.'

Samir plumped his chest and tossed his gutrah over his shoulders, grinning with the pride of someone in possession of a nugget of office intrigue. The 'phone rang. It continued ringing as they both stared at it on the desk.

'Should we answer it?' asked Gabriel, approaching the 'phone. She looked at the screen, it said 'PJ calling'.

The ringing stopped and the screen scrolled to 'Missed Call'. A breathless Mubaarak burst through the office door.

'You had a missed call.'

'Thank you, Samir.' Mubaarak snatched up his 'phone, looked visibly relieved to see the screen and dashed outside.

Samir and Gabriel's eyes locked in wordless exchange.

Haiku 35 – Jeddah to Market Hamilton via email
Samir is great guy
Keeping me sane. Doctor
Gets mystery calls!

Haiku 36 – Market Hamilton to Jeddah via email
Intriguing re calls
Maybe a secret lover!
Muslims at it too!

CHAPTER 15

Jeddah, Saudi Arabia and London, United Kingdom

1993 to 2000 (Gregorian calendar)

The pressure of expectation on eighteen year old Mubaarak was murderous. He had to get the grades for Oxford; there was no viable alternative. As his parents' only child, with a hoard of widowed or barren aunts, the responsibility for making the family proud weighed leaden. He desperately wished his father would take a second, younger wife to deflect some of the attention. One of his friends at college had said that his own father was taking delivery next week of a young Russian. They had selected her from many blonde, skinny possibles on the internet. Mubaarak had asked him to send the link; it had to be worth a try. But Mubaarak had other problems too, weighing on his eighteen year old, Saudi shoulders.

Six months previously, while his parents were out, Emilio the Philippino house-boy had seized the moment and knocked on his bedroom door. He was delighted to see that the little prince Mubaarak was sitting at his desk near the window, studying as usual.

'Sir, I have brought you a glass of cool water while you study, it will help your beautiful, clever brain.' He always spoke to his employers in English. The Arabic came in very useful when they thought he couldn't understand. Emilio stood close to Mubaarak, pressing his thigh against the little swot's upper arm, leaning over him to place the water slowly on the desk. Mubaarak would be sure to smell his spicy scent and gentle perspiration through the historical drama costume they forced him to wear. He would let him feel his smooth, coffee coloured cheek, with just the tiniest hint of stubble, brushing Mubaarak's dark face from which appalling, rough hair grew with such vigour.

Emilio felt Mubaarak grab clumsily at his firm, slender waist before he even had time to stand upright. He had expected a couple more warm-ups before the little prince was up for it. Athletically, he retrieved his balance and pressed Mubaarak towards the bed. There was no time to use many of his tricks. The spoilt little brat was gagging for it.

The little prince was, in fact, so gagging for it, that whenever his parents were out over the next few months, Emilio stood to earn a lucrative flow of tips. The tips from the men in this particular household were proving to make it one of his best positions since he had come to Saudi. He would be able to return to the Philippines soon, buy a piece of land, build a house, take a beautiful, meek Philipina wife and live the good life. If money was short, he could always turn a few tricks now and then with the visitors, just to keep things ticking over. The Arabs always tipped best and by now, he knew what they liked.

After the first glorious encounter, Mubaarak prostrated himself and prayed with such intensity that he bruised his nose and forehead on the floor. For the next week, he did not miss a single one of the five daily prayers, rising every day at 4a.m. to start the Fajr before daybreak. The following weekend he announced to the surprised household that he intended to travel to Mecca to perform the Hajj. Immediately after that Hajj, the wedding planning had started. Did his father suspect something, he wondered?

The visitations from the house-boy became more frequent, timed to coincide with his parents' regular absences. Each time, Mubaarak prayed intensely afterwards to annul the evil and each time he looked forward with greater hunger to the next opportunity to devour his Philippino delight.

A few weeks before the exams, Mubaarak's father's boss at the bank identified a suitable wife for Mubaarak. Mubaarak's parents had been introduced by the boss to sixteen year old Sureya's parents. They had discussed the suitability of the union for both families and finalised the dowry, which Mubaarak would be required to pay. One evening, when he returned from college, the stench of stress in the house was even greater than usual. Mubaarak found his father, the boss, his mother and aunt sitting on the low couches in the majlis with two strangers. They were drinking Arabic coffee and imbibing sweet snacks. The men were smoking and the ladies, in the presence of men who were not close blood relatives, were entirely concealed, except for their eyes, behind niqab.

The ladies precariously raised their tiny coffee cups behind their veils to take a sip of the pale, dizzy unroasted coffee. Mubaarak's Philippino delight, fetchingly costumed and delicious, stood to attention near the door. The men waved at him periodically and in response he handed dates, more fiery coffee and sweets to the party, passing round tissues so everyone could spit out their date stones, collecting them again and putting them in a discreet vessel by the door.

'Ah Mubaarak, there you are. This is Mr Saleh and his wife, Sureya's parents,' said the boss in jolly spirits. Having taken on the mantle of matchmaker, it was his role to see the union through to its conclusion or risk losing face with both families, together with a nice cut of the dowry.

'We are planning for you to meet Sureya at Mr and Mrs Saleh's home on Thursday afternoon,' said Mubaarak's father turning his straight face, cold as steel towards his quivering, terrified son.

'I – I – I would be honoured to meet your daughter, Mr and Mrs Saleh,' Mubaarak stammered.

Emilio shuffled slightly, understanding every detail of the proposed transaction. The next time he handed round the dates and snacks, he hesitated just a little longer than necessary before Mubaarak. He raised one black, sleek far eastern eyebrow and moved on.

Mubaarak dropped his coffee which soaked the front of his thaub and dripped down onto his sandaled feet, to the overt fury of his frowning father and simpering female relatives. Emilio smirked.

Mubaarak was expected to take a gift when he went to visit Sureya. On the morning of the visit, his mother and aunt called the driver and ushered him into the back of the car. The threesome was deposited at the yawning mouth of the Mall, and a suitable establishment identified, close to the entrance. Mubaarak was disposed of on a chair by the counter as his mother and her sister pointed, demanded, held items up to the light. Their abayas undulated around their Rubenesque forms and they resembled two crows fighting over nesting material. Mubaarak's opinion was hurriedly sought as an afterthought, when the ideal bijoux had already been chosen.

'Very nice,' he said as the point of no return was reached and debit card swiped.

Mubaarak sat in the back of the car between the crows, a perfumed package topped with numerous ice cream shaped bows, balanced on his knees. His mother and aunt had festooned him as he got into the car, in a dark cloak with golden edging over his thaub. He was hot, uncomfortable and conscious that he stood on the edge of an awful abyss from whence he would be unable to climb.

The car arrived at Sureya's parents' home. The driver spoke into the grill and the electric gates parted like curtains to a charnel house. Mubaarak felt fright grip his guts; an actor about to go and assume a role to which he was unsuited, unrehearsed. His mother and his aunt lowered themselves from the car onto the front step of the mansion, arranging their abayas and niqab before smoothing and plucking at Mubaarak's conspicuous costumerie.

An oriental house-boy bowed at the door. Mubaarak sweated and shivered, trying to tear his eyes away from the pert-buttocked, eastern beauty, clothed in an appealing fifteenth century French uniform. White tights, patent shoes, golden breeches, the irresistible European promise of fancy, the French lover boy's tricks and tickles leading him towards his doom.

Sureya sat in the majlis facing the low, square table, with her back to the door. Her long, straight, black hair hung down her back over an abaya embroidered with gold, swirling leaves and flowers. Her hijab had been removed for the visit so Mubaarak, his mother and aunt could see what they were getting for the dowry. Sureya's mother sat on the couch at right angles to her daughter's. The two crows descended towards the burning Oudh just inside the doorway, flapping their sleeves over the silver stove so the sickly, choking fumes impregnated their clothes and flabby, female bodies.

Mubaarak stood back, bearing the preposterously wrapped gift in his shaking, damp hands, tense and breathless with excitement at the proximity of the French lover boy. His mother and aunt prodded him forwards towards the couch upon which Sureya sat. He proffered the gift in both hands, trying to force his features into the crescent of a smile as he approached Sureya's back.

Sureya turned her face slowly towards him. He realised with a jolt that she was aesthetically delightful, a petite, classic Arabic beauty, a sweet little sister. Her dark eyes penetrated, deep into his mind. Was it possible that there could be some sort of understanding between them? Might there be a way out of this disastrous situation? Surely it was too much to hope for, he was fooling himself. He was the last person to have insight into the minds of young women but he had a horrific inkling about how they might react when they discovered that their betrothed, or worse still their husband, was a Sodomist.

The French fancy was still milling around the guests, making Mubaarak sweat and shuffle in his seat. Increasingly breathless, he plucked at the neck of his thaub and tossed his gutrah over his shoulders. He silently begged Allah to intervene, to explain the situation to Sureya via some divine channel, before it was too late. Was it too much to hope for that she might be prepared to help him sort out this abysmal mess?

Under the suffocating scrutiny of the crows and her mother, Sureya unwrapped the gift. Competently she dealt with the lacy festoons of paper and ribbon, piling them in a neat mound on the table then nodding gently to the house-boy who collected them. She opened the box, looked at Mubaarak and thanked him in a gracious, clear voice.

'Mubaarak, this is a beautiful gift. I am honoured that you have chosen to give it to me.'

'Sureya, it is my pleasure,' he stammered, under the weight of expectation. 'I am soon to go to Oxford University in the United Kingdom for three years. It is one of the best universities in the world.' He glanced towards the crows who were nodding encouragingly. With no viable alternative, he continued to play to his audience; a part which he would never be able to sustain.

Throughout, Sureya listened politely, nodding, encouraging. 'I too am very interested in academic study and read extensively, Mubaarak.'

Sureya's family and the crows stiffened, lips tightened. Tension suffused the room.

'I know that I will not go to university though,' Sureya went on, 'because my duty is to be a good wife and to remain here in Saudi with my family and my husband's family.'

The party relaxed again and nodded once more at one another in approval.

Sureya went on to explain that she would like to continue reading at home if her husband would allow it, and was also, with the help of a set of cassette tapes, ordered via the newspaper, trying to perfect her English.

'Sureya, when I am in Oxford, I will be able to buy for you the very best English books and send them to you here in Saudi. This way you can continue your learning while doing your duty as a wife.' Mubaarak recognised the chink of an opportunity. Perhaps he would be able to do some sort of bizarre deal with this girl. If he helped Sureya, would it be too much to ask, please Allah, that she would help him in return?

The crows and Sureya's mother were nudging one another, wordlessly reacting to every syllable the young couple uttered. The conversation between the two young people had not followed the expected path but all seemed to have gone well, their body language suggested.

Every one of them had completely missed the unspoken undertone; Mubaarak's silent prayers and fervent hope that Sureya would have some inkling of the message he needed so urgently to convey to her. He had a sense of being swept along in the slipstream of a juggernaut, gathering speed across the desert, in an unstoppable passage towards the terrifying, bleak Empty Quarter.

'Sureya, I am not sure I can handle this, for various very important reasons which I cannot discuss with you. Please believe me though, Sureya, that as your brother, I would give you the peace and freedom to spend your time however you wish in our home so long as you are able to accept me as I am and do not demand that I am a full and proper husband.'

In his desperation, he willed that he saw, in Sureya's dark eyes, a silent message of understanding in return.

'Mubaarak, if you would please take me now, I will ask nothing of you. Whatever you are so afraid of does not concern me. All I ask is that you are able to give me quietness and space to read and that you do not question my wish to continue to study and develop myself academically in the privacy of our home after we are married.'

Everyone except Mubaarak left Sureya's parents' mansion later that afternoon with a happier heart than when they had arrived. Mubaarak himself was tortured by the fact that the understanding he hoped he saw in Sureya's eyes was probably a figment of his exhausted imagination. What if this girl expected him to actually… to actually… Mubaarak shuddered and retched at the thought of being forced into marital relations with this beautiful young sister, all because of a misunderstanding following the bizarre interaction this afternoon. Was it too late to put a stop to the juggernaut which was gathering speed, a cloud of sand in its unstoppable wake? He glanced at the crows and concluded that there was no way out. They were already scribbling guest lists on the return journey in the car.

Mubaarak's father and the boss were delighted when the visiting party arrived home. They embraced Mubaarak, clapping him on the back, kissing him on both cheeks, congratulating one another at their excellent collaboration. The juggernaut thundered onwards over the desert.

The house-boy lurked at the back of the room, his hands brushing Mubaarak's with exaggerated frequency, his dancer's movements as he passed and cleared, disturbing the air, close, close, closer in front of Mubaarak's face.

The wedding was hastily arranged by his father and the boss. Mubaarak had a growing sense that his father suspected something and was becoming more and more certain that it was this which had motivated the intensified sense of urgency. The crows were heard espousing that Mubaarak would be leaving for Europe soon and the families wanted Sureya installed and settled in his family's house in advance. Mubaarak would be away for at least three years, the crows needed her in place so they would have plenty of time to mould young Sureya into the family's ways.

The next three months supped greedily at Mubaarak's energy. The crows were cawing and spinning in a vortex of lists, visits and preparations. The exams vacuumed up eight three hour chunks of his life, each of which punctuated the journey towards the dreaded junction: success or failure, which would set the irrevocable direction for the rest of his life. Alongside all of these, Mubaarak suffered an intensifying obsession with the house-boy, his delicious firm body and boundless creativity, each taste of which demanded a flurry of prayer and pilgrimage.

The house-boy's demands on Mubaarak's physical energy were surpassed only by his demands on his purse. Within a three week period, Mubaarak had bought the boy a watch, a laptop computer and a business class ticket to fly back to the Philippines for two weeks in the winter. He had not yet told his father that he had authorised the two week vacation and had no intention of ever mentioning the 'plane ticket. With Mubaarak's financial responsibilities towards the dowry and wedding being almost entirely funded by his father, it was easy to hide the house-boy's presents among the staggering ebbs and flows of his bank account. Mubaarak was not an unintelligent person and he was conscious that he was being taken for a fool but at the time, inexperienced and adolescent, he was powerless to stand on the tracks and halt what had been unleashed.

The wedding itself was surprisingly a relief, some time off from all the exhausting demands of the previous weeks. After several hours celebrating and dancing with the male guests, he was allowed to join Sureya and the fluttering female relatives. Sureya's kind face was like healing ice on a burn. All he yearned for was the quiet, peaceful companionship of his beautiful sister Sureya after the frenzy of the last few months. But what if she wanted more? What if she expected more of him when they were alone? He felt himself retch again and sat silent and brooding beside her as the wedding continued around him.

In the morning, when they were able to leave the wedding without causing offence to their families, Mubaarak and Sureya were finally alone. Mubaarak tensed as they entered the palatial surroundings of their freshly decorated and sumptuously linened bedroom, on the top floor of his parents' home. Exhausted and with a hammering head, Mubaarak collapsed. He positioned himself, facing towards the wall, on the far side of their expansive bed and tensed every muscle, willing Sureya not to touch him. He must have fallen asleep and slept more peacefully than he had for many weeks, until late in the afternoon. When he awoke, Sureya was sitting beside him reading. She smiled silently and her cool hand gently touched his head as though she was checking him for fever. After several minutes, she spoke,

'I will call the house-boy and ask him to bring you something to drink,' she said quietly.

'No Sureya, please,' said Mubaarak, just a millisecond too quickly.

Sureya's suspicions were confirmed. She had already decided to let it pass, it was irrelevant to her anyway; it would not interfere with her plans.

'Let's just be here, Sureya, together, you and me please for now. You read your book and I will just lie here and rest, please Sureya.' Mubaarak's face assumed a slight frown as he tried to work his way through the confusion. 'I will care for you, Sureya, for your whole life,' he finished, trying to explain, to unravel the mystery of how he would navigate the complex course of this marriage.

'Mubaarak, don't worry, I understand. I know I am young but I have read more than most people will read in their whole lives. I have prayed to God every day for wisdom and intelligence and I am ambitious, Mubaarak.'

'What do you read, Sureya?' Mubaarak was genuinely interested. The only women he had met in his eighteen years were his mother and other female relatives, all of his parent's generation. Their education had been such that the only reading they had ever undertaken in their lives had been the Qur'an. He wondered what else a women might be interested in. He realised suddenly that he had never spoken to a woman of his own age before Sureya.

'I read about the history of the world, Mubaarak, to the extent that I have been able in my parents' home. I read about the Islamic scholars in mathematics, geometry, science. I have learned about how the Christian and Islamic faiths split and travelled in different directions several hundreds of years ago. Now that I am here with you and when you are in Europe at University, I will ask you to send me more books, books I cannot buy here, to help me learn more about the implications of this and to help me to be more wise and intelligent. Then when you come back, I will be able to talk to you about wise, intelligent things when we are at home. Our partnership, Mubaarak, will be academic, founded on wisdom and intelligence.'

'I will send you books from Europe, Sureya. I will send you whatever you want and when we are together again, we will talk every evening about whatever interests you. I thank God that you are my sister and my wife.'

Within the next few weeks, Mubaarak's exam results arrived, were excellent and preparations for his departure to Oxford University in the United Kingdom swung into full force.

He and Sureya lived together like brother and sister on the top floor, both accepting the way things were and both happy to be rid of the unbearable expectations of their respective families. With Sureya installed, the frequency of the house-boy's visits had diminished substantially, limited now to the fortnightly occasions when Sureya, his mother and aunt visited Sureya's mother and sisters, and the house was empty. Mubaarak found himself surprisingly relieved that the frequency of the irresistible temptations of the house-boy and subsequent need for atonement had diminished. The house-boy, his alternative income stream shrinking, had started to become sulky and difficult. Mubaarak would be relieved to be away from him and his demands, even though he would miss the delight and fulfilment yielded by his glorious, skilled body.

Shortly after Mubaarak's departure, Emilio returned to the Philippines. He had tried to reason with Mubaarak's father, explaining that the old man's tips needed increasing to compensate for the departure of his other client in the household. Sadly the patriarch of the house didn't see it the same way and was impervious to any threats to make the sins of both father and son public. In truth he was probably sensible, whenever such matters came into the open, it was always the Arabs who came out smelling of roses while the servant classes were normally executed within the week. He didn't need them anyway, he had enough money saved up at home. It was time to call it a day, start building a house and looking for a Philipina wife. He looked at the Rolex on his wrist. He would enjoy showing the guys in the bars in Manila what he had.

Philip Jones was one of the lecturers at Magdalen College. Having been a child genius, he was only a few years senior to the majority of his students, and junior to a substantial minority. Philip noticed Mubaarak's olive skin, fine Arabic profile and irresistible vulnerability, from day one when the new students gathered for the welcoming events. Mubaarak, the only Arabic student, kept himself at a small distance from the rest of the loud, attention-seeking students, each trying too hard to assert their personality on the group. Only the brilliant and talented Gabriel took the time to try to include him in conversation, Philip noticed.

Philip was delighted to an extent which pushed the boundaries of professionalism, when providence divined that Mubaarak would be one of the students under his personal tutelage. While Mubaarak studied for his first degree, Philip successfully controlled the urge to pursue anything other than a tutor / student relationship. After graduation, however, with Mubaarak installed in the more adult ranks of the PhD cadre, Philip suggested dinner.

Mubaarak accepted, and despite coming from opposite worlds, conversation was comfortable, easy. There were more dinners, walks in the college grounds, trips to the theatre and then towards the end of Mubaarak's first post graduate year, Philip suggested a trip to a London theatre and a stay at his apartment in town. Mubaarak accepted again, sensing that a milestone had been reached and a corner was about to be turned. He had kept all his promises to Sureya, happily installed at his parents' home, progressing well with her English course and delighted to receive his frequent packages of learned reading from Europe. Mubaarak considered that he must be both the bookshop and the Post Office's best customer in Oxford.

Mubaarak and Philip travelled to London in the car together. Philip's careful, accurate driving rendered the journey a pleasure. Mubaarak tried to explain to him en route, the chaos of Jeddah's highways and the blood-bath risked by travellers each time they started their engines. The conversation flowed, Philip had not realised that women drivers were prohibited in Saudi Arabia. He had strong views on the subject which he expressed in a balanced, thoughtful way enabling Mubaarak, for the first time, to engage in the debate with a Westerner without lapsing into defensiveness.

They reminisced about Mubaarak's undergraduate years.

'Do you keep in touch with anyone you studied with?' asked Philip.

'Not really. The only person who I felt able to talk to was that tall woman, Gabriel. I'm not sure why. She just seemed more accepting, more intellectual too, than the other students.'

'Yes, she did always strike me as a good person. A brilliant undergraduate too. Highest marks in the whole of her year.'

'Well yes, but that doesn't mean she was necessarily the best student. She didn't go on to do a PhD or anything,' replied Mubaarak tersely.

Philip sensed a slight rise in tension and deduced that Mubaarak had become tired of talk about Gabriel's brilliance. Philip decided not to mention that Gabriel had probably returned home without pursuing further studies, to recover from the sudden death of both her parents. He shuddered as he remembered hearing the news.

As they drove past rainy London squares and spires, Mubaarak reflected on the conversation about his undergraduate contemporary, Gabriel. He resolved to get back in touch as soon as he was employed in Saudi Arabia after his PhD. Someone as brilliant as Gabriel would certainly be useful to him in furthering his ambitions. He thought too about Sureya, her books and her desire for wisdom. In the months they had been together before he left for Oxford and during his infrequent returns to Saudi Arabia over the summer breaks, they had never once engaged in physical marital activity. If Sureya was disappointed, she didn't express it but instead accepted the friendship and devoted generosity which Mubaarak offered as an alternative.

This weekend would be a turning point; Mubaarak was clear where the relationship with Philip was going, where he wanted it to go. In the UK, he felt protected, no longer needing to atone for his transgressions, whether actual or intended. How would Sureya react to the news that he had a lover? Would she be happy when he said he wanted them to carry on in Saudi Arabia just as they were? Did he have to tell her at all? He pictured her putting her hand on his forehead, looking at him with her sweet accepting eyes and being satisfied with sisterhood for the rest of their lives?

Philip's London flat was warm when they arrived and the fridge was full, thanks to his elderly neighbour who kept an eye on things while he was in Oxford.

'Philip, this is a beautiful apartment. How can you bear to leave it every weekend and travel back to Oxford?' Mubaarak immediately felt relaxed and comfortable in the efficient space behind the wide, rippled windows yielding an impressionist's view of the flowers in the park opposite. Philip had chosen a Moroccan colour scheme and amidst the modern functionality were filigreed, onion-domed lamps and artefacts, reminding Mubaarak of his mother's beloved memorabilia at home.

Philip ordered from a local vegetarian fine food emporium that delivered directly to the flat. Philip had wine and Mubaarak water. Mubaarak, whose natural inclination was to hector the drinker, pork eater or dog owner, felt able to accept readily whatever the wonderful Philip chose to do. They spent the night in Philip's bed, between crisp, cool Egyptian cotton sheets. In the morning, they drank Yorkshire tea and read the newspapers.

Many times over subsequent years, Mubaarak battled with his perfectionist mentality, his unerring capacity to quibble and disapprove of the actions of others, his dislike of the majority of the human race. He occasionally wished he were a better person, able to make friends, engage in small talk and humour, have patience. However hard he battled, the truth was that he was only truly relaxed in the equally unique and soothing company of either Philip, his lover or Sureya, his sister and wife.

CHAPTER 16

Market Hamilton, Yorkshire, United Kingdom

February 2013

Every morning since completing her final exams, Rosemary had visited the coffee shop at number 53 High Street. Every morning she sat at the same table and replayed an identical routine. The whole thing was becoming embarrassing. During her final year at school, when everyone else was marking radii on the map to define the acceptable minimum distances between university and their parents at home, Rosemary had made the enormous mistake of telling everyone that she was staying in Market Hamilton, would move out of her latest foster home into a flat, and become a writer. Why had she done that? What an idiot she was! Whatever had made her think that after seven years studying and indeed excelling at English literature under the competent but unimaginative tutelage of Mrs Pothelswaite, all she would need to do was sit, notebook on her knees, biro in her hand, and the ideas would flow?

Earlier in the year, she had seen a documentary about the enviably successful (and attractive) JK Rowling. Rowling had explained that she sat in a café in Edinburgh, day after day, and just wrote and wrote and wrote. The ideas came infinitely, one after the other like a train of wildebeest, to Rowling in the warm, condensation-infused atmosphere of the café. Rosemary had decided then that she would emulate Ms Rowling and repair to the coffee shop on the High Street which would be certain to catalyse her creativity. So far it hadn't, and worse, people were asking embarrassing questions about progress.

After several weeks, the blooming, blousy coffee shop proprietress was onto her. She knew, just as Rosemary did, that the great novel was going nowhere. Not only going nowhere but hadn't even left the garage to start the journey. Blousy, who had loathed school with all its irritating rules and restrictions and had left as soon as she could, was always keen to sneer at anything smacking of the intellectual. She had taken to glancing over Rosemary's shoulder and raising a single, pencilled eyebrow at the blank page in the notebook when she came over with coffee. That morning she remarked, laughing, in her broad brogue, 'Still not started the great book then, love. Shall I give you a few ideas to get you going? I read a lovely erotic novel last week. Is your book going to be an erotic novel, love?'

Blousy glanced round the café, her silky, scarlet top bulging and splaying across her vast bust, checking that her gentlemen customers had heard her clearly.

Rosemary wished the woman would just shut up. Why hadn't she chosen her venue more carefully when she had decided to follow the coffee shop approach? Surely Ms Rowling in her Edinburgh café hadn't been beset by such vulgar humiliation. Rosemary's mind felt as if it had been held between two hard hands and squeezed like a sponge. Squeezed until all the ideas had come out and run away out of reach down a hungry, stinking drain where they would rot with all the other detritus. She had no ideas, she could not write, she was a failure.

She picked up her recently brewed coffee and distractedly took a thirsty gulp. The coffee must have been heated in something resembling the Hedron collider, she reflected briefly, as the evil burning liquid seared at the roof of her mouth and removed the covering from her tongue. She couldn't spit it out in public so instead embarked on a frenzy of open mouthed huffing, trying to create a cooling breeze over her melted mouthparts. The clientele of the café turned to stare. A young woman panting in their midst offered outstanding entertainment in light of the proprietress' recent revelations about her literary preferences.

Shylah crossed the High Street to call at the café occasionally when demand for bakery products was uncharacteristically high and stocks at Bennets ran low. Celeste, the flamboyant owner, was always happy to oblige, selling her top-up stock at a tidy mark-up on suppliers' rates. Shylah pushed at the rattly door, setting off the old-fashioned doorbell which had been wired by one of Celeste's gentleman conquests. Shylah immediately saw that the young girl, who frequently occupied the corner seat, appeared to be having some sort of seizure. Celeste and the other customers were staring, faint expressions of amusement on their faces.

'Someone get her a glass of water,' Shylah barked in the general direction of Celeste, who immediately gathered herself and hurried to the sink.

Shylah shot a firm glance around the rest of the coffee shop's clientele, all of whom swiftly turned back to their tables, papers, victuals and conversations. She strode to Rosemary's table and sat down.

'Are you OK? What can I do to help?' she asked, placing her hand flat on Rosemary's back, between her shoulder blades.

'Drank my coffee too quickly,' replied Rosemary continuing to pant in a further effort to cool her mouth. The water arrived, borne by a contrite Celeste, and Rosemary gulped thirstily at the soothing, clear purity, her breathlessness abating.

Still sitting next to Rosemary, Shylah explained the main purpose of her visit to Celeste who, now in penitent mindset, bustled to the back of the shop to gather the required additional stock for her fellow High Street vendeuse.

'Are you feeling better now?' Shylah asked as the crisis subsided and Rosemary's face started to assume normal, Caucasian colouring.

'Yes, thanks,' replied Rosemary and Shylah sensed a small quiver in the young woman's voice and on her chin.

'Are you sure you're alright?'

'Can I buy you a drink to thank you for your kindness?' Rosemary asked, talking awkwardly around a tongue which felt like it had grown to elephantine proportions.

'That would be lovely, thank you. Celeste, may I have a ginger tea please?'

'On the house, Shylah.' Celeste's contrition was lasting longer than Shylah had expected.

'I've seen you in here before, haven't I?' Shylah turned back to Rosemary

'Yes. I have been coming every morning for ages now. Also, I sort of knew your son when I was little. We weren't at the same school but it's a pretty small town, isn't it?' Rosemary chose not to mention the constipated writing project.

Shylah had the manners not to ask why someone of her age would choose to spend every morning among the pensioners of Market Hamilton, for no apparent reason.

'So if you're a local, you'll know that I run the shop opposite, Bennets, with Colm. We have a partner in the business but she's abroad at the moment so it's just me and Colm this year.'

Rosemary saw the fissure of an opportunity open before her and felt herself drawn to leap into its darkness. She would have no confidence left at all if she carried on as she was and whilst the woman didn't seem to recognise her, she was sure that she would remember her in time. It was time to do something other than try to be a writer. Even if she didn't know what she was letting herself in for, it couldn't be worse than maintaining the status quo.

'Do you need any help? Just while your partner isn't around? I learn quickly. By the way, my name is Rosemary.'

Shylah did not need help. She and Colm had always managed Bennets between them while Gabriel pursued her other interests. However that grey morning, the coalescence of concern for the vulnerable Rosemary, along with a feeling with which she had awoken, that it was time to try something new, precipitated her response.

'I may do, do you want to come over to the shop for a chat?'

Rosemary tried to pay for her coffee but Celeste declined with much lowering of false, black lashes and flapping of her hand.

'It's the least I can do, love, and I didn't know you were Shylah's friend before. Special treatment for fellow shopkeepers and their friends, love.'

Rosemary picked up the cardboard box bound for Bennets and followed Shylah out of the shop.

'Take care crossing here. My mother could be about,' smiled Shylah. 'You should be safe today actually, the merry widow's on another cruise,' she smiled warmly again as Rosemary's expression sank into confusion.

'Come through the shop, we have a little office at the back and we can have a chat. Hi Colm, we have the bread and croissants. Pop the box on the counter please, Rosemary, Colm will deal with it.'

'You took your time, Mum. I've had two people in here asking for them while you were out. I said I'd drop them round in the car this afternoon, they both live close and they're regulars,' he grinned at Rosemary, recognising her from their infrequent and distant encounters over the last few years, and shook his head. 'She was talking to the lovely Celeste, I suppose.'

Rosemary smiled back and flinched, her mouth still sore.

Ella liked the smell of the person who came into the office with Shylah. She put her nose to the person's shoes as she sat down at the table and took a few deep doggy 'huffs' just to check all was well. Someone who likes making food in a kitchen from the smell of it, Ella concluded, flopping her solid, black form on the feet of the new person when she sat down at the table. The new person's feet were still and warm, not twitchy and fidgety like some people's feet. This was good news; Ella closed her eyes, snuggled into the nice, warm, still feet and had a little snooze while the new person spoke to Shylah.

Sat together at the table in the office, in the company of the gently snoring Ella, Shylah told Rosemary the story of

Bennets. Their original ideas, born in Oxford, about local sourcing, organic products and unusual fare, were even more resonant now with the evolving population of Market Hamilton than they were fifteen years before. Business was going well. Colm had always been good with computers at school and since leaving, had computerised the entire operation.

The Bennets website had recently been brought to life and Colm was managing the internet orders which were starting to flow nicely. As she talked, Shylah realised that she was describing a scenario in which Colm was the day to day driving force behind the business. While Colm had been at school, she had managed the whole operation herself, met with suppliers, managed deliveries and manned the shop, with the help of various temporary assistants. Now she had no idea how to operate the computerised stock, ordering or accounting systems and found the website aesthetically delightful but commercially mysterious. Rosemary listened intently and took notes, writing in tight, neat script, starting on the first page of her empty notebook.

'I will need to mention this to Colm, but he will be fine, I am sure. Can you start tomorrow?' asked Shylah

'I can start now if you like,' replied Rosemary.

Ella awoke startled, from a delicious dream about the new person making food in the kitchen upstairs and dropping lots and lots and lots of it on the floor. Ella knew that food on the floor was subject to a wholly different set of, much more relaxed strictures, to food anywhere else.

A frazzled Colm had overheard their concluding sentence from the shop. 'Is this a new assistant, Mum? Great news if you are, I know we've seen each other around the town, but I've forgotten your name, I'm really sorry.' Without waiting for an answer, the frazzled Colm continued, 'I have to go and deliver the loaves and take Ella out now, you could do with some help here, Mum, I've been run off my feet all morning.'

Rosemary continued to make copious notes all afternoon, watching Shylah's caring way with the customers, Colm's infectious, if clumsy, enthusiasm for the products and the competent, tidy organisation afforded by the computerised processes and records. The notebook was filling, page after page, asterisks, references, lists and reminders. Rosemary's enthusiasm for her new job was growing as each page was covered. By the end of the afternoon, she was working the till, loading items into bags and carrying them out to the cars for elderly customers. Her presence afforded a delighted Colm the opportunity to deal with the internet orders during opening hours and by six o'clock, they were all ready to finish.

'It's been great having you here today, Rosemary,' said Shylah. 'We normally don't finish until at least eight on a Saturday because I have to stay and help Colm with the orders.'

'Too right, it's been really helpful, thanks so much, Rosemary,' added Colm. 'I'm doing a roast tomorrow, would you like to come and join us, as a thank you? It'll be just Mum and me while Gabriel is away. We can celebrate the success of your first day, assuming you're happy to come back Monday after all your hard work. We normally cook at Gabriel's cottage instead of here on a Sunday to make sure the place is aired and everything. Shall I write down the address for you?'

'Thank you, I'd love to come. Write the address in here for me please, Colm.'

Rosemary handed over the notebook which was immediately passed to Shylah, whose writing was deemed more legible.

Rosemary tucked the notebook into the pocket of her coat and held the pocket tightly closed. The book was nearly half full following the afternoon in Bennets. A clear, sweet feeling of pride flooded like honey from the top of her head down to her feet. No more mornings failing in the fuggy atmosphere of the coffee shop among the sweaty pensioners. She felt proud, excited and, for the first time since leaving school, was looking forward to the future.

The following day at exactly midday, Rosemary finished walking the short distance to the cottage and arrived at the start of the garden hedge, alongside the pavement. She hadn't needed to consult the internet for directions. As soon as she read the address, in Shylah's deliberate, rounded handwriting, she realised that she had walked by the cottage hundreds of times before, on her way from her foster parents' home to school and back. Twice each day for the last seven years, she had looked over the hedge and craned her neck to see into the garden at the back; much easier in winter than in spring, autumn or summer when the leaves on the big apple tree, positioned at the back corner of the house prevented all but a slotted view of the sunny, colourful garden beyond.

On a school day, whenever she had reached the little iron gate, she would glance down the path towards the thick, dark green door and imagine who lived inside. There was frequently an ancient mini, in a matching green, parked in the road. When it was getting dark or the weather was cool in the afternoons, a drift of cloudy wood smoke floated from the chimney and tickled her nose.

That Sunday, Yorkshire early country springtime was doing its very best. A milky sunshine was easing away the chill, having melted the silvery frost, the air was still and silent. The green mini was in its usual position outside on the road, she noticed. The leaves on some of the trees, shrubs and hedge had just started to emerge from their buddy bundles and a puddle of golden aconites had flooded the front lawn. Scattered between the aconites was a flurry of snowdrops. She opened the gate, walked along the path and rang the bell: silence. She waited until it was safe to deduce that the incumbents had not heard, and rang the bell again: silence.

In a muddle of disappointment and shyness, Rosemary walked around the back of the cottage, towards the apple tree. An elderly gentleman was standing in the back garden. She couldn't remember seeing him before despite her frequent forays past the cottage; perhaps he was a relative of Gabriel, whom Shylah and Colm had said lived there.

'Good afternoon,' she called into the still, cool air, raising her hand in friendly greeting. The old man stood still and silent, he had no tools so wasn't working in the garden, she noticed, just standing enjoying the springtime, looking silently, calmly towards her.

'Are Shylah and Colm in the cottage? I am a friend of theirs, they asked me to lunch today,' she smiled, determined to charm and not offend whoever this was, the old man would probably be the fourth guest at their lunch.

He raised his hand and waved back at her, still silent, and smiled. His smile held such depth and warmth that Rosemary stood still, her feet heavy, sinking into the damp lawn and felt a sensation of strength and peace flood though her.

Colm rapped on the window, just as the robin started to sing above her head, from the apple tree. Three shrill arpeggios, before its whirring wings stirred the top of her hair as it flew away. The old man was no longer standing in the garden.

'Hi, glad you found us, has the bell broken again?' smiled Colm having managed with a swift kick to the bottom corner, to ease the swollen French door open.

'Yes, I couldn't hear it ring so I came round. Is the elderly gentleman joining us for lunch?'

The look of surprise blew across Colm's face, swift and barely noticeable, like thin cirrus across the blue sky on a summer's day.

'What gentleman, Rosemary?' he asked standing in the doorway, looking earnestly into her eyes.

'There was a gentleman standing over there by the bare piece of earth. I waved and he waved back.'

'Come in, Rosemary, you'll get cold.' Colm put his long, angular arm around her shoulder and drew her into the sitting room. She looked around fascinated at the richness, the colour, the patterns of the myriad artefacts and souvenirs lining the walls. He left his arm where it was as she looked and closed the door behind him with his other hand.

Ella bustled into the sitting room. What a very nice surprise, the person with nice kitchen-smelling, warm, still feet was at the cottage today. She had been at the shop yesterday too. Ella sniffed her shoes and hoped this was going to be how the days were from now onwards. It would be very nice, very nice indeed. She was distracted as she sniffed the lovely kitcheny feet by something in the corner of her ears and nose. They had registered someone in the garden outside, a long way down the garden, a familiar smell, nothing dangerous, but there in the garden all the same. She went to the window and issued a single, brisk bark, just to let everyone know that she had noticed.

Shylah decided to remain in the kitchen. She had heard the French door opening and an exchange which she assumed must be Colm letting Rosemary into the back of the house and explaining the behavioural problems of the bell. She could hear the rise and fall of their voices in the sitting room. Rosemary laughed and Colm's voice interrupted, quiet, lifting and falling. Shylah reflected how it may have been nice to have met someone by now to share her life with, someone with whom she could have cosy, laughter filled conversations in Gabriel's sitting room. Would Gabriel have been there with Shylah and whomever, or not? Was Gabriel, in fact her life partner and should she be content with simple friendship?

While Shylah had been pregnant and in the early years following Colm's birth, she had spent many hours with Sister Anthony, talking through her fears and feelings following the event of which she had no memory. Sister had pledged and maintained the Seal of the Confessional, had supported Shylah in her wish to avoid involving the police further and moreover had enabled her to isolate that night into a capsule, sealed in lead, unable to contaminate anything else around it.

'Shylah, do not confuse what happened with love. Love is from God and is a beautiful thing. When you find love, its beauty will shine separate from the evil darkness of that night, just as your love for Colm is separate from what happened.'

Sister spoke with eloquence and depth on the subject of love. Frequently her face would assume a dreamy quality and her eyes would be focused on something in the distance.

Over ten years ago while she was still young, settled in the flat above the shop, away from the horror of Hull, Shylah felt that was the time when it might have happened, but it didn't. Days were just so full with Colm and Bennets. There had been so many good times with Gabriel, too, when she was home. If Shylah was honest, no one had ever turned up who would have fitted into the tight unit which Gabriel, Colm and Shylah had created. Was it too late? She was only in her thirties, surely there was a chance that something might happen, someone might happen, even now. She had been doing a lot of thinking lately. There were things she would like to do, things unrelated to the puzzling question of a partner, or another partner, in life, ambitions she had allowed to drift into her mind and then rationalise away with a myriad of reasons why they couldn't be achieved. If she didn't get on and do them, at least some of them, soon it would be too late.

Ella hurtled into the kitchen and crashed into Shylah's knees, turned through one hundred and eighty degrees and hurtled out again to the sitting room. She repeated the circuit twice more and then flopped, heavy and exhausted, dribbling onto the cool kitchen floor.

'What am I going to do with you, Ella?' Shylah asked fondly as Colm and Rosemary entered the kitchen and Colm resumed ministering to his roast. Rosemary stood alongside him, chopping, peeling, stirring under Colm's fussy guidance. Shylah poured them all a glass of wine and left them to it, going to lay the table.

The blue and white striped files, their contents depleted and dissipated, were still in place on top of the bureau. Their beloved progeny, Bennets, having been brought to life many years before and well on the way now to adulthood. It was definitely time for Shylah to think about the next phase of her life. She took a blue and white striped folder down, emptied its contents, placing them in a bundle on top of the bureau, used an ancient rubber, sourced from the bowels of the stationary tin, to erase the pencilled label 'Bennets', sat down and started to make some notes on a sheet of lined, A4 paper.

Later that afternoon, the lunch having been declared a delicious triumph, the three of them sat together in Gabriel's sitting room. Colm and Rosemary had discovered a mutual interest in the lyrics of Leonard Cohen and were engaged in an exclusive argument about the song Hallelujah, while Shylah scrutinised the eclectic mix of literature in Gabriel's bookcase, twitchy for inspiration. The A4 sheet of paper with its list of ideas was in the pocket of her jeans. A theme was developing in her thinking and Shylah was hungry to make some progress. In a flash of inspiration, she decided to contact Sister Anthony for advice.

'Colm, I need to do a couple of emails, do you mind if I take the car and go back to the flat for a while? You two can stay here as long as you like, I don't want to rush you.'

'Of course, Mum, no problem, we'll finish the clearing up and then see you back there later.'

Shylah suspected more than a soupcon of delight in Colm's voice at the prospect of spending the rest of the afternoon alone at the cottage with Rosemary.

Sister Anthony

I am sorry that I haven't connected now for over a week and very much hope things are still going great in Ghana. I am sure you are continuing to draw on your own special brand of strength, to enable you to cope with the harrowing sights you must see every day.

I have been thinking for a while about trying to make a few changes in my life. Colm is doing most of the running of Bennets now and we have a new assistant called Rosemary who started last week. She's a local girl who has lived in the town all her life, you may recognise her when you eventually see her, although she didn't come to the school. She seems to have picked everything up at lightning speed so there's not so much for me to do now! I am only in my thirties, Sister, I feel like I need to take on something new before it is too late rather than hang around and hold Colm back!

Do you know of any jobs which might be available or any organisations whom I could contact about voluntary opportunities? What I am really interested in is something which would help to create opportunities for women, either in the UK or abroad. Gabriel is doing great things in Saudi Arabia; women who have been virtually excluded from the workplace due to the restrictions of the Saudi society, are now able to start careers in Saraco thanks to Gabriel (oh and of course the good Doctor!). You are doing great things helping the African people to emerge from their difficulties. I feel like it is time for me to contribute to the world too, Sister, to use my talents... Just as you taught us to when we were at school!

As always, your wisdom and guidance will be very welcome, Sister

Your friend Shylah

Haiku 47 – Market Hamilton to Jeddah via email
Found shop assistant.
All done by six this evening
I'll be redundant!

Colm arrived back at the flat alone later that evening. He sat down, opened his laptop, closed it again, and then looked intently at Shylah.

'Mum, have you ever seen anyone in the garden at Gabriel's cottage?'

'Not as far as I know. Has someone been going in there while she's been away? I've not noticed anything being disturbed.'

'It's just that Rosemary and I have both seen someone. The same person. I last saw him a long time ago and I'd sort of forgotten but then Rosemary saw him today, before lunch.'

'Who did you see, Colm? Are you worried about it?'

Their conversation was interrupted by a 'ping' from Shylah's laptop.

'Hold on, Colm, I need to go and check if I've had a reply from Sister Anthony.' Shylah opened the laptop.

My dear Shylah

Thank you so much for your mail. I am delighted that you are at last getting time to yourself and have been able to think about the future. You have done such a great job at the shop and you can be very proud of the business you created, from nothing. You are a great example of someone who had difficult things to deal with but who has made a success of her life and created something which Colm can now take on for the future.

There are so very many opportunities for you to contribute through voluntary work. I have sent you some links below to have a look at but please do not commit yourself to anything too long term. Gabriel will be back from Saudi in the not too distant future and I feel certain that you and I will be called upon by God to help her with what comes next. I am working with someone here in Ghana too who will help her when she returns and look forward to introducing you.

There is so much for us all to do, Shylah. We will need your help and are delighted that you will be available to support us.

With love

Sister Anthony

Shylah was surprised, and a little irritated. Sister Anthony appeared to be labouring under such comparative clarity and to have something mapped out for them all already for when Gabriel returned. As far as Shylah knew, there was no date yet for a return from Saudi and Shylah certainly had not expected Sister Anthony back from Africa. She had not even realised that Gabriel and Sister Anthony were in regular touch again. The extent of irritation she felt at being left out of some loop of communication, excluded from some sort of plan was irrational, she told herself.

Haiku 48 – Jeddah to Market Hamilton via email
Redundancy eh?
I should be very surprised
You're in great demand.

Shylah decided not to reply to the Haiku until she was feeling more relaxed. Distracted and uneasy, she poured a glass of wine and returned to sit with her son.

Colm recognised immediately from her manner that now was not the time for further discussion on the subject of visions in Gabriel's back garden.

CHAPTER 17

Jeddah, Saudi Arabia

April 2013 (Gregorian calendar)

'Mubaarak, it is not a great time for you to decide to go to the UK,' said Gabriel, horrified at his unheralded announcement. 'We have ladies starting every week now and induction courses running one after the other. We are already stretched and with just Samir and me here, we won't be able to cope.'

Samir sat silently at the desk, reluctant to address his senior, the Doctor. Having already shared his concerns about their workload with Gabriel, he was delighted to have her as spokesperson.

'Gabriel,' Mubaarak was becoming tense, a triangle of sweat gathering above his top lip, his hand shuffling, straightening the papers on his desk. 'I need you and Samir to step up here. I have private matters in the UK I have to deal with.'

'How long are you going to be away, Mubaarak? We agreed that none of us would take any leave until there were a hundred ladies in place and fully trained. What is so important that you need to go now? We all have private matters to deal with but we made an agreement.'

'Gabriel, I am the boss and I am going to the UK. I expect you and Samir to continue to run the project here. I will be back as soon as I can but I have to help someone who is ill.'

Gabriel exhaled and raised her eyes. Mubaarak was intent on remaining mysterious and despite her protestations, she and Samir would be left to handle the growing workload without him. She looked towards the door, already a small queue of newly recruited ladies were waiting outside needing help, no doubt, with one thing or another. What would the queues be like when there were more of them in place? Mubaarak flounced out of the office, past the surprised group of ladies, leaving Samir and Gabriel alone.

'This is something to do with the 2.30 'phone call, Gabriel,' said Samir.

'What makes you think that?' answered Gabriel exasperated.

'Well, he took the 'phone call today, went out of the office as usual then he's been stressed and distracted ever since. As soon as the three of us were alone, we had the conversation we've just had.'

Gabriel ran through the afternoon's events in her mind. Samir was right. That morning, before the daily call, the three of them had been planning who would cover which induction event, filling in their names on a table on the white board in the corner. Now, by the middle of the afternoon, everything had changed.

'What on earth is going on, Samir? It must be pretty important if he's changed his mind that quickly,' she said.

Samir shrugged his bethaubed shoulders.

'Whoever calls him every afternoon must either be from the UK and is ill or know the person who is ill.'

Gabriel remembered the initials 'PJ' which had flashed onto the screen of Mubaarak's 'phone a few weeks before. Who was PJ she wondered? Was she or he the person in London? Were they anything to do with his elusive domestic arrangements when she and Mubaarak had met there in the winter?

She never had the opportunity to ask. Mubaarak didn't come back into the office that afternoon and by six o'clock, Samir and Gabriel concluded jointly than he had already left. They stayed behind together to rewrite the plans for next week.

Haiku 49 – Jeddah to Market Hamilton via email
Good doctor on form
Unexplained trip to London
Overwhelmed by work!

Haiku 50 – Market Hamilton to Jeddah via email
Typical Doctor
Avoids work, takes the glory
At least there's Samir! ☺

Over the days that followed, Gabriel and Samir continued the Herculean task of managing the project with only two thirds of an already stretched workforce. They had received not a single call from Mubaarak and their emails to him remained unanswered.

'I'm going to have to call him again, Gabriel, I need the password for one of his files in the shared project drive.' Samir's exasperation was starting to get the better of him and Gabriel suspected that his wife, recently endowed as she had been with their first child, was none too pleased about Samir's new, extended working patterns.

'His 'phone is off again.' Samir threw his own 'phone onto the desk and put his head in his hands.

'OK Samir, let me try him.' Gabriel was running out of ideas. If they were unable to get to Mubaarak soon, their bosses at Saraco would start to suspect that something was wrong with the project, its leader having upped sticks unannounced. Gabriel had already had to cover for the absent Mubaarak at a couple of meetings with the board and draw on some of her very deepest creative powers to explain his absence.

Mubaarak's 'phone switched immediately the answer 'phone.

'You don't think something's happened to him, do you? Should I contact his wife? We could be calling and calling suspecting him of avoiding us when all the time he has had some sort of accident.' Gabriel would need some indication of when the good Doctor intended to return if she was going to keep Samir motivated and the Saraco board happy.

'I can tell you where they live, if you like, but I don't have a number for the house or for his wife,' said Samir. 'He keeps his private life very private. She's some sort of academic. She spends all her time in their house working, something to do with history, I think. We asked them to our wedding and to come over to see the baby but every time, there's some excuse. They aren't very sociable. They don't seem to have any friends.' Samir shrugged.

'Good idea, give me the address, Samir, or some directions and I'll go and see if I can speak to the family or his wife, if she'll see me. She may know how to get hold of him or if not, at least we can let her know we're worried.'

Samir removed an immense sheet of paper from the flipchart stand and embarked upon a complicated and unnecessarily detailed depiction of the location of Mubaarak's house. He stood back several times throughout his endeavours to admire his handiwork.

'I wanted to do art at school, you know, but my parents wouldn't let me. I had to do useful subjects instead,' he shared as Gabriel wondered how Priyantha would cope with following the cartographical masterpiece when he came to pick her up.

'I should get on your way now, Gabriel. The afternoon is the time you will most likely to get his wife to see you, I would think.'

Gabriel called Priyantha who immediately recognised the location of Mubaarak's marital home, without need for lengthy consultation of the masterpiece, and they set off.

'Ma'am, I haven't seen Thanuja for a little while, have you seen her this week?' asked Priyantha as soon as they were underway.

'No sadly, I have been working very late this week, Priyantha, and she has been finding it very difficult to get out of the house lately so I've only seen her briefly in the evenings over the last few weeks. I think Mrs Taha is unwell.'

'Yes ma'am, Thanuja has told me about this. I am worried about her. Thanuja is not a nurse and Mr Taha will not allow anyone else to come and help Mrs Taha. Thanuja can look after the baby, but it is too hard for her to look after both of them.'

Gabriel reflected on her interactions with Sister Anthony. There was definitely a good chance that they could help Thanuja to escape from her servitude at the Tahas, continue her education and be reunited with Sean.

With everything else going on, the problem had been finding the right time to talk to her.

'Priyantha, I will try to speak to Thanuja this evening and ask her to get in touch.'

The car drew to a stop outside a pair of impenetrable metal gates set into a fifteen foot high wall topped with razor wire.

'This is the house, ma'am. I need to speak to their security on the intercom. What do you want me to say?'

'Can you just say I would like to see Doctor Mubaarak's wife about her husband?'

'I don't think so, ma'am. I think it would be better for me to announce that you are a lady executive from Saraco who needs to discuss some important business while Doctor Mubaarak is not here. They will not be used to women they do not know calling at the house, especially to talk about their mistress's husband.'

Priyantha left the car, spoke in Arabic into the intercom and returned. The monolithic, incarcerating gates clunked then swung open to reveal a mansion, the first impression of which was that of a gingerbread house. The house was surrounded by a lush garden in complete contrast with the grassless, littered, grey of the city outside.

'How on earth do they keep all this watered, Priyantha? It never rains and there's not so much as a blade of grass outside.'

'They have pipes and sprinklers, ma'am. All the biggest mansions in the city do. It costs lot of money.'

As she looked more carefully, Gabriel noticed cats of miscellaneous shapes, sizes and colours, basking, weaving and playing among the lush, tropical shrubs and flowers. The overall effect was fantastical, the colours exaggerated like a cartoon. The feline, fairy-tale mansion was absolutely the last place she would expect to find the humourless, obsessive Doctor Mubaarak.

Priyantha drew the car into a shaded canopy as an elderly Indian gentleman clad in a business-like suit opened Gabriel's door and gestured towards a vast hallway. A slim, Arabic woman emerged smiling from the recesses of the hallway, her hand outstretched in welcome. As she walked, she scintillated like a butterfly, wide crimson trousers emerging from beneath a deep purple, silk dress.

'Hello Gabriel, I am Sureya, Mubaarak's wife.' Her English accent betrayed no hint of her Arabic heritage and her long, black hair swung in a unified curtain as she spoke.

Gabriel stood silent, transfixed, and felt goose bumps rise beneath the prickly abaya. Mubaarak had never spoken about his wife. She had been unprepared for the powerful energy which emerged, pulsating from the woman holding Gabriel's right hand between both of her own.

'I am sorry, Sureya, to call unannounced. I didn't know how to contact you here at home. Mubaarak is a very private man.'

'I understand, Gabriel, and I know that you have been a support to him professionally for many, many years. I am very grateful to you, Gabriel. Please come, we will have some coffee and talk.'

Sureya nodded slightly towards the suited gentleman who discreetly melted into one of the doorways. Gabriel felt a light touch at her elbow and Sureya encouraged her towards a high, bright salon, the four walls of which were lined floor to ceiling with books. In its centre was an immense desk strewn with papers and keyboards over which two large plasma screens loomed. Sureya gestured beyond the desk towards a horseshoe of tasselled couches, embroidered in gold, sweeping patterns. An oriental maid in a navy suit passed them, wheeling a silver serving tray towering with pots, cups and cakes. A second maid, in white overalls gathered two enormous cats from one of the couches and retreated, her petite form staggering beneath their bulk.

'I'm not sure if you like cats. Mubaarak said you and your family had dogs in the UK but I wasn't sure about cats. It will do those two no harm to be outside for a while.'

Gabriel noticed Sureya's fond smile, the girlish laughter in her eyes as she discussed her cats.

'Please sit, Gabriel, my team will leave us to talk privately now.' She nodded and the maid disappeared again, closing the door quietly as she left.

'Would you like coffee or tea? We have American coffee and English tea with milk, if you would like.' She smiled again with what appeared to be a hint of childlike enthusiasm. Gabriel reached out and placed her hand on Sureya's arm.

'Sureya, we cannot contact Mubaarak and we have been worried about him. There are passwords he has which we need for some of the project files and I need to know how to explain his absence to the board at Saraco.'

Sureya's answer was unexpected. 'Gabriel, I have the password backups here. Mubaarak always leaves them with me just in case anything happens to him. He is very dedicated to his work and its continuity. We will go through them together and I will give you what you need.'

Sureya stood and turned to the wheeled tray.

'English tea with milk please, Sureya, thank you.'

'Gabriel, to answer your second question, I need to understand how much you know about Mubaarak and his life. He and I have reason to believe that some of the people in the country who are very much against the principles of what he is doing at Saraco, are who looking to cause trouble for him.'

'Against the principles of providing opportunities for women, you mean?' Gabriel was horrified, particularly as the government and Saudi royal family were so overtly behind the concept of equality in the workplace.

'There are still many hard-line Muslims in Saudi, Gabriel. They do not support the principle of equality at all and will take action against those whom they consider are flouting their concept of Islam. Mubaarak has received threats, Gabriel, against himself and his team.'

'That's awful. He hasn't mentioned anything to Samir or to me. These people, whoever they are, are they happy to challenge the royal family and the government?'

'Gabriel, these hard-liners are very powerful and many people in Saudi have suffered at their hands. They don't care about the visible and public wishes of the government. They work to their own agenda.'

Gabriel looked intently into Sureya's face. This was a whole fresh seam of complexity of which she had not previously been aware.

Sureya went on, 'You have known Mubaarak and been a professional colleague for longer than anyone else, I am certain I can count on your discretion and your help to protect him should these hard-liners ... extremists if you like, wish to do him harm or ruin his reputation.' Sureya's eyes were suddenly hard, business-like, her head still and face taut as she looked at Gabriel's eyes.

'You can count on my complete discretion, Sureya,' she answered quietly, experiencing a flicker of suspicion about what was imminent

'Gabriel, Mubaarak is in London with his friend, Philip. Philip is very ill and Mubaarak needs to be with him. Mubaarak told me that you knew Philip, Philip Jones one of the lecturers while you were both at Oxford together.'

Gabriel's mouth opened and closed involuntarily. She felt memories, conversations, rumours about Philip Jones tumbling and landing in a more ordered manner in her mind. Sureya must have seen her hesitation and continued.

'Gabriel, I know this may seem surprising to you, but I am very happy to be Mubaarak's wife and to accept his … friendship with Philip. I have my work, that is my passion, and I am in contact from here with all my colleagues around the world.'

'Sureya, Mubaarak has never spoke to me about you or your relationship and of course, he never mentioned his other … I mean his other friends or his private life.' Gabriel realised immediately how clumsy she sounded but Sureya's calm voice of acceptance continued.

'Gabriel, from the moment I met Mubaarak, when I was sixteen, we knew that God had brought us together. My desire to succeed professionally as an academic and to run my household as I do, was almost as unacceptable at that time, as Mubaarak's lifestyle would have been. We have both had to find ways to work together as a team and fight our way around the restrictions we face. I am sure I do not need to explain to you, however that if his private life were made public by the people who wish to do him harm, things would be … difficult, very difficult.'

'I am sorry, Sureya, I had no idea how difficult things were for you. I realise that the government here is trying to create opportunities for women now, but I never really thought about women like you who came before and did not have those chances. I certainly did not realise the extent to which the extremists would go to fly in the face of current government direction either.'

'Gabriel, don't feel sorry for me, I have fought hard for what I have and I am very content with my life. I run my office from here, the staff are my support team. Mubaarak's acceptance of me and his encouragement have made my life whole and fulfilled. I was pleased when he found Philip too, a permanent part of his life whom I could accept, and someone incidentally, who has been very helpful to me in my work. My fear though, and Mubaarak's fear too, is that the extreme elements of our society may try to expose him … us … all of us, Gabriel.'

Gabriel reflected in silence, allowing Sureya's words to sink into her consciousness. Was there some sort of innuendo in Sureya's final words? She was suddenly startled as Sureya jumped to her feet, craned her head to the left as if looking for something under the desk and threw her hands in the air with a small shriek.

'You naughty boy, you were hiding there all the time, come out.' She knelt by the desk, head near the floor, trim behind raised, and hauled a large, ginger feline from the lower recesses. She carried the sleepy, fluffy bundle back over to the couch.

'Do you mind cats on your knee, Gabriel?' asked Sureya, a little late.

'No, not at all. I miss the animals we had in the UK.'

Sureya plopped the heavy, marmalade creature on Gabriel's lap where it shuffled slightly and resumed its slumbers.

'Sureya, I am sorry but I have to be honest with you. I have never seen the Mubaarak you describe. He has always been so strictly Muslim and … and his lifestyle is so contrary to what I understand of that faith.'

'Gabriel, like all of us, he has many conflicts and tensions in his mind and his heart which he is trying to navigate as best he can. He loves God and the teaching of Muhammad but none of us is perfect. It is my duty to help him. In public though, he overcompensates because you know what would happen here if his … his lifestyle were made public.'

'Yes, I think I understand.' Gabriel remembered the horrific execution site in the distance, outside the office, and shuddered. She had heard the team at Saraco discuss the coach loads of voyeurs who attended events on a Friday and the creativity of the executioners when dealing with misdemeanours of a sexual nature.

'Gabriel, please do not labour under the mistaken belief that homosexuality, alcoholism, prostitution and any number of activities forbidden by Islam and by law, do not happen here in Saudi Arabia. They happen just as they do anywhere else but people deal with them in the best way they can. Is it so very different in the UK?'

Gabriel reflected for a moment and thought of Shylah and her parents. The Cooks had been looked upon by so many in Market Hamilton as the perfect, united Roman Catholic family but underneath the surface, those close to the situation knew the truth.

'No Sureya, it's not so very different,' she concluded.

Sureya stood again. 'Come, let me show you the garden, Gabriel. You do not need to wear abaya here, we dress modestly and professionally, just as the Qur'an requires but do not observe the additional demands of the worldly leaders of our country. Take it off if you like, it's covered in cat hairs now anyway.'

Sureya smiled again and linked her delicate yet steely arm through Gabriel's as they walked around the fairy-tale garden. Underneath her abaya, Gabriel had taken to wearing a simple combination of jeans and tee shirt. It was the first time she had been anywhere outdoors except for the walled garden in the compound, wearing normal clothes for many months. She felt the viral power of Sureya and her fantastical surroundings. She was refreshed and free in Sureya's beatific company yet something resembling fear lurked somewhere in her consciousness, parts of the fairy-tale picture simply did not mesh together and there was something frightening about the woman's steely determination.

Sureya pointed out plants and flowers but her passion was the cats. She knew the name and progeny of every one and explained how one of the staff and two of the rooms in the house were dedicated to their care.

'Sureya, I do need to know what you would like me to say about Mubaarak's absence. Especially in light of the threat you believe he faces. In fact, Sureya, I think you're telling me that we're all under some sort of threat.' Gabriel struggled to focus on the underlying reason for her visit as they walked.

'Please tell them that he is with a family member who is unwell and that he hopes to be back by the end of next week. I will take your mobile number from you, Gabriel, when we are back in the house and we can keep in touch by email. It is very difficult for him to interact with anyone at work while he is with Philip.'

'I understand and thanks so much, Sureya, for being so helpful with the passwords. Will you tell Mubaarak we have had this conversation today?'

'Of course I will, Gabriel, we spoke about you when he left for London. If you had not been in touch by this weekend, I would have called you. I really am very grateful for the loyalty you have shown to Mubaarak over the years. His professional life would have been measurably more challenging had it not been for you. He and I both need to be able to rely on you now also, Gabriel, to protect him in light of the confidential matters I have shared with you. There are things which neither of you would wish to be exposed while you are here in Saudi, Gabriel.'

Gabriel shuddered at the intensity of Sureya's gaze. Mubaarak had never expressed his gratitude directly to her before, something Gabriel had found mildly frustrating. That afternoon, Gabriel started to understand how despite the years of knowing one another, she had only engaged with the tip of the iceberg which was Mubaarak. Today, Sureya had parted the seas and enabled her to glimpse what lay beneath, the part to which Mubaarak was too frightened to allow anyone but Sureya and Philip access. Despite the revelations, Gabriel remained unsure. Beneath the sea, at the base of the iceberg, something mortal lurked in the darkness.

With a set of passwords and Sureya's contact details on a memory stick, Gabriel returned to the car and Priyantha.

'Did your meeting go well, ma'am?' he asked.

'Yes, very well thank you, Priyantha. I think we should go back to the compound now, it is a little too late for the office. I will see if I can meet Thanuja in the garden this evening and find out if she needs your help with Mr and Mrs Taha.'

Gabriel texted Samir on the way, telling him that she had the passwords and that he should try to get an early night. They had a week at the absolute minimum before Mubaarak would return.

She texted a quick Haiku to Shylah

Haiku 51 – Jeddah to Market Hamilton via text
Met Mubaarak's wife.
Cat lady, gingerbread house
Things not adding up.

Back in the apartment, she hastily dumped her bags on the couch, picked up a can of drink, pocketed her book and turned again to leave for the walled garden. She sat down among the whisper of the tall grasses and tried to concentrate on reading. The graceful, intelligent, eccentric Sureya and their conversation that afternoon repeatedly broke into her mind. She had been seduced by Sureya's charm, her intellect, her support of Mubaarak and his tensions but felt a growing sense of fear and unease.

Mubaarak's obsessive personality and overemphasis of his religious observance had always challenged and confused Gabriel. She had been baffled by his avoidance of all discussions regarding his private life at university; his disappearances at the end of the working day in London were a mystery and his reaction to her casual enquiries at the compound restaurant several months previously had been completely unexpected. Sureya had painted in some of the missing parts of the picture yet there was a duplicity underlying the ideal, fairy-tale arrangement enjoyed by Mubaarak and Sureya. If challenged or under threat, Gabriel wondered how the indivisible partnership would react. How far would they go to protect the veneer of compliance with the demands of the society in which they lived? A veneer which was now, indeed, under threat. How far would they go to avoid the terrible consequences which public discovery of Mubaarak's lifestyle would evoke? Why had they decided to share the secret with Gabriel today and ask for her help in keeping Mubaarak's lifestyle secret? Did they imagine that today some sort of 'deal' had been struck?

She was jolted from her thoughts by the arrival of a distracted and stressed Thanuja.

'Hello ma'am, I saw you through the window. I am sorry I have not been to see you for some days.'

'Don't worry, Thanuja, I know things are hard with Mrs Taha's illness. It is lovely to see you tonight though.' Gabriel smiled, looked into Thanuja's young face and saw the grey pallor of her skin, the new dullness which had sucked the light from her eyes. 'You look very tired, Thanuja. Priyantha is worried about you, he says he has not heard from you for a while.'

'Ma'am, things are very difficult. Mrs Taha is very ill, she says she hates the baby.' Thanuja paused to absorb the horrifying concept of her employer hating her child when she herself longed desperately to be with Sean. 'Mr Taha is not home but Mrs Taha is sleeping now. I am very sad. I do not know what to do. I do not have time to call Priyantha.'

'Thanuja, why don't you use my 'phone and call Priyantha now to ask for his help with your sponsor? I do not think you can carry on looking after both Mrs Taha and the baby.'

Gabriel dialled Priyantha's number and handed the 'phone to Thanuja who immediately started talking in Sinhalese. Gabriel could understand nothing but felt it right to leave Thanuja to talk to her cousin in privacy. She walked out of the garden and stood with her back and head flat against the outside of the wall. She looked upwards and shuddered; the Tahas' house was in darkness, a cold silence exuded from its blackened windows and grey, impenetrable walls.

When the scream started, it was as though the devil had descended to earth unseen, hidden himself in the Tahas' garden and then chosen his moment to unleash his terror into the darkness, when least expected. Gabriel, only a few metres from the Tahas' house leapt in shock. The piercing shrill could not initially be identified as anything which might emanate from a human. After a few seconds, however, the depth of anguish it conveyed became clear, along with its human provenance. Thanuja shot from the garden like a bullet from a gun, dropping Gabriel's 'phone on the ground as she went. The Tahas' garden gate swung a metallic toll reminiscent of a warning bell heralding death at sea.

Gabriel stood motionless, she had been told before by Thanuja that the Tahas would not accept visitors but surely in an emergency, things were different. She picked up her 'phone but the face was shattered, a long shard of glass fell onto the top of her foot. Gabriel felt the clammy fist of panic squeeze around her heart and tried to brush the shard of glass away. It lodged itself searingly into the palm of her right hand. She ran towards the Tahas' villa clutching one throbbing hand in the other and cried out Thanuja's name to the closed gate in the impenetrable wall. The screaming, now coming from inside the villa, continued, its source had no need to draw breath for longer than an instant. Gabriel cried out to Thanuja again, ran into the garage beneath the building and tried the door into the basement. It was locked.

She was unable to use the ruined 'phone to contact Priyantha and she didn't know his number; it was somewhere in the bowels of the 'phone's memory. She lamented that her backup disciplines lagged far behind those of Sureya and realised she had absolutely no idea what to do.

Gabriel ran up the stairs to her apartment, flooded her hand with water and picked out as much of the glass as she could. It disappeared with a spiral of blood down the sink. She searched in her chest of drawers and found an old gentleman's handkerchief and wrapped it around her bleeding hand. She opened her laptop, inserted Sureya's memory stick, hastily scribbled down Sureya's number and ran back down the stairs and outside. She coursed through the compound walkways, between the anonymous, concrete walls, holding the handkerchief tight to staunch the bleeding. She saw no one except for a couple of maids outside in the darkness, hosing their boss's cars, creating lakes of grey, oily-filmed water across the ground. Gabriel splashed through the filth towards the clubhouse complex and entered the restaurant.

A handful of diners glanced up at the stranger with a blood-soaked bandage around her hand, mildly surprised at her dishevelled and breathless state. Gabriel approach a couple at the nearest table to the door.

'Please, I am so sorry to trouble you but I think something terrible has happened in one of the villas. My 'phone has broken, please may I borrow yours?'

The man looked, slow, sidelong at the unwelcome interruption. 'I've not got much battery left,' he sneered.

'I don't mind, I only need to make a very short call.'

'It's not international, is it?' His wife pursed her lips at the intrusion into their tidy, tax-free, compound lifestyle.

'I can pay you for the call,' said Gabriel, desperately searching through her pockets and handing over a 50 Riyal note. The man's face brightened and he passed over his 'phone, its battery fully charged, from where it lay between them on the table.

She called Sureya's number which switched immediately to voicemail.

'Sureya, it's Gabriel, we met this afternoon. My 'phone has broken and I need your help, please Sureya, it's important. I need to contact the driver whom Mubaarak found for me, his name is Priyantha. Please would you be able to email me his number. Thank you, Sureya.'

Gabriel ended the call and met the couple's four, cold, mocking eyes.

'I recommend you get yourself better organised in future so you don't have to disturb people having a quiet meal,' carped the woman in lightly accented English before tutting and returning her attention to her food.

Gabriel felt acid-tears sting her eyes and the ache of imminent loss of self-control clutch at her throat as she turned. The complacent disapproval of the small, close-knit clique of diners in the restaurant burned holes in her back as she left.

On her way back to the apartment, she passed two disaffected house-boys, sitting on the ground, heads hung, sharing a cigarette. They ignored her. The Tahas' house had been consumed again by steely, cold silence and someone had shut and padlocked the gate. She re-entered her apartment.

Haiku 52 – Jeddah to Market Hamilton via email
Terrible evening

'Phone broken, hand cut, headache
Problem with Thanuja

Haiku 53 – Market Hamilton to Jeddah via email
I'm so sorry friend
Paracetamol and sleep.
Sureya sounds odd!

Haiku 54 – Jeddah to Market Hamilton via email
Good advice my friend
Things look better in mornings!
Will keep you posted

After a hot, tortuous night in the apartment, Gabriel climbed shaking and sweating from her bed. She looked down at her hand, stinging and sore. The gentleman's handkerchief was still there, stuck to her hand with dried blood. She saw the navy blue 'W' embroidered in its corner and felt the calm, solid strength of her father flood through her body. It was time to get a grip of herself, she was not here on earth to be weak.

Stable, reliable Priyantha called in the car to collect her and she relayed the events of the night before.

'Ma'am, I know there is problem. Thanuja's call to me was cut off last night but she was very worried. I will contact Thanuja's sponsor today and we will make sure everything is OK at the Tahas' home.'

'Thank you, Priyantha, I am completely cut off without my 'phone. Please let me know as soon as there is any news'

'I am so sorry, ma'am, that Thanuja has broken your 'phone. I will take this for you to the shop.'

'No Priyantha, I am sorry, I didn't meant that I blame Thanuja for the 'phone. It's just that without it, I feel so isolated and unable to be of any help. I would be so grateful if you would get me a replacement, if you have time today, Priyantha.'

Gabriel felt the tears sting again as they arrived at the office, felt in her pocket for the handkerchief and steeled herself.

Later that morning, a security guard delivered a new 'phone to her desk. It had already been set up by the Sri Lankan store assistant, a distant cousin of Priyantha's, to exactly replicate the old one.

An email from Sureya, bearing Priyantha's contact details, eventually arrived, too late.

Samir and Gabriel relayed appropriate messages regarding Mubaarak's temporary absence to visit a family friend in the UK together with an aspirational return date one week hence. Reinvigorated with the requisite passwords, they made good progress with the project.

There was no news at all that day or for several thereafter about either Thanuja or the Tahas.

CHAPTER 18

Accra, Ghana

May 2013

It was four o'clock in the morning and Sister Anthony prayed intensely, kneeling on the cold, black and white chequered lino floor by her bed. Her eyes were clamped shut, her mouth fervently shaping silent words. Her knees by now, were inured to the hardness, her spine and hips moulded and strengthened to bear the unnatural, kneeling posture. She appealed to God for another successful and valuable day. Every single life which she and Michael were able to turn around among the AIDS-riddled, Ghanaian community was of greater value than the whole world's riches and she had been given the greatest gift; to be involved in saving those lives. She had never been so happy as she had been since arriving in filthy, colourful, fantastic Africa and to God she was permanently thankful.

Sister Anthony had opened her mind and heart completely to Him for so long now that she could physically feel his steer at every turning point in her life, a warm urging at her shoulder, a cool blue flow, helping her shape the right words when she was hesitant. Sister Anthony understood and accepted completely that all she had to do was be intelligent, watchful and open to His messages, listen to what He was saying and place her complete trust in Him. He required, and had always had, her unquestioning obedience.

Sister Anthony had a feeling that God would call upon her to leave Africa soon. The recent direct contact from Gabriel in Saudi Arabia, after so many years of second-hand news had been His sign. She and Gabriel were now in regular touch about the girl, Thanuja. Sister Gabriel prayed every day for Thanuja; she feared that God's plan involved high expectations of the young Sri Lankan mother. God had told her that Gabriel would need Sister Anthony's help and that it was her role to support and guide both Gabriel and Michael.

Blue Dragon House, where she and Michael boarded was in a muddy, orange road close to the new Accra Mall. While the house had been there for some fifteen years, it had recently been surrounded by identical rows of flimsy, rectangular apartment buildings. The apartments had been hastily erected to tempt Accra's exponentially expanding population away from the filth and disease which was rife among their asbestos and cast iron shacks.

The yard outside the house was surrounded by a high wall topped unnecessarily, in Sister Anthony's view, with hoops and spirals of rusty barbed wire. It was as though the house and garden were marooned on an impenetrable island which had been swept ashore during a storm and landed in a foreign country.

Within the confines of the imprisoning walls, hens pecked among the sparse, piercing grass and something which may once have been a banana tree lolled, brown and rotting in the corner beside the industrially-sized, black plastic dustbin. Cats bearing all permutations of skin disease, coupled with the spectrum of more permanent disfigurements hopped in and out of the bin avoiding, to the extent they were able, the razor talons of the vultures. The vultures loped and squabbled over discarded food scraps from the house and if there were no food scraps, they satisfied themselves with packets and boxes. Every morning, the yard would be covered with remnants of the vultures' pilferage. At six o'clock, Nsowaa the house girl, would run shrieking from her hut, waving her broom to scare the birds away and to recommence the ineffectual task of returning the rubbish to the bin.

The boys from the apartments had sprayed graffiti over the entire outside surface of the wall. The overall effect was reminiscent of the verdant batiks worn by the local women so that, from a distance the house looked like a majestic headscarf casually cast aside by an African giant among the apartment buildings. The boys kicked their footballs against the outside walls all day long and well into the night. Occasionally when she had had enough or needed to let off steam about an entirely unrelated matter, Miss Joyce, who ran the boarding house, opened the gate, put her head outside and screamed at the boys. Every time, they laughed, made lewd gestures depicting the most fulsome contours of Miss Joyce's feminine form and carried on exactly as they had been doing before the banshee intervention. Miss Joyce returned muttering, to the corrugated plastic contraption she referred to as a veranda, to continue reading the Western romances which Sister Anthony was able to borrow from some of the charity parcels. While reading she sucked thirstily on the cigarettes with which the Western tobacco conglomerates were so kindly flooding the market tables and corner stores of the poor African nations.

Miss Joyce was delighted that the English Sister Anthony and the handsome Kenyan charity worker, Michael, were staying at Blue Dragon House. They had been with her for several years now and the ladies at the church were jealous, very jealous indeed that Miss Joyce had secured such high quality, Christian tenants. Previously an irregular visitor at Mass, Miss Joyce had stepped up her attendance since their arrival, proudly donning her family cloth and precarious, pleated matching headscarf and setting out enthusiastically to recount the latest stories about the good Sister and the great charity worker. When stories were scarce, Mrs Joyce was not averse to using her poetic licence and making up a few tales to entertain her lady friends.

Sister Anthony and Michael always stood at the back of the church with the lower-class parishioners. Miss Joyce made clear to her lady friends that the charity for whom they worked demanded such concessions. She would never normally allow anyone who fraternised with the lower classes past the colourful walls of Blue Dragon House.

Sister Anthony came down to breakfast in Miss Joyce's kitchen, at six thirty every morning after prayers. Nsowaa served her fruit, juice, bread and coffee on the mottled, heavy plates which may once have been white. Miss Joyce preferred to keep nocturnal hours and waited until her guests returned from work to make an appearance at dinner time. When the internet was in action, Sister Anthony would sit quietly and work while she ate until Michael joined her. Nsowaa was happy with the arrangement; she would much prefer to talk to their guests when the glorious Michael was present. Michael was late that morning; he had been on the 'phone in his room.

'Morning Sister, Nsowaa, how are you ladies today?' He bounced across the small, grubby kitchen and gingerly positioned his solid strength atop the tiny stool.

'Fine, thank you, sir,' answered Nsowaa sashaying towards the table with fresh juice and coffee for Michael who (to Nsowaa's grave disappointment) turned his attention swiftly to Sister Anthony.

'I've just had a call from the Chief. She says the charity wants us to identify some local people to whom we can hand the work over. It's something about building local skills and sustainability, making best use of scarce charity resources i.e. us.'

'We know that makes perfect sense, Michael. You have delivered your message here and we both know we need to move on soon. Did she have any ideas about candidates or timescales?'

'She is sending someone over later in the week, a Dr Mensah, a Ghanaian who trained in London, specialising in the spread of sexually transmitted disease. The Chief is saying we should aim for the end of next month.'

'So about four weeks to hand everything over to him after he arrives. That sounds reasonable. I expect we should help him to identify his team too.'

'Sister, Dr Mensah is a woman,' laughed Michael slapping his thigh and throwing his head backwards on its supple hinges, to the surprise and delight of the ever proximal Nsowaa. 'But yes, we should help HER to identify HER team. I never thought I'd see the day Sister, never thought I'd see the day when you made a mistake like that! He punched Sister Anthony lightly on the arm eliciting from her a gentle, embarrassed laugh and from Nsowaa, a delighted, flutter of mirth. Sashaying with refreshed amplitude, Nsowaa dissipated her pent up energy by battering a tribe of cockroaches (the third of the morning) to death in the corner of the kitchen.

Sister Anthony spent the morning at the senior school alongside the charity counsellor while Michael was working at the hospital in the AIDS clinic. At lunchtime, they met in the hospital canteen to partake of the free staff meal before setting off to meet with the prostitutes who congregated in the afternoons outside the Western hotels to bribe the security staff and gain entry. Every day, the predictable hospital staff meal consisted of fufu, the mountainous white dumplings topped with grizzly gravy fashioned from a creative range of unidentifiable livestock and vegetable matter. To drink, the hospital provided a choice between two equally psychedelically coloured, fizzy chemicals in grubby bottles.

Sister Anthony allowed herself a moment to reflect on how she would not miss Ghanaian lunchtimes, before steering her mind back to a more righteous course of gratitude to God for providing adequate nourishment. With four weeks to go in Ghana, she felt the familiar urging at her shoulder. The time was ripe to raise the subject of the future with Michael.

'Michael, have the charity given you any indication of what they need you to do next?' she asked, trying to sound relaxed and casual.

'Well, the first priority is to settle Dr Mensah in here.' Michael speared the fufu with his fork as if he were killing a giant jellyfish. It was rubbery, unyielding and skidded across the plate, splashing its watery surrounds onto the table.

'Any idea what is in store after that?' Sister Anthony did not immediately meet Michael's fiery, intense eyes as he looked slowly upwards from his plate towards her.

'You and I need to go and help Gabriel, Sister, and then I will return to Africa. We are both clear about what we are required to do.'

'We are both clear, yes.' Sister Anthony was relieved. 'But to be open with you, Michael, so far I am light on details. Gabriel has only recently got back in touch with me after a break of well over ten years. I told her that you and I were working together and I suspect that she already realises who you are.'

'I understand, Sister, but let's go through what we have. Gabriel was your pupil in the UK and a brilliant student, am I right?'

Sister Anthony nodded.

'And she is now in Saudi Arabia, immersing herself in one of the most extreme Islamic societies on the planet. She is involved with one of the largest oil companies, one of the biggest revenue earners in Saudi bringing young, qualified women into the workplace to work alongside men. Do I have it right, Sister?'

'Yes, Michael, that's right.'

'So what she is doing in Saudi right now is in direct conflict with the prevailing beliefs and restrictions of the vast majority of Saudi men. In fact, in direct conflict, too, with all extremist Muslims in the world. Am I right, Sister?'

'You have it, Michael, but having women in business is not in conflict with the Qur'an nor the teachings of the prophet Muhammad. As you and I both know, Muhammad's wife Khadijah was always described as a businesswoman in the Qur'an.'

'So it is really about reinforcing the teachings of Muhammad and the Qur'an. The teachings which have been bastardised, for whatever reason, by the people wielding power in Saudi.'

'Yes Michael, but not only Saudi. This is about reversing the trend of extremism and its divergence with the roots of Islamic teaching.'

Michael sat back in his chair and inhaled deeply. The bright yellow, child-sized, plastic piece of furniture started to buckle alarmingly under his weight.

'Sister, Gabriel's going to need help. Maybe I should have got in touch with her before now, but we have just had so much to do here. It felt like there wasn't time but I do feel like Gabriel's time is imminent.'

He shook his head and pushed the unyielding fufu away, defeated by its fork avoidance tactics.

They sat in silence for a few minutes, drinking the sour, psychedelic concoctions through leaky paper straws.

'I'll email Gabriel later if we have connectivity at the house,' said Sister Anthony finally. 'We should find out when she will be finishing in Saudi. God willing, it will coincide with us handing over to Dr Mensah.'

Back at Blue Dragon House that evening, seizing a patchy interlude of internet availability before dinner, Sister Anthony contacted Gabriel.

My dear Gabriel

I haven't heard from you in a little while and am wondering how the young girl you spoke of, Thanuja, is getting on. Will it be possible for her to take advantage of any of the educational programmes we found for her? I feel certain too that if we can get her settled, we will be able to work with the Sisters in Colombo to reunite her with Sean. Do let me know, Gabriel.

On another note, I have been speaking with my colleague, Michael, here in Ghana. I mentioned Michael to you in one of my previous emails. He and I will be finished here in Ghana in the next few weeks and the charity for whom he is working is giving him a break from Africa for a while. Michael is ready to join me, Gabriel, in helping you take your own work forward. Do you know when you will be finished in Jeddah?

I am very much looking forward to seeing you again.

God's love and strength are with you, Gabriel, and we, your friends are here to support you.

Sister Anthony

Miss Joyce was in fine form that evening, having secured a monstrous snapper from the market, fried it until crispy and covered it in hot, red sauce.

'Where else but Blue Dragon House would you get nutritious, traditional Ghanaian food like this, Sister, Mr Michael?' she exclaimed proudly as she laid the concoction before them with flourish and waved both hands ceiling-wards in heavenly thanks. Nsowaa followed, bottom and hips waving, with a dish of floury plantain and they all sat down together on the stools, which were creaking and by now definitely on the last of each of their sets of legs.

Evening conversation was usually dominated by Miss Joyce's tales about her many guests over the years or ribald reveries concerning the latest exploits of the ladies at the church. Michael and Sister Anthony found such discourse, in the absence of any alternative entertainment in the house, strangely therapeutic after a hard day's work. That evening was no exception and Sister Anthony and Michael nodded, oooh'd and aaah'd in all the right places.

Gabriel's email response managed to navigate the tricky corridors of Accra's internet connectivity later that evening. Sister Anthony, who was allowed to keep her laptop with her during dinner, following special dispensation from Miss Joyce several months previously, showed the email to Michael.

Sister Anthony

Thank you so much for your mail. It is lovely to hear from you again. Sadly I do not have good news to share about Thanuja. The family for whom she works has been having problems over the last few weeks; the mother has some sort of depression. This has placed a big strain on Thanuja herself who has been looking after not only the baby but also his depressed mother. In the circumstances, it has not been possible to make any progress with discussing the opportunities you so kindly identified for her. Sadly, a few nights ago, there was some sort of incident at the house where she works and Thanuja had to return there urgently. Whatever it was must have been serious as I have not seen her since.

I will keep going to the garden where we normally meet in the evenings after she has put the baby to bed. As soon as things are calmer at the house, I am sure she will be able to come and join me again. I am also in close touch with Thanuja's cousin, Priyantha, who is trying hard to get in touch with her too.

The project at Saraco is going well. Our boss is away at the moment but we expect him back soon. I am expecting to be here a few more months yet but would like to meet up with you and with Michael soon if I possibly can.

I will speak to the boss as soon as he is back and will email with more news soon, Sister.

With Love

Gabriel

'Hmm, Sister, doesn't sound like she is going to escape from Saudi to coincide with our leaving here,' said Michael thoughtfully 'It's proving really difficult to connect with her. What do you think we should do?'

'Leaving here? You're not leaving are you?' interjected a horrified Miss Joyce.

'We were planning to let you know this week, Miss Joyce, and to very sadly give our notice but the work we are doing here is coming to an end. A new leader, a Dr Mensah, is arriving next week,' added Sister Anthony swiftly.

Miss Joyce, ever a lady with an eye for opportunity, replied immediately. 'Please contact your Dr Mensah and tell her she will be made very welcome here at Blue Dragon House, Sister, Mr Michael. I will make sure the large room is aired before she arrives. We have had doctors before as I may have mentioned.'

Sister Anthony reassured Miss Joyce that they would recommend her most heartily and were indeed well acquainted with her vast experience of caring for the specific needs of those endowed with doctorates.

'It will be a shame to see you go, Sister and you too of course, Mr Michael…'

Miss Joyce had just drawn breath ready to embark upon a new thread when the air was cleaved by a tragic shriek from her left. Nsowaa leapt up from her stool, flung her arm across her face so her forearm stemmed the gush of tears which had sprung, apparently from nowhere and ran from the room sobbing at deafening volume. The stool wobbled for a few seconds then clattered into several pieces across the floor.

'Silly girl, and just look at my lovely dining chair,' tutted Miss Joyce, to the wide- eyed astonishment of her dining companions, at which point the power went off and they embarked upon their well-rehearsed routine, bearing torches and essential belongings, retiring to their respective bedrooms in the warm, black, velvet darkness.

CHAPTER 19

Jeddah, Saudi Arabia

May 2013 to June 2013 (Gregorian calendar)

Mubaarak eventually returned to the office after several weeks, rather than the single week which he and Sureya had predicted. His return coincided with an Arab News press conference. The press conference had been scheduled for the Saraco board and a representative from the project team had been requested; a fact which Mubaarak must have learned about via Sureya, to whom Gabriel had been instructed to send daily updates on project progress. Gabriel reflected that either Philip's illness had miraculously subsided or the lure of personal glory in the press, superseded even the good Doctor's concern for his beloved. Mubaarak arrived wearing what was evidently a new suit, undoubtedly purchased from a smart London tailor. He placed his bags on the desk, bade Gabriel and Samir a cursory, 'Good morning,' and left immediately for the press conference.

'He didn't want to miss an opportunity like this,' whispered Samir.

'It would have been nice to have been told that he was definitely coming back. I spent the whole weekend preparing, just in case I needed to stand in for him,' replied

Gabriel, wondering why Sureya had not emailed, even if Mubaarak was busy travelling.

Mubaarak returned later that day beaming and with face aglow. The press conference had clearly been a great success and Gabriel suspected that the Doctor had maximised the opportunity to secure personal credit for the excellence of the project. Gabriel reflected that he probably had not even acknowledged the existence of his small team, much less their contribution.

'I'm going to leave early tonight as I have been away from home,' Mubaarak announced grabbing his unopened bags and heading for the door. 'Oh, Gabriel, I would like to invite you to dinner at my home tomorrow night after work. Seven o'clock, please. I think you know where I live now.'

Without waiting for an answer he left again leaving Samir and Gabriel in astonished silence.

'I wonder if he actually intends to do any more work at any point,' muttered Samir. 'I think you need to have a word with him, Gabriel.'

Gabriel smiled. Despite his clear irritation, there was still no chance that the submissive Samir would challenge a superior.

'Have you heard anything from Thanuja today, Priyantha?' asked Gabriel as she climbed into the car that evening, hauling the morbid burden of her abaya behind her.

'No ma'am. I am very worried. I have spoken to Thanuja's sponsor and he has tried to contact the Tahas. There is no one at their house, he called round two times today but the family are not there. We do not know where they have gone and we do not know where Thanuja is.' Priyantha bit his bottom lip and his hands gripped the steering wheel, his knuckles blue, as he drove. They sat in silence, both crushed under the burden of mounting concern for Thanuja, their minds conjuring horrific scenarios which neither wished to commit to speech.

'I don't know what to suggest, Priyantha. I will go to the garden again tonight but I don't really think there is any point. I haven't seen her now for over two weeks. I suppose if I go, at least if she does return, she knows where to find me in the early evening.'

As she got out of the car, a flock of mynahs were pecking at something on the ground just outside the door to the apartment. Brazen, they stayed put as she passed close by. She looked down and saw that they were dissecting the fresh corpse of a rat, larger than the ginger kitten which had been kicked to death by the drivers, several months before. Gabriel gasped and some of the mynahs flew off. Those that were left followed her into the building with their icy, black eyes.

Gabriel shuddered as she remembered the conclusion she had drawn that awful day when the kitten was killed in the office car park. Saudi did indeed operate on the moral principles of a boys' boarding school; she was living in the land of The Lord of the Flies. She reflected that she now understood only a little more clearly than she had back in December, why it was taking so long for things in the country to change.

After eating the remainder of the risotto she had made the night before, she gathered her papers and returned to the walled garden. There was no sign of the rat, the mynahs had greedily devoured every molecule of its being. She shuddered again.

Haiku 55 – Jeddah to Market Hamilton via Blackberry
Mubaarak returns!
Rats infesting the compound
Still no Thanuja.

Haiku 56 – Market Hamilton to Jeddah via email
Mubaarak and rats
Are these connected events?
Hush my naughty mouth!

She sat for a while in the quiet of the garden, the grasses rustling gently, closed her eyes and saw Thanuja's beautiful face, felt the warmth of her familiar touch. She remembered Thanuja's soft palm, always flat on Gabriel's forearm, connected rather than the usual, more distant touch of a Westerner who would use only the fingertips. Gabriel stood, resolute and walked the short distance to the Tahas' villa.

The padlock was still in place on the gate, the villa was silent, shrouded in thick darkness. She walked underneath the canopy of the claustrophobic car port. The Tahas' car wasn't there. Sandy, grey dust and a couple of pieces of litter had gathered in the right angle between the driveway and the wall, they agitated in the gentle breeze. Gabriel noticed an A4 piece of paper, covered in Arabic writing, Sellotaped crookedly to the door from the garage into the house. She squinted at the undecipherable loops, dots and curves and tried the door. It was locked. She carefully picked at the corners of the Sellotape and peeled the paper away from the door. She ran upstairs to her apartment, powered up her scanner and made a copy before running back downstairs to reattach the paper exactly where it had been before.

Haiku 57 – Jeddah to Market Hamilton via email
Have started spying!
Thanuja's place deserted
Letter on the door

Haiku 58 – Market Hamilton to Jeddah via email
What does letter say?
Where can Thanuja have gone?
Back to Colombo?

Haiku 59 – Jeddah to Market Hamilton via email
Not to Colombo.
Priyantha would know by now.
Can't read Arabic.

The next morning she handed the photocopy to Priyantha.

'Priyantha, Thanuja did not come to the garden last night. I had a look around the house and there is no one there. Thanuja must have gone somewhere with the Tahas, they've taken the car. I did find a sheet of paper stuck to the door but I can't read it. Can you?'

'No ma'am, I can speak some Arabic but I cannot read or write in Arabic. I can take it to Thanuja's sponsor though tomorrow to translate, he is not here today.'

'I think that would be a good idea, Priyantha. I don't want to give it to anyone at Saraco in case it is something sensitive.'

'I understand, ma'am.' Priyantha's voice had lost its melody, his face had lost its glow and navy-blue shadows had developed, over the previous week, beneath his eyes.

'Are you OK, Priyantha? You don't look well.'

'I am very worried for my little cousin, ma'am. I have worked in this country many years. It is not a…' Priyantha hesitated, searching for the right word. 'It is not a gentle country, ma'am.'

'No, Priyantha, you are right. It is not gentle. Not gentle at all,' Gabriel agreed. Gentleness was indeed an alien concept in the land of The Lord of the Flies.

Later, Priyantha conveyed Gabriel to Mubaarak and Sureya's house and through the now familiar entry fortifications to arrive at the front door at exactly seven o'clock. Mubaarak stood, his expression uncomfortably benevolent on the steps, his tense hand outstretched to shake Gabriel's.

'This is a beautiful house, Mubaarak. Sureya kindly showed me the garden when I visited while you were away.' Gabriel was surprised to feel a pang of unease, unused to being alone with Mubaarak outside their professional environment, particularly among the fairy-tale surroundings of his marital home.

'Sureya is just finishing a video conference with one of the universities in the US. She couldn't schedule it any earlier because of the time difference. She may join us later, let's go inside and have something to drink while I speak to you.'

Across the hallway, the doors to the office, scene of Gabriel's interaction with the mysterious Sureya, were firmly shut. As they entered the next room along, Mubaarak irritably waved away the maids who were arranging plates and jugs on the low table. He reclined himself on one of the vast couches.

Hesitant, Gabriel assumed an upright, seated stance on the other couch. Mubaarak's socked feet were raised, their soles pointed uncomfortably proximal to Gabriel's face. Mubaarak fixed his cold eyes upon hers.

'Gabriel, Sureya took the decision to speak to you recently about things which must, at all costs be kept absolutely confidential,' Mubaarak spat the words and tapped his right index finger thrice into the palm of his left hand with 'at all costs'.

'I understand, Mubaarak, I have no intention of betraying your confidence.' Gabriel endeavoured to sound sincere, fearing that she had achieved the opposite as a result of trying too hard. Her unease was mounting, trapped inside Mubaarak and Sureya's fortified, feline, fairy castle. She longed for the arrival of Sureya, hoping another presence might help to dissipate the tension.

'I had expected that I would need to spend longer in the UK. Sureya and I concluded that there was a danger of unwanted speculation, particularly since a vocal minority are expressing such concern about the project at Saraco. We decided that the lowest risk option was to take you into our confidence, Gabriel,' Mubaarak continued. 'We need to deflect any unwanted intrusion into our lives at all costs and you are the person best placed to help us do that. Also Gabriel … there are things about you which I am sure you would not wish to be in the public domain.'

'Mubaarak, as I said, you have my complete assurance of confidentiality. I hope Philip is very much better now.' Gabriel shuffled, uncomfortable both at Mubaarak's innuendo and moreover, the proximity of his stockinged feet.

'Thank you, Gabriel, he is. I hope we are both clear where we stand,' Mubaarak looked again into her eyes, unsmiling, unsettling. After a hard, silent pause, Mubaarak passed her a plate and napkin.

'Help yourself to food, Gabriel, there's humus, tabouleh and cold mezze. Sureya and I don't normally eat until around ten o'clock, so I will not join you now. Can I offer you some mint tea?'

'I didn't realise that you wouldn't be having anything to eat, Mubaarak.' The situation was becoming more bizarre and uncomfortable as each minute passed.

'You go ahead please, Gabriel.' Mubaarak flapped his hand and looked surreptitiously at his watch. They sat in silence as Gabriel tried to force a sufficient volume of food down her tight throat so as not to cause offence.

Mubaarak's cold eyes remained focussed on her face. There was still no sign of Sureya.

As soon as she had finished her plateful, Gabriel tried to turn the conversation towards less choppy waters.

'How was the press conference, Mubaarak?'

'Ahhh, it was a great success, Gabriel. The government and the Royal family are delighted with what I am achieving at Saraco. All targets are being met. It is a slow journey, Gabriel, and very difficult to make progress like this in Saudi against such opposition. It is however, a journey which will ultimately bring those involved a great deal of kudos. So long as messages are managed, Gabriel, and confidentiality is preserved about … peripheral matters.'

Mubaarak appeared to have forgotten that Gabriel was familiar with the project's challenges, many of which she had personally overcome, as he lectured. He closed his eyes periodically, presumably to re-envision the glory of his performance at the press conference.

There followed a further episode of tense small talk about the project and yet a further round of reiterating how extensively she was being relied upon to maintain Mubaarak and Sureya's confidentiality. After a further thirty minutes and with no sign of Sureya, Gabriel tentatively suggested that she would leave them to get on with their evening.

Mubaarak seized upon the suggestion with a level of enthusiasm which verged on the impolite.

'Actually, before I go, Mubaarak, there is one small thing you could help me with,' she added. Mubaarak had already set out at a canter towards the door.

'Yes, Gabriel?' answered Mubaarak over his shoulder, consulting his watch again.

'I have made friends with a Sri Lankan girl in my compound and I am worried about her.'

Mubaarak's face dissolved into an expression of disinterested disbelief.

'The mother of the family she works for has been ill and she has been looking after the mother as well as the baby for whose care she was originally employed. There was some sort of incident the other night and I have not seen…'

Mubaarak held his hand in the air, palm towards Gabriel, shaking his head.

'Gabriel, why are you troubling me with the problems of a low class Sri Lankan servant?'

Gabriel reeled. 'Mubaarak, she is my friend and I am worried about her. It is only right to try to help another human being whom you think may be in trouble,' she replied, her irritation with the events of the peculiar evening and the non-appearance of Sureya bubbling to the surface.

'Well, you shouldn't be making friends with servants, Gabriel. If this becomes known at Saraco, it will reflect badly on the project. I refuse to become involved in conversations about these people.'

He sneered as he uttered the words 'these people' and started again for the door.

'Mubaarak, I cannot believe you are reacting like this. She is a human being and she may need help.'

Mubaarak turned, his face suddenly angry. 'Gabriel, do not presume to lecture me on right and wrong. I have warned you, it will reflect badly on the project if you are seen to be fraternising with the lower classes. Leave them to look after themselves.'

He stalked through the hallway, spoke in sharp, rapid Arabic to a maid standing by the door and left Gabriel with her to wait for Priyantha on the doorstep.

'Good evening, ma'am, how was your evening?' Priyantha endeavoured to maintain normal courtesies in the face of their shared stresses.

'It was very strange, Priyantha. I think I will get an early night. We can get that paper translated by Thanuja's sponsor tomorrow. Hopefully that will help us track Thanuja down,' she replied.

'I hope so too, ma'am,'

They travelled in silence back to the compound.

Haiku 60 – Jeddah to Market Hamilton via email
Ate in Fairyland.
Mubaarak predictable.
Sureya no show.

Haiku 61 – Market Hamilton to Jeddah via email
Sureya is cat
Woman? Colm is so happy,
Rosemary superb.

The next morning, Priyantha went to see Thanuja's sponsor immediately after dropping Gabriel at the office.

The sponsor wore a grubby gutrah and sat behind his vast desk in the darkness. An ashtray erupted grey matter, sweet papers and brown cigarette butts which flowed like lava across the wooden surface. White circles, relieved of their varnish intersected in Olympiad patterns partially hidden under mountains of paper.

'I've been to look for the girl twice already. I'm losing patience with her.' He barked, irritated as Priyantha entered.

'Habib'bi, I am concerned that something has happened to her. Please would you take a look at this? It may help us find her, Insha'Allah.'

The sponsor impatiently snatched the photocopy and glanced at it. 'This says the house is back in the hands of the landlord. The Tahas' second rent cheque for the year must have been dishonoured by the bank or they've just gone away without paying and he's going to re-let. I doubt I'll ever get what they owe me now either.' The sponsor was furious, threw the paper on his desk and shook his head.

'Does it say anything about where they've gone, habib'bi? I need to find my cousin.'

'No it doesn't. And I need to find my money.'

Priyantha sat on the chair in the sponsor's office and put his head in his hands. The two men maintained an icy silence until eventually the sponsor shattered the surface.

'I have things to do today, Priyantha. You have always worked well for me and I am always happy to help your family get work here but these girls disappear all the time. They disappear and we get a new one from abroad. That's how life is, Priyantha, they are just foreign girls who come to work for the Saudis. You have to let it go, habib'bi.'

Priyantha felt his stomach churn. He knew he was about

to succumb to the days and nights of stress, to lose control. He was unsure how the loss of control would manifest closeted with the sponsor in his dark, stinking office. He had made the mistake of selling his loyalty and his soul to the sponsor many years before, bringing girls and boys over to Saudi from Sri Lanka and enjoying a steady flow of introduction fees into the bargain. Nothing had gone wrong before, everyone had earned enough money to make a big difference to their families back home. At that moment he realised the extent of his enslavement, his powerlessness. The life of a foreign girl was worth less to these people than the life of a dog. It was time to rethink what he was doing. He felt himself quiver and was horrified to experience, for the first time in many years, the warm flow of tears on his face.

'Thank you for your help, my friend,' Priyantha stammered, blindly groping and gathering his 'phone. He ran from the suffocation of the office to the car.

While Priyantha was with the sponsor, Samir and Gabriel were waiting in the office for a tardy Mubaarak.

'Where is he this morning? Gabriel, you're going to have to speak to him, we have a meeting with the board in an hour and he hasn't given me his presentation yet.' Samir was relying on his go-between as usual in times of potential conflict. Gabriel smiled, what would she have done without Samir to support and entertain her in the office?

'Don't worry, Samir, we can manage on our own if he doesn't make it. You know all this now like the back of your hand. It could be your chance to shine.'

Samir was swelling gently with pride as Mubaarak hopped through the door and plopped a copy of Arab News on the desk.

'There is very positive coverage of the progress Saraco are making with employing women in Arab News this morning. The board and I did a great job at the press conference.'

'That's excellent news, Mubaarak, may I have a look?' Gabriel pulled the newspaper towards her and raised an eyebrow at the photograph of the CEO shaking Mubaarak's hand before a row of veiled ladies and a conspicuously positioned Saraco logo. The article was indeed excellent, Mubaarak was right.

'Samir, I will be finished in a minute, you should look at this and be very proud,' she said.

Before she had finished reading, her eye was drawn down the page to the next article. The headline beneath the picture of beaming Mubaarak, caught her eye. She gasped as she read on, grabbing the newspaper off the desk, bringing it closer to her face, to Samir's evident surprise.

Baby drowned in Bath by nanny – Arabian Villas Compound

On al-'ahad: 3. Djumada l-Akhira 1434 (Gregorian calendar 14th April 2013), police were called to a house on the Arabian Villas compound, Jeddah at 8.30p.m. On their arrival, they found a three month old baby dead in the villa. He had been drowned in the bath by his nanny. The nanny, from Colombo in Sri Lanka, was immediately arrested, detained in the police station in the city and then executed at the square by the Queen's building last Friday.

The baby's parents, Mr and Mrs Taha understandably did not grant clemency in view of the seriousness of the crime and the devastating effect it will have on them and their family for many years to come.

We pray that God will be merciful and care for Mr and Mrs Taha and their family at this terrible time.

The intensity with which Gabriel slammed the newspaper back down onto the desk was such that not only Samir and Mubaarak, who were in the office, but also others on the same floor of the building were jolted from what they were doing. Gabriel would be the subject of conversation in Saudi Arabia for many years to come. The thunderous clap when she slammed down the newspaper would assume greater prominence in subsequent accounts than the extent to which she contributed to the more balanced workforce at Saraco and the pride and praise enjoyed by the board as a result of her efforts.

'Whatever is the matter, Gabriel?' Mubaarak's tone was ninety nine percent irritation and one percent concern.

'It's Thanuja, they are saying she drowned the Tahas' baby. She's been executed.'

Speaking the words did not make them more believable. She tried to rationalise the situation, to grasp a tiny thread of golden hope that there had been some mistake, that Thanuja was still alive, that the world was a logical, compassionate and merciful place.

The events of the night in the compound had haunted Gabriel. Thanuja had been excessively concerned about Mrs Taha's state of mind that evening. There had been no indication that Thanuja had just fled from the scene of a drowning. If she had, she would not have come to the garden where she could easily be found, she would not have stood where she could easily be seen and made 'phone calls to her cousin. Certainly, if she had just drowned the Taha's baby, she would not have run back to the villa as she had. Gabriel pictured Thanuja dropping the 'phone and running back to the villa after the never-ending scream. As her mind coursed again and again through the chain of events, she concluded categorically it was inconceivable that Thanuja was guilty.

Gabriel forced herself to think further, blocking out Mubaarak's hectoring drone. Samir had long since disappeared on pretext of an errand. Gabriel had run away from the walled garden to the clubhouse to make the 'phone call. She was away from the proximity of the Tahas' villa for around twenty minutes. Long enough for the police to come and take Thanuja away. Someone had closed and locked the gate by the time she got back. Had they closed it and locked it behind Thanuja who could, by then, already have been on her way to prison?

'These foreign girls are sometimes untrustworthy with the children the Saudi citizens allow into their care, Gabriel. They have to be punished when their careless actions lead to something terrible like this. I suggest you take the rest of the day off until you have calmed down and are able to behave in a proper and professional way.'

Mubaarak's bleating popped up like the ridiculous head of a meerkat from somewhere in the recesses of Gabriel's consciousness. She looked up at him to see him shake his head and look down at the screen of his laptop.

'Mubaarak, Mrs Taha was suffering from depression, no one would allow her to see a doctor. She was alone with the baby when this happened. I heard her scream from the house and Thanuja ran back to see what was wrong. She would have had no idea that the baby had died when she went back to the house. Thanuja was a very intelligent young woman, if she had just murdered a child, why on earth would she run back to the scene of her crime?'

'Gabriel, in this country, the penalty for death is death. You will recall that murderers were executed in Britain until comparatively recently.'

'But only after a trial, Mubaarak, not just at the whim of a depressed woman and her disinterested husband. The husband was at work most of the time, leaving Thanuja to look after his wife and the baby. I reiterate, Mubaarak, just in case you are still not clear. There is no way Thanuja murdered that baby. There is no justice when there is no evidence and no fair trial.'

'Gabriel, the Tahas are a respectable, Arabic family. This girl was just a young maid from abroad who had the privilege to be here working for them. I told you before not to become involved with these people. Please be sensible, go back to your compound and come back to work when you have calmed down sufficiently to behave in a professional manner.' He picked up his 'phone and started to make a call. After a short while someone answered.

'Priyantha, is that you? Please come to the office now and collect Miss Gabriel. She will be returning to the compound early.'

He started to tap on his keyboard, shaking his head slowly from side to side as Samir re-entered the office. Gabriel looked in Samir's direction but he avoided her eyes, head tucked into his chest, sorting fervently through the papers on the desk. When he noticed that she was still staring at him, he stood up and hurried again from the office.

When she and Mubaarak were alone again, Gabriel forced herself to speak, her voice searing as though broken glass was lodged in her throat. 'Mubaarak, you expected and have enjoyed my loyalty and confidentiality, even though your lifestyle is one which is contrary to everything your religion teaches. When I ask for loyalty and a tiny measure of human compassion from you, you refuse. How does that work, Mubaarak?'

Mubaarak's eyes narrowed and his voice assumed a razor edge. 'Gabriel, if you try to make trouble for me or for Sureya, I will personally ensure you are arrested and deported for your...' he hesitated, his mouth working to form a word '...your lesbianism,' he spat eventually.

Gabriel's mouth fell open and she felt a vacuum form in her chest as though all her organs descended to the floor. 'I am not a lesbian, Mubaarak, this is your obsession not mine. You are a hypocrite, your whole life is a fairy tale and a lie, your outward observance of Islam and the teachings of the prophet are all a hideous act of deceit. You disgust me and I never wish to see or hear from you again.'

Mubaarak's teeth shone like steel as a shaft of sunlight leaked behind the sunshade and caught the side of his face, throwing sharp, angular shadows across his cheekbones. 'Be very careful, Gabriel, you are a non-Muslim, a woman and a foreigner. You have no power here in Saudi Arabia and you are making me very angry. Very, very angry.'

Gabriel shoved her belongings into her bag and ran from the office, gathering her abaya around her knees so she did not trip as she tackled the emergency staircase, rather than wait for the ladies' lift. She flew out of the door into the car park just as Priyantha drew through the gate. She gasped as she realised she must now calm herself and tackle the awful task of breaking the news about Thanuja to Priyantha.

Priyantha stood and walked around to open the door. His gait was stooped, his step stiff as though he had aged over thirty years in the previous two weeks. Gabriel sat in the back of the car, placed her bags gently beside her. As she started to speak, Priyantha raised his eyes so she was looking directly at him in the mirror. The blurred intensity of their reflected connection was insufficient, she concluded, for the task in hand.

'Priyantha, I need to talk to you. I cannot speak to the back of your head. Please park the car at the side of the road and I will come and sit beside you.'

'Ma'am, this is not possible. If the police see us talking together in the car, I will be arrested and so will you.'

Gabriel raised her hands and shrugged in despair, her patience exhausted with the meaningless strictures and restrictions while the gentle, balanced teachings of the Qur'an and the prophet were being flouted and abused.

'Priyantha, please then will you drive to the compound as quickly as you are able and we will speak there behind the walls.'

'Yes, ma'am, of course. I did have the paper translated, ma'am, by the sponsor.'

In despair at the futility, Gabriel enquired as to the result.

'I do not think it is good news, ma'am. The Tahas' house has been passed back to the landlord and he will be letting to new tenants. No one is able to trace the Tahas or Thanuja.'

Gabriel hung her head, willing the journey to be over.

When they reached the compound, Priyantha stopped the car by the apartment as he had done every evening for the previous six months.

'Priyantha, please come into the garden with me, Thanuja and I used to talk there every evening.'

They walked the short distance in silence, sat on the bench together and Gabriel turned to face the grey, tense ghost of her friend and former driver.

'Priyantha, Thanuja has been executed. There is an article today in the Arab News. The Tahas accused her of drowning the baby and she was executed last Friday. She had been in prison, which is why we could not find her.'

Priyantha made the sign of the cross, bowed his head, closed his eyes and allowed the tears to course down his face and drip unstaunched onto his shirt and then his hands, joined between his knees. They sat in silence together except for the occasional shriek of a mynah and the omnipresent whisper of the grasses in the garden.

Eventually Priyantha spoke. 'Will you stay, ma'am?'

'No, Priyantha, I will leave as soon as I can get a flight back to the UK.'

Gabriel had not been conscious she had already made the decision to return but realised as she spoke that her purpose was clarifying. She needed to get out of Saudi, back to the UK and meet with Sister Anthony and Michael as soon as she could.

'Ma'am, I will take you to the airport and then return to Colombo to speak to Thanuja's family.'

'Will you come back again to Saudi, Priyantha?'

'I am not sure, ma'am. I will pray to God tonight and ask him to help me with this. I need to…' he hesitated, again searching for the words, '…to make so much bad, good again.'

'I understand, Priyantha.'

They sat together in Thanuja's garden until Priyantha felt it was time for him to leave. He stood, slow, awkward, a shocking contrast with the leonine athleticism of the new young driver who had arrived several months before, following the incident with the ginger kitten in the office car park.

'Shall I collect you in the morning, ma'am?'

'No thank you, Priyantha, I will prepare and hand over the documents for the Saraco project from my apartment and let you know the time of my flight as soon as I can.'

As Priyantha walked away, the moon glimpsed above the wall into Thanuja's garden and bathed the grasses in its luminescence. In response, thousands of golden threads shimmered and danced in the gentle breeze. Golden threads reminiscent of Thanuja's golden threads of hope.

Gabriel vaulted from the bench and ran after Priyantha, catching him just as he was getting into the car.

'Priyantha, I know how you can make the bad good again. Thanuja has a son, Sean. She has never been happy about him living with her parents. She wanted a good education for him and a different future to the one she was able to have. That is what she was working for. That is how we can make this right.'

Priyantha smiled, the golden moon warming the glimpses of his teeth and eyes amidst the cold, stony grey of his face.

'Thank you, ma'am. I will pray about this tonight.'

Back in the apartment, Gabriel opened her laptop and started her preparations to leave the land of the lord of the flies.

Sister Anthony

I am afraid I have had some very bad news today about Thanuja. In my last email, I mentioned that she had gone missing after some sort of incident with the family for whom she was working. I was horrified to read in the newspaper earlier today that she has been in prison and was executed last Friday. The newspaper report says that the baby in her care was drowned in the bath and that Thanuja murdered him. Sister, I am certain that this is not true but there has been no evidence and no trial here, the execution happened within days, seemingly based solely on the Tahas' account of events.

When I expressed my concern about this to Mubaarak, he was very clear that this is how things happen here. If the parents do not wish to show clemency, quite frankly there is nothing a young, foreign servant can do and as this all happened so quickly and subversively, no one else had the opportunity to intervene.

Sister, this event and the reaction of the press and local people here is a message to me. I have taken the decision to return to the UK as soon as I can and to work on raising awareness of the appalling divergence between the balanced teachings of the Qur'an and the prophet Muhammad and the thuggish, bullying behaviour of the Muslims here in real life in the twenty first century.

Sister, you mentioned that you and Michael were finishing your work in Africa soon. When will you be in the UK so we can meet?

With love

Gabriel

Haiku 62 – Jeddah to Market Hamilton by email
Greatest tragedy
Radiant beauty gone. Rebuild
Goodness, compassion.

Haiku 63 – Market Hamilton to Jeddah by email
Whatever happened?
When can you call me today?
You're worrying me.

Mubaarak

We now have one hundred ladies working at Saraco, our processes and procedures are in place. Everything is now set up to enable the company to grow and develop their female workforce. In the circumstances, therefore, I feel that the time has come to hand over my role in the project to one of the local people to ensure continuity and sustainability of the good work we have all done.

I plan to return to the UK soon but over the next few days will prepare all materials to enable that handover to happen. I will remain contactable over the coming weeks to support the project remotely should this be required.

The events of this week and indeed the last few months have clarified for me that there are other priorities on which I must now focus. I anticipate,

Mubaarak that you are familiar with the Hadith of Gabriel and would respectfully request that you spend some time reflecting upon it. Sadly I feel that what I have experienced in Saudi is a microcosm of a widespread divergence between the true framework of Islam, Iman and Ihsham and the behaviours of some of those who represent themselves as Muslims.

I hope that you and Sureya will be well

Gabriel

Gabriel never received a reply to her email and had no direct contact with Mubaarak ever again. She received a reply from Sister Anthony within hours.

Gabriel

This is terrible news and a tragedy.

Thanuja is in mine and Michael's prayers. We are arranging for a mass to be said for her here at the local church in Accra before we leave for the UK. Doctor Mensah who will be taking over from us here is an impressive lady. It has taken her no time at all to become well-installed and respected by her team around her. We are therefore hoping that we will be free to leave next week.

Michael and I will be staying at the convent in Market Hamilton when we return. I will email you details of our arrival and we look forward to seeing you soon.

Take care, Gabriel, and may the strength of the Lord help you in your sadness

Sister Anthony

CHAPTER 20

Jeddah, Saudi Arabia

July 2013 (Gregorian calendar)

Gabriel spent her final, solitary days in the chocolate apartment, working on her handover notes in a foggy daze. Her limbs were leaden, her joints ached and as she worked, she frequently retired to lie on the unwelcoming couch, to close her eyes in an attempt to relieve herself of the chiselling headache vandalising her skull. The horror of Thanuja's execution and the acceptance of those around her, that the murder of a servant girl provided closure, tested her both emotionally and physically.

She managed to secure a flight for her return and packed as many of her possessions as was possible in the two suitcases she had brought when she arrived. She telephoned Priyantha to advise him of her plans.

'Hello Priyantha, I have a flight arranged, can you come and take me to the airport at eleven p.m. please on Saturday evening?'

'Yes ma'am. I too will book my return next week. I have spoken to the sponsor about this. He is angry but he understands that I will go home now.'

'That is good news, Priyantha. Do you need any help with anything? I have a contact in Sri Lanka called Sister Mary, she is Thanuja's old teacher. We were working together to try to find some charitable funding to enable Thanuja to continue her education … before all this happened.'

Gabriel realised that she had not contacted Sister Mary to advise her of Thanuja's death. She wondered also whether Priyantha would have let Thanuja's parents know, whether anyone would ever talk to Sean about what happened to his mother when he grew up.

'Ma'am, thank you for your help. When I get to Sri Lanka, I will visit Thanuja's parents. My sister and her husband are good people and they will be happy to look after Sean. I will make the…' he hesitated, searching for an appropriate word in English, 'the deal, ma'am, with Thanuja's family when I am back home. I hope Sister Mary will be able to help my sister and her husband with Sean's education.'

'I am sure she would be happy to do anything she can, Priyantha. I will tell her you will call on her at Thanuja's old school when you get back.'

Gabriel stuffed those belongings which would not fit into the suitcases into two plastic bin liners and heaped them in the small hallway. She wrote a note to the compound facilities manager advising of her departure, reminding him that her rent was paid until the end of the year and asking him to donate her possessions to a workers' charity of his choice.

Early on Saturday evening as she sat alone amongst her luggage, a car drew up in the parking area outside the apartment. Its black windows reflected the harsh, angular distortions from the setting sun. As Gabriel watched from her window, she witnessed Sureya climb from the car and approach the building with feline grace. The intercom shrieked and she picked up the handset.

'Gabriel, it is Sureya, please may I come in.'

Gabriel pressed the buzzer, opened the utilitarian front door, stood and waited.

Sureya exited the lift and stalked the short distance across the corridor in silence. She was wearing a heavy, black abaya which wove a fluttering wake as she walked. Her face was covered with a pair of immense sunglasses and her hair enshrouded beneath a veil. She raised her hand to her temple and the needle points of her polished nails reflected the light from the small staircase window. She took off her sunglasses, wordlessly passed Gabriel who stood in the doorway and entered the apartment. In the sitting room, she claimed the space as her own, then turned to face Gabriel.

'Gabriel, thank you for seeing me. I will be brief. When we met before, I thought we had created an understanding between us. I must confess to being shocked that you find it acceptable, at this point, to leave Mubaarak at Saraco with no notice. This is making things very difficult for everyone, Gabriel.' Sureya's face was still, the razor tips of her small, sharp teeth showed between blood-red lips as she enunciated each word in her faultless, upper class English accent.

'Sureya, I am not sure what Mubaarak has told you but I am unable to stay here after the events with Thanuja. I need to return to the UK and do what I can to change things from there.'

Sureya twitched, her flaming eyes turned their full power upon Gabriel's face.

'What do you mean, change things? Who are you, Gabriel, to decide what requires changing and what does not?'

'Sureya, Thanuja was executed without a trial for a crime which I am certain she did not commit. Her employer and his mentally ill wife were able to pass unfettered judgement over whether she lived or died. Moreover, the press and everyone I speak to in this country appear to consider this an acceptable form of justice.'

Sureya stepped closer to Gabriel, her hot, red breath pulsed on Gabriel's face as she licked her lips with a flick of her pointed tongue.

'Gabriel, let me be very clear. I am sure Mubaarak explained to you that these people are privileged to get visas and work permits to come and work for us here in Saudi. Our courts are managed under Allah's guidance and according to his law.'

'Sureya, I am afraid that I do not agree. The teachings of Muhammad and the words of the Qur'an are a very long way away from what I have seen here in Saudi. There are some small things changing but while the rulers and the majority of the men behave as they do, and the women continue to put up with it, things will never change quickly enough.'

Sureya continued to stare into Gabriel's eyes in silence. Gabriel sensed her adjust something in her hands, there was a sharp metallic 'click' and for a moment Gabriel's chest constricted with cold fear. She glanced downwards and was relieved to see that Sureya was unwrapping her sunglasses rather than handling more murderous equipment.

'Gabriel, you are a Christian and a foreigner, you know nothing of Muhammad, the Qur'an, nor indeed of justice.'

Gabriel hesitated. How much should she reveal to this woman? Was it too soon? A gentle, invisible urging at her shoulder bade her proceed.

'Sureya, I know every single word of the Qur'an. I know also Muhammad's reaction to each when it was dictated to him.'

Sureya's face assumed an expression of sneering astonishment. She slowly turned her head from side to side. 'Gabriel, I tend to agree with my husband that your mind appears to have become unbalanced. Perhaps the project at Saraco is beyond your capabilities and you are suffering from stress. Maybe it is better for everyone if you do leave, after all.'

'Sureya, I leave with a clear conscience. Do you and Mubaarak have clear consciences?' she hesitated before continuing. 'I will not let this rest, Sureya. I will continue with what I have started here when I return to the UK.'

They stood opposite one another in silence for several seconds; two lionesses, circling one another, weighing up the consequences.

'Gabriel, Mubaarak and I have a lifestyle and privileges here which we will fight to protect. Be clear that I will stop at nothing and I mean absolutely nothing if you or anyone else threaten our stability or security in any way. The servant girl is dead, no one takes any notice, because it is not important. If girls allow babies in their care to die, they will be punished.' Sureya spat as she spoke her final words: hot, acidic droplets stung onto Gabriel's lips. Sureya raised her hand and replaced her sunglasses, closing the door on her burning eyes. She turned swiftly, her morbid garment swirling like a deadly, black mist around her back as she let herself out of the apartment.

Priyantha arrived at eleven as agreed. Gabriel left her key in the lock, descended with her suitcases and bags in the lift and took her final journey through the filthy streets and perilous traffic of Jeddah. Despite the hour, at the start of Ramadan the roads were packed. On the pavements, queues of men spilled from the fast-food outlets, gorging under cover of darkness. Once the sun rose again, they would recommence their fasting for another fifteen hours until the next night of gluttony.

At the seething airport, Priyantha placed her suitcases on a rusty trolley borne by a skinny, twitching Indian porter. Gabriel extended her hand, and she and Priyantha stood, hands joined in silence for several seconds.

'I am very happy, ma'am, that you were Thanuja's friend. Thank you.'

'Thank you too, Priyantha. I will contact Sister Mary next week. Please will you let her know how I can get in touch with you in Sri Lanka? We are all going to support you and your sister to get help with Sean and provide him with everything he needs for the future.'

'Thank you, ma'am, you are a very good person. God bless you.'

They ignored for several seconds, the stares, spits and hisses from the crowd, disapproving of the woman with the uncovered head, interacting so intimately in public with someone who looked, for all the world, like her driver. Eventually Gabriel let Priyantha's hand go, he dropped his head, turned and got back into the car, tears splashing onto his shirt, trails of mucus unchecked on his upper lip.

Gabriel slept throughout the flight; a sweating, fitful sleep interrupted by chilling hallucinations featuring the executed Thanuja's corpse with the orphaned Sean, climbing onto her body. Just before landing she awoke as someone gently laid their hand on her arm.

'We're nearly there, sister. You have been very uneasy and seemed hot while sleeping on the flight, are you feeling OK?' Her neighbour was a young Saudi woman, about Thanuja's age dressed in a black abaya and veil.

'Yes thank you, I am fine. I do hope I didn't disturb you. I am a bit ... stressed about a couple of things and was probably dreaming as a result.'

'I am sorry to hear that, sister. Do not worry about disturbing me, I am fine. I have a car booked to pick me up and take me into Manchester from the airport if you need a lift anywhere, to save you waiting while you are feeling so ... tired.'

'Thank you, I am fine, I have a taxi arranged,' answered Gabriel

'That's good, sister,' said the young woman, gathering her belongings as the plane landed. 'Please take care of yourself and get well soon, Insha'Allah.'

She walked away, straight-backed, assertive, head held high and proud, into the crowd; a portent of hope for the future.

CHAPTER 21

'Bennets', Market Hamilton, Yorkshire, United Kingdom

July 2013

Gabriel sat and finished her coffee and Lebkuchen in the security of Shylah's office, or was it Colm's office now? She wondered. She helped herself to a couple more scrumptious Lebkuchen from the crimson and gold packet. The last few weeks had pummelled her mind and body; comfort food and being back in Yorkshire would soon do the trick. The visions of Thanuja's broken body, with Sean clutching at the mangled remnants of his mother, crept repeatedly onto her shoulder, round her neck and into her eyes. She closed them and shook her head, the surface of the vision cracked, shattered and fell in sharp, cubic particles. As time passed, the vision's intensity was waning. It crept upon her less frequently now.

Ella stood and rested her head on Gabriel's thigh, a hint of panic in her deep brown eyes as Gabriel started to eat the last Lebkuchen in the packet. That was a whole box gone and Ella had received nothing so far. Not so much as a crumb! She nuzzled a little more insistently.

Gabriel looked down and caved in immediately to the innocent, imploring Ella. Shylah would be horrified.

Checking to make sure that neither Shylah nor Colm were within spying distance, she tucked the final half biscuit between Ella's gentle, velvety lips.

'Don't tell them, Ella,' she whispered.

'Don't tell who, what?' Gabriel was unsure whether the slender, female silhouette in the doorway who spoke had actually seen the misdemeanour or simply caught its protagonist silencing the primary witness.

'Umm, I was…'

The silhouette interrupted, saving Gabriel the necessity of fabrication.

'I'm Rosemary,' it said, 'Gabriel, it is great to see you. Shylah, Colm and Ella never stop talking about you so I recognised you straightaway from their description. Oh, and I've seen your Dad in your garden at the cottage a few times, too, but he doesn't talk, obviously. Are you back for good or is this just a visit?'

On hearing Rosemary's voice, Gabriel realised with delight that she and the silhouette had met before; more than once, in fact many times, in many places. For the third time, Gabriel hastily confirmed that she had returned from Saudi for good. She opened her mouth again, hoping to continue the conversation, rebuild their connection, but the silhouette continued.

'I'm going to take over from Shylah in the shop now, give you two some time to be together and chat. We'll catch up again another time.'

The silhouette retreated from the doorway and Gabriel remembered with affection that Rosemary, whatever the time or place, was not a great one for letting others get a word in edgeways.

Ella looked from one woman to the other, made her (difficult) choice and slumped down again on top of Gabriel's feet. Gabriel leant down, placed her hand on top of the dog's velvet head and smoothed her warm fur. She noticed the cut from the glass in the 'phone, sustained in Thanuja's garden on the night of Mrs Taha's scream. It was nearly healed; already only a small, barely perceptible scar remained. Within a couple of days, it would be gone.

Once Gabriel had told her that she didn't want to be alone, Shylah had immediately made the decision to move out of the flat above Bennets and into Gabriel's cottage. Sister Anthony had already said in her email that there was work for them all to do and that she would need Shylah's help. Gabriel had also mentioned that Sister Anthony and indeed, to her great surprise, the glorious Michael were due to return from Africa next week. Despite having been completely out of touch for years, it seemed that Gabriel had become Sister Anthony's number one confidante! Shylah was surprised that she no longer felt so much as an iota of irritation at the interesting realignment of allegiances. Perhaps she was getting old; perhaps she was so secure in Gabriel and Sister Anthony's affections that rivalry was irrelevant; perhaps she was just excited and looking forward to whatever was to come. She felt energised, buzzing and something as yet undefined loomed upon the horizon, was it something good or something which would test her to the limit? Either way, she was confident that everything would become clear very soon.

Shylah spent all day Monday packing her clothes and the small number of other possessions which would be of no use at all to Colm or Rosemary; everything else she would need was already at Gabriel's cottage. The activity was oddly cathartic, a new beginning, spreading like the vast skies and muted landscape of the escarpment of East Yorkshire from the Wolds. The artist David Hockney flew into her thoughts. His landscape paintings were a reflection of her state of mind. She laughed to herself. Such erudite thoughts were more like those of Gabriel rather than practical, dependable, smiling Shylah.

'Mum, you don't have to leave. We are all fine here, the three of us. It feels like we have been making you feel unwelcome,' Colm was concerned and Shylah had the distinct impression that Rosemary had insisted he convey the message as a matter of priority.

'I know I don't have to go, Colm, but I want to make some changes. Bennets has been my whole life, along with bringing up my wonderful son, for years now. It's time for a change.'

'But Mum, you can have a change without feeling like you have to leave your home.' Colm's anxious face precipitated a tug deep in Shylah's womb. His expression was that of the small, anxious, clumsy boy who had been so delighted to start his new school in Market Hamilton; who had so proudly worked behind the counter in Bennets with his Mum and Aunty Gabriel; who had successfully launched the online business and who had recently announced that Rosemary and he were together.

'Colm love, that's not how I feel. The cottage has always been like a second home to us both anyway and if I am honest, I think Gabriel needs me at the moment. I want to give you and Rosemary some space too. It is a tiny bit like being a gooseberry at the moment in the flat,' she smiled, willing Colm to join in the joke.

He smiled weakly and shrugged his shoulders, accepting rather than jocund.

'Would you help me carry these things to the car?'

Colm picked up the bags and walked towards the door. Rosemary was waiting immediately outside.

'You've made your decision,' she said, the upward inflection of her voice questioning rather than a statement.

'Yes, decision made, and very happily made. Thanks to you both, I have the opportunity to go and do something different now, knowing everything will be fine here.'

Rosemary picked up one of the bags and started down the stairs to the car. Midway she stopped with a small shriek.

'You're not taking Ella, are you?' There was a note of panic in her voice.

'Don't worry, Ella will always call this home and we're only a walk away anyway, I'm sure she'll come and play in the garden just as frequently as she does already.'

The next day, Colm called to see Shylah at the cottage immediately after closing the shop.

'I've just to make sure you're settled, Mum,' he said as he entered, passing Gabriel in the hallway, 'is there anything else you need me to bring over? I found a couple of your books so I've got them in a bag for you here. Is there anything else?'

Gabriel seized her opportunity. 'Colm, do you mind if I just pop over to the shop and buy one of those packets of Lebkuchen from you. Is Rosemary there at the moment to let me in?'

'Yes, that's fine, Gabriel. Have you developed some sort of addiction while you were in Saudi?' he laughed, handing her the keys. 'I can ring the doorbell when I get back. Take these, just in case Rosemary is in the cellar and doesn't hear you.'

'Thanks Colm. Why don't you and your Mum sit down for a while and have a coffee or a glass of wine.'

Gabriel walked towards the town, stroked by the warmth of the still, summer evening. It was still light but as she looked up, the sky darkened and swirled in churning, black spirals. The thousands of starlings dipped, whistled and flung across the sky. The energy and beauty of the murmeration stopped her in her tracks. That was the sign I have been waiting for, she reflected, and quickened her pace towards Bennets.

When she reached 45 High Street, she let herself into the shop. Everything was in darkness except for a shaft of halogen light from the cellar staircase.

'Rosemary it's me, Gabriel,' she called towards the staircase. She didn't want to creep up and scare the life out of Rosemary in the cellar. 'I've just come to collect some biscuits to take to the cottage but could we have a quick chat while I'm here, please?'

Rosemary's head appeared above the steps and she clicked the light switch.

As the bulb warmed up, before Rosemary's eyes, Gabriel's imposing presence was flooded from behind by a luminescent rainbow, first blue and violet then steadily brightening to embrace the full spectrum. Her backlit hair glowed silver and the golden fabric of her diaphanous garment shone luminescent like burnished gold. Gabriel loomed like a Brocken spectre above Rosemary as she stood, paralysed, close to the top of the cellar steps.

'Do you know why I am here, Rosemary?' Gabriel's voice echoed, more resonant, more musical than usual. The scent of ginger lifted on the air, carried by a gentle breeze.

'I am not quite sure, Gabriel, not one hundred percent sure.' Rosemary heard her own voice, echoing from somewhere else, as though she were outside her body, observing the scene from a distance.

'Rosemary, you have a role to play which is of greater significance than any one on earth can even imagine. The joy you will encounter in the future will be immeasurable, Rosemary, but there are challenging times ahead for us all. You more than most must be strong.'

Rosemary climbed the remaining stairs from the cellar and entered the shop. A comforting warmth emanated from the luminescent Gabriel. Rosemary felt herself relax. The tension of anticipation had been with her for many years. Now that it had happened, she was flooded with warm relief which outweighed the fear of what was to come.

'Gabriel, I am sorry but I do not understand fully yet what is required of me this time.' It was as though someone else were speaking the words simultaneously with the rush of strength which coursed through her body, 'I am willing to do what is asked of me but I am confused about exactly what that is.'

'That is all that is needed for now, Rosemary. Do not worry, everything will become clearer very soon and there will be people with you to support you.'

Rosemary stayed silent, trying to make sense of what she had been told. She shook her head in confusion as she looked back at Gabriel and was surprised to find herself disappointed rather than relieved that the spectacle of a few moments ago was gone. Gabriel's appearance had returned to that of the strong, handsome woman whom she had met briefly that afternoon. The two women smiled, a gentle, silent connection before Gabriel turned to leave. As she opened the door, the cool breeze rustled again through the shop bearing the scent of ginger.

'Gabriel,' called Rosemary.

Gabriel turned as Rosemary picked a red and gold packet from one of the shelves and approached the door.

'Don't forget your biscuits,' she said, handing the packet to Gabriel who tucked them into her bag, smiling broadly and waving on her way out.

Colm and Rosemary expanded their possessions and daily activities to absorb the enhanced accommodation of the whole flat above Bennets, surprising themselves as they realised how much they enjoyed the extra space and feeling more than a little guilty about the extent to which they enjoyed being alone, without Shylah. They discussed a future which included them both, united in the face of whatever challenges life had in store. Bill came frequently to the cottage garden and the robin sang his encouraging three arpeggios from the apple tree each day.

Ella settled into a dual-location lifestyle which suited her very well indeed. She had lots of time to spend with all her favourite people and plenty of opportunity to ferret in the garden at the cottage where several new and exciting small mammals had taken up residence in a fascinating network of burrows and mounds. Every burrow and every mound would, in due course, require thorough investigation and Ella considered herself up to the task. An added bonus was that everyone was so very busy talking or working these days that they seldom remembered to check with one another whether she had already been fed. Double helpings were on the menu more frequently than before. All very satisfactory.

CHAPTER 22

Gabriel's Cottage, Market Hamilton, Yorkshire, United Kingdom

July 2013

Gabriel and Shylah seamlessly resumed the rhythm of their long friendship without missing a beat. Alone for several days with Gabriel, for the first time in her life Shylah felt able to vocalise what she believed to have happened on the night of the party, over twenty years before. While her logical memory remained blank, undoubtedly due to an alien substance added by someone to her wine in the kitchen, the passage of time and the love of those around her had smoothed the jagged edges of the incident. This, coupled with the wisdom of age enabled her to draw inevitable conclusions from the mosaic of shattered images which she was able to piece together. They sat and talked long into the night in the protective womb of Gabriel's sitting room.

'The worst thing is, I still have no idea who Colm's father was. Those boys were all strangers, older than we were, probably students. As far as I know, I never saw any of them again.'

'Does Colm ever ask about it?'

'No, to be honest, he's never even mentioned it. Is that odd, do you think?'

'I don't know. I'm not really an expert, but if he was that worried, surely he would have said something before now.'

Shylah shrugged and they sat in silence, thinking together for several minutes before Shylah spoke again.

'I don't know what I should do for the best. I'd love to be able to give Colm a name of a father so he could at least get in touch and maybe even build some sort of relationship with him if he chose to do so. I feel like I've denied him that choice.'

'Yes, I can see what you mean but you don't know who his father is and probably won't be able to find out now. If he's happy as things are, what good will it do to start raking up the past?'

'You're right. He's never asked about it and he is so happy at the moment. I suppose if it's not broken, don't try to fix it.'

Over twenty years on, with a son whom she loved, she and Gabriel eventually concluded that the best approach was to bury the evening's events under the soil and concentrate instead on the beautiful roses which had grown, flourished and covered their resting place for ever.

In her Yorkshire cottage, Gabriel felt herself re-inhabit a familiar, comfortable, yet stronger and more resolute version of herself. She accorded the transformation to the extended physical distance between herself and the scene of Thanuja's execution coupled with the razor-sharp clarity with which she was now able to envision her future. She knew that these precious hours at the cottage, before she met with Sister Anthony and Michael on their return, was a prelude before her overture.

By Thursday evening, after an exhausting journey from Accra, Sister Anthony had reinstalled herself into her old room at the convent. Unpacking her few possessions from her small suitcase had taken less than five minutes, providing her with time to return to the familiar peace of the convent chapel and sit in contemplative silence for an hour. She was joined later by the Sri Lankan Sisters Magdalene and Eve, who were delighted to introduce themselves to the woman about whom they had heard so much. The three nuns sat in joyful, prayerful silence until the two Sri Lankan Sisters suggested that the exhausted Sister Anthony retire to bed.

The following day, with a little time available to circulate, Sister Anthony was delighted to find that the convent had blossomed under the competent management of the two Sri Lankan girls who had arrived as noviciates and were now fully-fledged Sisters. Rather than decline as the elderly community dwindled one by one, as had been expected, the number of residents had burgeoned. Elderly nuns from all over the United Kingdom had heard about the saintly devotion the two Far Eastern Sisters lavished on the elderly in their care and had schemed by all manner of means to be transferred to Yorkshire in their dotage. Additionally, there was a steady stream of women and a few men who took up temporary residence on retreat or just on a break from whatever blows life had dealt them.

The arrival of Michael at the convent provided unimaginable excitement and much matronly fluttering among the elderly nuns. Their excitement was surpassed multifold however by that of the current cadre of schoolgirls at the adjacent St Anne's. Crowds of navy-uniformed scholars loitered more frequently than usual at the intersection between school and convent with an ever more creative list of excuses for their presence. The new convent headmistress, a well-educated lay woman by the name of Ms Bowman, was not averse herself to lingering by her office window, before returning to her early morning paperwork, to be rewarded by the sight of Michael on his daily run.

It seemed that the only people within the convent/school complex unaffected by Michael's many attractive endowments were Sister Magdalene and Sister Eve who stewarded daily operations at the convent like clockwork, wondering at how the peculiar behaviour of Westerners could still continue to yield surprises after so many years.

On Friday morning, Sister Anthony stepped out into the cool morning, waved at Ms Bowman standing at her office window, nodded 'Good morning, girls,' to the small posse of students milling around the school gate and set out for the cottage. She walked along the High Street, trying to remember how things had been before, wanting to identify what had changed since she left for Africa. Several of the older establishments were still in place and alongside them she was delighted to see new signage, unfamiliar names and feel a fresh vibrancy in the heart of the small town. She approached Bennets and was delighted to see a tall, slender young man whom she concluded was the adult Colm. As she entered the shop, Colm looked up and smiled a smile which shone phosphorescent through his eyes and face.

'Your smile reminds me of your Mother, Colm,' said Sister Anthony.

'Sister, you look exactly the same as I remember you. What's your secret?'

Sister Anthony allowed herself a girlish laugh at Colm's gentle flattery.

'I'm serious, Sister. If you tell me the secret, we'll sell some of whatever it is in the shop! Rosemary was only suggesting yesterday evening that we start a line of ecological cosmetics. Maybe there's something magical you found in Africa which will make us all rich!'

'I found lots of magical things in Africa, Colm, but sadly nothing to make us rich. Do you have any of those biscuits that Shylah told me Gabriel likes? I'm going to pop into the cottage and was hoping I'll be offered a cup of tea while I'm there.'

'You're lucky we've got any left, Sister. Gabriel's been hoovering them up since she got back. You won't be turned away if you take another packet with you, Colm's guarantee.' He reached to the back of the shelf where a single red and gold packet of Lebkuchen remained.

Sister Anthony furtled within her habit for her purse.

'On the house, Sister,' said Colm raising his hand slightly and waving away the proffered five pound note. 'You'll be lucky if you get one of these anyway with Gabriel around. Anyone would think they don't have food in Saudi Arabia.'

'Thank you, Colm, I appreciate that. I hope we can spend some more time together now I'm back and I'd like to get to know Rosemary again, if I can. Shylah told me all about her in her emails.'

Colm hesitated, wondering whether Sister Anthony was aware of the surreal interaction between Rosemary and Gabriel the previous evening. He and Rosemary had sat awake, running through events until the early hours, trying to piece together the fragments of what had happened, to create some iota of clarity about what Gabriel might have been predicting. Exhausted, Rosemary had stayed in bed that morning, pale faced and drained by the encounter and the subsequent lengthy analysis, Colm presumed. He decided to say nothing, sensing that the concurrent return of Sister Anthony and Gabriel signalled the start of a new, energy-sapping chapter for them all and confident that everything would become clear in good time.

Gabriel heard Sister Anthony's knock at the cottage door. She took a moment on the landing to appreciate the exquisite, golden gentleness of the framed early 14c Byzantine icon, one of many depicting the Archangel Gabriel in female form, at the Annunciation. She tipped her head beneath the beam as she turned to descend the narrow staircase, allowing her mind to wander towards the fond memory of her parents, who had given her the picture on her thirteenth birthday.

She opened the door, allowing the electric arc joining the two women through the open doorway to form and connect them. They stood still, watching one another.

'Are you ready, Gabriel?' asked the small, strong, balanced nun.

Gabriel saw that Sister Anthony was suntanned from the African sun, slightly greying around the temples but otherwise exactly how she remembered her.

'Yes, Sister, I am ready. Please come in.' Gabriel stood back, allowed the older woman to pass, gently closed the door and followed.

Rather than bound to the door as was her usual wont, Ella sat, calm, restrained and followed the pair quietly into the kitchen where Shylah was replacing the fuse in the plug of the kettle.

'Sister Anthony, it is great to see you. Why don't you sit down, we're just about to have a coffee. This'll be done in a sec.'

As she sat, Sister Anthony turned her electric eyes again towards Gabriel. 'Have you been able to talk to Shylah this week about what needs to be done, Gabriel?'

Shylah looked up from her own electrical endeavours as Gabriel shook her head slowly in response. Sister Anthony nodded once in acknowledgement and started to speak. Her steady, clear voice penetrated the space in the room, subsuming all distraction, quelling any other thoughts. Gabriel was reminded of the day when Sister Anthony had stood at the front of the class and in an identical tone had explained the implications of Heisenberg's uncertainty principle.

'Shylah, we need to talk today about something very important. You will recall how I mentioned in one of my emails that we would be called upon to help Gabriel.' Sister Anthony paused as Shylah nodded, a hint of confusion suffusing her face.

'Well, that time has come, Shylah, and there are a few things you need to know. Firstly, Gabriel is not an ordinary human being, like you and me. I have always known that Gabriel is someone special, someone from whom God will demand more than an ordinary human can give. We need to talk about the roles which we will play in supporting her.'

Shylah's lips parted and her eyes opened wide with astonishment as her knees buckled beneath her. She sat, heavily onto one of the kitchen chairs which shuddered in response. The majority of previous exchanges with Sister Anthony focused exclusively on practical matters. Sister had been a science teacher at St. Anne's, concentrating on the rational, the logical and nothing more. In fact, if Shylah was honest, she would classify Sister Anthony among the most unimaginative of her acquaintances.

The fact that having returned from Africa, within the first two minutes, Sister Anthony was leading a conversation towards something which was starting to sound ethereal at the very least, was fascinating but, she suddenly realised, not so great a shock as she would have expected. Forces within the room sequestered Shylah's voice, forcing her to concentrate exclusively on Sister Anthony's explanation.

'When Gabriel joined us at the school, Gabriel's dear late parents spoke to me. In Gabriel, we are privileged to know an archangel, one of God's special messengers. Archangels and angels live among us here on earth, Shylah and very few of us know their identity. All her life, Gabriel has been working towards the time when she will carry one of God's divine decrees to the world.'

Shylah's mouth silently opened and closed again like a goldfish as she looked to Gabriel and then back at Sister Anthony.

'Did you know about all this, Gabriel? Are you absolutely certain this is true?'

Gabriel nodded silently.

'And you obviously knew all about this too, Sister? Did no one ever think it might be an idea to talk to me about it? Especially if you are now asking for my help with whatever it is Gabriel has to do. This isn't some sort of joke, is it Gabriel? It sounds a bit far-fetched, you being an archangel. You haven't got any wings for a start.'

Sister Anthony was the next to speak as Gabriel remained silent, concluding that allowing Sister Anthony to assume the role of spokesperson had the greatest chance of dissipating Shylah's mounting irritation.

'This is all true, Shylah. Gabriel is particularly special and we are particularly privileged. She is one of only two of

God's archangels who stand both before God in Revelations and who are also recognised by name in the Qur'an.'

'Yes, that's all well and good and if it is true, I can sort of see that it's a privilege to have a special archangel rather than just a run-of-the-mill one, but no one's answering my questions. Why didn't either of you tell me? Who else knows about all this? Most importantly, is this all some sort of joke and you're both about to fall about laughing at my expense?'

'This is absolutely true, Shylah. No one is joking and the only people who know this are here in the cottage now, Shylah. We four and Gabriel's dear late parents are the only people on earth who know.'

'Four? There are only three of us here, Sister, or do you mean Ella? Are you telling me even the dog knew about this before me?'

A small shuffle against the door jamb to her left, made Shylah turn her head in surprise. The imposing outline of a tall African man, dressed casually in jeans and a white tee-shirt, towered above her from the kitchen doorway. In the early morning light, his skin shone like gold, the hairs on his muscular arms glowed like saffron. He moved silently to the fourth chair at the table. Shylah's mind flitted momentarily sideways. She wondered briefly why Ella had remained stationary, sleeping in the doorway as the stranger had silently entered the cottage and passed her in the narrow hallway.

Michael sat down with the women. As he did so, Gabriel felt a prickling warmth on her skin. She had thought about him so many times over the preceding months but the power of his physical presence at this their first meeting, had sucked the air from her lungs.

'Oh my God,' exclaimed Shylah, recognising Michael from the plethora of media coverage. 'What on earth is he doing here? How did he get in? Have you been hiding him in your bedroom, Gabriel?' Shylah raised a single mischievous eyebrow towards a silent, breathless Gabriel, before Sister Anthony went on.

'Shylah and Gabriel, I think you already know that this is Michael. There has been a lot of media coverage over the last few years around his work to reduce the spread of AIDS in Africa. He is, as a result, very well connected in the religious and media worlds and has come to work with us here in Yorkshire.'

'What? So not only do I find out that my closest friend of over twenty years is an archangel, my old teacher and … and … guardian knew about it all along, but also he, Michael has suddenly appeared in our kitchen. Frankly, this is a bit much to take in all at once.'

Shylah put her elbows on the table and rested her head on her hands, closing her eyes, trying to absorb.

As Shylah opened her eyes and turned again to look at her friend, now seated beside Michael, she felt her heart quicken and beat more forcefully in her chest; such was the power of Gabriel and Michael's joint presence. Luminous warmth radiated from them as they sat close together, their shoulders and upper arms touching. It burned Shylah's skin, forcing her to gasp and raise her hand to her smarting cheek. At that moment Shylah realised that Gabriel and Michael's archangelic partnership was real. It must have endured since the creation. How had she not realised something before today? She was plunged suddenly backwards in time to the self-conscious uncertainty she had felt as a girl at St Anne's.

'Gabriel, have you known all this for the last, god knows how many years of our friendship and just decided not to tell me about it?' Why was she always the one who didn't quite get it, needing explanation from someone more intelligent, more involved in all the exciting stuff going on at the school, in the world?

Eventually Gabriel spoke hesitantly, aware that she must choose her words with precision to protect her relationship with Shylah, who was clearly reeling in the face of the revelation.

'I have always known that I am an angel, Shylah, and that, at the appointed time, I will be required to pass a divine message to the world. When we live on earth as angels or archangels, the full details of our purpose and the content of our message only become clear to us over time. It is like a process of maturing, a learning process. God demands that we use our intellect and talents and that we exercise our free will while we are here.' Gabriel looked down at her coffee, a blush infusing her skin, her mouth quivering slightly. 'I loved everything as it was, Shylah, I loved you as we were. I just wanted to enjoy our friendship and keep everything simple for as long as possible.' Gabriel raised her shoulders, looking briefly towards at Michael for reassurance.

'Well, you've made me look a right fool, thank you, Gabriel. Even Ella seems to know something's going on, lying quietly in the hall like that instead of coming in here, jumping all over everyone.' Shylah set her mouth into a thin, silent line, closed her eyes and breathed deeply several times.

They all sat around the table in silence looking at her until she stood, rearranged her features into a warm smile, and looked in turn at everyone. 'I am just going to have to come to terms with all this, aren't I? The last thing I want is to be left out of all the drama and excitement of whatever is about to happen while you all go and … and … do whatever it is you're going to do without me. I'll deal with it, I've handled worse shocks in my life. Within the hour, I'll be back to my old self.'

She stood and walked over to the kettle again and looked back over her shoulder at the group around the table. 'Come on everyone, let's get on with it. Divine messages don't just deliver themselves, you know. You archangels clearly need a bit more get up and go. Another coffee, anyone?'

Michael's smile illuminated the room. Sister Anthony pulled her laptop from her bag and placed it on the table. Shylah, who knew the majority of Gabriel's human habits and proclivities, interjected again.

'Sister, are you ever going to open those biscuits or are they just for you to take back to the convent and trough by yourself in your room? Gabriel will be getting desperate before long. Didn't you know about the post-Saudi archangelic biscuit obsession?'

CHAPTER 23

Market Hamilton, Yorkshire, United Kingdom

July 2013

Spurred on by Shylah's sense of urgency, led by the irrepressible drive and unparalleled intellect of Gabriel and tempered by the outstanding organisational skills of Sister Anthony, the team made rapid progress that first afternoon. By the evening, they had a plan for what they would do over the next two weeks. Shylah's meticulous minuting of everything they discussed, meant that the walls of the cottage were soon covered in Post-It-notes, plans and lists of actions.

It took Michael no time at all to mine his extensive network, assemble a virtual team from across the world, secure the best advice and call in the help they would need. Together they would bring Thanuja's tragic story into the international spotlight and from there engage the leaders of all faiths in the debate about extremism, the biggest contemporary threat to world peace.

Michael's media connections and network were not limited to Africa. Concerns about AIDS and interest in the enormous success of the African programme, for which he was the popular and revered figurehead, had attracted global interest. Nor were his connections limited to the

Christian Church. Many of the Muslim leaders, struggling with the challenge of the growing threat of AIDS, found Michael's messages of self-respect and abstinence more palatable than previous approaches to the issue. Michael was considered responsible for the initiation of the AIDS debate in the Muslim world; superseding the abject denial and the resurgence of established taboos which had characterised their response in the past.

Following discussions with Michael's impressive team of Islamic advisors from nations crossing several continents, the decision was taken to launch Thanuja's story and to follow up with Gabriel's broader messages to the Muslim world, the day after. Gabriel's message would be timed to coincide with the Eidd Al-Fitr festival, the end of the Islamic observance of Ramadan and the time when Muslims around the world celebrate their common goal of unity.

The cottage buzzed with activity, day and night throughout the weekend and into the following week. International conference calls were arranged, messages were written, reviewed by experts, edited and re-edited. Press releases and sound bites were created, transcribed, translated, appraised and critiqued. Spokespeople embracing the Catholic and Jewish traditions, Hindi and Muslims were approached; messages and commentaries were rehearsed, re-rehearsed and honed.

They decided to use Priyantha and Sister Mary as their key contact points in Sri Lanka, Thanuja's home.

'Gabriel, is that you, ma'am?' Priyantha's voice echoed on Gabriel's old Saudi mobile.

'Hi, yes Priyantha, thanks for calling me back. I take it you got back to Colombo safely?'

'Yes, everything went fine with the journey and I have met with Sister Mary already, as we discussed.'

'That's great, Priyantha. I am working with a team of people here in the UK so we can give publicity to Thanuja's story, the injustice of her execution and the plight of others like her who have been executed without trial in Saudi Arabia.' Gabriel was conscious that she was shouting to overcome the shortcomings of the signal. She left the room to give Sister Anthony, Michael and Shylah some peace, installing herself in the sanctuary of her chair in the sitting room.

'I hope we can help other girls avoid similar trouble, ma'am. I trust you to do the right thing. You are very experienced and respected. How do you need me to help you from Colombo?'

'Priyantha, we would like you and Sister Mary to host the reporters and photographers in Colombo who, by next week, will want to know about where Thanuja lived, what her background was like, who her family are. We will speak on a conference call every day so you are both clear what will happen when and exactly what is needed. Are you happy with that, Priyantha?'

'Yes, ma'am. I am happy. I do not feel confident in this task, I am only a driver, ma'am, but I know that you and Sister Mary will help me.'

'That's great, Priyantha, thank you. Do not worry, I know you're up to the job.'

Gabriel provided Priyantha with more reliable contact details for the future and stayed in the sitting room, enjoying the view of the garden for several minutes after their call ended.

As Gabriel had predicted, Priyantha did indeed rise to the challenge. He worked tirelessly thereafter with Sister

Mary in Colombo, sourcing and transmitting pictures of Thanuja, testimonies from those who knew her, pictures of the small apartment in which she had lived with her family.

Thanuja's father, who barely flinched when Priyantha had imparted news of his daughter's death, became immediately enthused by the project and his daughter's posthumous notoriety. He offered to host TV crews at the apartment for a suitable fee. He was already the proud owner of a new moped funded from the joint good fortunes of Thanuja's wages, sent weekly via Western Union from Saudi, and the generous settlement arranged by Priyantha, to enable handover of baby Sean to his new family. Thanuja's mother stayed inside the apartment, unwilling to participate in discussions concerning her late daughter yet similarly unwilling to forego the new luxuries endowed by the family's recently improved fortunes.

Colm and Rosemary made frequent trips to the cottage, despatching the ingredients for delicious meals, snacks and drinks sourced from the shop and prepared in the kitchen at the flat. The six of them coined the phrase: 'A team of Archangels only work with full stomachs.'

On reflection, a pretty weak joke but one which kept them all laughing throughout the coming days.

For a day or two, Rosemary struggled to recover full strength following her encounter with Gabriel. She found herself frequently overcome by waves of tiredness which left her feeling as though her every movement was impeded by a sea of treacle. A concerned Colm sent her to lie down on their bed in the cool light of their freshly painted bedroom. If there was no improvement by next week, he would insist on a visit to the doctor.

At lunchtime on Monday 29th July, Michael, who had been on the 'phone most of the weekend, called everyone together for an international conference call.

'Thank you so much to everyone for working so hard over the last few days, and especially over your weekends,' he started. 'As you all know, we plan to release Thanuja's tragic story to the world to coincide with the end of Ramadan. We will raise awareness of the issues girls like Thanuja face, the injustice frequently meted out to them and in doing so we will grab the attention of the world.'

The international attendees on the call were vocal in their support.

Gabriel continued. 'The next day, to coincide with the start of Eidd, we will build upon Thanuja's story to question more fundamentally how Islamic extremism such as that prevalent in Saudi, conflicts with the mercy and compassion taught by the prophet Muhammad and reiterated in the Qur'an.'

Again, the international 'phone lines buzzed with approval and support as Gabriel went on:

'On Thursday 8th August, the first day of Eidd, in the late afternoon – UK time – a press conference has been arranged in the Hyde Park Hilton. Thanuja's story and the direct message to the communities involved will have been in circulation by that time for twenty four hours.'

'How can we be sure that Thanuja's story will have had a real impact by then, Michael?' asked one of the US team members

'For a start, I will personally stand behind Thanuja's story,' answered Michael.

Sister Anthony continued. 'Michael is already renowned for having a substantial and positive impact on the world and is referred to in the popular media as 'Michael, Africa's Prince of Light'. If Michael is backing the story, the world will listen,' she concluded confidently.

World leading IT expertise had been engaged, again leveraging Michael's connections, to ensure consistent proliferation of the messages via the full scope of social media channels in addition to the traditional press, TV and radio networks. The irony around the location for the press conference was not lost on Gabriel who remembered with crystal clarity her meeting with Doctor Mubaarak and the Saraco board some nine months previously. She allowed herself to wonder, but only momentarily, what Mubaarak and Sureya would make of her post-Saudi activities.

On Wednesday 31st July in the afternoon, Gabriel and Shylah set out for York railway station to take the train to Kings Cross. Michael had suggested that they spend time working from London, preparing for the press conference and meeting with the UK- based journalists, presenters, religious and political leaders who would be helping them. He and Sister Anthony were already in London by the time Gabriel and Shylah left and well underway with briefings and discussions with relevant parties.

'Do you remember, Shylah, that the last time I was here in the station, I saw your father?' Gabriel recounted how she had tried unsuccessfully, to attract the attention of a distracted, tired-looking Peter on the morning of the day he died.

'Yes, I remember the 'phone conversation we had while you were on your way back. I didn't realise it was the last time you had been here though.' Shylah settled herself into a sofa in the corner of the small café on Platform three.

'Did you ever find out why he was on his way to Edinburgh that day?' asked Gabriel.

Shylah was silent for a minute or two. 'Well, while you were away, I had a lot of time to think about it. I have an idea about it all, but I'm still not sure.'

'And you accuse me of keeping secrets! What's the idea then?'

'Do you remember that Scottish lady who comes into the shop? She works sometimes for the Council in York but she lives in Edinburgh. She mentions Dad every time she comes in. She was very sad when he died. I think some of the people at the Council had called her to let her know. Actually she always did mention him in some small way or another when she called at the shop, ever since she started coming to us on the day we opened. Everyone else has forgotten about him now, Gabriel, even though it's less than a year since he died.'

Shylah's resigned face turned towards Gabriel who silently chastised herself for having mentioned such a sensitive matter in such a public place. 'I'm sorry Shylah, I shouldn't have brought it up here.'

'No, it's OK, Gabriel, it's actually good to talk about it. Dad and I saw one another frequently in the shop over the last few years and he did form a relationship with Colm. Not exactly your ideal grandfather to grandson relationship but certainly better than nothing. I would be really happy, actually, if Dad had found some sort of company, some happiness. It was certainly in short supply at home, although he never spoke about any of it either to me or to Colm.'

'Are you going to ask her, the Scottish lady, whether you're right?'

'I'm not sure. I'll see whether it feels like the right thing to do next time she comes into the shop. Although, to be honest, I don't expect I'll be there much any more, now Colm and Rosemary are in control and we have so much to be getting on with!'

CHAPTER 24

London, United Kingdom

July to August 2013

As Shylah and Gabriel travelled from Kings Cross, in a black London taxi, Gabriel's Saudi 'phone bleeped.

'It's a text from Fatima,' she said. 'She says she has moved to London with the guy she met on her English course, that's quick work!'

Gabriel reminded Shylah about Fatima who worked in the little shop owned by her uncle and aunt in Bradford. She explained how Fatima had provided Gabriel's first insight into Saudi life and imparted her own eclectic take on Arabic and Islamic culture. She took the small postcard from her bag with Fatima's 'Five Big Rules' which she had so carefully written out for Gabriel. Fatima had been unfamiliar with Latin script at that time hence the childish loops and jagged curls.

'We must go and visit her while we are here, Gabriel, it would be fun for you to see her again.'

'Yes, it would be nice, let's see how things go.'

In London, Shylah, Gabriel, Sister Anthony and Michael all stayed at the hotel which Gabriel had used on her previous trip to meet Mubaarak and the Saraco board. The Hilton Metropole was situated on the Edgware Road; a busy, nocturnal melting pot of cultures. None of them felt able to justify the colossal price of the rooms at the Park Lane Hilton and there was a manageable distance between the two.

That evening, they all ate together at a small Italian restaurant, within walking distance of Edgware Road. Michael's notoriety had reached London some time before and several groups of adoring well-wishers approached their table as they ate their pasta and drank their rich, red wine. A few paid brief attention to Sister Anthony whose name had frequently been associated with Michael but no one took any particular interest that evening in the other two women with them.

One week later, when well-wishers remembered the evening, they would recall that one of the women was tall and striking and one shorter, attractive and with smiling eyes.

After the meal, when they returned to the hotel, a small crowd had gathered in the foyer of the Hilton Metropole. Michael stopped to talk and allowed them to take photographs. Gabriel waited with him, allowing herself to be photographed too, shaking hands and exchanging pleasantries. The small group in the foyer would look back on the encounter and recount how the physical and energetic presence of Michael and Gabriel transcended anything they had encountered before. Their charisma and intellect radiated, filling the cavernous reception area, attracting passers-by to the extent that the crowd swelled multifold within minutes.

'You come across very well, Gabriel, you build a real connection with people. That will really help us to create the right buzz over the next few days.' Michael looked deep into Gabriel's eyes and smiled as he spoke. Gabriel chastised herself silently as she felt herself weaken at the knees, reflecting that this was probably not the best stage of life to fall in love for the first time.

The next morning, a few UK and European editions carried reports about Michael in London. Several also mentioned Michael's tall, handsome lady companion and speculated on the nature of the relationship between the two.

'Have you seen that you're in the paper, Gabriel?' cried an excited Shylah through the interconnecting door between their hotel rooms. 'Everyone on the tube and in the taxis this morning will be reading about you in the Metro! This is fantastic.'

Gabriel took the paper and read the brief paragraph under a picture of herself and Michael smiling broadly amidst a crowd.

'They are making it look like I'm Michael's partner. Do you think that's OK? Is it likely to help us?'

'Well you two do give out an amazing energy when you're together. I'd say it can't do any harm even if it's not quite the truth … yet!'

'Yes, I think you're probably right. Everyone likes a bit of a romance, so even if there isn't any real romance, it makes a good story.' Gabriel looked at Shylah and smiled gently, shrugging her shoulders.

'Would you like there to be some romance, Gabriel?'

'I'm not sure. I don't think it's really on the cards, do you?'

'Well, I'm not an expert on archangels and their love lives but I must admit it doesn't feel like the best time right now. It's a nice picture of you both though.' She smiled her warm, gentle smile and Gabriel was reminded how complete her life already was, without the complications of romance.

Over the following two days, interest in the presence of Michael, 'The Prince of Light in Africa', in the United Kingdom grew. Speculation in the popular media about the reason for his visit to London was outstripped multifold by speculation about the relationship between Michael and Gabriel and the origins of Gabriel's striking and unique style of dress.

By Tuesday 6th August, media interest was fizzing. An excellent launch pad for Thanuja's story, which was released, precisely as planned on Wednesday 7th August at one minute past midnight, UK time.

By the morning and throughout the next day, newspapers, TV channels and social media the world over, were carrying various colours and complexions of one story:

Innocent Teenage Au Pair, executed without trial near Holy City of Mecca

'How can this be allowed to happen in the twenty first century?'

Asks Michael, Africa's Prince of Light

As Michael and his phalanx of international experts and advisers had predicted, the brutal killing of a beautiful, young, Far Eastern woman was an ideal attention-grabbing headline. The burgeoning interest in Michael and Gabriel in London had served well as a forerunner to the story and Michael's endorsement of it.

In Jeddah, Samir sat with Mubaarak in the office on the third floor at Saraco. Mubaarak frowned and twitched as he scanned, yet again, the pages of Arab News. Samir saw him find what he was looking for and fold the paper to a more portable size so he could sit back in his chair and absorb. Samir raised his eyes skywards and reflected that ever since Gabriel's departure, rather than pitch in and help with the ever expanding project workload, the Doctor had spent the majority of his time reading papers, surfing the internet or dashing in and out of the office on his mobile 'phone speaking in increasingly panicked tones to someone or other.

In Samir's opinion, the Doctor was getting the whole issue of Gabriel's new notoriety out of proportion. He could understand that Mubaarak might be jealous but other than that he was at a loss to see why it was such a problem. If Gabriel wanted to campaign for the rights of the servant girls, so long as she was doing it from her own country and not Saudi, why shouldn't she?

He said nothing as Mubaarak tutted, twitched and then sprung to his feet, his mobile 'phone glued to his ear. As Mubaarak bolted from the office yet again to find somewhere private to talk, Samir heard him say,

'Sureya, this is too risky, we have to do something…' before the door slammed and he was out of earshot.

Once Mubaarak had gone, Samir seized the newspaper. He turned to the back and started to trawl the situations vacant. Without Gabriel to support him, things were becoming intolerable at Saraco.

In Manila, Emilio was just closing the bar after a disappointingly quiet day. The meek wife he had chosen some years before, on his return to the Philippines had turned out to be a carping harpy. He allowed his mind to wander back to the days in Saudi when fulfilling the perverse fantasies of his employers was a far easier way of life, certainly easier than putting up with his wife's nagging and running a bar for the tourists.

He picked up a newspaper which had been left behind on the bar and noticed that some woman in the UK was kicking up a fuss about the treatment of servants in Saudi Arabia. With a wry smile, he reflected that his own time in Saudi had been the most lucrative and enjoyable in his life; easy money certainly, what was there to complain about?

He read on. From her picture, the woman called Gabriel looked like a right handful. She had worked at Saraco, the big Saudi oil company, running an equal opportunities project with someone called Mubaarak. Mubaarak … now that was a name from the past. He had never before or since come across anyone else called Mubaarak. What if it was the same guy? It had to be, how many Mubaarak's were there in Jeddah?

Emilio was sick of the late nights and aching feet, a far better idea started slowly to crystallise in his mind now that Mubaarak had earned himself some notoriety by proxy via this Gabriel woman. As soon as he got back to his apartment, he resolved to look out the small box of Polaroid pictures he had kept of that little git. He had a few of Mubaarak's Dad, the wrinkly old bastard, too if his memory served him well.

Blackmail had come a long way since Emilio's days in Saudi, the advent of the internet was a very good thing indeed in his eyes. He could have the pictures going viral in no time at all if they didn't do what he wanted.

As the day went on, international news reports started to expand their coverage of Thanuja's story to explore the extent to which current 'Extreme Muslim Culture', had become divergent from 'true Islam'.

Execution an Insult to our Culture

… Spokesperson Khaled AlSaud declared the recent execution, without trial, of an eighteen year old girl in Saudi Arabia to 'fly in the face of Islam,' adding that "God is Compassion and Mercy' is the phrase mentioned at the start of every chapter but one in the Holy Qur'an'…

- CNN Reporter – Marion Butler

Many bulletins carried similar stories and commentators frequently went on to discuss how women in the Muslim world had become marginalised rather than 'two halves of one whole' as also written in the Qur'an.

The inevitable conclusion drawn by the majority of reports was that current practice was leading to the development of a thuggish, male-dominated culture, damaging to the principles of the underlying Islamic faith and creating ever growing tensions with the Western world.

Michael, Gabriel and the international team were delighted. Everything was going to plan.

'Thank you all for joining a conference call again at such short notice, and thanks particularly to those of you joining during the night in your time zones,' Michael opened with the team. 'As you will all be aware, Thanuja's story has absolutely had the impact we had hoped for and your outstanding management has definitely steered the discussion in the direction we were aiming for in advance of the press conference later today.'

There were sounds of approval from across the globe, before Michael went on to outline plans for the press conference.

'Gabriel and Michael, Thanuja's story has gone viral. Newspaper sales have rocketed and social media is buzzing. Are you confident the press conference can be accommodated in the hotel in London?' Some participants, particularly from the US, were anxious.

'Shouldn't we move it to somewhere like the Excel Centre which has more capacity?'

'Please may I answer that, Michael,' interjected Gabriel thanking the US team for their question. 'Shylah met with the Hyde Park Hilton team yesterday and we have formally invited sufficient press representatives from across the world to fill the venue. Only invited representatives will attend the actual conference. Arrangements are being made right now to transmit the conference to an audience outside in the park nearby. In addition, an international team will field questions online in real-time.'

Again the 'phone lines buzzed in electrified agreement.

'This is just the start, team. If we manage to get this message understood and taken seriously, we will have a real and positive impact on the world and make it a better place for future generations. Let's talk again later, after the press conference,' concluded Michael before taking more questions and closing the call.

By lunchtime in the UK, as the United States was awakening, social media was alive with the story and teams of cameramen were filing into the Park Lane Hilton to talk to Gabriel and Michael. By then the pair had been installed in one of the hotel conference rooms. Michael's contacts were managing the frenzy with calm competence under the watchful eye of Sister Anthony. Shylah was keeping detailed track of the schedule, ensuring that every team kept to their allotted time-slot and had read the briefing papers in advance.

Interviews with, and footage of, the two articulate, attractive, charismatic individuals continued to exert a direct positive impact on readership and ratings throughout the day and by mid-afternoon, the media excitement was fuelled ever further by commentaries from senior figures in the Christian and Muslim faiths. Foreign media despatched teams to Heathrow to ensure they received first-hand accounts and the very best pictures.

At five p.m. (UK time), Shylah met with the hotel management and agreed that the scheduled press conference should be relocated from the conference room to the substantially larger banqueting hall. Michael's team and the hotel staff, used to the challenges of handling last minute changes of plan reacted immediately. The giant TV screens had been erected during the day, in nearby Hyde Park. Crowds were gathering during the afternoon despite the cool breeze coursing along the Thames.

At six p.m. the technicians, from their vantage point on the balcony, could see that the banqueting hall was teeming. Individuals bore their recording and photographic equipment, filed into chairs, formed groups, dispersed, reformed, dispersed. Their perspective resembled that of a group of naturalists observing an ants' nest, frenetic individuals united by common purpose. The energy level in the vast room sustained as every seat was filled and hordes of cameramen filed in front of and behind the rows of seats taking their positions.

Gabriel waited with Michael in the small ante room beside the banqueting hall, sipping a room temperature, Hilton-branded bottle of mineral water and finalising her notes on the hotel note pad. They sat close together at the corner of the table. Gabriel's body touched Michael's as they leaned together over their notes. An electrical charge fizzed between them, from shoulder to shoulder, through each arm, thigh, knee, ankle. Gabriel could hear the raucous cacophony outside but was unable to disentangle the individual sounds or voices. The sheer volume made it clear to them both that well over one thousand people were waiting. Gabriel had been informed that there were more outside in the Park, watching the conference on giant TV screens. Many millions more were watching across the world via live satellite links.

'OK, two minutes now until we start. Would either of you like to go to the toilet?' Ever practical, Shylah, bearing her minute by minute schedule had been sent in with the warning.

'No, I'm OK, thanks Shylah,' Michael answered smiling broadly, calmly, slowly, imbuing the crackling air with confidence.

'I'm fine too. A bit nervous though. It sounds like a lot of people out there,' answered Gabriel, wondering to herself why she was always compelled to state the blindingly obvious in times of stress.

They rose from their seats together, ready to go, their eyes met and Michael leaned towards Gabriel, allowing his lips to brush the side of her mouth. Gabriel gasped as she experienced the electric shock of desire, felt the hot intensity of Michael's hand on her forearm.

One of the hotel staff arrived and led them onto the wooden platform erected at the front of the room. Gabriel's footsteps echoed like a drumbeat, up the large, strong bones in her legs, into her chest, around her cranium, deafening despite the background noise. She hesitated momentarily as she entered the banqueting hall. She had heard the crowd but had been unprepared for the sea of expectant faces, the honeycomb of camera lenses. The staff member seated them competently on adjacent chairs. The technical team approached to adjust their microphones, crouched down as if in reverence, and backed away when they were done. One of Michael's press managers sat beside Gabriel, turned and smiled.

'All you need to do is answer the questions slowly and clearly. You are both well prepared so there is nothing to be nervous about.' He turned to the crowd. Cameras flashed. The noise level subsided.

They were ready to begin.

'May we have the first question, please?' he glanced down at his briefing note. 'From Kate Boyd on behalf of The Times, UK.'

Gabriel answered each question clearly, slowly, articulately; her confidence growing with every answer she gave. Michael's interjections had been rehearsed, designed to draw helpful parallels, reiterate key points, give his endorsement to Gabriel and her message. Not once did Gabriel or Michael interrupt one another. Not once did their messages conflict. The two strong, charismatic orators were like a masterful pas a double. They reinforced, re-emphasised and supported one another such that the impact of them together was exponentially greater than the already compelling separate parts. Dictaphones and cameras whirred, flashbulbs continued to pierce the air as Gabriel and Michael filled the cavernous hall with their resonant voices. Every person within, those in the Park outside, and the millions across the world heard a clear, consistent message, relevant to their time and their lives. Notes were scribbled, conclusions drawn, points summarised, opinions formed. Press releases, reports and broadcasts were prepared in real time as Gabriel and Michael spoke:

'…Thanuja's death is a shocking symptom of a more significant underlying issue poisoning our world…'

'…Islam and Christianity are both in danger of losing their integrity in today's world…'

'…The behaviours of many who purport to act in God's name are an insult to him…'

'…It is up to all of us, from every religion and tradition, to show humility and reflect carefully on the qualities of compassion and mercy before the world suffers further…'

Gabriel was shocked to realise that after around fifteen minutes, she was enjoying herself. The pressure of preparation had paid off. Everyone was listening intently as she and Michael held them in awe. She felt God's hand, warm on her shoulder, calming, comforting, reassuring her that he was pleased.

'We have time for one final question,' said the press manager eventually.

A man in the third row stood as the microphone was handed to him. He was about Gabriel's height. He wore an ankle-length thaub; black rather than the usual white or cream to which Gabriel had become accustomed in Saudi Arabia. His hair was black as a crow, similarly feathery, blue-brilliant and equally oily. His eyes were like coal, his face dark and with a scarred complexion. From his chin, a beard resembling a thunderous, black cloud, pregnant with an imminent electrical storm billowed across his chest, falling down the front of his thaub to the level of his heart, where it stopped dead.

'Mr Abbas from Zarb E Momin. Please go ahead.'

As the man stood, Gabriel recognised the look of acidic contempt and blind hatred which she had encountered several times while abroad. The look had usually come from those in the workplace, whom she had only just met, before they had learned that she presented no threat. One exception was her first driver with whom the look had remained until the kitten kicking incident. She shuddered, cold, as the man began to speak. She drew breath, leant her shoulder closer to Michael and regained her composure.

'Madam. You speak eloquently about the mercy and compassion espoused in our holy Qur'an and by the messenger of God, the Prophet Muhammad – Peace be upon Him. We are … grateful … that you have clearly studied the subject in such detail. Please would you be able to tell us though, how a woman, a Christian and a non-Arabic speaker is able to presume to understand our religion and draw such conclusions as you have presented today?'

Gabriel felt Michael stiffen beside her. He reached out his hand as if to touch her forearm and then withdrew it again. She felt the gentle warmth again at her shoulder, transcending the energy even of Michael's presence. It encouraged her, urged her forwards. To the surprise of the press manager and Michael beside her, she stood; a smooth, measured ascent.

She closed her eyes and inhaled deeply, listening to the new, clear voice inside her head, prepared to do its will.

'Sir. I thank you for your question. I understand the Qur'an in such depth and am confident in its meaning because it was Jabril, the archangel who dictated the Qur'an to the Prophet Muhammad.'

She continued to stand, locking the bearded man's eyes and surprisingly suffused with relief. She felt a gentle pressure on her shoulder. It was done.

An electric arc pierced the air between Gabriel's eyes and those of the man in the crowd. She thought she may have seen him sneer with victory, a slight rearrangement of his facial expression, invisible to all but himself and Gabriel. He raised his fist, as if in slow motion, swung it, punching the air as he shouted 'Haram, haram, haram.' His voice became louder, now a scream rather than a chant. He continued to pummel the air as if flattening an unseen enemy, battering the life from an adversary. A small group of similarly clothed, long-bearded men stood up around him, punching the air, pointing at Gabriel, screaming hysterically 'Haram, haram.' into the otherwise silent auditorium.

Two security teams simultaneously surrounded two groups in the banqueting hall. The bearded man and his comrades were carried, horizontal yet still chanting, to the rear of the room.

Gabriel who had involuntarily grasped Michael's hand found herself swept away and her hand wrenched from his. Two men, one at each side bore her swiftly off the stage and seated her back in the ante room. She listened to the sound coming from the banqueting hall, and through the window from outside. The volume was louder than before the conference but this time, the words were clear. 'Mercy and Compassion, Mercy and Compassion'

It was late in Saudi Arabia. Mubaarak had been glued to the television all evening. He had managed to convince Sureya to go and visit her Mother and sister so at least she was out of the house and he had some privacy. He had suffered from indigestion before. He was now and it was agonising, waves of excoriating pain from chest to bowel, one after the other.

Not only did he have Philip's illness to worry about but the extreme Muslims were giving him a hard time in Saudi Arabia about the work at Saraco; now Gabriel, the stupid ugly bitch, was stirring them up in the UK. He saw the expression, frozen on camera tonight on the BBC World Service, on the Pakistani guy's face. It would only be a matter of time before things would start to get very uncomfortable, very uncomfortable indeed. Sureya knew all about Philip but there was a far bigger problem. She knew nothing of the male prostitutes, gigolos and servants and they certainly hadn't discussed HIV and its implications. What if one of them recognised his name and started to cause trouble? What if Gabriel's new-found fame somehow led back to him? He leant forward and folded his arms across his stomach as another wave of acidic pain swept through his body.

Shaking, he stood and retrieved his laptop. He opened the browser and started to search for flights from Jeddah to London.

A few hours later, it was morning in Manila and Emilio was in front of a laptop too. His friend Dilvan was really good at computers and all that sort of thing and had agreed to meet him at the bar before opening time to give him a hand.

They had already scanned the Polaroid pictures on Dilvan's portable scanner and would definitely be done with the text about Mubaarak and translation into English before Emilio needed to open the bar.

CHAPTER 25

London, United Kingdom

8th August 2013

Shylah and Sister Anthony entered the ante room and the security team took their positions outside the door.

'That was amazing, Gabriel and Michael. You had every single person in that room in the palms of your hands,' Sister Anthony's face shone with pride and joy.

'Except for that weirdo at the end but security dealt with him and his cronies,' cried Shylah, her face alight with excitement.

'Thanks, it was a bit scary at the end but overall, I think it went OK. What do you think, Michael? Did I say too much?'

'It was absolutely great, Gabriel. Your honesty and the point about the Hadith of Gabriel or Jabril, was brilliant. Did God guide you to reveal the truth?'

'Yes, Michael. Were you aware that was what He wanted me to do?'

Michael shook his head slowly as he spoke.

'No, Gabriel. God is speaking directly to you here. It is you who is making the difference, I am just here to support you and carry on your work … afterwards.'

He hesitated, they looked into one another's eyes and he leaned over to kiss her again.

'What you said will have been heard clearly by those learned in Islam, Iman and Ihsham. It will challenge their misconceptions and make them think carefully. That's exactly what we wanted.'

Michael held her hand and she leaned against his glorious, firm body in silence, closing her eyes and breathing deeply.

'You need to be strong now, Gabriel. Do you understand?' said Michael eventually

Gabriel felt a surge of energy prickle from her knees, through her thighs, to her chest. Suddenly gripped by fear, hot tears burned behind her eyelids but she set her mouth firm, sat up straight and returned his gaze, squeezing his hand a little tighter.

'I understand, Michael. I'm so glad you're here.'

'Why don't you go back to the hotel for a few hours and get some rest while I meet the team here and work out our next steps?' Michael continued to hold her hand, willing his strength to permeate her arm.

'No, I'm happy to stay,' she replied, simultaneously fearful and reluctant to miss any of the excitement.

Shylah met Michael's eye and took control.

'Gabriel, it could be a very long night. Remember it is still only the afternoon in the States. Michael's right. Let's go back to the hotel, take a few hours off, and then we can come back here later on when you're needed again.'

Reluctantly Gabriel rose to her feet and followed Shylah, looking back over her shoulder to meet Michael's eyes and smile, one final time.

The security team outside flanked the pair as they walked through the corridors to the cries of the crowd, and settled them into the car.

The London rush hour traffic was heavy and they edged frustratingly slowly around Hyde Park Corner, to Marble Arch and through the melee of the Edgware Road, safely anonymous behind the blackened windows of the car. Gabriel put her head back on her seat, breathed deeply and closed her eyes as they sat in exhausted silence. When they eventually reached their destination, there was no sign of the security team who had left the Park Lane Hilton in an identical car behind them.

'Let's just dash up to our rooms, Shylah. They could be ages in this traffic. We can't wait around for them for ever.'

Shylah checked briefly out of the car window. Gabriel did have a point, the traffic was awful and the journey had taken far longer than before. She glanced around and noticed that the hotel foyer was deserted except for a few nondescript guests filing in and out through the smoked glass, rotating doors. Certainly there was no sign of the teeming crowds and cameras they had left behind. She concluded that despite the dire warnings of the security team, it looked safe enough to make a dash for it, if they were very quick.

'Come on then,' she said, opening the car door for Gabriel, directing her towards one of the two rotating doors and leaping into the other door herself.

As Gabriel pushed at the glass, someone stepped forward behind her, forcing themselves into her compartment of the door. For one or two seconds, she and whoever it was, were pressed tightly, breathlessly together, squeezed between the right angled, smoked glass panes. As Gabriel escaped from the uncomfortable confinement and entered the foyer, she turned back, intending to ask what the hurry had been about. Her rotating door companion had not exited with her and their glass partition continued on its circular journey. Gabriel saw the shadowy, black figure run away, largely obscured behind the tinted foyer window.

She shrieked suddenly with surprise, a hot pain like a needle piercing her leg.

'Did you see that, Shylah? What a nerve, I've just been crushed in the door with a complete stranger and now he's run off. Ouch, and I think I've been stung by a wasp. Ouch, oh my God, it stings!'

Shylah watched in horror as Gabriel jumped from foot to foot, clutching and rubbing her thigh. She had only been alone in the door for a matter of seconds, surely nothing untoward could have happened in that time, and the area had been all but deserted.

'It must have been some sort of pervert who enjoys pressing up against women in confined spaces. Anyway he's gone now. Where have you been stung? It's a bit late for wasps, isn't it?'

'Here, on the top of my leg. It must have got up inside my clothes. Ouch. Oh my God, Shylah, it's agony.' Gabriel was vigorously rubbing at her thigh.

'Gabriel, for goodness sake, stop making such a fuss. Colm and I have been stung by wasps hundreds of times.'

'But I've never been stung before, oh my God, this is awful.' Gabriel was pulling at her clothes.

'Gabriel, this is not a great time to be getting wasp stings. Let's get up to our rooms, we'll need to run quickly and we can sort you out. Wait there, where I can see you for a minute and I'll ask someone to bring some vinegar up or something.'

'Shylah, I'm going up to the room, you follow. I've got to get these clothes off the sting. You'll be up in a second, there's no queue at reception and there's no one around. I'll be fine.'

Shylah tutted, turned around and headed for the reception desk.

Gabriel entered the lift, leaving Shylah in frantic discussion with the Eastern European reception staff who appeared to have very strong views on the appropriate treatment for wasp stings. Predictably, their methods looked to be significantly divergent to those of practical Yorkshire women like Shylah. The request for vinegar was being dismissed with a flippant wave of a slender Slavic hand as the lift doors closed.

Gabriel's leg started to numb. She counted the floors out loud, tracking the progress of the lift as it ascended to the third floor. She dragged her throbbing limb behind her as she struggled across the landing and leaned on the opposite wall for support. Painstakingly, she felt her way along the wall, counting the doors to her room, her key card clutched in her hot, sticky hand. She reflected briefly that the sting might have been a hornet rather than a wasp, possibly even one of the new breed of Asiatic hornet reputed to be sweeping across Europe. Maybe she was allergic to wasps … or hornets. Her head throbbed as she struggled to rationalise how such a substantially proportioned insect could have made its way unseen inside her clothing and then flown away again. At that moment, as she struggled onwards, the possibility occurred to Gabriel that the agony had been caused by something more sinister than an insect.

The pain and swelling increased with her every movement. A cold sweat broke out on her face, she gasped to force air into her lungs which grew more constrained and resistant with each breath. Gabriel felt herself become dizzy, unbalanced. She forced herself to blink rapidly, trying to clear her progressively deteriorating vision. She pressed her face to each door, trying to decipher the room numbers as she struggled onwards. Three two zero, three two two, only one more to go until she reached three two four, interconnecting with Shylah in three two six.

She slumped against the door of her room, feeling for the locking mechanism, unable to see, sweat now soaking her clothes which clung to her body. She inserted and retracted the key card. Her knees buckled and her upper body fell heavily into the room between the door and its frame.

Shylah soon managed to extract herself from the discussion with the reception staff and ascended in close pursuit of Gabriel. As she exited the lift, she saw a pair of legs and a crumpled lower body strewn, several doors down the corridor, across the carpet. The legs assumed unnatural angles, inhuman contortions. The body had been slammed at the waist in the heavy mechanism of the fireproof door to room three two four. Gabriel's head and face were completely obscured from view behind the door, inside the room.

'On my God, Gabriel, are you OK?' Shylah screamed and heaved the door open, pushing the weight of Gabriel's upper body behind it as she did so, forcing it to move against the friction of the carpet. Shylah needed only to look briefly at Gabriel's purple face, staring, bloodshot eyes and grotesquely swollen lips to realise that it was too late to save her archangel.

'Gabriel, wake up,' she screamed, lifting Gabriel from behind into a sitting position, securing purchase under her arms and dragging her motionless bulk across the room towards the bed. The door slammed shut with a crash which echoed around the room and down the corridor with chilling finality.

Shylah sat on the carpet, her back against the bed, wracked and weeping; tears and mucus streaming down her face. She cradled Gabriel's head in her lap, hiding the swollen, ruined features against her chest. She was unable to lift the solid body onto the bed and reflected that the endeavour would be pointless anyway.

Shylah sat against the bed with Gabriel until the convulsions which had consumed her whole being gradually subsided. Tentatively, she allowed Gabriel's face to fall away from her chest and swim into view. She maintained her hold on Gabriel's head, cradling it in her arms and forced herself to look downwards into her beloved's face. For the only time in her life, Shylah kissed Gabriel full on her lips. Afterward, as she lifted her head away, she realised it had been an empty gesture; the disfigured corpse already bore no relation to her Gabriel. She gently moved aside, lifting the head away from her lap as she did so to lay the body straight, flat, orderly, respectfully on the floor of the room. She removed the quilt from the bed to cover it and knelt, waiting for an inevitable knock.

Someone from the hotel's room service team arrived with a trolley bearing ice, vinegar, lemon juice, baking soda, a small blowlamp and a pair of knitting needles.

'Thank you, but you're too late,' said Shylah blocking the doorway to the room with her body. 'Please call the Hilton Park Lane and ask Michael and Sister Anthony to come urgently to this room, number three two four.'

She had to repeat the message several times before the bewildered young man understood what was required. He left again, still bearing his trolley of bric-a-brac and Shylah returned to sit in silence on the side of the bed keeping watch over Gabriel's body.

The two security men who had followed in the car behind were next to arrive, in the company of the hotel reception staff. They opened the door and stood motionless, absorbing the sight of the serene, attractive woman sitting, hands joined on the bed. She presided over what they concluded was a body covered with something white.

'What happened?' asked the taller of the two security men tenderly, sitting down beside Shylah.

'She said she'd been stung. I told her to come up to the room. When I got here she was dead. I moved her body from the doorway.'

The second security man knelt down by the body, lifted the edge of the quilt, looked down, turned and nodded to his colleague.

'Did you see whatever it was that stung her?' asked the man.

'No, she just said she'd been stung,' Shylah replied, 'although to be honest, she said she'd never been stung before so … I suppose she could have been mistaken.'

The security man nodded at his colleague again.

By the time Sister Anthony and Michael arrived, the police had descended and Shylah could hear an immense crowd forming in the street outside the window.

'Michael will deal with everyone now, Shylah. Come down the corridor to my room and we'll get some peace.' Sister Anthony took Shylah's hand. She felt fragile, brittle like the small, frightened, pregnant teenager in the competent, loving care of someone who always knew exactly what to do.

Sister Anthony sat on her bed, her back against the headboard, her legs straight out in front of her. Shylah lay beside her, her head in Sister Anthony's lap, silent as Sister Anthony stroked her hair.

'What happened, Shylah?' asked Sister Anthony eventually.

'She said she'd been stung. But I'm not sure now. There was someone who pushed himself into the revolving door when we were coming into the foyer. I should have been looking after her, but there was no one around when we arrived and I thought we could just run up to the room. He ran off. I don't know how this will affect what we are doing here. It was so important to Gabriel. I loved her so much, Sister. She was everything to me and Colm.'

'Gabriel's work is already a success, Shylah. The Muslim and Christian leaders have already set the date for a World Summit to agree how they will resolve the escalating tensions created by extremism. You have nothing to blame yourself for, you were Gabriel's rock throughout her entire life and especially in these last few weeks. The news of Gabriel's death will bring even greater media attention to the issue and accelerate the cause.' Sister Anthony's voice was calm; the rhythm of her hand stroking Shylah's head uninterrupted as she spoke. Shylah looked up into Sister Anthony's strong, tearless face.

'Are you saying that Gabriel dying, or being killed, is what was meant to happen, Sister?' Shylah was horrified.

'Yes Shylah, Gabriel has done what she was here to do this time. You, Michael and I need to finish her work now.

She'll be back to earth again when God decides we need her. His other angels will continue to come and go in the meantime.'

They stayed together where they were. Shylah wept until her eyes became desiccated. Sister Anthony maintained her comforting, prayerful silence. The chanting crowds outside the window continued into the night from one side of the bed. The sounds of people running, shouting, banging in the corridor endured similarly outside the door on the other.

At around three o'clock in the morning, Shylah was the first to speak.

'Sister, I think I'd better have something to eat. We have a lot to do if we're going to continue Gabriel's work after tomorrow. You haven't got any of her biscuits in your bag have you?'

CHAPTER 26

Market Hamilton, Yorkshire, United Kingdom and Colombo, Sri Lanka

Friday 9th August 2013

Colm and Rosemary moved their TV from the flat into the office behind the shop. They were determined to stay abreast of everything going on in London during the week. Shylah had warned them that they would be busy and there would be no time for emails or 'phone calls. Despite the difficulty Colm and Rosemary would have in connecting directly with either Shylah or Gabriel, they did not intend to miss a single thing.

Bennets was busier than it had ever been. Everyone wanted to call in and see the shop owned by Gabriel, suddenly one of the most televised and talked about women of the decade. For years it had been run by her loyal companion, the attractive Shylah whose supportive presence and pretty face alongside Gabriel, had become equally familiar throughout the week.

Adventurous journalists who had made the journey north as far as Market Hamilton lamented at Gabriel's lack of blood relatives. They had hoped for some interviews with the family. They settled instead for footage of Colm and his radiant partner, Rosemary, in the shop. He was the nearest they were likely to get to a proper relative they reasoned, being the son of Gabriel's constant companion, Shylah.

Market Hamilton's High Street was buzzing. With the unparalleled interest in two of its long term residents, Yorkshire's tourists had amended their schedules to call at the small market town. Celeste's café had started to sell take-out coffees as demand outstripped the extent of its seated accommodation. Celeste herself had been bowled over by the attentions of one of the photographers from The Guardian who had travelled from Manchester and needed overnight accommodation in a hurry.

The two Sri Lankan Sisters, Sister Magdalene and Sister Eve, were expertly fielding inquiries at the convent from the multiple curious about the solid Sister Anthony, omnipresent in the background during interviews with Michael and Gabriel. The Sisters' pictures also appeared in the press flanked by several of the livelier of their elderly charges.

Several schoolgirls had been filmed giggling outside the headmistress, Ms Bowman's, window as journalists asked them questions about Michael and the impact of his short stay next door to their school.

Rosemary had woken on Friday morning feeling more energetic than she had felt for years. She entered the kitchen to find Colm staring silently at his 'phone. His eyes were red and trails of mucus descended from each nostril.

Rosemary placed her hand on his shoulder. She had known that the message would arrive somehow, at some time that morning.

He handed the 'phone silently to Rosemary.

Colm and Rosemary. I did not want to wake you so please, please, please forgive me sending this via a text. Sadly, Gabriel died last night. Circumstances were suspicious and I will call you in the shop as soon as I know more.

'I am so sorry, love. I need to go now but I'll be back soon. I must keep the appointment with Dr Brookes this morning. I'll be back soon to help you. We need to be here for your Mum after this.' She turned to look at him again briefly as she left.

The news announcing Gabriel's death and the likelihood of a post mortem was broadcast on the radio, several minutes later. As the full realisation sank in, Colm sat down heavily on one of the flimsy chairs, clutched his head in his hands and wept with loud, convulsing sobs. His tears flowed like they had many years before when a small frightened boy was the victim of bullying in one of the roughest schools in Hull.

Three lady American tourists, surprised to find Bennets deserted, heard wails of anguish coming from the rear of the premises. They tentatively investigated and resolved to help the young Englishman in distress. One made Colm a cup of appallingly weak tea and busied herself at the sink. The second sat and held Colm's hand explaining how she was 'visited regularly' by her late Aunt who had moved over to 'the other side' some years previously. The third stood guard over the shop at Colm's request, awaiting Rosemary's return.

Shortly after the arrival of the Americans, a dishevelled, middle-aged woman smelling of alcohol entered the shop demanding to know the whereabouts of Colm. The third

American was caught completely by surprise and led the woman to the office where a distraught young man was being fussed over by her two companions. He looked up.

'Oh God, Mary, what do you want? Mum's not here at the moment.'

'I know she's not here. I just saw the telly. She's in London, I know. I just...' Mary hesitated, hauling a sodden tissue from the recesses of her sleeve to wipe her dripping nose. 'I just thought that she might need me now. God knows, I haven't been much of a Mother to her so far. I don't know what she'll do without that Gabriel.'

Mary sat down in the office opposite Colm, dripping from every facial orifice. Colm put an awkward arm around her bony shoulders.

In Colombo Priyantha was visiting his sister's apartment. Sean was able to sit up now and his adoptive parents had bought him some bricks which he was studiously piling one on top of the other.

'He's very clever for his age, you know,' said Priyantha's sister, 'just like his Mummy was.'

Priyantha crouched down and helped Sean build his tower higher and higher. His sister turned on the radio just as the announcer moved onto the story of Gabriel's death. The words floated into Priyantha's consciousness, took several seconds to arrange themselves into anything comprehensible and were then followed by the numbness associated with the early stages of grief. Priyantha carried on playing with Sean for a few more minutes. There was no need to upset either him or his sister, neither of whom would grasp the significance of a story about someone as far away as the United Kingdom. He maintained his composure until it was time to leave, walked slowly, dignified to his car, sat down behind the wheel, put his head in his hands and wept.

As Gabriel's solicitor, Mr Betteridge considered it his duty to listen carefully to the reports about his client throughout the week. One callow reporter followed another, standing in the street outside Bennets and talking in overenthusiastic tones about 'Gabriel's delicatessen'. Mr Betteridge reflected that he was probably the only person aware that it wasn't actually 'Gabriel's delicatessen' any longer. She had been to see him privately, a little over seven years previously and transferred the title of the freehold into Colm's name.

On Friday morning, Mr Betteridge saw the news of Gabriel's death on the Reuters scroll at the top of his screen. Gabriel had been very particular in her will about how things should be administered on her death and how title of the cottage should transfer jointly to Shylah and Colm. Mr Betteridge took his duty to his clients very seriously indeed. He immediately set out for the cottage to check that all was well.

When Mr Betteridge arrived, the cottage was already besieged by photographers. He noticed with irritation that people had trampled Bill's garden in their enthusiasm to get pictures through the cottage windows. Now though, the police had erected a blue and white striped plastic ribbon around the perimeter and placed a Special Constable on guard.

The robin, horrified by the intensified activity had already flown away from the apple tree in search of somewhere more peaceful from whence to sing.

Mubaarak saw the news about Gabriel on the continuous BBC News 24 transmission as he cleared the desk at the Business Class Lounge in Jeddah Airport. He threw down his bag in frustration. The ticket to Heathrow had cost him $3,000 which had now been a complete waste of money.

Someone else had got there before him to put an end to the bloody woman, her blasphemous outpourings and her troublemaking. Despite the rankling $3,000, he breathed a sigh of relief and mopped his soaked brow with a tissue. He turned on his Blackberry and was aghast to see 22 missed calls, from somebody calling from somewhere with the country code +63.

EPILOGUE

August 2013

Market Hamilton, Yorkshire, United Kingdom

In Market Hamilton, somewhere between Bennets and the Surgery, Gabriel fell into step with Rosemary. They were in a small side street, deserted and silent except for the two women and the echo of their concurrent footsteps.

'Hello, Gabriel. Thanks for coming to say goodbye, I appreciate it,' Rosemary quickened her step and smiled at her tall companion as she spoke.

'That's OK. Do you know when the baby is due?' asked Gabriel.

'Not exactly, I'm just going to the doctor now to get everything set up. I should find out very soon.'

Gabriel smiled as she put her arm around Rosemary's shoulders and hugged her briefly.

'He will be a boy, Rosemary. You will call him Raphael,' she said.

'Thanks, Gabriel. Don't worry. Everything's in good hands here. I'll email Michael and Sister Anthony as soon as I'm back from the doc's. See you next time.'

Rosemary walked on for another five paces, heard a robin sing, three shrill arpeggios from a tree in the small courtyard outside the entrance to the surgery.

She turned briefly and saw that the road behind her was empty, as she had known it would be.

Biography

Clara now divides her time between Yorkshire in the UK and The Charente in France. In the past, she has worked internationally in the Financial Services and IT industries. Clara spent several years working in Saudi Arabia, where she is one of only a handful of western women to have held a senior position within a government owned institution.

Since 2006, Clara has published several poems and short stories in journals and online, both in the UK and the US. In late 2013, Clara stepped back from the corporate world to complete a master's degree in creative writing at York, St John University, in the UK, and to finish her first novel. The novel, all events and characters therein are fictional but the story is informed by Clara's love of Yorkshire together with her first hand experiences in the Middle East, Far East and Africa.

www.clarachallonerwalker.com